BRUTAL
OF THE
MOUNTAIN MAN

BRUTAL NIGHT
OF THE
MOUNTAIN MAN

WILLIAM W. JOHNSTONE
with J. A. Johnstone

PINNACLE BOOKS
Kensington Publishing Corp.
www.kensingtonbooks.com

PINNACLE BOOKS are published by

Kensington Publishing Corp.
119 West 40th Street
New York, NY 10018

PUBLISHER'S NOTE
Following the death of William W. Johnstone, the Johnstone family is working with a carefully selected writer to organize and complete Mr. Johnstone's outlines and many unfinished manuscripts to create additional novels in all of his series like The Last Gunfighter, Mountain Man, and Eagles, among others. This novel was inspired by Mr. Johnstone's superb storytelling.

All Kensington titles, imprints, and distributed lines are available at special quantity discounts for bulk purchases for sales promotions, premiums, fund-raising, educational, or institutional use. Special book excerpts or customized printings can also be created to fit specific needs. For details, write or phone the office of the Kensington sales manager: Kensington Publishing Corp., 119 West 40th Street, New York, NY 10018, attn: Sales Department; phone 1-800-221-2647.

PINNACLE BOOKS, the Pinnacle logo, and the WWJ steer head logo are Reg. U.S. Pat. & TM Off.

ISBN-13: 978-0-7860-3555-7
ISBN-10: 0-7860-3555-2

First printing: December 2016

10 9 8 7 6 5 4 3 2 1

Printed in the United States of America

First electronic edition: December 2016

ISBN-13: 978-0-7860-3556-4
ISBN-10: 0-7860-3556-0

THE JENSEN FAMILY
FIRST FAMILY OF THE AMERICAN FRONTIER

Smoke Jensen—*The Mountain Man*
The youngest of three children and orphaned as a young boy, Smoke Jensen is considered one of the fastest draws in the West. His quest to tame the lawless West has become the stuff of legend. Smoke owns the Sugarloaf Ranch in Colorado. Married to Sally Jensen, father to Denise ("Denny") and Louis.

Preacher—*The First Mountain Man*
Though not a blood relative, grizzled frontiersman Preacher became a father figure to the young Smoke Jensen, teaching him how to survive in the brutal, often deadly Rocky Mountains. Fought the battles that forged his destiny. Armed with a long gun, Preacher is as fierce as the land itself.

Matt Jensen—*The Last Mountain Man*
Orphaned but taken in by Smoke Jensen, Matt Jensen has become like a younger brother to Smoke and even took the Jensen name. And like Smoke, Matt has carved out his destiny on the American frontier. He lives by the gun and surrenders to no man.

Luke Jensen—*Bounty Hunter*
Mountain Man Smoke Jensen's long-lost brother, Luke Jensen, is scarred by war and a dead shot—the right qualities to be a bounty hunter. And he's cunning, and fierce enough, to bring down the deadliest outlaws of his day.

Ace Jensen and Chance Jensen—*Those Jensen Boys!*
The untold story of Smoke Jensen's long-lost nephews, Ace and Chance, a pair of young-gun twins as reckless and wild as the frontier itself . . . Their father is Luke Jensen, thought killed in the Civil War. Their uncle Smoke Jensen is one of the fiercest gunfighters the West has ever known. It's no surprise that the inseparable Ace and Chance Jensen have a knack for taking risks—even if they have to blast their way out of them.

CHAPTER ONE

El Paso County, Texas

The Eagle Shire Ranch was second in size only to the King Ranch in Southwest Texas. Silas Atwood, owner of Eagle Shire, had been ruthless in building his ranch. He began the process by buying, from the bank, the mortgage paper on many of the smaller adjacent ranches. If a blizzard or drought or some other calamity would happen to cause the smaller ranchers to miss payments, Atwood was merciless in foreclosing on them immediately. In this way he continued to expand his already large holdings.

Bo Willis, Tony Clinton, Abe Creech, and Danny Reed rode for Atwood, though they couldn't exactly be called cowboys since their positions for the ranch called for a set of skills that were different from those required by working cowboys. Atwood called such men his "special cadre." At the moment, Willis and the others were at Glen Creek, a year-round stream that supplied water for this part of the county. They were near the spillway where, even now, water was pooling into a widening lake behind gate number one. Closing the gate stopped the creek from flowing onto the Double Nickel Ranch. A medium-size ranch, the Double Nickel had, so far, managed to survive blizzards and droughts.

Bo Willis took a leak against an ocotillo cactus, aiming at a sunning frog as he did so. He laughed when the creature, caught in the stream, hopped away. Buttoning his pants, he walked back over to the others.

"See anything yet?" Willis asked.

Clinton spit a wad of tobacco before he answered. "Nope," he said. "I'm not sure anyone will be here."

"Oh, someone will be here all right. Either Dumey or some of his men," Willis said. "They're goin' to want to know what happened to the stream."

Reed laughed. "When they find out, I don't reckon Dumey is goin' to be all that happy about it."

"Yeah, well he can bitch all he wants, Mr. Atwood has a court order allowin' us to close the gate, so there's nothing he can do about it. Nothing legal, that is. That means that if he, or any of his men, show up, it can only be to cause us trouble. And remember, when they do arrive, they will be trespassing, which means we have every right to shoot them down."

"Hey, Bo," Creech said. "Looks like we've got company comin'."

Creech pointed out three riders.

"All right, you fellas stay out of sight," Willis said. "Have your rifles loaded and ready. When I give the signal, shoot 'em."

"Shoot at them?" Reed asked.

"No, shoot them," Willis said. "You got a problem with that? 'Cause if you do, it may just be that you'll need to find another place to work."

"No, I ain't got no problem with that," Reed insisted. "I just wanted to be sure that's what Mr. Atwood wanted, is all."

"He give us fifty dollars apiece to come out here 'n do just that," Willis said. "I don't intend to go back 'n tell 'im the job didn't get done. So if you ain't got it in you, just go on back now, 'n I'll take your fifty dollars."

"Like hell you will," Reed said. "You just give me the word, then step out of the way so they don't none of them fall on you."

Clinton and Creech laughed at Reed's comment.

"Go on, then, 'n get out of sight," Willis ordered.

Clinton, Creech, and Reed got out of sight behind an outcropping of rocks. Willis walked out to the middle of the road and stood, waiting until the three riders came close enough for him to identify them. One of them was Gus Dumey, son of the owner of the Double Nickel. The other two were Paul Burke, who was the foreman of the Double Nickel, and a man named Poke, who was one of the Double Nickel riders. Poke was the only name Willis knew him by.

"That's far enough!" Willis called out, holding his hand up to stop the riders. "You three men are trespassing on Eagle Shire Ranch property."

"Is that you, Willis?" Burke asked.

"Yeah. What are you three doin' here, Burke?"

"Our crick has run dry," Burke said. "We're tryin' to find out why."

"It's run dry 'cause we closed the gate," Willis said.

"What?" Dumey shouted. "Why the hell did Atwood do that?"

"It ain't Mr. Atwood's doin'," Willis replied. "Judge Boykin ordered it shut down so as to divert some water to the other ranches because of the drought."

"There aren't any other ranches serviced by Glen Creek except Eagle Shire and the Double Nickel," Dumey said angrily. "And there isn't a drought."

"Well, then, if their ain't no drought, you got no need for the crik, do you?" Willis said with a smug smile.

Dumey started toward the gate.

"Where do you think you're a-goin'?" Willis asked.

"I aim to open that gate," Dumey replied.

Willis looked toward the concealed men and nodded. Shots rang out and Dumey, Burke, and Poke all three went down as a cloud of gunsmoke drifted up over the rocks.

Clinton and the others came out then. "Dead?" Clinton asked.

"Yeah," Willis replied.

"Let's get 'em throwed over their saddles, then take 'em into Marshal Witherspoon. Mr. Atwood wants this done all legal-like."

Big Rock, Colorado

Smoke Jensen and Cal Wood were standing in the crowd of some fifty or so spectators, watching the horseshoe-pitching contest. They were here to support their friend Pearlie, who was representing Big Rock in the Eagle County championship match. Pearlie was defending his position as county champion, but he was facing stiff competition this time from Jim Wyatt, who represented Red Cliff.

The two men were tied, and Wyatt, who was up, held the shoe under his chin, studied the pit at the far end, then made his toss. His shoe hit the stake and lay there, in contact with the stake.

"Good toss, Wyatt," someone called.

"Yeah? Watch this one."

Wyatt threw his second shoe. There was a loud clang as the horseshoe hit the iron stake, then fell. The judge made a quick examination of the shoe, then called back, "The ends are all the way through. It's a ringer."

"That gives Wyatt twenty-one points, Pearlie," someone shouted. "Looks to me like you ain't a-goin' to be the horseshoe-throwin' champion of Eagle County no more."

The man who called out was Beans Evans, one of the wagon drivers for Big Rock Freighters.

"Don't count 'im out yet, Beans," Cal said. "He's got two more throws."

"He ain't hit a ringer in the last ten tosses," Beans replied. "He ain't likely to do it now."

Pearlie threw the shoe. It hit the stake and then whirled around. Pearlie held his breath until it dropped.

"It spun off," Wyatt said.

"No, it didn't," the judge replied, examining the

shoe. "Mr. Wyatt's ringer is canceled, and there is zero score for either man."

"You're at nineteen points, Pearlie. Another ringer is all you need."

"I bet you five dollars he don't get it," Beans said.

"Now, Beans, I know you don't really want to bet that much," Smoke said. "Suppose we just bet a beer on it."

Beans laughed. "Yeah," he said. "I was gettin' a little carried away there, wasn't I? All right, I'll bet you a beer."

Sugarloaf Ranch

Sally Jensen was sitting on Eagle Watch, the high escarpment that guarded the north end of the ranch. She had found this place shortly after she and Smoke were married, and she came here quite often to enjoy the view. From here she could see the house, a large two-story edifice, white, with a porch that ran all the way across the front. It had turrets at each of the front corners, the windows of which now shined gold in the reflected sunlight. Also in the compound were several other structures, including the bunkhouse, cook's shack, cowboy dining hall, barn, granary, and other outbuildings.

Now was bluebell season, and at her insistence some of the meadow was left free of any livestock so she could enjoy the tulip-shaped blooms and their rich color from deep blue, to almost purple. Although Sally had grown up in New England, she was now living the life of her dreams; married to the man she loved.

Smoke Jensen's reputation reached far beyond the Colorado state lines, far beyond the West. He was someone whose reputation as a rancher, and as a courageous champion of others, was the stuff of heroes, and indeed, there had already been many books written about him.

Even as such thoughts played across her mind, she looked down onto Jensen Pike and smiled at the sight of three approaching riders. They were, she knew, Smoke, Pearlie, and Cal. Pearlie and Cal were their two top ranch hands, but they were much more than that. The two young men had been with them for a long time, having come to the ranch when they were relatively young. As a result, Smoke and Sally looked at them more as if they were members of the family than just employees.

Sally mounted her horse, then rode back down the trail to meet them, arriving back at the house at about the same time Smoke, Pearlie, and Cal did.

"I made some bear sign," Sally said. "I figured they would be good as consolation in case you lost, or as a celebration in case you won. Which was it?"

Pearlie reached down into his saddlebag, then, with a big smile, pulled out a brass cup.

"We'll be celebratin'," he said, holding the cup up so she could see it.

"My," Sally replied. "I do believe that one is even prettier than the other three."

"It is, isn't it?"

"They all look just alike," Cal said.

Smoke laughed. "I believe you have just been subjected to a bit of Sally's sarcasm."

Eagle Shire Ranch, El Paso County

There were two separate bunkhouses on the Eagle Shire Ranch. The larger of the two bunkhouses was for the men who were actually cowboys, men who rode the range, kept the fences repaired, pulled cattle out of mud holes, and maintained the wagons and equipment. The smaller bunkhouse was for Silas Atwood's cadre of gunmen. It was because Silas Atwood was so successful that he justified the presence of his own personal army of gunmen. He suggested that a man of his wealth and prominence was always in danger of being attacked.

The working cowboys weren't jealous of the special cadre. In fact, honestly they gave the gunmen little thought.

"They have their job, we have ours," is the way Miner Cobb, the foreman of the ranch, explained it. Because of the decreasing number of area ranches, the working cowboys of Eagle Shire were just thankful for the job.

Steady employment was not the norm for the cowboys working at any of the few remaining ranches. It was not only that none of the other ranchers had the economic clout as Silas Atwood, it was that many of the smaller ranches that had started the year under the ownership of one man had changed hands when they found the challenge of trying to survive in the shadow of a huge ranch, like the Eagle Shire, to be more difficult than they could handle.

Some sold out to Atwood on his first offer. They were the lucky ones. Those who insisted that they could survive sometimes found that their source of water was compromised, or mysterious fires burned away their grass. Also, because Atwood owned so much land, he had the smaller ranches blocked so that passage in and out of town was possible only by paying high toll fees. Most gave up, and abandoned their ranches with only what they could carry with them.

It wasn't just the ranchers who were having to deal with Atwood, several of the businessmen of the town of Etholen found their livelihood threatened as well.

"Do you know anything about the old feudal system of England?" Atwood once asked. "Men who owned large areas of land, and who controlled the village, became members of the peerage. We don't have peerage here, but I intend to have as much power as any duke in the realm."

Atwood already controlled the law in Etholen, not only the marshal and his deputy but the city council and the circuit judge as well. It was Atwood's control of the law that allowed him to bring in the bodies of Gus Dumey, Paul Burke, and Poke without having to face any consequences.

The only official in town that Atwood did not control was Mayor Joe Cravens. But he intended to take care of that in the next election.

CHAPTER TWO

The most popular saloon in town was the Pretty Girl and Happy Cowboy Saloon. If he could gain control of that saloon, Atwood felt that it would give him influence over much of the rest of the town. The Pretty Girl and Happy Cowboy Saloon was enjoying a peaceful Saturday afternoon. There was a friendly card game going on at one of the tables, and the teases, touches, and flirtatious laughter of the girls who gave the saloon its name were in play all through the room. The owner of the saloon, Kate Abernathy, was sitting at a table with Mayor Joe Cravens and Allen Blanton, the editor and publisher of the *Etholen Standard.*

Rusty Abernathy, Kate's son, was playing the piano, his music adding to the ambience of afternoon. Unlike the pianos in most saloons, this wasn't an upright . . . this was a Steinway Grand Piano, and, unlike most saloon piano players, Rusty had natural talent, great skill, and classical training. It was relatively rare when he played classical music, but even when he played the saloon classic songs, such as "The

Old Chisholm Trail," "The Cowboy's Lament," or "I Ride an Old Paint," he offered a melodic poignancy that made the musical experience in the Pretty Girl and Happy Cowboy to be quite unique.

"Atwood said that young Dumey, Burke, and Poke came out there to tear down the gate, and when they were challenged, they opened fire," Mayor Cravens said. "They said they were killed in self-defense."

"You don't believe that, do you, Joe?" Blanton asked.

"Not for a minute. But Witherspoon believed it. And so did Judge Boykin, so that's the end of it."

"I don't think that Witherspoon or Boykin believe it any more than we do. They're both in Atwood's pocket. You know that," Blanton said.

"Yes, well, it doesn't matter whether Boykin absolved Willis and the others out of belief or graft, he's made his ruling, and there's nothing we can do about it."

"You're the mayor," Kate said.

"I can't do a thing without the backing of the city council, and Atwood controls them as much as he does Witherspoon and Boykin."

"Maybe you can't do anything, but I've got the newspaper and freedom of the press," Blanton said. "And I intend to use it."

"You're a good man, Allen," Mayor Cravens said.

"Thank you. And, speaking of the paper, I've got some advertising copy I have to set, so, if you two will excuse me."

"I'll come with you," Mayor Cravens said.

The two men stood, then turned toward Kate. "Kate, my dear," Cravens said, taking her hand and lifting it to his lips. "It has been a pleasure visiting with you. You are like a long, cool drink of water in the midst of a blazing desert."

"Damn!" Blanton said. "And here I am supposed to be the one with a facility for words."

Kate laughed. "You gentlemen make my day."

Silas Atwood never went anywhere without at least two of his gunmen. Tonight, when he rode into town, he took Jeb Calley and Tony Clinton with him. He never hired anyone unless he knew quite a bit about them. Calley had deserted the army and robbed a stagecoach up in Wyoming, before drifting down to Texas. Clinton was wanted for murder back in Arkansas. The fact that Atwood knew so much about the men he hired for his special cadre helped him exercise control over them.

Kate saw Atwood and his two men come into her saloon, and she braced herself because she knew that Atwood was going to come to her table to talk to her. She also knew what he was going to talk about, because the subject came up every time Atwood came in. The Pretty Girl and Happy Cowboy Saloon was more than a mere saloon. It was almost like a country club, so that even women of the town could come in without being scandalized. The Pretty Girls of the saloon were just that, pretty girls who acted as hostesses and who provided the cowboy customers with what, for most of them, was their only opportunity to ever have a pleasant conversation with a woman.

Because of the popularity of the Pretty Girl and Happy Cowboy Saloon, Atwood had made it a point to try to buy it. He wanted to control the entire town, and it was his belief that control of the Pretty Girl and Happy Cowboy would give him enough of a presence, and influence over the town, that he would be able to realize his ambition.

As she expected, Atwood, leaving his two body-guards standing at the bar, came over to Kate's table.

"You may as well sell out to me, Kate," Atwood said. "You must know that no decent woman would ever own a saloon. I have made you a very generous offer."

"I appreciate the offer, Mr. Atwood. But my late husband opened this saloon, and I intend to manage it for as long as there is breath in my body."

"I'm sorry to hear you say that. I fear that you may find that remark to be most prophetic."

"Prophetic. What do you mean by that?"

"Let's just leave it at that, shall we?"

Atwood got up to leave, but on his way out, he stopped to say something to a man who was standing at the end of the bar that was nearest the door. As Atwood left the saloon, Clinton left with him, but Calley stayed behind.

Kate was sure Atwood had ordered him to stay behind, but why? After Atwood left, Calley looked directly at her, and with that glance, Kate was certain that their brief conversation had had something to do with her.

For a few moments after Atwood left, Calley continued to stand at the bar, then he shouted over to Rusty, "Hey you! Play 'Wait for the Wagon'!"

Rusty held up his hand, nodded, then played the

song Calley requested. After he completed the song, he started another one.

"Play 'Wait for the Wagon'!" Calley called again.

Rusty chuckled, waved, and continued with what he was playing.

"Play 'Wait for the Wagon'!" Calley shouted.

Rusty nodded again, then hurried through the song he was playing. "Mr. Calley, do you really want to hear it again?" he asked.

"Yeah," Calley replied.

"All right, here it is again."

Rusty played the song through to the end, even adding a few of his own flourishes. Then, he started another song.

"Hey, you! Play 'Wait for the Wagon'!" Calley demanded.

Rusty continued with the song he was playing.

"I told you to play 'Wait for the Wagon'!"

Rusty stopped in the middle of his song and turned around to face his heckler. "Mr. Calley, I have played that song for you, twice. There are other people who have asked that I play something for them, and I'm going to honor their requests. After that, I will play your song again, but that will be the last time tonight."

"If you don't commence a' playin' that song by the time I count to ten, I'm goin' to draw my gun and shoot you dead," Calley said menacingly.

There were fifteen other people witnessing the event, counting the customers, plus Kate and the "girls" who worked for her. One of the fifteen was Deputy Tim Calhoun, but he couldn't exactly be called a witness, since he was sitting at a table in the back of the room, too drunk to be aware of what was going on. At Calley's words, all conversation came to a halt as they looked at the drama that was playing out before them.

"Mr. Calley, surely you don't mean that," the bartender said.

"Peterson, you got that scattergun under the bar?"

When Peterson didn't answer, Calley drew his pistol and pointed it at the bartender.

"I asked you a question. Do you still have that scattergun under the bar?"

"Yeah," Peterson replied quietly.

"Pull that gun out by the barrel 'n lay it up on the bar," Calley ordered.

With shaking hands, Peterson reached down under the bar, then came up with his hands wrapped around the two barrels of the double-barreled, twelve-gauge, Greener shotgun. He put the gun on the bar.

"Good for you," Calley said. Then, with a grin that could only be described as malevolent, he turned back to Rusty.

"Piano player, you ain't started playin' yet," Calley said.

"I've no intention of playing 'Wait for the Wagon' again," Rusty said resolutely.

"Then I aim to commence a' countin', 'n if you ain't a' playin' that song by the time I get to ten, I'm goin' to shoot you," Calley said. "One!"

Rusty stood up, then moved out from behind the piano bench. "Mr. Calley, I wish you wouldn't do this," he said.

"Deputy Calhoun, do something, please!" Kate

said, calling back to the deputy marshal, whose head was on the table in front of him.

"Ha!" Calley said. "You think that drunk's goin' to be able to do anything?" He added to the count. "Two."

"Mr. Calley, as I am sure you are fully aware, I'm not a gunman," Rusty said. "Perhaps you have noticed, by now, that I'm not even wearing a pistol. I don't think you want to shoot an unarmed man, do you?"

"You," Calley said, pointing to one of the other customers. "Take your pistol over there, 'n lay it on the bench beside 'im." Calley laughed, though there was little humor in his laugh. "He's right, I don't want to shoot an unarmed man, 'n when I kill 'im, I don't want no one to say I wasn't bein' fair."

"That ain't fair, Calley," the customer said. "Like Rusty said, he ain't no gunfighter. Hell, all he does is play the piano and help his ma around the place."

"Take your pistol over there 'n lay it on the bench beside 'im like I told you to, or use it yourself," Calley said menacingly.

"You got no call to make me do that," the customer said.

"Either do what I told you to do, or draw your gun when I get to three." Calley smiled, an evil smile. "And mayhaps you mighta noticed, I'm already up to two."

"All right, all right!" the customer said, holding his hands out in front of him. "I'll do it!"

"Walk over there, take your gun out just real slow like, 'n put it on the bench alongside of 'im, then get out of the way. I wouldn't want you to maybe get yourself shot when I kill the piano player here."

Under Calley's watchful eye, the customer walked over to the bench. "I'm sorry, Rusty," the customer said. "But you can see how it is. What else could I do?"

"That's all right, Doodle, I understand," Rusty replied.

Doodle pulled his pistol, put it on the piano bench, then stepped back up to the bar.

"Three," Calley said after Doodle stepped away.

Rusty felt a hollowness in the pit of his stomach, and his throat grew dry.

"Four."

Calley continued to count. When he got to seven, he interrupted the count for a moment.

"Boy, if you think I'm just foolin' you, then you got another think comin'. By the time I get to ten, I'm goin' to kill you. Onliest chance you got is to pick up that gun 'n try 'n beat me. You ain't goin' to beat me, but you can at least try. Eight."

"Calley, what you're a' doin' is murder, pure 'n simple!" one of the other customers said.

"I tell you what," Calley said to Rusty. "If that whore mama of your'n would be willin' to sell this place to Mr. Atwood, why maybe I wouldn't kill you."

"Wait a minute! Is that what this is all about?" Kate asked. "This is so I'll sell my place to Atwood? I saw Atwood talking to you just before he left. Did he put you up to this?"

Calley turned to look toward Kate. "Nah, he didn't say nothin' like that to me. But I know he wants to buy this place, so I figure, if I could talk you into it, why he might just be real thankful for me doin' 'im a favor like that."

Out of the corner of her eye, Kate saw Rusty moving his hand slowly but steadily toward the pistol that Doodle had put on the piano bench. She decided to keep Calley's attention as long as she could.

"You can tell Atwood for me that I have no intention of selling my place to him."

"Well now, that's pure-dee a shame, ain't it?" Calley said. "I guess I'm just goin' to have to continue with the countin'. Nine . . ."

Suddenly the room was filled with the explosive sound of a gunshot. Blood squirted out from a bullet hole in Calley's temple, and he went down quickly, dead before he hit the floor.

Rusty stood there in shock, staring at the body of the man he had just shot. He was still holding the pistol, and he could smell the gunsmoke that curled up in a thin stream from the barrel.

"Damn!" Peterson said.

"Rusty!" Kate yelled, hurrying over to her son. She embraced him.

"I . . . I shot him, Mom," Rusty said, speaking the words in quiet awe. "I've never shot anybody before."

"You didn't have any choice, boy," Peterson said. "The son of a bitch was about to shoot you."

By now several people were coming into the saloon from the street, some drawn by the sound of the shot, and some because word of what had happened had already begun to spread.

One of those who came in was Marshal Witherspoon. He saw Rusty standing there holding the gun.

"Did you do this?" Witherspoon asked.

"Yes," Rusty answered.

Witherspoon walked over to take the gun. Rusty offered no resistance.

"You're under arrest for murder," he said.

CHAPTER THREE

Judge Henry L. Boykin rapped his gavel on the bench of the Circuit Court of Etholen.

Rusty looked over at Emil Cates, his court-appointed defense counsel. Rusty could smell whiskey, and Cates was so drunk he could barely hold his head up. He groaned when he saw the makeup of the jury. He recognized Willis, Clark, Booker, Creech, Walker, Pardeen, and Clinton, all members of Atwood's special cadre.

"Mr. Cates, can't you do somethin' about the jury?" Rusty asked. "Seven of them ride for the Eagle Shire Ranch."

"But five of them are citizens of the town," Cates replied. "Four are members of the city council, plus the manager of the bank is on the jury. They are all outstanding citizens, and it would do no good to challenge."

"Atwood owns the bank, and everyone knows that he controls the city council."

"Court will now come to order," Judge Boykin said. "Are counsels for prosecution and defense present?"

"Prosecution is present," C.E. Felker said.

"Defense?"

"Present."

"I want another lawyer," Rusty said.

"Mr. Cates has been appointed to defend you," Boykin said.

"I don't need a court-appointed attorney. I've got enough money to hire my own lawyer. I'll get a lawyer from El Paso."

"You are out of order. This trial is about to commence. Prosecutor, you may make your case."

"Prosecution calls Marshal Witherspoon," Felker said.

After Witherspoon was sworn in, he told about coming into the saloon and seeing Jeb Calley's body lying on the floor. He also testified that he saw Rusty Abernathy holding a gun.

"Did you question the defendant?" Felker asked.

"Yes, I asked him if he killed Calley."

"What was his answer?"

"He said yeah, he did it."

"Your witness," Felker said.

"No questions," Cates replied.

"Wait a minute!" Rusty said. "What do you mean, no questions? I told him I did it in self-defense."

Boykin began banging his gavel on the bench. "You are out of order! Witness is dismissed."

"Your Honor, prosecution rests," Felker said.

"Mr. Cates, do you have any witnesses?"

"No witnesses, Your Honor."

"What do you mean, no witnesses?" Kate Abernathy screamed from the gallery. Her protest was joined by a dozen others, all of whom had come to testify on Rusty's behalf.

"Order!" Boykin shouted. "If there is one more outburst, I will have this court cleared." Boykin turned back to Cates who, at the moment, was drinking from a whiskey flask.

"Are you prepared to present a case for the defense?" Boykin asked.

Cates corked the bottle, wiped the back of his hand across his lips, then stood, shakily.

"Your Honor, the boy said he did it in self-defense." Cates burped. "Defense rests, Your Honor."

It came as no surprise that after a deliberation of less than two minutes, the jury returned a verdict of guilty. Boykin dismissed the jury, then pronounced sentence.

"It is the sentence of this court that the defendant be held in jail until Friday next, at which date, with the rising of the sun, he is to be hanged by the neck until dead."

"No!" Kate screamed.

"Court is adjourned."

Big Rock

Smoke, Pearlie, and Cal had left Smoke's ranch, Sugarloaf, earlier this morning, pushing a herd of one hundred cows to the railhead in town. Shortly after they left, Sally had gone into town as well, but she had gone in a buckboard so she could make some purchases. Her shopping complete, she was now on Red Cliff Road halfway back home. The road made a curve about fifty yards ahead, and, for just an instant, she thought she saw the shadow of a man cast upon the ground. She had not seen anyone ahead of her, and the fact that no man materialized after the shadow put her on the alert. The average person would have paid no attention to the shadow, but one thing she had learned in all the years she had been married to Smoke was to always be vigilant.

"I've made a lot of enemies in my life," Smoke told her. "And some of them would do anything they could to get at me. And anyone who knows me also knows that the thing I fear most is the idea that you might be hurt because of me."

Smoke had also taught Sally how to use a gun, and she was an excellent student. She once demonstrated her skill with a pistol by entering a shooting contest with a young woman by the name of Phoebe Ann Mosey. The two women matched each other shot for shot, thrilling the audience with their skills, until, at the very last shot, Miss Mosey put a bullet half an inch closer to the center bull's-eye than did Sally. It wasn't until then that Sally learned the professional name of her opponent. It was Annie Oakley.

Sally pulled her pistol from the holster and held it beside her.

As the buckboard rounded the curve, a man jumped out into the road in front of her. His action startled the team of horses, and they reared up, causing her to have to pull back on the reins to get them back under control.

Sally had not been surprised by the man's sudden appearance, nor was the fact that he was holding a pistol in his hand unexpected.

"Is this a holdup attempt?" Sally asked. "If so, I

have very little money. As you can see by the bundles in the back I have been shopping, and I took only enough money for the purchases."

"Nah, this ain't no holdup," the man said. "You're Smoke Jensen's wife, ain't ya?"

"I'm proud to say that I am."

The man smiled, showing crooked, tobacco-stained teeth. "Then it don't matter none whether you've got 'ny money or not, 'cause that ain't what I'm after."

"What are you after?" Sally asked.

"I'm after some payback," the man said.

"Payback?"

"The name is Templeton. Adam Templeton. Does that name mean anythin' to you?"

"Would you be related to Deekus Templeton?"

"Yeah. What do you know about 'im?"

"I know that he took as hostage a very sweet young girl named Lucy Woodward, and held her for ransom."

"Yeah, he was my brother. I was in prison when your man killed him."

"Actually, it wasn't Smoke who killed him, it was a young man by the name of Malcolm Puddle."

"It don't make no never mind who it was, Jensen was there 'n as far as I'm concerned, it's the same thing as him killin' my brother."

"Why did you stop me?"

"Why, I thought you knew, missy. I plan to kill you. I figure me killin' you will get even with him."

"Will you allow me to step down from the buckboard before you shoot me?" Sally asked.

Templeton was surprised by Sally's strange reaction, not so much the question itself as the tone of her voice. She was showing absolutely no fear or nervousness.

"What do you want to climb down for?"

"I bought some material for a dress I'm going to make," Sally said, "and I wouldn't want to take a chance that I might bleed on it."

Templeton laughed. "You're one strange woman, do you know that? What the hell difference would it make to you whether you bleed on it or not? You ain't goin' to be makin' no damn dress, on account of because you're a-goin' to be dead."

"May I climb down?"

"Yeah, sure, go ahead."

Holding her pistol in the folds of her dress, Sally climbed down from the buckboard, then turned to face Templeton.

"Mr. Templeton, if you would put your gun away and ride off now, I won't kill you," Sally said. Again, the tone of her voice was conversational.

"What? Are you crazy? I'm the one holdin' the gun here. Now, say your prayers."

Suddenly, and totally unexpectedly, Sally raised her pistol and fired, the bullet plunging into Templeton's chest. He got a look of total shock on his face, dropped his pistol, then, as his eyes rolled up in his head, collapsed onto the road.

Cautiously, Sally walked over to look down at him.

Templeton was dead

Leaving Templeton's body lying on the side of the road, Sally turned the buckboard around and went back to town. Stopping in front of the marshal's

office, she went in to tell Marshal Monty Carson what
had happened.

Unaware of Sally's adventure, Smoke, Pearlie, and
Cal were pushing cows up the loading ramps into the
four stock cars that were parked on a side-track, doing
so at a rate of twenty-five animals per car.

"When will they be picked up?" Smoke asked. "I
don't want them to be in these cars any longer than
they have to be."

"The engine is already here," Gus Thomas said.
"They'll be out of here by one this afternoon, 'n
they'll be in Kansas City three days from now."

"Three days?"

Thomas chuckled. "Sure beats the old days of long
cattle drives, don't it?"

"It does at that," Smoke said.

It took no more than half an hour to finish loading the cattle, then Smoke took Pearlie and Cal to
lunch at Lamberts Café.

"Heads up!" someone shouted just as they stepped
inside, and Pearlie reached up to grab a biscuit that
came sailing through the air. *Tossed Biscuits* was a
trademark of the café.

"Why, there's Sally," Smoke said. "I wonder what
she's doing here."

"I hope there's nothing wrong," Pearlie said.

The three men joined her.

"I thought you were going back home," Smoke
said.

"Something came up," Sally said. She told him
about the encounter with Templeton on her way back.

"Where is he now? Templeton, I mean?" Smoke asked.

"I stopped by the marshal's office and Monty sent someone out to pick up the body."

"Smoke, before I go back to the ranch, I'd like to run down to the gunsmith shop," Pearlie said after lunch. "Seabaugh ordered a new pistol for me, 'n I'm pretty sure it's in by now."

"What did you get?" Cal asked.

"A Smith and Wesson Model Three," Pearlie said.

"Colt isn't good enough for you?"

"I like the Smith and Wesson," Pearlie said. "The way it breaks down, it's easier to load."

"I'll come with you," Cal said. "I need to buy a box of shells."

"And I've been wanting a new shotgun," Smoke said.

"You three go have your fun in the gun shop," Sally said. "I still have a buckboard full of purchases to unload. I'll see you when you get home."

CHAPTER FOUR

Etholen, Texas, Thursday night

"How does it feel, knowin' this is your last night on earth?" Witherspoon asked, standing just outside Rusty's cell.

Rusty glared at the marshal but said nothing.

"You ever seen anyone hang?" Witherspoon asked. "I have. Sometimes their eyes bulge out so far that you can just near 'bout pluck 'em out with your fingers. Well, wait until tomorrow mornin', 'n you'll see what I'm talkin' about. Oh, wait, you won't be able to see nothin', will you, 'cause it'll be your eyes that's all popped out like that."

Witherspoon laughed, a cackling laugh, then he walked back into the front of the office, just as Deputy Calhoun came in.

"Watch over him, Calhoun," Witherspoon said. "This is his last night, you know."

"Marshal, I ain't said nothin' 'bout this before, but do you think the boy really had a fair trial?"

"What difference does it make whether the trial

was fair or not?" Witherspoon asked. "Truth is, there warn't really no need for a trial in the first place, seein' as he told me his own self that he was the one that kilt Calley."

"Yes, but everyone who saw it said the boy didn't have any choice."

"You were there," Witherspoon said. "What do you think?"

"I . . . uh . . . didn't actually see what happened," Calhoun replied.

"No, you didn't see it, 'cause you were drunk. I don't know why I keep you on as deputy anyway."

"You keep me on because no one but me will deputy for you, and the only reason I will is 'cause I can't get work nowhere else."

"Yeah, well, seein' as you was drunk, if I was you, I just wouldn't be makin' no more comments about the trial. Besides which, Kate will probably wind up sellin' the saloon to Atwood before she lets her boy hang, 'n then it'll all be over."

"If that's all it takes to save 'im, wonder why she ain't done it yet?" Calhoun asked.

"Maybe she thinks Atwood is bluffing, and she's going to play it out to the last minute," Witherspoon suggested.

As soon as Witherspoon left, Calhoun walked over to a window, pulled a flask of whiskey from behind the shutter, then sat at the desk.

Over in the Pretty Girl and Happy Cowboy Saloon, Cletus Murphy and Doodle Higgins, who were not only regular customers of the saloon but friends with

Kate, were meeting with her back in the saloon office. Dolly was there as well.

"I told you Cletus and Doodle would be willing to do it."

"You don't have to do it, you know," Kate said. "Atwood has told me that if I would be willing to sell out to him, he would see to it that Rusty is set free. I've been waiting, hoping he was just running a bluff and would let Rusty out before he was actually hanged. That was no more of a trial than it was a church service, and if they actually did hang him, why it would be murder."

"Yes, ma'am, it would be murder," Cletus said. "But don't you think, for a moment, that Atwood ain't the kind of person who would murder someone. Remember what happened to young Gus Dumey and Burke and Poke. They was all three murdered, there ain't no doubt in my mind."

Kate nodded. "Yes, I believe you. That's why I'm going to tell Atwood that I'll sell out to him."

Doodle shook his head. "Ain't no need for you to do that. We'll have Rusty out of here and gone before mornin' ever rolls around."

"But it will be dangerous for you to do that . . . not only for you, but for Rusty as well."

"Calhoun will be watching him tonight," Cletus said. "Like as not, Calhoun is passed out drunk already."

Kate walked over to a cabinet, opened a door, and took out a box. "Here is one hundred dollars," she said, removing the money from the box. "This is all the cash I have on hand at the moment. Give this to him, and tell him I'll try and get more money to him later."

"Yes, ma'am," Doodle said, taking the money. "And don't you worry about a thing. Rusty will be long gone before anyone even misses him."

Five hours later, when the clock struck midnight, Calhoun didn't hear it. He also didn't notice when Cletus Murphy and Doodle Higgins came into the office. Doodle walked over to the desk.

"Asleep?" Cletus asked.

"Passed out drunk," Doodle answered.

Cletus reached up to take the ring of keys down, then, while Doodle kept an eye on Calhoun, Cletus went into the back of the jail. As it turned out, Rusty was the only one incarcerated at the moment.

"Rusty!" Cletus said as he opened the cell door.

"Cletus?"

"Here's a hundred dollars," Cletus said, giving Rusty the money. "There is a saddled horse out back. Go on up to Rattlesnake Springs; I've got a brother that owns a bakery there. Give 'im this letter."

"I need to see Mom before I go."

"No, it would be better if you just got on out of town now. She knows about this. Where do you think the one hundred dollars came from? Just go on up to Rattlesnake Springs and wait. We'll get your ma up to see you in a few days, then you all can figure out what you want to do next."

Rattlesnake Springs, Texas

Francis Murphy not only helped Rusty find a room, he also gave him a job, telling all the locals that Rusty's name was Terry Cooper and that he was his cousin from Fort Worth.

Rusty had been there for four days when he looked up to see Cletus coming in through the front door of the bakery. Rusty's broad smile at seeing him faded when he saw the expression on his friend's face.

"Cletus, what is it? What happened?"

"It's your ma, Rusty."

"My mom? What's wrong? What happened?"

"She's in jail. They say if you don't come back within a month, they'll hang her in your place."

"Then I'm going back!"

"No, don't, your ma doesn't want that. She's afraid if you come back they might just hang both of you."

"Well I'm not going to just stand by and let her hang. Can't you break her out of jail the way you did me?"

"Witherspoon is being a lot more careful with her. Anyway, if I broke her out and she left town, Atwood would wind up with the saloon, and she could sign over the saloon to him and save her own life now. But she doesn't want to do that unless it is absolutely necessary."

"Well, she's going to have to do that," Rusty insisted. "Because I'll be damned if I'm going to let her hang."

"Do you have an Uncle Wes?" Cletus asked.

"Yeah," Rusty said. "I've never seen him, but I do have an Uncle Wes."

Cletus gave Rusty a piece of paper. "You ma said this is where you'll find him."

Sugarloaf Ranch

When Smoke, Pearlie, and Cal dismounted in front of the house, Sally stepped down from the front porch to meet them. There was a young man with her, younger even than Cal.

"Hello," Smoke said.

"Hi, yourself," Sally replied with a smile.

"Looks like you've got company, Smoke. Give me your reins, and I'll take Seven to the barn," Pearlie said.

"No, Pearlie, let Cal take care of the horses," Sally said. "You come on inside, too. This concerns you."

"This concerns me?" Pearlie replied with a confused look on his face. "How does it concern me? What is this about?"

"We'll talk about it inside," Sally said.

"Damn, Pearlie, have you done somethin' you don't want anyone to know about?" Cal asked.

"I've done lots of things I don't want anyone to know about," Pearlie replied as he turned over the reins of his horse to Cal. Smoke and Pearlie followed Sally and the young man into the house.

"Pearlie," Sally said when they went into the parlor. "This is Rusty Abernathy. He has come to see you."

"Do I know you?" Pearlie asked.

"No, but you know my mom."

"I know your mother? What do you mean, I know your mother? What is her name?"

"Her name is Abernathy now. But you would know her as Kate Fontaine."

"What?" Pearlie gasped. He sat down quickly. "Katie is your mother?"

"Yes, sir, she is. Hello, Uncle Wes."

Pearlie was silent for a long moment. "How did you know where to find me?" he asked.

"You came to Texas not too long ago to deliver some horses to Mr. Tom Byrd. Do you remember that?"

"Yes, I remember that," Pearlie said.

"Mom knew you were there, 'n she almost went to see you then. But she said you were in some trouble when you were real young, and she wasn't sure you would want to see her."

"She's right about that," Pearlie said. "Oh, not about me not wantin' to see her," he added quickly. "I mean she's right about me being in trouble when I was young. But it was more than *some* trouble, I was in a hell of a lot of trouble."

Cal came in then.

"Dooley said he'd take care of the horses," Cal said. "I thought I'd come in and see what was going on in case you needed me for something."

"We don't need you for anything, Cal," Sally said. "This concerns Pearlie."

"No, Miz Sally, please, let 'im stay," Pearlie said, lifting his hand. "I'm about to tell you all a story, and being as Cal is my friend, he may as well hear it at the same time you and Rusty do. Smoke, you can listen, too, of course, but you already know the story. I told it to you a long time ago, back when I first come to work for you."

Smoke nodded. "Yes, I remember the story."

"I asked you then not to tell Miz Sally, 'cause I didn't want her thinkin' bad of me, but I guess she's pretty much made up her mind about me now, no matter what, so I figure I may as well tell it."

"Pearlie," Sally said. "I don't think there's anything you could tell me about your past that would change how I feel about you. You and Cal are both very special to me."

"Yes, ma'am, I know that, and I appreciate it more than I can say. But I guess this is as good a time as any to get this off my chest.

"My folks died when I was thirteen years old, and I got on as a cowboy, riding for the B Bar B brand. It was hard work, but I discovered then that I liked being a cowboy, and I became a pretty good hand, even if I do say so myself. I made a lot of really good friends with all the other cowboys at the B Bar B, and one night when I was fifteen, I went into town with some of the boys, and we went to a saloon."

"Pearlie, you were in a saloon when you were only fifteen?" Sally asked.

"Yes, ma'am, but you don't have to worry any about that, because the only thing I was drinking was lemonade. Only as things turned out, it would have been better if I had been drinking beer or whiskey, 'cause it was drinking the lemonade that started the trouble."

"I don't see how just drinking a glass of lemonade could start trouble," Sally said.

"Yes, ma'am, you wouldn't think so, would you?" Pearlie replied. "And if Miller had been a decent kind of man, why, there wouldn't have been any trouble."

"Someone named Miller gave you trouble just because you were drinking lemonade?"

"Yes, ma'am. Emmett Miller, his name was."

As Pearlie continued, he spoke with such feeling and such intensity that the story played out in front of the others as if they had been actual witnesses.

CHAPTER FIVE

Southwest Texas, several years earlier

There were four others who had come into town with Pearlie, whose real name was Wes Wesley Fontaine. The other four ordered beer, but Wes ordered a glass of lemonade.

"Ha, lemonade? You come into a man's bar and order lemonade?" one of the saloon patrons taunted.

"I like lemonade."

"That ain't much of a man's drink now, is it?"

Wes, realizing that the man was trying to pick a fight, didn't respond.

"What's a kid like you doin' comin' in here with the men? Ain't they someplace you could go to be with the other children to drink lemonade?"

"Why don't you back off and leave him alone, mister? He ain't botherin' you none," one of the other B Bar B riders said. "Wes is as good a worker as any rider we have."

"Yeah? Well tell me, has he been weaned yet? Or

do you boys carry a sugar tit around for him?" the heckler taunted.

"Here's your lemonade, Wes."

"Thanks," Wes said.

"Tell me, kid, can you drink that without a nipple?"

Wes set his lemonade down and turned toward the cowboy who was riding him.

"What is your name, sir?"

"Well now, this kid called me sir. Maybe does have some manners after all. Or, maybe he thinks that if he's just real nice to me, I won't turn him over my knees and give him a spanking."

"My name is Wes. Wes Fontaine. You haven't told me your name, sir."

"His name is Miller," one of the other B Bar B riders said. "Emmett Miller."

"Well, Miller," Wes started.

"That would be *Mister* Miller to you, you snot-nosed little brat," Miller said, emphasizing the word "Mister."

"Mr. Miller, I'm going to ask you now, in the nicest possible way, to leave me alone."

Miller laughed. "You're asking me in the nicest possible way, are you? And if I don't leave you alone, what are you going to do?"

"It may be that I have to kill you," Wes replied in a quiet, matter-of-fact voice. "I don't want to, but if you don't leave me alone, it may come to that."

"What did you just say?" Miller shouted at him.

"I said that if you don't leave me alone, I'm going to kill you," Wes repeated. "But, in the nicest possible way, of course," he added with a sardonic grin.

"By God! I don't have to take that from no snot-nosed, big-mouthed kid!"

"No, you don't have to take it," Wes said. "You don't have to take it at all. All you have to do is shut up, go your way, and let me go mine. Then we can act as if none of this has even happened."

"No, by God, I ain't goin' my way!" Miller said, reaching for his gun even as he was shouting the words.

What neither Miller, nor even any of the other B Bar B riders, realized was that Wes, knowing that he was younger than most of the others, had decided his best way of protecting himself would be with a gun. And because of that, he had been practicing with his draw for some time now. And though Miller started his draw first, Wes had his gun out and shooting before Miller was even able to bring his gun up to aim. Miller fell back on the saloon floor with a bullet in his chest.

"Son of a bitch!" one of the B Bar B riders said. "Who knew the kid was that good?"

Although he was good with a gun, this was the first time Wes had ever shot at another man, and now as he looked at the man he had just killed, lying on the floor, he felt a little nauseous.

"Mr. Poppell, I think I would like to have a whiskey," Wes said.

"You ever had yourself 'ny whiskey before, Wes?" one of the other B Bar B riders asked.

"No."

"Then take my word for it, you don't want none now, neither. Wait till you get a mite older afore you start on somethin' like that."

"Jimmy's right," one of the B Bar B riders said. "Folks that get started too early sometimes wind up as drunks, 'n you sure as hell don't want nothin' like that."

"I'll give you a whiskey if that's what you want, boy," Poppell said. "But I think you should listen to your friends and stick to lemonade."

"All right," Wes said. He picked up the lemonade Poppell had put in front of him earlier.

"What the hell's goin' on in here? I just heard a gunshot!" someone said, pushing in through the batwing doors. He was wearing a badge.

"Hello, Marshal Gibson, I was about to send for you," Poppell said.

Marshal Gibson had a bad reputation; some said he had been a cattle rustler before coming here. Others said that he had sold his gun to the highest bidder. Pinning on the badge had not made an honest man of him, because it was well known that he was selling protection to the honest businesses and taking a cut from the dishonest businesses. He stared down at Miller's body.

"Someone want to tell me what happened?" Gibson asked.

"Miller got hisself kilt," someone said.

"Hell, I can see that. What I want to know is, who done it?"

"I did," Wes said. He didn't look at the marshal. Instead, he stared into his glass of lemonade.

Gibson laughed out loud. "Are you kidding me? I'm askin' a serious question here. Now, who was it that kilt Miller?"

Wes turned toward the marshal. "I told you, Marshal, I killed him."

"The kid's tellin' you the truth," one of the other saloon patrons said.

"But he didn't have no choice, Marshal," the bartender put in quickly. "Miller kept ridin' the kid, for no good reason. Finally, the kid stood up to him, 'n when he did, Miller drawed on 'im."

"Are you tellin' me that Miller drawed first, but the kid kilt 'im anyway?"

"Yeah," Poppell said.

"I don't believe you."

"That's right, Marshal. Ever'thing Poppell is tellin' you is right," another patron said, and every one of the B Bar B riders said the same thing.

"So you kilt 'im, did you?" the marshal said, finally coming to the understanding that Miller had drawn first.

"Yes, sir. I didn't want to kill 'im, but he didn't leave me any choice."

"Get out of my county, kid," the marshal said.

"What?"

"You heard me. I said get out of my county."

"But I live here. Where would I go?"

"I don't give a damn where you go, just as long as you leave."

"Why?"

"Why? Because the last thing I need is some young punk who thinks he's a gunfighter."

"You heard everyone, Marshal. I didn't start this fight, Miller did. Anyhow I don't want to leave. Like I said, I live here, and I have a good job and good friends."

"You don't understand, do you, kid? I don't really

give a damn whether you want to leave or not. I'm *orderin'* you to leave, and you ain't got no choice."

"Yes, sir, I do have the choice of leavin' 'cause the truth is, you've got no right to force me. I'm tellin' you right now, I don't have any intention of leavin'. So if you want to arrest me, why you just go right ahead. I'll come peacefully, then I'll take my chances with a trial."

"There ain't goin' to be no trial. With all these people testifyin' for you, you'd more'n likely get off, then you'd still be in my county, and I don't plan on that happenin'. So I'm going to tell you one more time, to get out of my county."

Wes shook his head. "I ain't goin'."

"You got no choice, boy. You either get out of my county now, or get ready to die."

"Wait a minute. You're plannin' to draw on me? Why? I haven't done anything wrong. You heard everyone in here tell you that I was in the right."

An evil smile spread across the marshal's face. "Boy, I don't know if it's your brain or your ears that ain't workin'. I told you to get out, 'n you're either goin' to do that, or I'm goin' to kill you right here, 'n right now."

At those words, everyone in the saloon stepped out of the way to give the two room. They hadn't done so with the first shooting, because it had happened too quickly, and by the time they realized there was going to be a shooting, it was too late. Not so now, as a shooting seemed inevitable.

"Marshal, I ain't leavin'," Wes said. "So if you're plannin' on shootin' me, I reckon you better just go ahead and try."

"You think you can beat me, do you?" the marshal asked.

"I reckon I can," Wes said. "I sure didn't plan on it goin' this far, but yeah, if it comes down to it, I can beat you."

With a triumphant smile, the marshal's hand dipped toward his pistol, but before he could clear leather, Wes had already drawn and fired. The marshal, with a surprised look on his face, went down.

Sugarloaf Ranch, the present

Pearlie stopped his story there and was quiet for a long moment, realizing that Sally, Cal, and Rusty were hanging on every word. Smoke was listening quietly as well, though he already knew the story.

"Do you understand what I'm saying?" Pearlie asked. "Within ten minutes' time I had killed two men, and one of the two men I killed was a lawman."

"I knew about the story because Mom heard it," Rusty said. "You left right after that, didn't you?"

"Yeah, I left right after that. I didn't have two dimes to rub together, but the other men took up a collection, and even the bartender and the soiled doves added to it. I left town with forty dollars, which, at the time, was the most money I had ever held in my hand at one time."

"You were older than fifteen when you came here," Sally said.

"Yes, well, I . . . uh . . . didn't come here right away," Pearlie said. "I wandered around for a while, and I did some things that I'd just as soon not talk about, things that I'm not very proud of."

"Mom has been wanting to write to you, to tell you that there was nobody looking for you anymore," Rusty said. "She was upset with herself for not coming to see you when you were at the Byrd Ranch. So after you left, she found out where you lived and was planning on maybe coming to see you sometime. That is, before this happened."

"Before what happened?" Pearlie asked.

Rusty took a deep breath, held it for a moment, then let it out in an audible sigh. "Well, like you, Uncle Wes, I killed someone. And, like you, it wasn't something I set out to do, it was self-defense."

Rusty explained how a man named Silas Atwood controlled most of El Paso County, and how he was now trying to take over the town of Etholen as well. He told of his encounter with Jeb Calley, and the subsequent jailbreak.

"Was anyone killed during the jailbreak?" Smoke asked.

"No, sir, there wasn't even anyone hurt. You see, they came by in the middle of the night and Calhoun, he's the deputy that was supposed to be watching me, was passed out drunk. All they had to do was take the cell keys down from where they were hanging on a nail alongside the calendar. They opened the cell door and let me out, just slick as a whistle."

Pearlie nodded. "It's good to have friends," he said.

"Yes, sir, friends, and relatives."

"By relatives, you mean me, don't you?" Pearlie asked.

"Yes, sir, I do mean relatives, and since you're the only relative that I have, I mean you. Uncle Wes, Mom is in jail now."

"Katie is in jail?" Pearlie asked, the expression on his face showing his shock at the pronouncement. "Why on earth is Katie in jail?"

"Atwood blames her for helping me escape."

"Well, I wouldn't worry too much about her," Smoke said. "It'll be hard for him to make the case that she helped you escape."

Rusty shook his head. "You don't understand how crooked a judge Boykin really is. Mom has already been tried and found guilty of accessory to murder, and helping a condemned murderer to escape. Judge Boykin says he will keep her in jail for thirty days, though he also says he will set her free if I come back and turn myself in."

"Well, then all you have to do is stay away for thirty days, and they'll let her loose," Sally suggested with a bright smile.

"No, ma'am, it isn't like that. It isn't at all like that. What Atwood plans to do is hold her for thirty days, then hang her."

"Why, that is outrageous!"

"You said Atwood was going to hold her for thirty days," Smoke said. "Don't you mean this judge . . . Boykin that you're talking about, is the one who is going to hold her?"

"Boykin does exactly what Atwood tells him to do," Rusty said.

"What makes this Atwood person think he can get away with something like that?" Sally asked.

"He don't just think he can get away with it, Miz Sally, he knows he can get away with it. It's like I said, Atwood controls all of El Paso County, and a lot of Reeves and Presidio Counties as well. To be honest, I doubt if Atwood even wants me to come back. Because if they really do hang Mom, then he'll be able to buy up the saloon at a public auction."

"How many days has Katie been in jail, so far?" Pearlie asked.

"She's been in jail for over a week now, maybe even a few days longer. As soon as I found out about it, I took a train and came up here to see you."

"That means we've only got three weeks left," Smoke said.

"We?" Rusty asked.

"Of course, we," Smoke replied. "You did come up here to ask for Pearlie's help, didn't you?"

"Yes, sir, but I didn't figure anyone other than Uncle Wes would get involved."

"Rusty, here is something you are going to learn about us," Cal said. "If one of us is involved, all of us are involved."

CHAPTER SIX

After a two-day trip down from Big Rock, the train rolled into the station in Gomez, Texas, where they were told that the train would have a half-hour wait.

"Are you in any danger of being recognized here?" Pearlie asked his nephew.

Rusty shook his head. "I hardly think that anyone would know me here. Only way I could get recognized would be if I happened to run into someone from Etholen who was visiting, or if someone had come to Etholen and heard me play the piano."

"Play the piano?" Sally asked, perking up at that information.

"Yes, I play the piano in Mom's saloon. Anyway, I've never been here before, so I'm reasonably sure I won't be recognized by anyone."

"That's good to know. How are you fixed for money?" Pearlie asked his nephew.

"Oh, don't you worry about that, I'm in good shape," Rusty replied. "Mom and I have more'n five thousand dollars in the Etholen Bank."

"No, you don't," Smoke said.

"What do you mean, we don't? We sure do have money in that bank."

"Oh, you may have money there, all right," Smoke agreed. "But you aren't going to be able to get to it until this is all cleared up."

"How much do you have on you, right now?" Pearlie asked.

"About twelve dollars," Rusty said. "I had a hundred dollars when I left town, but I've used most of it up."

"Here's another hundred dollars," Pearlie said, pulling the money from his billfold and giving it to Rusty. "We've been talking it over and we've decided it would be better for you to stay here until we get this all settled."

"What do you mean you want me to stay here? That's my mom in jail in Etholen, and they're planning on hanging her if I don't show up."

"Yes, and if you show up now, they'll hang you *and* your mother, which means I'll be losing a sister I just found, and a nephew I never knew I had," Pearlie said. "And I'm not willing to do that, so I want you to listen to what I'm telling you. You are going to stay here, in Gomez, until we send for you."

Rusty shook his head. "No, I don't think you understand. Witherspoon is the marshal, and he's only got one deputy. But the real power, I told you, is Silas Atwood. Atwood has a whole bunch of hired guns working for him. That's how he keeps control of everything. You'll be badly outnumbered if you go in there, with just the three of you."

"Four of us," Sally said.

"Four of you? But, you're a woman."

Pearlie chuckled. "Damn, Miz Sally. Did you know you were a woman?"

Sally smiled. "I've been told that."

Smoke chuckled. "Rusty, don't you worry about Sally being a woman. That's never stopped her before."

Sally put her hand on Rusty's shoulder. "I know it's going to be hard on you, honey, but I've been around these three for a long time and I learned, a long time ago, to have faith in them. They will get things taken care of, and we will send for you."

"All right," Rusty agreed. "I'll wait here, but I'm going to be on pins and needles until I hear from you."

"I plan to visit Kate as soon as I arrive," Sally said. "I'll let her know that you are all right."

"Good, that'll take some of the worry away," Rusty said.

Sally smiled. "I expect she'll be surprised by a visit from a stranger."

"Oh, she knows who you are, Miz Sally. Don't forget, she'd been makin' plans to come up 'n see Uncle Wes ever since you all took them horses down to the Byrd Ranch. And she is the one that got word to me that I should come up and get Uncle Wes."

"Good, then I shouldn't have any trouble getting in to see her."

"Unless Marshal Witherspoon stops you," Rusty said. "You be careful of him. He's about the biggest crook there is."

"We'll be careful," Sally promised.

* * *

During the two-hour trip from Gomez to Etholen, Smoke, Sally, Pearlie, and Cal came up with a plan. Execution of the plan, however, would depend upon Kate's approval.

"What if Kate doesn't believe I'm who I say I am?" Sally said. "What if she thinks I don't even know Pearlie, that I'm working for Atwood?"

"Tell her that one night she and I went over to Mr. Rowe's farm and stole a watermelon," Pearlie said. "Then, Mr. Rowe came out of his house and shot at us with a shotgun, and I put myself in front of her, to protect her, so that I was the one who got hit."

"Oh, heavens, Pearlie! You were shot with a shotgun?"

Pearlie laughed. "Yeah. The shells had been loaded with strips of rawhide, so it stung like the dickens when it hit me, but it didn't do much more than wound my pride."

"What happened to the watermelon?" Cal asked.

This time it was Sally who laughed. "Leave it to Cal to worry about the watermelon."

"I dropped it and it broke open," Pearlie said. "So, Kate and I just scooped the heart out, then ran."

Prior to leaving Big Rock, Smoke had made arrangements to lease a special stock car to be attached to their train. The purpose of the car was to provide transportation for the horses, and when the four of them reached Etholen, the job of taking care of the horses fell to Cal. Smoke, Sally, and Pearlie took the luggage to the Milner Hotel where they arranged for the rooms. Then, from the hotel, Sally went to the jail to visit with Kate, while Smoke and Pearlie went to the Pretty Girl and Happy Cowboy Saloon.

When Sally stepped into the jail, it smelled of cheap cigar smoke, and the origin of the smell was quickly and easily ascertained. A thin man, with what looked like a week's growth of scraggly whiskers, sat behind a desk with a lit cigar clenched between his teeth. He was dealing poker hands, but he was the only one playing since he was alone in the jail.

"Marshal Witherspoon?" Sally asked.

Sally had entered the room so quietly that she hadn't been seen, and when she spoke, the man behind the desk was visibly startled.

"Jesus, lady! Who the hell are you, and how did you get in here?"

"I opened the door and walked in," Sally replied. She purposely omitted giving her name. "Are you Marshal Witherspoon?"

"Nah, I ain't the marshal. I'm Deputy Calhoun. What do you want?"

"I wish to visit one of your prisoners," Sally replied.

"One of 'em? Ha! We only got us one prisoner."

"That would be Mrs. Abernathy?"

"Yeah. You know Kate, do you?"

"You call her by her first name?"

"Ever'one does. Hell, she runs a saloon. Any woman that runs a saloon don't expect to be called by nothin' else. Are you one of her whores? 'Cause if you are, I ain't never seen you before."

"No."

"Then why do you want to see her?"

"We have a mutual acquaintance."

The deputy squinted his eyes. "Yeah? That mutual acquaintance wouldn't be her son now, would it? 'Cause, maybe you don't know nothin' 'bout it, but Rusty Abernathy, he's wanted for murder."

"No, Rusty Abernathy isn't the name of the person we share in common."

"Well, who is it then?" the deputy asked.

"Why would you need to know who it might be?"

"On account of 'cause I'm the law, 'n I got a right to know things like that. It's all a part of investigatin' 'n all, you know, so as we can find out where Rusty Abernathy is."

"The mutual acquaintance we share is her brother."

"Ha! Now I know you're lyin'. She ain't got no brother."

"Where was Kate born?" Sally asked.

"What? How do I know where she was born?"

"If you don't know where she was born, then you don't know everything about her, do you? She could have a brother, and you would know nothing at all about it."

Calhoun ran his hand through the scraggly growth of whiskers on his chin and stared at Sally for a long moment.

"You're wearin' a pistol."

"Oh, for heaven's sake, Deputy, you aren't afraid of a woman, are you?"

"All right," Calhoun finally agreed. "Let me have

your pistol and you can go on back there; you can talk to her. But I plan to listen to everything you talk about."

"Well, you are certainly welcome to do that," Sally replied as she handed her pistol over, butt first. "We have no secrets."

When Sally stepped into the back of the jail, she saw a woman sitting on the edge of her bed.

"You got a visitor, Kate," Calhoun said.

"Who are you?" Kate asked, looking up in curiosity.

"Wes Fontaine sent me," Sally said.

Kate gasped. "Wes?"

"Yes."

"Say, Kate, do you know who this fella Wes Fontaine is?" Deputy Calhoun asked.

"Yes. Wes Fontaine is my brother."

"All right then, you wasn't lyin'. You two go ahead and talk, I'll just listen in."

"Wes wanted me to tell you about the new quilt I made for him," Sally said. "Which do you like, Cactus Wreath? Or Country Stable? Of course, I also like Sassy Sunflower. But then, Tile Tangle is nice, too."

At first, Kate was puzzled, then, when she saw the expression on the deputy's face, she realized what Sally was doing.

"Well, I've always liked Lilies of the Field. What sort of stitch are you using? Stitch in the Ditch, or Outline?"

"Stitch in the Ditch; I know it's more difficult, but it makes a much more beautiful quilt. Why I . . ."

"Is this all you two are going to talk about?" Calhoun asked with a sigh.

"Oh, but Deputy Calhoun, you should see the

quilt. Why, if I say so myself, it's the most beautiful quilt I've ever made."

Calhoun shook his head in disgust. "There ain't no way I'm goin' to stay back here 'n listen to you two prattle on about quiltin' and such."

Calhoun left, then closed the door behind him so that the two women were alone in the back of the jail. They looked at each other and laughed.

"At first, I wasn't sure what you were talking about," Kate said. "That was a good way of getting rid of him. How is Wes doing?"

"He's doing just great. He got your message, and he's here, in town."

"What about . . ." Kate stopped in midsentence, then looked toward the door to make certain that the deputy wasn't listening. "Wait a minute. How do I know you are who you say you are? It could be that my message to Wes was intercepted, and you're somebody Atwood paid to pretend to know Wes. I think it would be better if we didn't talk."

"What happened when you and your brother tried to steal watermelons from Mr. Rowe?" Sally asked.

For a moment Kate was surprised by the question, then a broad smile spread across her face.

"Mr. Rowe had loaded some of his shotgun shells with bits of rawhide, and he shot Wes." She laughed. "There's absolutely no way you could possibly know that if Wes hadn't told you. You are who you say you are."

"I am indeed. And we are here to help you."

"Have you seen Rusty?"

"Yes, and he's fine," Sally said. "He's the one who told us about your problem."

"Oh, but, he isn't here, in town, is he? It's much too dangerous for him to be here."

"No, he is nearby, but he isn't here. We'll get you together when it is safe to do so."

"We?"

"My husband, Pearlie, Cal, and I."

"By Pearlie you mean . . ."

"Your brother," Sally said, answering before the question was completed. Sally reached through the bars, and Kate took her hand.

"Yes, I heard that he was calling himself Pearlie now."

"Just sit tight, and don't worry about a thing," Sally said. "We are going to get you out of this."

CHAPTER SEVEN

"I'm told a lady owns this saloon. Is that true?" Smoke asked as he and Pearlie stepped up to the bar to order a drink. Smoke was well aware that it was true, but he asked the question so that he could measure the bartender's reaction.

"Yes, sir, and a fine lady she is, too," the bartender said as he drew two beers.

"Lady, hell? She ain't much more'n a whore," one of the drinkers at the other end of the bar said.

"That ain't true, 'n you know it, Pardeen. Miss Kate is not a whore," the bartender said.

"What do you mean, she's not a whore? She's got whores that works for her, don't she? That's the same thing. What she should do is sell this place to my boss."

"Why should she do that?" the bartender asked. "Miss Kate is a fine woman, and she treats all of us real good."

"Yeah? Well what are you goin' to do when they wind up hangin' her in place of her son, on account of he run away after he murdered Calley."

"Rusty didn't murder Calley. You forget, I was here, and I saw what happened. That shooting was self-defense, pure 'n simple," the bartender said.

"The hell it was. Calley warn't even a' lookin' at Abernathy when he got shot. I was on the jury, remember, 'n that's how come we found 'im guilty. 'N that's how come Judge Boykin sentenced him to hang."

"Hell, Pardeen, Calley was countin' out loud, 'n he told ever'one in the saloon that he was goin' to kill Rusty when he got to ten. He was already up to nine when Rusty shot 'im, 'n if Rusty hadn't of shot him, Calley damn sure would've shot Rusty," one of the other patrons said.

"Yeah, but Calley was lookin' away from Rusty when Rusty picked up that gun 'n kilt 'im."

"That doesn't matter. There is nobody who saw it who would say that the shooting wasn't justified," the bartender said.

"Yeah, well I seen it, 'n I was on the jury, 'n we said what he done was murder," Pardeen said.

"Wait a minute," Smoke said. "Are you telling me that you were a witness to the event, and yet you served on the jury?"

"Yeah," Pardeen said. "That's what I'm tellin' you."

"There was no one on that jury except men who Atwood either controls or men who ride for him. And none of them were real cowboys, either. They were all gunhands, same as Calley," the bartender said.

"It don't make no never mind now whether Rusty is guilty or not," Pardeen said. "He won't never be comin' back here. 'N if he don't come back, the whore that owns this place is goin' to get her neck stretched."

"Maybe common sense will prevail," the bartender said.

"If there was any common sense, she woulda sold this place to Atwood when she had the chance. Now, she's goin' to wind up dead, that no-count son of hers is gone to hell 'n back, 'n that means they won't be nobody left to own this place. What's goin' to happen is the marshal will wind up takin' it over, then he'll sell it to the highest bidder, 'n that'll be Atwood."

"I'll tell you this, Pardeen," the bartender said. "If Atwood does wind up owning this place, he'll have to get a new bartender, because I sure as hell won't work for him."

"No, and neither will any of the girls," a nearby bar girl said.

"Ha," Pardeen replied. "Bartenders are a dime a dozen, 'n whores are even cheaper. You won't have to quit, Atwood will more'n likely fire ever'one anyway. Why, I might wind up tendin' bar myself."

"Yeah, you'd make a fine bartender. You don't know scotch from bourbon," the bartender replied.

"What is your name, bartender?" Smoke asked.

"The name is Peterson. Ray Peterson."

"Mr. Peterson, I like a man who is loyal to his employer. You're a good man."

The bartender smiled. "Why, I thank you, sir," Peterson replied. "But when you have a boss like Miss Kate, it isn't hard to be loyal."

The scoffing sound Pardeen made may have been

a laugh. "You beddin' her, Peterson?" he asked. "Is that why you takin' up for her like that?"

"You have a big mouth," Peterson said.

"You know what? I don't want you to quit. I want you to beg Atwood to let you stay on. I want to see him fire you."

"Mr. Pardeen, you keep talking about Atwood. Do you know him?" Smoke asked.

"Yeah, I know him. I work for him."

"You're a cowboy?"

"Cowboy?" Pardeen smiled. "Yeah, I'm a cowboy."

"He's no more a cowboy than I am," Peterson said. "He's one of Atwood's gunhands."

"I want you to take a message to Atwood," Smoke said.

"A message? What kind of message?"

"You can tell him that he is not going to buy this saloon."

"Oh? Who's going to buy it? You?"

"Nobody is going to buy it. It's going to stay in the hands of its current owner."

"Really? You bein' new here, maybe you don't know that Kate is in jail now, 'n she's more'n likely goin' to hang if her no-count son don't come back so's we can hang him."

"My sister isn't going to hang, and neither is my nephew. We aren't going to let that happen," Pearlie said.

"Your sister? Who the hell are you?"

"My name is Pearlie, and Katie is my sister."

Pardeen laughed. "Pearlie? What the hell kind of name is Pearlie?"

"It's my name," Pearlie said without any further explanation.

"And you're going to stop 'em from hanging, are you? Tell me . . . Pearlie, just how do you plan to stop that?"

"We're going to stop it by taking Atwood down. You might tell him that for us," Smoke said.

Pardeen turned to face Smoke and when he did so, Pearlie, recognizing the expression on Pardeen's face, stepped to one side.

"You're going to take Mr. Atwood down, are you?"

"Yes."

"It could be that I'll just take you down instead," Pardeen suggested.

"I wish you wouldn't do that," Smoke said.

"Yeah?" Pardeen said with an easy, confident grin on his face. "I'll just bet you do. Don't want to get shot, do you?"

"No, I don't want to have to kill you," Smoke replied. "I'd rather you stay alive so you can deliver my message to Atwood."

"You don't need to worry none about . . ." Pardeen didn't finish his sentence, and it was soon obvious that he had no intention of doing so, because the sentence was just a distraction. Pardeen snaked his gun from his holster in a lightning-swift move.

But Smoke was faster. Smoke intuitively knew that Pardeen was about to go for his gun, and even before Pardeen was able to bring his gun to bear, Smoke was pulling the trigger.

Pardeen pulled the trigger as well, but it was a reflexive action because as he went down with a bullet in his heart, the bullet from his gun punched a hole in the floor, in front of the bar.

There were a few gasps of surprise from some of the other patrons in the saloon, and they looked on in shock at the calmness the two men displayed as Smoke and Pearlie took their beers over to a table near the back wall, leaving Pardeen dead on the floor behind them.

"Who are those men?" someone asked.

"That one feller said he was Kate's brother, but I never heard her say nothin' 'bout havin' a brother. I don't have no idee who the other 'n is."

Smoke and Pearlie had chosen this particular table because its location meant that nobody could get behind them, and from here, both men could see everyone at the bar.

"Do you think that might shake Atwood up a bit?" Smoke asked.

"Yeah," Pearlie replied with a chuckle. "I think it might just do that."

Smoke noticed that a couple of the men who had been standing next to Pardeen when they first came in were now talking to one another in what could only be described as anxious whispers. They were joined by a third man.

"From the way those men are acting, keeping their conversation close and glancin' over here toward us, I wouldn't be surprised if the were plannin' somethin'," Pearlie said.

"I would say that is a good observation," Smoke replied.

Smoke and Pearlie continued to monitor the

three men, though doing so without being too obvious.

After their brief conference the three men separated, one standing at either end of the bar, and one taking his place at the middle of the bar. Then, as one, they all three turned to look back toward the table occupied by Smoke and Pearlie.

"Here it comes," Smoke said quietly.

"Mister, you've just committed murder," one of the men said. "And until the marshal comes, we intend to keep you from running away."

Smoke took a swallow of his beer before he put the glass down. "I'm not planning on going anywhere," he said.

That wasn't the answer the man was expecting, so he blinked his eyes in surprise. Then he continued to tell Smoke and Pearlie what he was thinking, just as if they had asked him.

"What I'm a' thinkin' is, Mr. Atwood is more'n likely not goin' to be too pleased with you killin' one of his men like that."

"Do you mean you work for Atwood?" Smoke asked.

"Yeah, we do."

"Willis, if I were you, I'd leave that gentleman alone," Peterson said. "There's not a soul in this room who didn't see what happened, and we'll give Witherspoon an earful when he gets here."

"There ain't goin' to be no need for you to be a' tellin' Witherspoon anything," Willis said. "I expect by the time Witherspoon gets here this will all be over with."

"Pearlie, I do believe these three folks are getting ready to draw against us," Smoke said.

"Do you think so?" Pearlie replied.

"I don't know, but it seems to me like they're trying to get up their courage to give us a try."

Smoke and Pearlie were talking about the potential life-or-death situation as calmly as if they were discussing whether or not it might rain. Their calmness in the face of this situation awed the patrons of the saloon and somewhat unnerved Willis and the two men with him.

But by then, Smoke and Pearlie had seen something that the three men hadn't seen. They had seen Cal come into the saloon just in time to take notice of the situation.

Pearlie smiled. "You know, I think it would be a big mistake for these men to draw on us," Pearlie said.

"Oh, don't be so hard on them, Pearlie. It's clear that Mr. Willis just hasn't thought this through. He doesn't realize that he could wind up getting himself, and his two friends, killed."

"What the hell are you two talkin' about?" Willis asked, his voice reflecting his growing nervousness. "If they's anyone that's likely to get kilt here, it's goin' to be you two. Maybe you didn't notice, but they's only two of you, and there's three of us."

Slipping his pistol from the holster and moving very quietly, and unnoticed, Cal stepped up behind the man who was standing at the end of the bar nearest the door. He brought his pistol down on the head of that man. Hearing him fall, Willis turned, only to see Cal holding a pistol in his hand.

"Now there are three of us, and two of you," Cal said.

"Now, Cal, it's not fair for you to be butting into this," Pearlie said as he brought his gun up. "We're the ones that loudmouthed son of a bitch has been picking on. That means I'm the one that gets to kill him. If you want to, you can kill the one that's down at the other end of the bar."

"Now wait a minute," Smoke said. "Cal already got his man. You can have the loudmouth if you want him, but I'll be killing the one at the other end of the bar."

Like Pearlie, Smoke had drawn his pistol during the distraction caused by Cal's dramatic entrance. He pointed it at the man at the other end of the bar, then cocked his pistol. As the hammer came back, the gear engaged the cylinder, making a loud clicking sound that filled the now silent room.

"What . . . what are we goin' to do, Willis?" the man standing at the opposite end of the bar asked. "My God! They're goin' to kill us! They're goin' to kill us, just like he did Pardeen." He held both his hands out in front of him as if, by that action, he could ward off any bullets. "No, no! Don't shoot me! Please don't!"

By now the man Cal had knocked out was coming to, and he groaned.

"Take off your pistol belts, and hand them to Mr. Peterson," Smoke said.

"What the hell! I ain't givin' up my pistol!" Willis said.

"Mr. Willis, you will either hand your pistol belt over to Mr. Peterson while you are alive, or I will

kill you and give him the belt after you are dead,"
Pearlie said.

"You better do it, Willis, 'cause I ain't standin' with
you!" the man at the far end of the bar said as,
quickly, and with shaking hands, he removed his own
belt.

"Booker! You cowardly son of a bitch!" Willis said,
but even as he was talking, he joined the other two in
taking off his pistol belt. Then the three men, after
turning their belts over to Peterson, left the saloon.

"Damn!" someone said. "I never thought I would
see any of Atwood's cutthroats be disarmed like that
and run off with their tails tucked between their
legs."

"If you two fellas want another drink, I'll be glad
to buy it," another said.

"We're good," Smoke said. "But you can buy one
for our friend. Step up to the bar, Cal, and tell Mr.
Peterson what you'll have."

With a broad smile, Cal ordered a beer, then,
saluting his benefactor by raising the beer toward
him, he joined Smoke and Pearlie at their table.

"I got the horses taken care of," he said.

"Good. Did you see Sally?" Smoke asked.

"Not since we separated at the depot."

CHAPTER EIGHT

"You need to get over to the Pretty Girl Saloon. Some son of a bitch just kilt Pardeen!" Willis said. He and the others had come straight to the marshal's office after leaving the Pretty Girl and Happy Cowboy Saloon.

"What do you mean, someone kilt Pardeen? You mean he shot 'im in the back?" Calhoun replied.

"No, he faced Pardeen down."

"I didn't think anyone could beat Pardeen."

"This feller did," Booker said. "He's the fastest I've ever seen."

"Who was it?"

"He has some funny name like Stoke or Shoke or somethin' like that."

Sally and Kate, in back of the jail, were unaware of the conversation taking part out front.

"I must be going," Sally said. "But I don't want you to worry anymore. Smoke says that we will get you out of jail, and I learned, a long time ago, to trust him when he is determined to do a thing."

"Sally, thanks for coming. And please ask Wes to come visit me."

"I'll send him right over," Sally promised.

When Sally reached the front of the jail, she saw three men there with Deputy Calhoun.

"He took our guns," one of the men said.

"He didn't take 'em, Booker. You give 'em up to 'im."

"Then you should thank Mr. Booker," Sally said. "By giving up your guns like that, Smoke didn't have to kill you."

"Who the hell are you?" the loudmouthed one asked.

"She says she's a friend of Kate's brother," Calhoun said.

"I am Mrs. Smoke Jensen."

"Smoke! Yeah, that was the son of a bitch's name that kilt Pardeen! It was Smoke!"

"May I have my pistol back, Deputy?" Sally asked.

Calhoun opened the drawer, took out the gun, and handed it to Sally.

"Thank you," Sally replied. She turned to the loud-mouth. "And your name, sir?" Sally asked.

"It's Willis."

Sally pointed her pistol at Willis.

"What the hell?" Willis cried out. "What are you doin'?"

"Mr. Willis, I would appreciate it if you didn't use such language around me. Especially about my husband. And I would appreciate an apology."

"Do somethin', Calhoun!" Willis said.

"What do you expect me to do?" Calhoun asked.

"Iffen we had our guns, she wouldn't be doing this," Willis said.

Sally cocked the pistol. "My apology?"

"I'm sorry!" Willis said desperately. "I'm sorry."

Sally smiled. "Your apology is accepted."

"If Witherspoon wants us, we'll be down at the Bull and Heifer," Willis said. "That is, unless you're plannin' on shootin' us," he added, looking back at Sally.

"No, as I said, your apology is accepted. You're free to go wherever you wish."

"Come on," Willis said to the others in a voice that could only be described as a growl.

Sally waited until the three men were gone before she slipped her pistol back into its holster.

"You probably shouldn'ta done that, Missy," Calhoun said. "It ain't good to have them boys as enemies."

"Well, I certainly wouldn't want them as friends," Sally replied.

Sally's response was unexpected, and after blinking in surprise, Calhoun laughed out loud. "I guess you have a point there," he said.

When Sally reached the saloon a couple of minutes later, she saw two men putting a body into the back of a wagon. The words WELCH UNDERTAKING SERVICE were painted on the side of the wagon.

As soon as Sally stepped into the saloon, she was met by Smoke.

"I hear I missed some excitement," Sally said.

"A little," Smoke said.

"A little? I did see someone being loaded into the back of an undertaker's wagon, didn't I? Tell me, Smoke, how can someone be a little dead?"

Smoke laughed. "Well, you've got me on that one, Sally, I'm not sure someone can be a little dead. Why don't you come join Pearlie, Cal, and me at the table?"

"I'd be glad to," Sally said.

"Mr. Peterson, a white wine if you please," Smoke called over to the bartender as he led Sally to the table.

"Yes, sir," Peterson said.

"Oh, Mr. Peterson, Kate said to tell you she is doing fine, and she thanks you for standing by her."

"You saw Kate?" Peterson asked, surprised at the comment.

"I did indeed."

Pearlie and Cal stood as Sally approached the table, then waited until Smoke pulled out a chair for her before they sat again.

One of the bar girls, having overheard Sally's comment to Peterson, approached the table.

"How is Miss Kate? Is she doing all right?" the girl asked.

"Yes. She doesn't enjoy being in jail, of course, but she is doing just fine, and of course, she is worried about all her friends here."

"Have you seen Rusty? I mean, if you have, you don't need to tell me where he is, or anything like that, I wouldn't want to put him in danger. I would just like to know if he is all right."

Sally reached up and put her hand on the girl's

arm. "He's doing just fine, dear," she said with a warm smile.

"Oh!" the bar girl said with a happy smile. "Oh, that's wonderful to hear! I mean . . . uh . . . well, all the girls who work here will be real glad to hear that. If you go see Miss Kate again, would you tell her that Dolly asked about her?"

"I'll be glad to," Sally replied.

"Do you think they really intend to hang her if Rusty doesn't come back?" Dolly asked.

"I will guarantee you that you don't have to worry about that," Smoke said. "We will not let that happen."

"And if Atwood insists on it?" Dolly asked.

"We will stop it."

"But, how? Atwood has so many men who work for him. To say nothing of Marshal Witherspoon. And there are only three of you."

"There are four of us," Sally said.

"What do you mean, four?" Dolly asked.

Sally counted off, pointing her finger at Cal, Pearlie, and Smoke. "One, two, three." She paused, then turned her finger to herself. "Four."

"Oh," Dolly said. "Oh, I didn't think . . . uh, that is, I mean you're a . . ."

"Yeah, I am," Sally said with a big smile.

"Did you have any trouble getting in to see Kate?" Pearlie asked after Dolly walked away.

"Not really," Sally said. "Oh, and Pearlie, Kate wants you to come see her."

"You mean now? She wants to see me now?"

"Yes."

A broad smile spread across Pearlie's face. "I'm

glad to hear that. After all these years, and with me making no effort to get in touch with her, I wasn't sure she would ever want to see me again, even if I tried."

"You aren't the only one who feels guilty," Sally said. "She blames herself for not trying to find you."

"You mean Katie thinks it's all her fault?"

"Apparently so."

Pearlie laughed. "Good, I'll let her think that, and I'll make her apologize to me."

"Pearlie, don't you dare!" Sally said.

"I was just teasing. I have to confess, though, that I am a bit nervous about going to see her."

"Don't be. She's as sweet a person as you would ever want to meet. Please, go see her now. I promised I would send you over there as soon as I could."

"All right," Pearlie replied with an assenting nod. "I reckon I'll just go on over there now."

"You ain't goin' nowhere, mister!" a loud voice called out. "There ain't nobody goin' nowhere till I say they can!"

Looking toward the man who had spoken, Smoke saw a man standing just inside the batwing doors. He was wearing a star on a shirt that strained at the buttons.

"Witherspoon, you ain't got no case here. Pardeen drew first," one of the patrons said.

"Cletus is right," Peterson said. "Pardeen drew first."

"That's the way it happened, Marshal," Dolly said, and she was backed up by all the other girls in the saloon.

"We ain't goin' to let you do to this man what you done to Rusty," yet another patron said.

"We'll . . . we'll see about that," Witherspoon said, jabbing his finger toward everyone. "We'll just see about that," he repeated as he backed out of the saloon.

Witherspoon's departure was followed by a loud burst of laughter from the throats of everyone present.

Pearlie followed Witherspoon out the door, and a moment later someone came in and stepped up to the bar to say something to Peterson. Peterson nodded, then stepped around the bar and led the man over to the table where Smoke, Sally, and Cal were sitting, Pearlie having just vacated his seat.

"Mr. Jensen, this is Slim Pollard," Peterson said. "He rides for the Eagle Shire."

"Atwood?"

"Yes," Peterson said. "But Slim here is a good man, I've known him for some time. And he's one of the real cowboys, he's not one of Atwood's gun-hands."

"What can I do for you, Pollard?" Smoke asked.

"I, uh, have come to pick up the guns for Willis 'n the two men that was with 'im," Pollard said.

"Where are those men now?" Smoke asked.

"They're down at the Bull 'n Heifer," Pollard said.

"They sent you after their guns, did they?"

"No, sir, I volunteered to come get 'em. I figured if they come for 'em, well, there could maybe be some more shootin'. But if I was to come 'n just ask for 'em real polite, there wouldn't be no more trouble."

"All right," Smoke said. "Mr. Peterson, give him the guns."

"I appreciate that," Pollard replied.

"Why don't you join us for a beer?" Smoke invited.

"Thank you!" Pollard said, this time with a broad smile.

Smoke held his hand out toward Sally. "This is my wife."

"Nice to meet you, ma'am," Pollard said.

"Tell me, Mr. Pollard," Smoke said after the beer was served. "If you are a good man, as Mr. Peterson says, and I don't doubt him, why are you riding for someone like Silas Atwood?"

"He's got cows and horses that need tendin'," Pollard replied. "And bein' as they're just dumb animals, they don't know what kind of man it is that owns them. Besides which, after Mr. Dumey left, the Double Nickel, which is the brand I used to ride for, wasn't no more, 'n I didn't have no job left. So when Miner Cobb offered to put me on, I took 'im up on it."

"Miner Cobb?"

"He's the foreman out at the Eagle Shire. 'N he's a good man, too, he ain't no gunhand like them others that Mr. Atwood has hired."

Smoke drummed his fingers on the table for a moment or two as he stared at Pollard.

"Mr. Pollard, for reasons that I'm not going to go into, actually for reasons I'm sure you already know, I plan to take Atwood down."

"Take him down? You mean you . . . you plan to

kill 'im?" Pollard replied with a troubled expression on his face.

"It is not my intention to kill him," Smoke said. "When I say take him down, what I mean is, disengage him from his hold over this town."

Pollard shook his head. "He ain't never goin' to just willingly give that up."

"Fortunately, my plan does not depend upon a willing relinquishment of his position of power. But I will bring that about, with, or without, Atwood's willing acquiescence."

"Oh," Pollard said.

"Where will you stand on that issue, Mr. Pollard?" Smoke asked.

"Well, sir, I've been a cowhand, man, and boy now for more'n twenty years," Pollard replied. "And I've always believed that a cowboy owes some loyalty to the brand he's ridin' for."

"I can understand loyalty," Smoke said.

"On the other hand, I was loyal to Mr. Dumey, too, but when he give up 'n left his ranch, I didn't think twice 'bout ridin' for the man that run 'im off. If it comes right down to a battle between you 'n Mr. Atwood, I won't be fightin' ag'in you, 'n I don't think any of the regular Eagle Shire hands will, either. I expect that about the onliest ones you're goin' to have to worry about will be them boys that lives in the special bunkhouse."

"Special bunkhouse?"

"Yes, sir, that's what the rest of us call the place where the gunhands, folks like Willis, 'n Clark, 'n Booker, and such live. That was where Pardeen lived, too, till you shot 'im."

"I see."

Pollard snorted what might have been a laugh. "Pardeen, well, he sort of lorded over all of us regular cowboys. I'll be honest with you, Mr. Jensen, I don't expect any of us is goin' to be all too broke up over him gettin' kilt."

CHAPTER NINE

When Pearlie stepped into the jail, there were two men inside and both were wearing a badge. One of the men was Marshal Witherspoon, who had just left the saloon.

"What the hell are you doing here?" the marshal asked. "Did you follow me?"

"No. Well, yes, I suppose I did, but not specifically. Marshal Witherspoon, my name is Pear . . . , uh, that is, Wes Fontaine. I'm here to see my sister."

"We ain't got nobody here by the name of Fontaine," Witherspoon said.

"Her married name is Abernathy. Kate Abernathy," Pearlie said.

"This here's the feller the woman mentioned when she was here a little while ago."

"Let me ask you something," Witherspoon said. "Were you in the saloon when Pardeen was shot?"

"Yes."

"Which one of you shot him?"

"What difference does it make who shot him? Pardeen drew first. You heard everyone in the saloon tell you that."

"I just want to know which one of you done it is all."

"Willis said it was the one named Smoke," Calhoun said.

"It was Smoke, but it could just as easily have been me, because if Pardeen had drawn on me like he did on Smoke, I would have shot him."

"Ha! You think you could've beaten Pardeen?"

"Yes."

"I doubt that. Pardeen was really good with a pistol."

"Is that so? Well, as it turns out, he wasn't good enough, was he?"

Pearlie's response quieted Witherspoon for a moment. "What's the purpose of your visit?" he asked.

"I told you, Katie is my sister. What other purpose would I need?"

The marshal stroked his chin for a moment, then he nodded. "All right. Shuck out of that gunbelt, 'n I'll let you go on back."

Pearlie unbuckled the gunbelt, then held it out toward Deputy Calhoun. The deputy took it, then pulled the pistol from the holster to examine it.

"What kind of pistol is this, anyway?"

"Smith and Wesson, Model Three."

"Don't think I've ever seen one like it."

"It's new. I don't have to tell you to be careful with it, do I?" Pearlie asked.

"No," Calhoun said as, self-consciously, he returned the pistol to its holster.

"Take 'im back there to see the whore," Witherspoon said.

Pearlie glared at Witherspoon but said nothing.

"What's the matter, Fontaine? You didn't know your sister was a whore?" Witherspoon asked with a chuckle.

"To be honest, Marshal, she ain't really a whore, 'n none of them girls that works for her is whores, neither," Calhoun said.

"Shut up, Calhoun. When I want your opinion, I'll ask for it," the marshal replied in a low, hissing voice.

When Pearlie reached the back of the jail, he stopped and stood there for just a moment, regarding the woman who was sitting on the bunk looking toward the window. He was able to remain unobserved because she had not yet noticed him.

Kate was five years older than Pearlie, and as he stood there, he recalled when he had last seen her. He was thirteen years old at the time.

"You ain't my mama," Wes said. "You ain't the boss of me."

"I'm your big sister, I have to look out for you," Kate said.

"You look out for yourself and I'll look out for myself," Wes said resolutely. "I'm goin' to go get me a job punchin' cattle."

"Wes, don't go," Kate pleaded. "You're too young."

"No, I ain't. I can ride as good as anyone."

"Please, don't go. You're not old enough, I'll be so worried about you."

That was the last time Wes had seen his older sister, but now, despite the passage of time, there was enough of a familiarity about her that he knew without question this was the sister he had left so long ago. He took a deep breath, then walked back to her cell.

"Hi, Katie," he said.

"Wes!" she said. She jumped up from the bed, then hurried over to the bars. "Oh, Wes!"

Her eyes filled with tears, and she stuck her hands through the bars to touch his face. "You have grown up so. What a fine-looking man you have become."

"Now, don't go embarrassing me first thing after we meet again," Pearlie said, though there was a smile in his voice as he spoke.

"There was a lady here, Sally Jensen, who said that you were in town. I was almost afraid to let myself believe her."

"You can believe it, 'cause here I am."

"She seems like an awfully nice lady."

"She's the nicest lady I've ever known. I know proper grammar, I've read books, good books, too, not just dime novels. Why, I can quote Shakespeare, did you know that? And you can even ask me a question about history. Miz Sally taught me."

"My brother, quoting Shakespeare. Who would have ever thought something like that?"

Pearlie assumed an affected position with hand over his heart, and the other arm extended. In a deep voice, he began to intone. "'*Tomorrow, and tomorrow, and tomorrow, creeps in this petty pace from day to day,*'" he broke his pose. "And it goes on from there."

Kate laughed. "You *can* quote Shakespeare. Oh, Wes, I'm so glad to see you. I have worried so about you over the years."

"Rusty said you knew I had come to Texas to deliver some horses to Mr. Byrd?" Pearlie asked. "How did you know that was me? I gave up the name, Wes Fontaine, a long time ago."

"One of the men you had ridden with at the B Bar B learned, somehow, that you were going by the name of Pearlie and that you were living in Colorado. Then, when I happened to be in San Vicente, I was told that there were some people who had brought some horses to Mr. Byrd. I saw you at dinner in the Marshal House, and I heard someone call you Pearlie. I studied you from the other side of the room and saw enough of the brother I thought I had lost that I just knew it was you. I almost walked up to you then."

"Oh, Katie, why didn't you?"

"I was afraid."

"Afraid of what?"

"It had been so many years since we had last seen one another. And when you left you were so adamant about being on your own. I don't know; I was afraid that you might reject me."

"I'm sorry. I suppose I can see why you might

think something like that. I mean, I certainly gave you every cause to be a little scared of me."

"As I thought more about it, I realized I should have come out to the ranch to see you. But, when Mr. Byrd's daughter, Katrina, was killed, I didn't want to impose on his grief. It wasn't until much later that I approached Mr. Byrd to ask about you. He told me that you worked for Smoke Jensen on the Sugarloaf Ranch near Big Rock, Colorado.

"I knew then that you had made a good life for yourself, and I was pretty sure you didn't need a long-lost sister to show up and complicate things. So, I made a vow never to bother you. And I never would have if this hadn't come up. I sent a message for Rusty to find you, and I see that he did."

"Well, I can tell you right now that I'm glad he did. Katie, I'm sorry we haven't kept up," Pearlie said. "I should have; it was my responsibility to do so because I knew how to get ahold of you, but you had no idea how to find me." Pearlie chuckled. "That is, not until we delivered those horses to Mr. Byrd. As it turns out now, I'm glad you happened to be in San Vicente that day."

"I'm glad as well, because it led to our finally meeting. But, Wes, or would you rather I call you Pearlie?"

Pearlie chuckled. "I've been called Pearlie a lot longer than I was ever called Wes, so if it's all the same to you, I think I would prefer to be called Pearlie."

Kate smiled. "All right, then, Pearlie it is. And, Pearlie, you did absolutely the right thing by not trying to get in touch with me. You have no idea how many times marshals and deputies questioned me about you when you first, uh, ran into trouble. And every time they came to see me I was able to tell them, truthfully, that I didn't have any idea where you were, or even who you were. Then, of course, I had never heard of anyone named Pearlie."

"Katie, it's important to me that you know those killings weren't my fault. Every witness in the saloon was willing to testify that both of them were in self-defense. But it's hard to make a case of self-defense when you kill a marshal."

"I know. Some of your friends from the B Bar B looked me up because they said they wanted me to know the truth about what happened. Our reunion, such as it is, has certainly been a long time in coming. I'm just sorry that, when we finally did meet again, it had to be like this, with me being in jail."

Pearlie smiled. "Don't worry about it, Katie. I can promise you that you won't be in here long. I know Rusty's story, too, and I know that he's no more guilty of murder than I was, so my friends and I are going to get both you and Rusty out of this mess."

"I appreciate your efforts, We . . . I mean Pearlie," Kate said with a wan smile. "But I don't see how you are going to be able to do that. It isn't just the marshal and the judge. The person who is really in charge is . . ."

"Silas Atwood," Pearlie said, interrupting her.

"Yes, and if you know about him, then you must know how many men he has working for him. He has his own private army."

Pearlie smiled. "He has one less now."

"What? What do you mean? Pearlie, you haven't killed someone on my account, have you?"

"It wasn't me, it was Smoke."

"Who?"

"Sally's husband. But don't worry about it, everyone in the saloon is willing to testify that Pardeen drew first."

"Pardeen? Pardeen is dead?"

"Yes."

"Oh. Well, I don't want to celebrate someone's death, but Pardeen was one of the worst of the lot. Does Atwood know about it yet?"

"He may know by now. As it turns out some of his other men were in there as well."

"That's unusual for so many of Atwood's people to be in there. Most of the time they can be found in the Bull and Heifer. They like the girls better there."

"What do you mean? The girls down at the Bull and Heifer can't possibly be prettier than the girls at your place."

Kate smiled. "It's not that they are prettier, it's that they will . . . uh, it's what they are willing to do."

"Oh," Pearlie said, understanding then what Kate was saying.

"Pearlie, be careful while you are here. Atwood is a very dangerous man."

"Don't you worry any about it, Katie," he said. "I've got a pretty good army with me, as well."

"You do?" Kate asked, surprised by Pearlie's comment. "How many men do you have with you?"

Again, Pearlie assumed the position of an actor on stage. "*We few, we happy few, we band of brothers; for he to-day that sheds his blood with me shall be my brother; be he ne'er so vile. This day shall gentle his condition.'"*

"What?" Kate asked.

Pearlie laughed. "I told you that Miz Sally had taught me Shakespeare. That's from *King Henry the Fifth.* Anyway, all you need to know is that there are enough of us to get the job done. But the first thing we're going to do is make bail so we can get you out of this jail."

"Judge Boykin won't give you bail," Kate said. "He's as much one of Atwood's toadies as is the marshal."

"We'll get you out of here," Pearlie repeated. "And we'll do it legally. You don't worry any about Marshal Witherspoon, Judge Boykin, or even Silas Atwood. We have a few strings and connections we can pull ourselves, if we have to."

"Oh, how I pray that you are right. By the way, how are Mr. Peterson and the girls doing, back at the saloon? I know they must be worried about what is going to happen to them."

"They seem to be doing as well as can be expected, but they are more worried about you than they are about themselves. Peterson, Dolly, and the young women who work for you all send their greetings. Katie, you have some very loyal people there."

"Yes," Kate agreed. "They are good people, all of them. I want you to do something for me."

"All right."

"You haven't heard what it is I want you to do."

Pearlie reached in through the bars and took Kate's hand into his own. "It doesn't matter what it is. If you want me to do it, I'll do it."

"I have left Mr. Peterson in charge of the saloon. I know that Atwood is going to try again to take over the saloon. I want you to help Mr. Peterson hold on to it for me."

"Atwood is not going to get the saloon. I promise you, it will still be there for you when we get you out."

CHAPTER TEN

When Pearlie walked back into the front of the jailhouse, Deputy Calhoun returned his holster and pistol to him.

"How is Miz Kate getting along back there?" Calhoun asked. There seemed to be a degree of actual concern in the deputy's question.

"She's doing all right. She'll be a lot better when I can get her out of here, though."

"Only way you're going to get her out of here is if that no-count boy of hers comes back so we can hang him instead of his whore mama," Marshal Witherspoon said.

Pearlie had just strapped his pistol belt back on and now, in a lightning-fast draw, he pulled his pistol and stuck the barrel into the marshal's mouth, doing so with such force that the front blade-sight cut Witherspoon's lip.

"*Whug . . . whug arg yug doig?*" Witherspoon mumbled, unable to say the words clearly because of the gun barrel in his mouth. His eyes were open wide in fright.

"You know, Marshal, I would take it just real

neighborly of you if you wouldn't call my sister a whore anymore," Pearlie said. Even though he was jamming his pistol into the back of the marshal's throat, he spoke the words quietly, and calmly, which had the effect of making them much more frightening than if he had raised his voice in anger.

"I won't, I won't!" Witherspoon said, but because the barrel of the gun was in his mouth, the words came out, *"Ah wug, ah wug."*

Smiling, Pearlie returned his pistol to his holster. "I thought you might see things my way," he said.

"I could arrest you for armed assault against an officer of the law!" Witherspoon said as a little sliver of blood oozed from the cut on his lip.

"Could you?" Pearlie replied.

"I'll . . . I'll let it go this time," Witherspoon said.

"Well now, I appreciate that, Marshal. I'll just be going then. But you do take care now, you hear?"

Witherspoon watched Pearlie leave, then he took out his handkerchief and dabbed it against the small cut on his lip.

"You just stood there and did nothing," Witherspoon said.

"What would you have had me do, Marshal?" Calhoun asked. "He had the gun stuck in your mouth. I was afraid that if I did anything he would've blowed the back of your head off."

"Get out," Witherspoon said with an angry wave of his hand.

"Where do you want me to go?"

"I don't care where you go, as long as I don't have to look at you. Go somewhere and get drunk. That's what you do, ain't it?"

"Marshal, I was just lookin' out for you is all," Calhoun said.

Witherspoon held the handkerchief against his lip and glared at Calhoun, but he said nothing.

A few minutes later, Calhoun showed up in the Pretty Girl and Happy Cowboy Saloon. He saw Kate's brother talking to two other men and the woman who had visited Kate earlier. He stared at them for just a moment, but he didn't approach their table.

"What can I get for you, Deputy?" Peterson asked, moving down the bar to stand in front of him. Peterson had a towel in his hand, and he made a swipe across the bar in front of Calhoun.

"Whiskey."

"I thought you said you were tryin' to quit. When you couldn't testify at Rusty's trial it was 'cause you were drunk 'n couldn't remember. Wouldn't you rather just have a beer?"

"Whiskey," Calhoun said again. "I need a drink."

Peterson shrugged his shoulders, then poured a shot. Calhoun tossed it down quickly, then pushed his glass out.

"Another one."

"Are you sure?"

"I want another one, damnit!" Calhoun said angrily.

Witherspoon had ridden out to Eagle Shire Ranch, and he was met by Atwood even before he dismounted.

"Willis told me Pardeen was killed today," Atwood said.

"Yes, sir, he was, by a man named Jensen. Smoke Jensen."

"Why didn't you arrest him?" Atwood asked angrily. "Pardeen was one of my best men, and this man killed him."

"It wouldn'ta done no good to arrest 'im," Witherspoon said. "Ever'one in the entire saloon said it was Pardeen that drawed first."

"Are you telling me that this man, Jensen, was able to outdraw Pardeen?"

"That's what ever'one in the saloon said."

"I don't believe it. Pardeen was the fastest gun of all my special cadre."

"Maybe so, but if I had arrested 'im, ever'one in the saloon would've testified that it was a fair fight."

"What difference does that make? They would've said the same thing about Kate's brat, too. We didn't let them testify."

"It's not the same thing," Witherspoon said. "Rusty Abernathy wasn't nothin' but a piano player, 'n he didn't have nobody that would be willin' to challenge us. But this here Jensen ain't alone. They's two others with 'im, and I figure that any one of them is ten times better than most men. I can't see them just standin' by 'n lettin' us do to another what we done to Rusty Abernathy."

Atwood stroked his Van Dyke beard for a moment. "Yes, well, it may wind up being better this way," he said. "Getting someone convicted and sentenced to hang doesn't always work out that well anyway, as we have recently seen. Perhaps it will be best for us to handle this in some other way."

"What other way? What are you talking about?"

"How do you fight a prairie fire?" Atwood asked.

"I don't know. I guess the best way is to set a back fire," Witherspoon said.

"Precisely. You fight fire with fire. Do you see what I mean?"

"Not exactly," Witherspoon replied, the expression on his face showing the confusion.

"You just let me worry about it."

Back in Etholen, Smoke and Pearlie were standing in front of the courthouse. They were able to find it, both by the flagpole and by the caisson-mounted thirty-two-pounder cannon that Peterson had told them to look for. Stacked up next to the gun were enough cannon balls to form a waist-high pyramid. A printed sign explained the display.

THIS CANNON

"OLD THUNDER"

WAS DONATED TO OUR TOWN
by the OFFICERS *and* MEN
of FORT QUITMAN

"Look at this," Pearlie said, running his hand over the smooth barrel of the artillery piece. "Do you think it would still fire?"

"I don't know why not," Smoke replied as he

examined it more closely. "The touchhole hasn't been spiked."

They were to visit with Judge Henry L. Boykin, and after a moment of examining the gun, Smoke and Pearlie went into the building where they were directed to Judge Boykin's office.

"Smoke Jensen? I understand you are the man who killed Rufus Pardeen," Boykin said.

"I am."

"Have you come here to seek some sort of official dismissal? If you have, you are wasting your time, because I cannot issue a dismissal. However, you shouldn't worry about it, as there has been no charge filed. As far as I'm concerned, you are free to go."

"I'm not in the least worried about it," Smoke said. "I'm here for a different reason."

"And what would that be?"

As Smoke began to make an appeal for bail for Kate Abernathy, Boykin blew his nose, then stuck his handkerchief back into his pocket, doing so in such a way as to indicate his complete disdain for the idea.

"Are you a lawyer, Mr. Jensen?" Boykin asked.

"No, Your Honor, I am not a member of the bar."

"But you have read for the law?"

"No, Your Honor, I have not."

"Then tell me, Mr. Jensen, what right do you have to apply for bail for Miss Abernathy?"

"That would be Mrs. Abernathy, Your Honor. And she has designated me as her personal representative."

"Well, Mr. Jensen, whether you have been designated her personal representative or not, I'll tell you here and now, that I'm denying her bail."

"For what reason?"

"Reason? Reason, Mr. Jensen? I don't need a reason. I am the judge, and it is within my purview to grant or not to grant bail. In this particular case I choose not to grant bail, and no further justification for my action is required. I know you have only the most rudimentary knowledge of the law, Mr. Jensen, but do you understand that?"

Smoke smiled. "I do, Your Honor. And I thought you might deny her bail."

"If you thought that, then why did you even bother to apply?"

"I guess I just wanted to see if it was true what people say, that you are a fawning sycophant who jumps at Atwood's bark. I can see now that you are."

"How dare you, sir!" Boykin said angrily. "If you were in my court right now, I would hold you for contempt."

"Funny you would say that, Judge, because we don't need to be in a court for me to hold you in contempt."

"Mr. Jensen, as our business is complete, I am going to ask you to leave my chambers."

"All right, I'll go. I guess I'll just have to find another way to get Mrs. Abernathy out of jail."

Boykin's eyes narrowed, and he pointed a bony finger at Smoke. "You wouldn't be suggesting that you are going to try to break her out of jail, would you, Jensen?"

"Judge, if I decide to do that, there won't be any *trying* to it. I will succeed."

"I intend to instruct Marshal Witherspoon to keep his eye on you."

Smoke chuckled. "Oh, I expect he is already doing that. Yes, sir, I'm quite aware of the marshal's scrutiny."

When Smoke and Pearlie returned to the Pretty Girl and Happy Cowboy, they were met by Cal.

"Miz Sally is back there, by the piano," Cal said.

"Hey, Mr. Peterson, what's the story with that cannon?" Pearlie asked.

"Just like the sign says, Pearlie. When Fort Quitman shut down, they gave the cannon to the town."

"Will it still shoot?"

"I'll say it does. We fire it off every Fourth of July. It makes one hell of a racket."

Pearlie hurried on to join Smoke, Sally, and Cal.

"So he said no?" Sally was asking as Pearlie joined them.

"He said no, but I wasn't really expecting him to say anything else," Smoke said.

"I was talking to Mr. Peterson," Cal said. "He told me that Boykin is as crooked as a dog's hind leg. I'm not surprised he found Rusty guilty and won't grant bail to Miss Kate."

"Well, we won't worry about Rusty yet," Smoke said. "He's safe for the time being. It's Kate we need to get out of jail. We'll do it legally if we can. But if we can't get it done legally, we'll break her out. There's no way we're going to let them hang her."

"Yeah, well, we're probably going to have to break Katie out because there's no way we can do it legally if Boykin won't even grant bail," Pearlie said.

"There's a federal court in El Paso," Smoke said. "I'm going to go over there and try to convince the federal judge to overturn Judge Boykin's ruling that put Kate in jail in the first place."

"How is a federal court going to help?" Pearlie asked. "They're holding Katie for accessory to murder, and murder is a state law."

"Going to the federal court was Sally's idea," Smoke said.

"Your idea?" Pearlie asked.

"Yes," Sally answered. "You are right, murder is a state law, but what they are doing here is a violation of the Fourteenth Amendment, which says that no state shall deprive any person of life, liberty, or property, without due process of law, nor deny to any person within its jurisdiction the equal protection of the laws. The incarceration of your sister, Kate, is in direct violation of that amendment, and that is all the justification a federal judge would need to order her immediate release."

"Yes, but even so, won't it just be our word against Boykin's word?" Pearlie asked.

"I suppose it will be," Smoke admitted. "But I've got to try."

"It need not be just our word against Boykin's word," Sally said. "Smoke, a moment ago, you said not to worry about Rusty yet. But if we can get Rusty's conviction overturned, that will automatically apply to Kate as well, wouldn't it?"

"Well, yes, I'm sure it would."

"I think we can get his conviction overturned under the same argument."

"How? I can see how your idea might work with Kate, she didn't get a trial."

"We can show that Rusty's rights to a fair trial were violated, so we can use the Fourteenth Amendment in appealing his case, as well."

"Do you have an idea how to do that?" Smoke asked.

"Yes, but we're going to have to talk to Mr. Peterson about it."

"I'll bring him over to the table," Cal offered.

A moment later Cal returned to the table with the bartender. "Yes, ma'am, Cal said you wanted to talk to me about somethin'?" Peterson asked.

"Mr. Peterson, you saw what happened in here the night Rusty killed Calley, didn't you?" Sally asked.

"Yes, ma'am, I saw every bit of it."

"Do you have a pen and paper?"

"A pen and paper? Well, I . . . wait a minute. Dolly does. She's always writing poetry and such."

"Would you ask her if she would bring paper and pen to me?"

"What have you got in mind, Sally?" Smoke asked.

Sally smiled. "I intend to validate the story we are going to tell him."

"We?"

"I'll be going with you," Sally said.

Chapter Eleven

"You wanted this, Miz Sally?" Dolly asked, bringing a pen and a few sheets of writing paper with her.

"Yes, Dolly, thank you," Sally replied. Sally looked up at Peterson.

"Now, Mr. Peterson, if you would please, tell us what happened that night, and be as accurate as you can."

Peterson began talking, and as he did so, Sally recorded his words. Peterson told the story in exact detail, chronicling how Calley had put a pistol on the piano stool, then began counting to ten, declaring that when he got to ten he was going to shoot.

"He looked away when he got to eight, 'n that's when Rusty grabbed the gun and shot him, just as he said 'nine.' But if he hadn't done that, Calley would have kilt him sure. You see, Calley had some reputation as a gunfighter and Rusty? Well, as far as I know there weren't nobody that ever even seen Rusty wearin' a gun at all. He didn't have no choice but to do what he done."

"That's true, Miz Sally," Dolly, who had been listening, said. "Calley would've killed poor Rusty, if Rusty hadn't taken the opportunity to shoot him when he had the chance."

"Then, when it come to the trial, Judge Boykin, he wouldn't let anyone who actually saw what happened tell their story," Peterson said in conclusion.

"How many others were in the saloon that night?"

"Well, Dolly 'n the girls was all here. That makes five. 'N there was at least six or seven more that was here that seen what happened."

"We, who affix our signatures hereto this document, do affirm that the particulars as recorded above are true and accurate in every detail," Sally said aloud as she penned the validating statement.

"Now," she said. "Let's get as many of the witnesses to sign this as we can, then we'll take this document to see the federal judge in El Paso."

"Sally," Smoke said with a big smile. "That is positively brilliant!"

"I just wish we could get them notarized," Sally said.

"Oh, you can get it notarized all right, there's no problem with that. I can do it for you," Dolly said.

"You can? How?"

"I'm a notary public," she said with a broad smile.

"You?" Sally asked in surprise. "You are a notary public?"

"Yes, ma'am, I sure am. Miss Kate asked me to do it so I could notarize things for her."

"That's wonderful!" Sally said.

Within an hour, they had the signature of every witness but one.

"Who's missing?" Smoke asked.

"Deputy Calhoun was here," Peterson said. "But it won't do any good to get his signature."

"Well, even if he rebutted the testimony of the others, it would still be," she counted the names, "eleven to one."

"Oh, he wouldn't refute it," Peterson said. "He couldn't. He was passed out drunk that night and didn't see anything."

"Besides, he most likely wouldn't refute it anyway," Dolly said.

"Why not?"

"Deputy Calhoun is a good man, don't get me wrong. I mean he is Marshal Witherspoon's deputy 'n all, but he isn't a mean man like Witherspoon."

"That's true," Peterson said. "Calhoun's actually a pretty good man."

"Why does he stay on with him, then?"

"To be honest, I don't think Calhoun could get a job anywhere else. And Witherspoon keeps him on because he's a drunk and easy for Witherspoon to control," Peterson said.

"He didn't testify at Rusty's trial," Dolly said. "He coulda said that Rusty murdered Calley, but he told the judge he didn't see anything."

"Who did testify against Rusty?"

"The marshal did."

"But he wasn't even here, was he?"

"No, he wasn't. But that didn't stop him from testifying," Dolly said.

"Lying, you mean," Peterson added.

Eagle Shire Ranch

Silas Atwood lived on the Eagle Shire Ranch in an antebellum house, three and a half stories high, topped by a large cupola, with Corinthian columns across the front. It was an exact replica of Colonel Raymond Windsor's mansion, Windsor Hall, on Moss Point Plantation in Demopolis, Alabama. Atwood had grown up on Moss Point Plantation, the son of the white overseer. Atwood hadn't built the house to honor Colonel Windsor, but to prove to himself that he was just as good as Windsor was.

Windsor had not treated Atwood's father any differently than he had his slaves, nor had he treated Atwood any differently from the young blacks on the plantation. That's not to say that Atwood was mistreated, because Windsor had actually treated everyone well, but that wasn't the point. The point was, Atwood was white, and he felt as if he should have been treated better than the slaves.

Raymond Windsor had supported the Confederacy to the point that he raised and equipped a regiment of cavalrymen from his own funds. But before he left for the war, he converted half of his money, which was a considerable amount, into gold as a hedge against the Confederate dollar.

Atwood and his father had both joined the regiment, and his father had been killed at the Battle of Tupelo in July of 1864. Five months later, Colonel

Windsor lay mortally wounded at the Battle of Franklin. He sent for Atwood, who he had recently promoted to lieutenant.

"Lieutenant Atwood," Windsor gasped. "I'm releasing you from the army now because I want you to take care of something for me. Return to Moss Point to look after my family. Wait until the war is over, and when everything has settled down, dig on the north side of the center silo. There, you will find the gold that I hid. Give it to my wife and children so that they aren't left destitute by this cruel war. And keep one thousand dollars for yourself."

"You are being very generous, Colonel," Atwood said.

"You have earned it, my boy. And if you do this for me, it will be money well spent. Do I have your word that you will do this?"

"You have my word, Colonel," Atwood promised.

Atwood returned to Moss Point, stayed for a few weeks, just long enough to earn Mrs. Windsor's trust, then, in the middle of the night, left with a horse and a pack mule. The pack mule was carrying one hundred fifty pounds of gold . . . or 2,175 troy ounces. At nineteen dollars and eighty cents a troy ounce, that came to just over forty-three thousand dollars.

When he arrived in Texas two months later, he was far from the closing battles of the war. And he was a rich man.

Now, more than twenty years later, Silas Atwood was much wealthier than he had been when he first arrived. At the moment he was sitting in a library, surrounded by books, none of which he had ever read, lighting a cigar and talking around puffs to Marshal Witherspoon and Judge Boykin.

"What do you know about these men who have come to town?" He puffed a few times until the end of the cigar glowed red, and his head was wreathed with aromatic smoke before he finished his question. "I am particularly interested in the one that killed Rufus Pardeen."

"That would be Smoke Jensen," Witherspoon replied.

"I was paying Pardeen more than any of my other special cadre because he had the reputation of being exceptionally good with a gun. This man, Jensen, did he beat him fair and square?"

"That's what all the witnesses in the saloon say," Witherspoon replied.

Atwood pulled the cigar from his mouth and examined the end of it. "One of the newcomers is Kate's brother, I understand?"

"Yes, and she is why they are here. Kate's brother, and Smoke Jensen, came to my office trying to get me to set bail for her."

"What did you tell them?"

"I said no, of course."

"Well, what with the shooting of Pardeen, and the humiliating and disarming of Willis and the two men who were with him, I'm sure that Kate's brother . . . what is his name?"

"Fontaine," Witherspoon replied. "Wes Fontaine, though he calls himself Pearlie nowadays."

"Pearlie," Atwood said. "Yes, Pearlie. Pearlie and Smoke, they with their colorful names, may feel that they have the upper hand for now. But when all is said and done, I'm sure Kate Abernathy's champions will give us no real difficulty."

"It may not be as easy as all that," Judge Boykin said.

"Why do you say that?"

"Apparently this man Jensen has earned somewhat of a reputation as a hero."

"A hero?" Atwood replied. "What do you mean, he's a hero?"

"When he came to visit me I thought that, perhaps, I had heard his name before, so I walked down to the newspaper office to look him up. There have been several articles written about his exploits, which have been notable enough to warrant syndication by the Associated Press. They've even written some books about him, I understand. He is quite well known in Colorado where it is said that there is no one who is faster, or more accurate, in the use of a pistol."

"Colorado?" Atwood removed his cigar and used it as he gestured. "Well, that may be. But he is in Texas now, and he is going to have to deal with me." The tone of Atwood's voice displayed his incredulity that anyone would dare challenge him.

"Yes, sir, he will have to deal with you, but he is already aware of your position here," Judge Boykin said. "He mentioned your name while we were in conversation."

Returning the cigar to his mouth, Atwood smiled around it. "He mentioned my name, you say? In what way was my name used?"

"He . . . uh . . . questioned the relationship I had

with you, suggesting that you may have an undue degree of influence over any judicial decision I might make."

Atwood chuckled. "You mean he knows that I have you by the balls?"

Boykin cleared his throat in embarrassment. "Well, uh, I wouldn't exactly say that."

"How would you say it?"

"I would say that, uh, your interests and mine coincide."

"Yeah," Atwood said, chuckling again. "You might say that. And Jensen pointed that out to you, did he?"

"Yes."

"Well, it could be that this man, Jensen, isn't as dumb as I thought. But what I want to know is, why is he getting involved in the first place? What does he have to do with Kate Abernathy?"

"Wes Fontaine works for Smoke Jensen," Marshal Witherspoon said. "Apparently he and his sister haven't seen each other in many years."

"If they haven't seen each other in a long time, what do you suppose made him show up now?" Atwood said.

Witherspoon smiled. "Well, he showed up now because, somehow, he learned that she was in trouble. And, I suppose he feels guilty about not seeing her for all these years. Who knows why he's here? Whatever the reason he is here, he and Jensen are bound to make trouble for us."

"You say Fontaine works for Jensen?"

"Yes."

Atwood studied the end of his cigar for a moment. "Then that's how we'll handle it. If we get rid of

Jensen, that will take care of Fontaine and the other man who is with them. To kill a snake, you cut off its head."

"Mr. Atwood, you aren't actually suggesting that we kill Jensen, are you?" Boykin asked. "That would be murder."

"Perhaps not," Atwood replied.

"What do you mean?"

"You did say that he is a well-known gunfighter, didn't you, Boykin?"

Upon hearing himself called by his last name, without the honorific title "Judge," there was just a flicker of resentment, though Boykin covered it up well.

"Yes, I did say that."

"Well, there's your answer then. Someone who is that good with a gun is bound to have had some paper out on him at some time in his past. All you have to do is find the wanted poster."

"And if I can't find one?"

"Make one up," Atwood said easily.

"I'd rather not make one up. I'm sure you are right; I'm sure that someone with his propensity for violence is bound to have a wanted poster out on him somewhere."

"Just make certain that it is a poster that says 'dead or alive,'" Judge Boykin instructed.

CHAPTER TWELVE

El Paso

When Smoke, Sally, and Pearlie arrived in El Paso, they saw that, unlike Etholen, which was a rather bucolic community, El Paso was quite a thriving city. There was a great deal of wagon and buggy traffic, and dozens and dozens of people walking along the plank walks that lined both sides of the streets. At intervals there were boards stretched all the way across the dirt streets to allow people a way to cross when the roads were full of mud. This seemed a totally unnecessary accommodation now, though, as it had been several weeks since the last good rain. As a result the passage of horses and wheeled vehicles stirred up the dust so that a brown-gray cloud seemed to hang in the air, no more than six feet above the ground.

"I'll ask that man over there where the federal court building is," Smoke said.

"No need to," Sally replied. "Look down there."

Sally pointed to a large and impressive brick and

stone building that stood three stories high, with a tower in the center that stretched up one additional story. Stone steps climbed up to a porch that had an array of impressive-looking columns. A sign attached to the front of the structure said, UNITED STATES FEDERAL BUILDING.

"I would say that's the place we're looking for," Sally said.

"And I would say that you are right," Smoke replied.

Tying their horses to a hitching rail out front, the three went inside, examined the directory, then walked upstairs to the office of the federal judge.

Ezekiel B. Turner was the judge of the West Texas Federal Court, and he greeted them courteously after the judicial clerk announced their presence.

"Which of you gentlemen is Smoke Jensen?" Judge Turner asked.

"I am, Your Honor, though my real name is . . ."

"Kirby Jensen," Turner interrupted.

The expression on Smoke's face reflected his surprise at the judge knowing his given name.

"I beg your pardon?"

"That is your name, isn't it? Kirby Jensen?"

"Well, yes, that is true. But how in the world do you know that? To the best of my memory, we've never met."

"No, we haven't. But I know you. At least, I know of you. That is, if you are the same man who was appointed as a Deputy U.S. Marshal by Uriah B. Holloway."

"Yes, I am that man," Smoke replied. "Although, that was several years ago."

Turner smiled and nodded. "I thought so. Uriah

and I are great friends from way back. He has spoken well of you."

"Marshal Holloway is a good man," Smoke said.

"That he is, Mr. Jensen, that he is. And this young lady?" Turner asked, smiling at Sally.

"This is my wife, Sally."

"Sally," Judge Turner said. "That is a beautiful name for a beautiful lady." He looked toward Pearlie.

"This is Pearlie," Smoke said.

"Pearlie?"

"That's what I'm called, Your Honor. My real name is Wes Fontaine."

"Now, Mr. and Mrs. Jensen, Pearlie, what can I do for you?"

"It's about Pearlie's sister. Pearlie is an employee of mine, and . . ." Smoke started.

"Smoke, Pearlie is much more than just an employee, and you know that," Sally interrupted.

"Yes, he is," Smoke said. "The truth is, Pearlie is more family than mere employee."

Pearlie smiled self-consciously at Smoke's beneficent description of their relationship.

"And you've always made me feel that way," Pearlie said. "But, Your Honor, my sister, Katie Abernathy, is why we're here."

"And Pearlie's nephew, Rusty Abernathy. Rusty was tried and convicted of murder."

Judge Turner held up his hand and shook his head. "I'm sure you realize that murder is a state offense."

"Your Honor, if I may," Sally said. "We are appealing to you on the basis of Judge Boykin's court violating Mr. Abernathy's rights under the Fourteenth

Amendment, and that makes it federal. His trial was improper; therefore, his imprisonment was improper."

Judge Turner nodded. "That is an interesting tactic for appeal," he said. "How was the trial improper?"

"To begin with, Your Honor, Mr. Abernathy was given no choice in selecting his own lawyer. His defense was appointed by the court."

"Yes, well, when an indigent defendant is appointed a lawyer, he rarely has any say in it."

"That's just it, Your Honor. Mr. Abernathy isn't indigent. He could well afford his own lawyer but was denied that right. In addition there was no voir dire of a jury that was packed with Atwood men, and the court did not allow so much as one witness to testify in Mr. Abernathy's defense."

"Were there eyewitnesses who could have provided cogent testimony?" Judge Turner asked.

"Indeed there were, Your Honor, but as I said, they weren't allowed to testify."

"Is Mr. Abernathy in jail now?" he asked.

"No," Smoke replied. "Rusty escaped, and the marshal arrested Kate, his mother. Now they are saying that if Rusty doesn't return by a date certain, they are going to hang his mother in his place."

"What? Why, that is outrageous!" Judge Turner said.

"Yes, sir, that's what we thought, too," Smoke said. "We applied for bail through Judge Boykin, but he turned us down."

"Boykin," Judge Turner said, practically spitting

the name. "If ever there was a man who dishonored the bench more than that miscreant, I have yet to hear of him. If you can get me some eyewitness accounts of the incident involving Mrs. Abernathy's son, I will, if those accounts justify it, overturn Judge Boykin and grant Mrs. Abernathy release on her own recognizance."

A broad smile played across Sally's lips. "We hoped you might say something like that," she said. Sally removed the paper she had recorded from the envelope, then handed it to Judge Turner. "Here is an affidavit, signed by every eyewitness to the event, and notarized."

Judge Turner read the document, reacting audibly to the part where it explained that no eyewitnesses were allowed to testify.

"You can forget about bail," Judge Turner said.

"What?" Smoke asked, surprised by the judge's announcement.

"There is no need for bail, neither for Mrs. Abernathy nor for her son. I am ordering the immediate release of Mrs. Abernathy, and I am officially vacating the conviction of Rusty Abernathy. I have never seen such a travesty of justice as this in all my days on the bench."

Smoke smiled and reached out to shake Judge Turner's hand.

"Your Honor, I don't know how to thank you."

"No, Mr. Jensen, it is I who should thank you and Mrs. Jensen for bringing this to my attention. Oh, by the way, you might have a little trouble with Boykin and the marshal there, so the two of you hold up your right hand." He was referring to Smoke and Pearlie.

Smoke smiled. "I was going to ask you if you would be willing to appoint us as officers of the court."

"I'm more than willing. I'm proud to do it," Judge Turner replied.

Smoke and Pearlie raised their right hands as Judge Turner swore them in as United States Marshals.

When Smoke and Pearlie stepped into the marshal's office later that same day back in Etholen, Marshal Witherspoon was the only one present.

"Look here," Witherspoon said, pointing at Pearlie. "I ought to lock you up for what you done last time you was here. You assaulted an officer of the law, what with you stickin' your pistol in my mouth like you done."

"I didn't do that because you were an officer of the law," Pearlie said. "I did that because you are a low-life son of a bitch and I didn't like the way you referred to my sister."

"Yeah, well, maybe I was a little out of line, callin' her a whore 'n all. So, I'm goin' to let it pass this time," Witherspoon said, speaking as if he had any control over the matter. "But you better not do anythin' like that again. I reckon you're wantin' to go back there 'n see her, so, if you 'n Jensen will just go over there 'n shuck out of them pistol belts, you can go on back."

"We'll keep our guns, because we don't plan to go back and see her," Pearlie said.

"What do you mean? You aren't here to see your sister?"

"Oh, we're here to see her all right," Smoke said. "But we won't be going back there to see her. You are going to bring her up here, to us."

"Now, why would I want to do a damn-fool thing like that?"

"You should do it because we have an order from the court that says my sister is free," Pearlie said. "So we expect you to let her go."

"The judge is setting her free, is he?" Witherspoon smiled. "Good, then she's agreed to sell the saloon to Mr. Atwood. That probably means the judge will more'n likely drop charges against the boy, too. Hell, if Kate hadda agreed to sell the saloon to Mr. Atwood in the first place, none of this would've happened."

"What makes you think she has agreed to sell the saloon to Atwood?" Smoke asked.

"You said the judge said to let her out, didn't you?"

"Yes."

"Then that means she's willin' to sell the saloon to Mr. Atwood. Atwood told me hisself that that's all it would take for him to agree to allow Judge Boykin to let Kate out of jail."

"Are you telling me, Marshal, that Judge Boykin, an officer of the court, takes his orders from Silas Atwood?" Smoke asked.

"Hell, we pretty much all do," Witherspoon admitted. "Without Mr. Atwood, there most likely wouldn't be none of us have our jobs, the judge included."

"It really comes as no surprise to us that you and Boykin are in Atwood's pocket," Smoke said. "I just wanted to hear you say it aloud. But Boykin didn't set Mrs. Abernathy free."

"Wait a minute. You mean she ain't been set free? Well, what did you tell me that for? Did you think I wouldn't check with the judge?"

"Oh, my sister has been set free, all right," Pearlie said. "But this court order doesn't come from Boykin, it comes from Judge Ezekiel B. Turner, in El Paso."

"El Paso? What does a judge in El Paso have to do with Etholen? He won't have any jurisdiction here. You'll need to get an order from Judge Boykin."

Smoke shook his head. "You don't understand. Turner is a federal judge. That means he has authority over Boykin, and every other judge in West Texas."

"Yeah? Well, I don't know about that," Witherspoon said. "I think maybe I should wait and see what Atwood thinks. I don't think I have the authority to let her go on my own."

"On the contrary, you have no authority to keep her on your own. I, on the other hand, do have the authority to see her set free," Smoke said. "And I intend to see to it that you do that, right now."

"You have the authority?" Witherspoon asked. "What authority do you have?"

"This," Smoke said, showing Marshal Witherspoon the paper. "And this," he added, pulling his pistol.

Smoke reached out to take the marshal's gun

from his holster. "Get the keys, Pearlie. The marshal, here, is about to become a guest in his own jail."

"What are you doing? You can't do this!"

"Yeah, I can," Smoke said with an easy grin.

With the keys in Pearlie's hand, and a pistol in Smoke's hand, the three men went into the back of the jail. When they got to the back, they saw Kate standing in her cell with her hands grasping the bars.

"Pearlie, I thought I heard your voice out there." She saw that the man with her brother was holding a pistol on the marshal, and she gasped in fear. "What's going on?" she asked.

"We're getting you out of here, Katie."

"No!" Kate said, shaking her head. "I don't want you to break me out of jail! Wes, I mean Pearlie, I don't want you getting in trouble because of me!"

"Relax, we aren't in any trouble," Pearlie said. "We've got a court order from a federal judge, ordering your release. The only reason we've come back like this is because the marshal, here, didn't want to honor the court order. So, we just took it on our own to enforce the order."

"But, even with that letter, you don't have the authority on your own, do you?"

"I'll have you know, Katie, that Smoke and I were both appointed as officers of the federal court. That gives us all the authority we need."

While Smoke and Pearlie were freeing Kate, Deputy Calhoun, unaware of what was playing out back at the city jail, was in the back room of the courthouse, surrounded by cardboard boxes filled with yellowed and sometimes crumbling paper.

PROCLAMATION
of the
GOVERNOR OF MISSOURI

WANTED
for ROBBERY *and* MURDER

THE JAMES GANG :
JESSE JAMES, FRANK JAMES, COLE YOUNGER,
JIM YOUNGER, *and* BOB YOUNGER

REWARD OF $5,000
$1,000 ea.

Calhoun found dozens of other posters that he knew were outdated because the principals had already been captured or killed. He was about ready to give up when he found one that did catch his interest. This poster was brown with age, and the edges were curling up. He was sure it had probably been withdrawn or it wouldn't have been in this box with all the other outdated posters. Besides, it was a poster from Colorado, so he wasn't sure it would be applicable in Texas anyway. But he would let Marshal Witherspoon decide.

CHAPTER THIRTEEN

"Miss Kate! You're out!" Peterson exclaimed in excitement when Kate, Pearlie, and Smoke stepped into the Pretty Girl and Happy Cowboy Saloon a few minutes later.

"Oh, Miss Kate! How good it is to see you!" Dolly shouted happily, running to her to give her an embrace. The other four girls did the same thing.

"Pearlie told me what all of you did for me," Kate said. "Sally, I thank you so much for writing up the paper telling what happened, and Mr. Peterson, Dolly, and all of you, I thank you for putting your names to it."

"It's only right," Dolly said. "Marshal Witherspoon had no business putting you in jail in the first place."

"Belly up to the bar, boys, and name your poison," Kate said. "Mr. Peterson, if you would, please, set everyone up with a drink of their choice, on the house."

"Thank you!" one of the patrons boomed in response, and all seventeen men present hurried to the bar to claim their drink.

"I'll bet Marshal Witherspoon is fit to be tied," Dolly said.

Kate laughed. "Funny you should mention that. Fit to be tied, I mean."

"Oh, oh," Sally said. "Smoke, what did you do? You didn't tie the marshal up, did you?"

"Why, no, there was no need to tie him up," Smoke said.

"I wouldn't put it past you."

"I mean, as long as we could put him in a jail cell, why bother to tie him up?"

"Smoke, you didn't!" Sally said, but she laughed as she made the comment.

"Did you say that Judge Turner overturned Rusty's conviction?" Kate asked.

"He sure did," Sally replied with a broad smile.

"Is there any way we can get word to him about that? I would sure like to have him come back home."

"I tell you what, Sis. I'll go get him and bring him back home," Pearlie said.

"Would you? Oh, that would be wonderful!"

"I'll go with you," Cal said.

"I suppose you folks will be going back home now that this is all straightened out," Kate said, though the tone of her voice indicated that this was not something she was particularly looking forward to.

"We have no intention of going back," Smoke said.

"Oh?"

"We don't have everything straightened out," Smoke said. "As I understand it, Atwood still wants to get control of your place, doesn't he?"

"I'm sure he does."

"Then, until he changes his mind, everything isn't

straightened out. And we won't leave here until Atwood changes his tune."

Kate shook her head. "Oh, I don't think Silas Atwood is going to change anything very soon."

Smoke smiled. "Well then, we'll just have to change his mind for him, won't we?"

"I got that information on Smoke Jensen you was lookin' for," Deputy Calhoun said when he stepped into the marshal's office. He glanced toward the other side of the room and saw that the marshal wasn't sitting behind his desk. "Marshal? Marshal Witherspoon, are you in here?"

"Calhoun! I'm back here!" Witherspoon called.

"All right, I'll just leave this on your desk."

"Get back here!" Witherspoon shouted.

"What's up, Marshal? You havin' trouble with Kate?" Calhoun asked, and, putting the flyer he had located on the marshal's desk, he walked back to the cell area. "I'll be right there."

When Calhoun got to the cell area, he expected to see Marshal Witherspoon standing just outside of the prisoner's cell. To his total shock, he saw him standing inside the cell.

"Lord, have mercy, Marshal! What are you doin' in that jail cell?"

"Get me the hell out of here!" Witherspoon demanded angrily.

"How did you get in there?"

"Never mind all that. Just get me out, now!"

Calhoun hurried out to the front of the office, got the keys, then came back to let Witherspoon out.

"Where the hell have you been?" Witherspoon demanded to know. "I've been locked up back here for at least two hours!"

"I was doin' what you told me to do, Marshal," Calhoun replied. "I was seein' what I could come up with on Smoke Jensen."

"And did you?" Witherspoon asked as they returned to the office.

"Well, I'm not sure. I found somethin', but I'm not sure it'll be of any use to us."

"You let me decide on whether or not it'll be any use to us. What did you find?"

"I got a wanted poster on him for murder. But it's from Colorado, it ain't from Texas."

Despite the ordeal of having just been locked up in his own jail, a huge smile spread across Marshal Witherspoon's face. "The hell you say."

"Onliest thing is, that poster has to be over twenty years old."

"That doesn't matter," Witherspoon said. "I'm no lawyer, but even I know that there's no statute of limitations on murder." Witherspoon looked at the wanted poster. "And, as you can see here," he said, thumping his fingers on the paper, "he's wanted for murder. And for ten thousand dollars. Oh, yeah, Mr. Atwood is going to be really happy about this."

WANTED

DEAD *or* ALIVE
THE OUTLAW AND MURDERER

SMOKE JENSEN

$10,000 REWARD
Contact the Sheriff—Bury, Idaho Terr.

"You mean he *was* wanted for murder," Calhoun said. "Since this is the onliest one on him I found, why, like as not, it's done been called back."

"Maybe it was called back from Colorado," Witherspoon said with an evil smile. "But it wasn't called back from Texas."

"How do you know it wasn't called back from Texas?"

"You found it, didn't you? If it had been called back, most likely it would've been destroyed, not just put away."

"So, what do we do with it now?"

"I'll see Judge Boykin 'n have him issue a new one," Witherspoon said.

"Even if it's been withdrawn?"

"That's for the judge to decide, not you," Witherspoon said.

"I don't know if I have the authority to reissue this," Judge Boykin said after Witherspoon showed him the reward poster on Smoke Jensen. "This was issued by some sheriff up in Idaho, and it is offering a ten-thousand-dollar reward. Suppose someone did kill him, how would we come up with ten thousand dollars?"

"Hell, Judge, we won't actually be reissuing this poster," Witherspoon said. "We'll just be reprinting it for that marshal up in Idaho. If somebody kills Jensen and wants the reward, they'll have to contact that sheriff."

"But this poster is over twenty years old. There's very little chance that the man who originally posted this reward would still be the marshal, and whoever is there now probably knows nothing at all about this. I doubt seriously that the reward would even be paid."

Witherspoon chuckled. "Well now, that ain't really goin' to be our problem, is it? Once Jensen is dead, he's dead, 'n whether the sheriff up in Bury, Idaho, whoever he is, pays this reward or not, it don't really matter none to us."

"But if I am purposely issuing a wanted poster on a man who isn't wanted, I could get into a lot of trouble," Boykin complained.

"Are you a' tellin' me that you ain't goin' to reissue the poster?"

"I'm just saying it could be risky."

"Tell me this, Judge, have you ever received any information saying that Smoke Jensen ain't wanted no more?"

"Well, no, but then, I wasn't the judge back when this dodger was first issued."

"Then you have no information telling you that it has been withdrawn. As far as you know, you're just doing the state of Colorado a favor by authorizing the reprint of this.

"And, I might add, Atwood wants this done."

Judge Boykin smiled. "Yes," he said. "Yes, you're right, I would just be doing a community service by reissuing this document, wouldn't I?"

"You write out somethin' sayin' you approve of this, 'n I'll go over to the newspaper office 'n have 'em print up some reward dodgers for us," Witherspoon said.

"I wouldn't go to the newspaper office if I were you," Boykin said.

"Why not? I need to get these things printed."

"You've read some of Blanton's editorials, haven't you? I can't say that any of them have been particularly supportive. You'd better find someplace else to have it printed."

"Yeah, you're right," Witherspoon said.

"How many did you have printed?" Atwood asked.

"So far there's just this one. I told him I'd need to see what you thought about it before I'd have him print any more."

Atwood nodded. "Yes, it looks good, but we don't need any more. This one will be enough."

"One?" Witherspoon questioned, surprised by Atwood's reply. "What do you mean we only need one? How are we going to get them out there for people to see them if we only print one?"

"No need for a lot of people to see it," Atwood said. "The only one who needs to see it is the one who is going to try and collect the reward."

"Uh, Mr. Atwood, you do know, don't you, that there might not be any reward at all? This was first printed a long time ago, and besides that, it was done up in Colorado."

"Paying the reward is not our problem," Atwood said. "According to this, it is the sheriff up in Idaho who will be paying the ten thousand."

"I suppose so. But I don't think Jensen is going to be all that easy to kill. It's not just that he killed

Pardeen, from what I've been able to find out about him, he's better with a gun than just about anybody."

"Just about doesn't mean everyone. I may know of just the man who can handle him."

"Who would that be?" Witherspoon asked. "I know you've got some good men ridin' for you, but I'll be honest with you, Mr. Atwood, I don't think you've got anyone who's up to handlin' Smoke Jensen."

"Do you think someone like Lucien Critchlow would be good enough to take the measure of Mr. Jensen?"

"Someone like Critchlow? I don't know. He might be. That is, if he really is as good as Critchlow."

Atwood smiled. "Oh, I expect Critchlow is as good as Critchlow."

"You've got Critchlow?"

"Not yet, but I'll get him."

Witherspoon smiled and nodded. "Yeah, you get Critchlow, and our problem will be taken care of. Oh, wait, that might not be such a good idea."

"Why not?"

"Critchlow is for sure going to want the ten-thousand-dollar reward, and like I told you before, there might not even be a reward out for Jensen now. It's more than likely that this here reward was took down years ago. Otherwise, there would be fresh paper out on 'im, and I can tell you for a fact, there ain't none. And Critchlow ain't exactly the kind of a man I'd want to have thinkin' we cheated him."

"You let me worry about that."

* * *

"Why is it you're willin' to hire someone else to take care of Jensen?" Bo Willis asked. "Ain't that why you've got folks like me 'n Clark 'n Booker 'n the others? We ain't exactly your ordinary cowhands, you know."

"You had your opportunity to deal with him, and it didn't turn out all that well, did it?"

"Yeah, well, it wasn't just him, it was three of 'em, if you recall. 'N one of 'em sneaked up behind us."

"I do recall," Atwood said. "Look, Willis, don't misunderstand the situation here. You, Clark, and Booker are too valuable to me and I can't afford to lose you right now. If Critchlow succeeds, and Jensen is killed, I will be able to continue with the long-range plans I have. But if Critchlow is killed, it will merely be a temporary setback. I can replace him easily. You, not so easily."

"Oh," Willis said, mollified by Atwood's explanation. "Oh, well, yeah, if you put it that way, I see what you mean."

"Now, do be a good man and go to Carrizo Springs for me. I'm told that is where you will be able to find Critchlow."

CHAPTER FOURTEEN

Bo Willis had never actually seen Lucien Critchlow, but he did have a good description of him, and when he stepped into the Bottom Dollar Saloon in Carrizo Springs, Texas, he saw someone standing, alone, at the far end of the bar. The man standing there had a narrow face with hollow cheeks and very thin lips. His eyes were dark, and deep—set beneath sparse eyebrows.

"What'll it be?" the bartender asked, stepping up to Willis.

"I'll take a whiskey."

The bartender poured a shot from an unmarked bottle.

"That man standing at the other end of the bar," Willis said quietly, as he paid for the drink. "Would that be Lucien Critchlow?"

"It might be. Who are you?"

"The name is Willis. I work for Mr. Atwood over in El Paso County, 'n he wants to make Critchlow an offer."

"What kind of offer?" the bartender asked.

Willis glared at him. "The offer is for Critchlow," he said.

"Yeah? Well, I wouldn't make 'im mad, if I was you," the bartender said as he walked away.

Willis tossed down his whiskey and looked over toward Critchlow. Nobody knew for sure how many men Lucien Critchlow had actually killed. Seventeen, some said. Twenty-three, others insisted. Critchlow knew, but he never spoke about it. He didn't have to; his reputation spoke for itself.

Willis set the glass down on the bar, wiped his lips with the back of his hand, then screwed up his courage to approach the gunfighter.

"Mr. Critchlow?"

"Yeah?" Critchlow replied without turning around.

"I work for a man named Silas Atwood. He wants to make you an offer."

"An offer?"

"He wants to hire you for a job."

"I don't come cheap."

"Mr. Atwood isn't a cheap man."

"What is this job I'm supposed to do?"

"Have you ever heard of a man named Smoke Jensen?"

"Smoke Jensen? Yeah, I've heard of him. He come down here not too long ago and got into a little brawl with that Mexican feller that was raisin' so much Cain here about. Keno, I think his name was."

"Is that all you know about 'im?"

"Folks say that he's good with a gun," Critchlow said.

"Yeah, that's what I heard, too."

"What about Jensen? Why are you askin' me about 'im?"

"I'd rather let Mr. Atwood tell you about 'im," Willis said. "I can tell you this, though. He told me to tell you that if you can do the job, it'll be worth a lot of money to you."

Critchlow said nothing, but turned back to the bar and stared down into his whiskey glass. Willis, not quite sure what he should do now, stood there for a moment, then turned to walk away.

"Where are you goin'?" Critchlow asked with a low growl.

"Well, I, uh, am goin' to go back 'n tell Mr. Atwood you ain't interested."

"Did I tell you I wasn't interested?"

"You didn't say nothin' at all."

"Then don't be tellin' 'im nothin' if you don't know what you're talkin' about."

"You mean, you will come see Mr. Atwood?"

"Yeah, you can tell 'im I'll be there."

"When?"

"When I get there," Critchlow replied.

A couple of Atwood's Mexican employees were replacing shingles on the barn the next day when they saw someone ride in and dismount in front of the big house.

"*Pistolero*," one of them said.

"*Si, hombre asesina*," the other replied.

The two men spoke so quietly that it was impossible for Critchlow to have overheard them, but as he looped his horse's reins around the hitching post, he looked up toward them.

"*Madre de Dios*," one of them said prayerfully.

"It is all right, Ramon. He goes to see Señor Atwood."

Critchlow was shown into the library where, without being asked, he sat in what appeared to be the most comfortable leather chair to wait for Atwood.

When Atwood came into the room a few minutes later, it was obvious by the expression on his face that Atwood had chosen his chair. Critchlow made no effort to relinquish the chair.

"Mr. Critchlow, thank you for coming," Atwood said, finding another, less comfortable chair.

"Yeah, well, this ain't exactly what you might call a social visit," Critchlow said. "I was told that you might have a job for me."

"I do," Atwood said. "That is, if you are willing to take it."

"So, you want me to kill Smoke Jensen, do you?"

Atwood coughed. "You, uh, do get to the bottom of things very quickly, don't you?"

"You said you have a job for me. I don't punch cattle, and I'm no handyman. You know who I am, and what I do, so there's only one reason you would want to hire me. Your man asked me about Smoke Jensen, so I figure he's the one you want me to kill."

"Yes, you're right."

"Why do you want him killed?"

"I have personal and business reasons for wanting Smoke Jensen out of the way."

"Reason enough to pay for murder?"

"It won't exactly be murder."

"How will it not be murder?"

Atwood showed Critchlow the recently printed poster stating that Smoke Jensen was wanted, dead or alive, and that a reward of ten thousand dollars was being offered.

Critchlow studied the poster for a long moment. "Ten-thousand-dollar reward?"

"Yes."

"That's a lot of money."

"Yes, it is. Do you know this man, Jensen?" Atwood asked.

"Yeah, I know who he is," Critchlow replied. "I didn't know there was any paper out on 'im, though."

"This is new," Atwood said. "If you know him, then you also know that he is a man who, shall we say, enjoys somewhat of a reputation as one who is quite skilled with a gun."

"Yeah, so I've heard," Critchlow replied.

"Will you take the job?"

"What do you mean, will I take the job?" Critchlow held up the poster. "From the way I'm seein' it, this ain't exactly a job. There's a reward out for him, so what you're sayin' is that you want me to compete with all the others who are going after him."

"No," Atwood replied. "This poster hasn't been issued yet. You are the first one to see it, so you won't be competing with anyone."

"Once I kill 'im, who'll be payin' the reward?"

"It's like the poster says. The reward will be paid by the marshal up in Bury, Idaho. I'll see to it that the body is properly identified and reported, though. I'll have the local marshal and the judge verify it. You won't have any problem proving that you killed him.

And of course, because Jensen is wanted, dead or alive, there won't be any unpleasant charges brought against the man who dispatches him."

"Who does what?"

"Who kills him."

"And you say that you've got personal reasons for wantin' 'im dead?"

"Yes."

"One thousand dollars."

"Ten thousand dollars."

"No, the reward is for ten thousand dollars, and in order to collect that, I'll have to contact some marshal up in Idaho. That means it could be a real long time before I get anything, if I ever get it at all," Critchlow said. "So when I say I want a thousand dollars, what I mean is, I want that thousand dollars from you, in addition to the reward. And I want it as soon as the job is done so I'll have some money while I'm waitin' for the ten thousand dollars to be paid."

"A thousand dollars? That's . . . uh . . . a lot of money."

"Yeah, well, if you want me to do the job, then that's what it's goin' to cost."

Atwood stroked his chin for a long moment before he replied. "All right, I'll meet your price. Just get the job done. Do you think you can handle Jensen?"

"I can beat 'im."

"You're sure you can?"

"Yeah, I'm sure."

"The reason I ask is, if, for some reason, you can't beat him, it might well come back that I'm the one who hired you."

"What do you mean, you hired me? Ain't you just showed me that there's paper out on him?"

"Yes, but still, I'm taking somewhat of a chance here."

Critchlow chuckled. "*You're* takin' a chance? I'm the one that's goin' to go up against him."

"Yes, I suppose that is true, isn't it?"

"I want the money now."

"I'll pay you when the job is done."

"Then you can get someone else to do the job." Critchlow turned to leave.

"Wait!" Atwood called to him. "What if I gave you one hundred dollars now and the rest of the money after the job is done? I promise you, I won't cheat you."

Critchlow moved his thin lips into what might have been a smile, though with a face like his, it was hard to tell. And if it was a smile, it didn't reach his eyes.

"Tell me, Atwood, do you really think I might be worried that you would cheat me?"

"No, I . . . I guess not."

"It's not 'cause I think you might cheat me. I just want a little walkin'-around money up front is all."

"All right," Atwood agreed. "I'll give you a hundred dollars now. But this one hundred comes off the one thousand."

"No. This one hundred dollars is what you might call expense money," Critchlow said.

"All right, all right. Kill Jensen, and I'll give you the entire one thousand dollars."

Ramon and Carlos saw Critchlow again as the *pistolero* rode away.

"He goes to kill someone, I think," Carlos said.

"*Si*," Ramon said. "I think so, too." Ramon crossed himself.

Gomez, Texas

"Really?" Rusty said as a huge smile spread across his face. "I'm not wanted anymore?"

"Judge Turner has overturned your conviction and has freed Katie as well," Pearlie said. He smiled at his nephew. "We've come to take you home to your mama."

"Thank you, Uncle Pearlie! Thank you!"

"I don't know about you two, but I'm kinda hungry," Pearlie said. "What do you say we find us a restaurant?"

Five minutes later Pearlie, Rusty, and Cal were enjoying their lunch at a café on Center Street called Susie's.

"Is Atwood still trying to take over Mom's saloon?" Rusty asked.

"He may try, but he won't get it," Cal said. "We'll make certain of that."

"By the way," Pearlie said. "Some of the customers at the Pretty Girl are wondering when you'll be back. It seems that they miss your piano playing."

Rusty smiled. "I miss playing it, too."

"Yeah, well I'd like to hear you play, so you can . . . damn!" Cal said. He had just started to take a bite when he spilled food all down the front of his shirt.

"Savin' some of your lunch for later, are you?" Pearlie teased.

"You think we have time for me to get a new shirt before we go back?"

"I think we need to; I sure don't want to be seen with a slob like you," Pearlie said.

"Hey!" someone called to them when the three men stepped out into the street. "You're Rusty Abernathy, ain't you?"

Rusty didn't answer.

"Yeah, I know you are. I've seen you play in the saloon over in Etholen."

Rusty smiled at the man who had called out to him. "Yeah, I'm Rusty. I hope you enjoyed . . ." that was as far as he got before the man, unexpectedly, drew his pistol and pointed it at Rusty.

"That's what I thought," the man said. "You're worth five hunnert dollars," he said.

"No, he isn't," Pearlie said. "A federal judge has set aside his guilty verdict. That means that the reward has been pulled back. He's not a wanted man anymore."

"Who the hell says so?" the man holding the gun replied.

"I say so," Pearlie said. "I was in the judge's office when he did that."

"Well, I've got a document in my pocket that says he's worth five hunnert dollars, 'n I intend to collect on it."

"I told you, that reward poster is worthless."

"Who are you?"

"I'm Rusty's uncle."

"Yeah? Well that tells me you're lyin' to save him.

Only it ain't goin' to work, 'cause I'm pointin' this gun directly at him."

Pearlie drew so fast that he was holding a gun in his hand before the man realized it.

"And I'm pointing this gun directly at you," Pearlie said.

"Are you crazy, mister? Can't you see I'm already pointin' my gun at Abernathy? I told you, he's worth five hunnert dollars to me."

"And I told you, the reward has been withdrawn." Pearlie smiled. "And even if it hasn't been, how are you going to spend five hundred dollars if you're dead?"

"I, uh . . ."

"Get his gun, Cal."

Cal reached out for the gun, which the man surrendered without resistance. Cal took out the cylinder, then handed the pistol, without the cylinder, back to the would-be bounty hunter.

"My friend is going to buy a shirt," Pearlie said. "When we're gone, you can pick up your cylinder over there, in the mercantile store."

"I want a red one," Cal said easily, as they headed toward the store, leaving the frustrated bounty hunter standing in the street, holding a useless pistol.

Back in Etholen, Sally and Kate were having lunch together.

"It has been a long time since I last saw my brother, but I must say he has made some wonderful friends."

"Pearlie has been almost a part of our family since we first met him," Sally said. "And over the years we have had to depend upon him more times than I can possibly count. He and Cal have been such a blessing to us."

"Yes, well, I don't know what would have happened to Rusty and me if he, you, Smoke, and Cal hadn't come along when you did. In fact, I don't want to know what would have happened."

Sally reached out across the table to lay her hand on Kate's hand. You don't have to wonder about it, because nothing bad is going to happen. We're here now, and Smoke told me he has no intention of our going back home until he is sure that you will be safe and not bothered."

CHAPTER FIFTEEN

With Sally and Kate having lunch at the Palace Café, and with Pearlie and Cal gone to fetch Rusty, Smoke found himself alone in the Pretty Girl and Happy Cowboy Saloon. He was well aware that Atwood might still try to cause some trouble for Kate, so he was sitting at a table that offered a commanding view of the entire room. He had just taken a swallow of his beer when he saw someone come in who piqued his interest. As soon as the man stepped through the batwing doors, he moved in such a way as to put the wall to his back while he studied the saloon.

This was exactly the way Smoke entered a saloon, and the way this man did it, easily and without calling attention to himself, suggested to Smoke that he was either a man on the run or someone who had made many enemies in his life. And it was Smoke's experience that anyone who had made a lot of enemies had probably killed a lot of men. Also, the way the man wore his gun, low on his right hip, and slightly kicked out, suggested that he was quite proficient in its use.

Smoke wondered why such a man would be in Etholen, but even as he wondered, he had a gut feeling that he wasn't here by chance. There had been nothing overt in the man's actions, but Smoke had long ago developed an intuition about such things. That intuition, almost as much as his prowess with a pistol, had kept him alive through the years.

The gunman, and that was how Smoke was thinking of him now, stepped up to the bar and ordered a drink. Although the man was standing with his back to Smoke, Smoke could see that he was using the mirror to make a very careful study of the room. Then, when the man found what he was looking for, his searching eyes stopped.

And they stopped on Smoke.

That action validated Smoke's notion that the man was here for him. This wouldn't be the first time that a gunfighter, trying to make a name for himself, had called him out. But, he was out of his normal territory, so he rather doubted this was such a person. He believed that this could well be someone who had been sent by Atwood.

A couple of times Smoke looked directly at the gunman's reflection, wanting to look him in the eyes, but the man cut his gaze away both times.

Finally the gunman turned toward Smoke.

"Mister, why is it that you're a-starin' at me in the mirror?" he asked. He spoke the words loudly, and he put more reproach into the question than was required.

"Was I staring?" Smoke said. "I'm sorry, I don't mean to make you uncomfortable."

"Yeah? Well you are making me damn uncomfortable."

"I assure you, sir, any thought that I am staring at you is unfounded. I'll make certain not to do so in the future."

The gunman twisted his mouth into what might have been a smile. "Well now, Mr. Smoke Jensen, what makes you think you're even goin' to have a future?" he asked.

Here it was. This was no casual encounter. This man had called Smoke by name, and that could only mean that he was after him in particular.

"That's enough, mister!" Peterson said. "This man ain't done nothin' to you, and he apologized even though he didn't do nothin'. Now back off."

The gunman held a hand out toward the bartender, though he didn't take his eyes off Smoke.

"This ain't none of your business, bartender. 'N if you don't keep your mouth shut, 'n stay out of this, I'll be takin' care of you, right after I take care of the famous . . . Smoke Jensen. That is your name, ain't it?"

"It is," Smoke replied.

"Tell me, would you be the same Smoke Jensen that a marshal from Idaho is offerin' a ten-thousand-dollar reward for?"

Smoke was rarely surprised by anything anymore, but this did surprise him.

"What?" he asked, practically shouting the response.

"You heard me. There's paper out on you from

Idaho, ain't there? 'N it's for ten thousand dollars. I know this, 'cause I seen the dodger with m' own eyes."

"Mister, now, how about telling me your name?" Smoke asked.

"The name is Critchlow. Lucien Critchlow."

"Critchlow!" someone said, and though it was a whisper, it was loud enough that everyone in the saloon heard it.

The name was repeated a few more times, and in as much awe as was used by the first to speak it.

The gunman smiled. "I see several here have heard of me. But then most people have. Of course, some of 'em hear of me a little too late, if you get my meanin'."

Smoke, who was still sitting at the table, made no reply.

"Critchlow, I've heard of you," Peterson said. "But I've heard of Smoke Jensen, too, and if you're thinkin' about takin' him on, you might want to reconsider. I believe you're about to take a bigger bite than you can chew."

"Is that a fact? This man, Smoke Jensen, he's supposed to be somebody, is he? I mean, other than a murderer 'n an outlaw that the marshal up in Bury, Idaho, is willin' to pay ten thousand dollars for."

"Critchlow, I don't know where you saw that, but that poster was issued more than twenty years ago," Smoke said. "And it was pulled soon after it was issued. There is no reward out for me, not here in Texas, not up in Colorado, not anywhere in the entire nation. So if you're prodding me so you can collect a reward, you're going to be disappointed, because nobody is going to pay you any money for my hide."

"Yeah? Well, now I know you're lyin', just tryin' to weasel your way out. I've seen the poster, mister, 'n the one I seen ain't twenty years old. Hell, it ain't hardly a week old, 'cause it was bright 'n shiny, brand new, which means that more'n likely it just come off the printin' press. Anyhow, why don't we let the marshal up in Idaho decide whether it's still any good or not?"

"I'm afraid Sheriff Reece isn't going to be able to tell you anything about this poster."

"Sheriff Reece? That's the lawman up in Bury, Idaho, that's wantin' you, is it?"

"He was the marshal when the poster was put out over twenty years ago. But he isn't there anymore."

"Yeah? Well he could be. I've heard of sheriffs bein' sheriffs for more'n twenty years."

"Not this one. He's dead."

"How do you know he's dead?" Critchlow challenged.

"I know he's dead, because I killed him."

At Smoke's words, spoken without inflection, there was another audible gasp of surprise from those present in the saloon.

"You'll never get your money, Critchlow."

Critchlow's mocking smile grew even wider. "So you're sayin' I ain't goin' to get the money 'cause you killed a marshal? Well now, it just so happens that the lawman in Idaho ain't the only one wantin' to see you dead. Turns out there's another fella willin' to pay for it."

The bartender, measuring the conversation, knew

that it had reached the pivotal stage and moved down to the far end of the bar.

Now it was Smoke's time to smile, and unlike Critchlow's forced smile, Smoke's smile was easy and confident.

"No. I'm saying you'll never get your money because if you actually try and go through with this, I'm going to kill you," Smoke said easily.

Critchlow was used to invoking fear in the men he faced. Smoke's calm, and almost matter-of-fact response unnerved him, and without saying another word, and without warning, the gunman's hand dipped with lightning speed toward his pistol.

Because Smoke was still sitting at the table, he was at a disadvantage, and Critchlow actually managed to draw his gun and get one shot off. The bullet punched a hole in the table just in front of Smoke. But Smoke had his gun out just as fast, firing at almost the same time. And unlike Critchlow, Smoke didn't miss.

Critchlow dropped his gun and grabbed his chest, then turned his hand out and looked down in surprise and disbelief as his palm began filling with his own blood.

"You . . . you was sittin' down! How the hell did you . . . ?" he started to say, but he was unable to finish his sentence. Instead, his eyes rolled back in his head and he fell back, then lay motionless on the floor with open, but sightless eyes staring toward the ceiling.

Gunsmoke from the two charges merged to form a large, acrid-bitter cloud, which drifted slowly toward the door. Beams of sunlight streaming in through the door and windows became visible as they stabbed through the cloud.

The other patrons in the saloon, shocked to have seen Critchlow beaten in a gunfight, and not only beaten, but by a man who was sitting down, moved with cautious awe toward the body that lay unmoving on the saloon floor.

"Did you see that?" someone asked.

"Hell, Cletus, we're in here, too," someone answered. "Yeah, we seen it. We all seen it."

"I seen it," another said. "But I ain't never seen nothin' like it."

"I thought Critchlow was fast."

"He was fast."

"Yeah? Well he warn't fast enough, was he?"

There were rapid and heavy footfalls on the wooden sidewalk outside as more people began coming in through the swinging doors. Marshal Witherspoon was one of the first ones to come in.

"What the hell happened here?" Witherspoon asked. Seeing that the dead man was Lucien Critchlow, Marshal Witherspoon nodded grimly. "I'll be damn. Someone got Critchlow."

"Yeah," Peterson said. He pointed to Critchlow's body. "And if there was ever anybody who needed killin' more than Lucien Critchlow, I don't know who it would be."

"Who done it?" Witherspoon asked.

"That would be me," Smoke said.

The marshal looked over at Smoke, who had placed his gun on the table, though his hands, also on the table, were clasped together.

"What'd you kill 'im for?" the marshal asked.

"I didn't have much choice, he drew on me." Smoke pointed to the bullet hole in the table. "Here is where his bullet went."

"You were sitting at the table?"

"Yes."

"Damndest thing I ever saw, Marshal. Critchlow drew first, and Smoke Jensen had to draw while he was sittin' down, 'n still he beat 'im," Cletus said.

"I never thought nobody would ever be able to beat Lucien Critchlow, neither," Doodle said.

"You ain't plannin' on arrestin' him, are you, Marshal?" Cletus asked. "Because I'll tell you right now, that ever'one in here will say what really happened. 'N we ain't goin' to let you 'n Boykin keep us from testifyin' this time."

"No, I ain't goin' to arrest him," Witherspoon said. He stared pointedly at Smoke. "This is the second man you've kilt since you come into my town. Killin' seems to be followin' you around, don't it?"

Smoke nodded. "Sometimes it does," he agreed.

Witherspoon looked back at Critchlow. "I'll get Welch down here to take care of the body," he added.

Cletus chuckled. "You don't have to be in too big a hurry, do you, Marshal? I expect there'll be quite a few folks who are goin' to want to come in here 'n see the body. Especially seein' as who it is."

"Yeah," Doodle said. "Hell, the Pretty Girl 'n Happy Cowboy will prob'ly wind up makin' twice as much money as they would have."

"Jensen, I'd advise you not to be leavin' town anytime soon," Witherspoon said.

"Oh, I'm not planning on going anywhere," Smoke replied. "Not until all this business with Atwood is cleaned up."

"What . . . what business is that?" Witherspoon asked.

Smoke chuckled. "You know what I'm talking about. Don't make yourself look any dumber than you have to, Marshal."

"Look here! You can't talk to me like that."

"Hell, Witherspoon, it looks to me like he just did talk to you like that," Doodle said to the laughter of the others in the saloon.

Clenching his fists in frustration, and with his cheeks flaming in embarrassment, Witherspoon spun on his heels and stormed out of the saloon.

CHAPTER SIXTEEN

Shortly after Witherspoon left the saloon, Deputy Calhoun came in. His reaction, when he saw Critchlow's body lying on the floor, was ample indication that he knew nothing about what had just happened.

"Good Lord a'mighty! Is that Lucien Critchlow?" he asked.

"It sure as hell is," Cletus replied.

"What happened?"

"We've just been through all that with the marshal," Peterson said. "Smoke Jensen killed him."

"But it was a fair fight," Doodle said, and his declaration was validated by several other comments.

"How come Critchlow took Jensen on like that? I mean, what started the fight?"

"There warn't no fight," one of the other saloon patrons said. He reached over to the bar and picked up a flyer, then showed it to Calhoun. "Critchlow come in here carryin' this reward poster sayin' that they was a ten-thousand-dollar reward out for Jensen, dead or alive."

"Can I see that?" Calhoun asked in a small voice.

"Yeah, sure," the patron said, handing the reward poster over to the deputy. "It come from Idaho, so I don't know what it's doin' down here in Texas. Jensen said it warn't no good, but Critchlow didn't listen to 'im."

With the dodger in hand, Calhoun walked over to talk to Smoke, who was sitting back at his table.

"Critchlow tried to claim this reward?" Calhoun asked.

"Yes."

"I told Witherspoon that I didn't think this was any good."

"You saw it before?" Smoke asked.

"Yeah, I'm the one that found it. Well, not this one," Calhoun said, holding up the paper to look at it. "This looks like a new one, and I don't know where it come from. The one I found was so old it was near 'bout fallin' apart."

"Where did you find it? And why were you looking for it?" Smoke asked.

"I was lookin' for it, 'cause Witherspoon told me to look for it. 'N I found it in the courthouse records, but like I said, I told Witherspoon that, like as not, it was no good."

"You were right, it isn't any good."

"You're the one that got Kate let out of jail, too, aren't you?"

"I didn't do it by myself. My wife and Kate's brother were both with me."

"When I come back, I found Witherspoon in jail," Calhoun said. He laughed. "He was fit to be tied, too."

"Was he?"

"Yeah, he was. You know you're becomin' a real pain in the ass to him, don't you? Him and Atwood both."

"Am I?"

"Yeah," Calhoun said with a chuckle. "You are."

"You don't seem particularly upset by it."

"Yeah, well, I don't exactly agree with ever'thing Witherspoon does." Calhoun looked around at the others in the saloon, then spoke quietly. "Truth is, I don't agree with much of anything that he does. Like, I never thought we had no business puttin' Kate in jail in the first place, 'n if it had been up to me, I wouldn't of done it. It's Atwood that's causin' all this, but then, I figure you already know that. Atwood says jump, 'n the marshal 'n the judge, they kinda see which one of 'em can jump the highest. So if you put a burr under Atwood's saddle, it don't bother me all that much at all."

"Deputy Calhoun, from what several people have told me, you're a pretty good man. Why do you stay with Witherspoon?"

"The way I look at it, with the way Witherspoon is, I mean him 'n Judge Boykin bein' told what to do 'n all by Atwood, seems to me like there ought to be someone who has the good of the town in mind. 'Course, when it come to Rusty 'n his mama, I wasn't able to do nothin' about it, seein' as I was drunk when Rusty kilt Calley, and I don't remember anything about it. And when it come to puttin' Miss Kate in jail . . . I tried to talk 'em out of it, but they didn't listen to nothin' I had to say. That's why I'm glad you come to town when you did."

"It's good to hear that I've got a friend in the enemy's camp," Smoke said.

Calhoun laughed again. "A friend in the enemy's camp. That's a good one." He was still laughing as he left the saloon, meeting Welch, the undertaker, on his way out.

"Deputy, I'm told there's someone in need of my services in here," Welch said, glaring at Calhoun.

"Yeah, he's lyin' right over there."

"Why are you laughing, Deputy? I hardly think levity is appropriate around a dead body."

"Depends on who it is, Mr. Welch. For some people, you just want to celebrate when they're kilt. And Lucien Critchlow is just such a person."

"You mean the famous gunfighter? Oh, my. To think that I'll be burying someone like Lucien Critchlow." Welch smiled in anticipation.

"You see what I mean, Undertaker? Sometimes you do want to smile."

"Hey, Marshal, I was just over in the saloon, and seen that Smoke Jensen killed Lucien Critchlow," Calhoun said when he stepped into the marshal's office a few minutes later.

"Yeah? Well, tell me somethin' I don't know."

"Here's somethin' you don't know. Or maybe you do know. Critchlow had a dead or alive wanted poster for Jensen."

"Did he now? Well, that's interesting."

"You want to know what's even more interesting? It was the same wanted poster that I found over at the courthouse, only, this here one wasn't all old and crumbly like the one I found. This here one looked like it was fresh off the press."

"You don't say."

"You know what I think?"

"What do you think?"

"I think maybe Judge Boykin took it on hisself to reprint that poster."

"Maybe the poster is still good," Witherspoon suggested.

"No, it ain't no good. If you ask me, the judge is just pissed off because Jensen went to the federal judge 'n got Miss Kate turned loose. 'N that's why he printed up a new poster."

"Could be," Witherspoon agreed.

"That wasn't right, Marshal. You know damn well that wasn't right. And now that I think about it, it was probably Atwood that put 'im up to it."

Witherspoon held his finger up. "I'll tell you this, Calhoun. You'd do well to remember who butters your biscuit."

"I'm not likely to forget that," Calhoun replied.

"See that you don't," Witherspoon said as he headed toward the door.

"Where are you goin'?"

"Out," the marshal snapped.

Even before Sally and Kate returned to the saloon, they had heard the news of the shoot-out. By the time they got back, though, the body had been moved and the small amount of blood had been cleaned up. There was nothing to remind anyone of the shooting other than the excited babble of conversation.

"You should've seen it, Miss Kate," Cletus said. "It was the damndest thing I ever saw. Critchlow drew first, and Jensen had to draw while he was sittin' down, 'n still he beat 'im."

"I never thought anyone would be able to beat Critchlow," yet another said.

"What did the marshal say?" Kate asked.

"We were all willin' to give a statement 'bout what happened here, I mean as to who drew first 'n all that, but the marshal didn't want it," Peterson said.

"Oh, dear. I hope he isn't planning on another trial like the one he gave Rusty."

"No, ma'am, we've already told 'im that we don't have any intention of lettin' 'im do that," yet another customer said. "He didn't like it much, but he seemed to take it without too much guff."

"You want to know what I think, Mr. Jensen? I think that even Witherspoon figures that you did us a favor, killin' Critchlow like you did," Peterson said. "He was a bad sort, but then I reckon you know about 'im."

"Truth to tell, Mr. Peterson, I had never even heard of Critchlow until right now."

"Really? You never heard of him, huh? It's too bad Critchlow didn't live long enough to hear you say that. He was about the most arrogant son of a bitch I've ever known," Peterson said. "I beg your pardon, ladies."

"Oh, heavens, there's no need to apologize, Mr. Peterson," Sally said. "As it so happens, that particular sobriquet is appropriate when applied to some people."

"Yes, ma'am, I suppose so," Peterson replied, not

entirely certain what Sally said, though satisfied that she held no fault with him.

"Heavens! I feel guilty that someone tried to kill you. I know it is because of me," Kate said.

"If it hadn't been because of you, it would have been for some other reason," Sally said. "You have no idea how often someone tries to kill Smoke."

"Don't you worry about him?"

"Kate, if I worried about every two-bit gunman who had it in his mind to make a name for himself by killing Smoke, I would never draw an easy breath," Sally replied. "I have boundless confidence in his ability to take care of himself." She paused for a minute before she added, "and me."

"I'm glad to hear you say that," Smoke said. "Knowing that I don't have to be concerned about you worrying about me gives me an edge."

Sally smiled and put her hand on Smoke's shoulder. "That's good to know, because even though I don't worry about you, I do like for you to have every edge possible."

"Howdy, ever'body!" someone yelled from the front door.

"Rusty!" Kate shouted happily, as Rusty, Pearlie, and Cal came into the saloon then.

"Hi, Mom," Rusty replied with a broad smile.

Kate ran toward Rusty with her arms spread wide, embracing him firmly. "Oh, I'm so happy to have you back!"

The other patrons in the saloon joined in the welcome back, including all the "Pretty Girls." Dolly was the only one of the Pretty Girls to add her embrace to Kate's, and she seemed to do so with particular vivacity.

As Smoke and Sally were witnessing the happy reunion, Smoke glanced over at Cal and smiled at the bright red shirt he was wearing.

"Whoa, that's some shirt you're wearing," Smoke said.

"You like it? I just bought it."

"You couldn't find one in red?"

"What are you talking about? This is . . ." Cal started to say, but he paused in midsentence, then grinned. "You're teasin' me, aren't you?"

"Maybe just a little," Smoke admitted, returning Cal's smile.

"Oh, is it safe for you to be here?" Kate asked.

"Uncle Pearlie says I'm not wanted anymore," Rusty said.

"Well, yes, but . . . who knows what Mr. Atwood might try next?"

"Katie, you and the boy can't be spending the rest of your life worrying about Atwood," Pearlie said. "For now the two of you just enjoy the fact that the law isn't after you anymore. You let us take care of Atwood."

"Take care of him? What do you mean, take care of him?"

"Take care of him," Pearlie said simply.

"Hey, Rusty, why don't you play the piano for us?" Peterson asked.

"Ha! So you have missed me, haven't you?" Rusty replied.

Peterson shook his head. "No, I can't say as we've

missed you. But we have missed listenin' to someone play the piano," he added with a laugh.

"Play 'Old Dan Tucker,'" Cletus said.

Rusty held up his hand. "I will," he promised. "But first, I'm going to play whatever Mom wants me to play."

Kate smiled through her tears. "You know what I want you to play," she said.

Rusty nodded and, crossing his arm across his stomach, made a production of bowing to the audience there gathered. Then, walking over to the piano, he made a motion as if sweeping his tails back, took his seat on the piano bench, and stared at the keyboard for a moment.

"Oh, my," Sally said. "Is Rusty a classically trained pianist?"

"Yes," Kate answered proudly.

"How wonderful."

The saloon, which was normally filled with the cacophony of loud conversation, booming laughter, and high-pitched squeals, now waited in absolute silence. One of the patrons moved his chair just a fraction to better his position, and half a dozen cast a censoring gaze at him for the resultant squeak.

Then, with a flourish, Rusty began playing Tchaikovsky's Concerto Number Two. The music, coming from this piano, as opposed to the upright pianos that were so common in most of the saloons, was so rich and deep that it was almost as great as the difference between the voice of a solitary singer and a full chorus.

Smoke looked over at Sally and could see by the gleam in her eyes, and the expression on her face, how much she was enjoying this. Although Sally had never complained about it, he knew that one of the things she missed by having lived so much of her life out West was the opportunity for the cultural events living back East had afforded her. Because of that, he had spent much of their married time together taking her to concerts and plays presented by traveling troupes.

Rusty played only the second movement of the concerto. It was the most melodious of the three movements, and was only a little over eight minutes long. The entire concerto would have been well over half an hour long, and though Sally would have appreciated listening to the whole piece, she knew the people here would not be able to sit still for the whole thing.

It was, however, obvious that they enjoyed what they did hear, because the applause was loud and enthusiastic at the conclusion of the number. He stood and, with a broad smile on his face, bowed again at the audience.

"This was wonderful," Sally said.

Kate wiped her eyes. "Oh, how I would love to hear him play a real concert, in a real symphony hall," she said. "Maybe Atwood is right. Maybe I should sell out to him. I feel I have done Rusty such an injustice by making him stay here."

"Rusty is a grown man," Sally said. "If he is here with you, it is because he wants to be here with you."

CHAPTER SEVENTEEN

As the patrons of the Pretty Girl and Happy Cowboy Saloon were enjoying the impromptu concert, Allen Blanton, editor of the *Etholen Standard*, finished setting the type on the article, then leaned back to read it. When he first came into the newspaper business, it took him a while to read type because of it being set in reverse. But now he could read backward as easily as forward, and he smiled as he read what he intended to be the lead story to run in this evening's newspaper.

Today, Lucien Critchlow, a man known for his skill with a pistol and his willingness, one might even say his eagerness, to employ that skill, met the fate that so often befalls someone of his ilk. He had the misfortune to engage in a gunfight with someone who was able to employ his pistol with even more effectiveness.

The result was that Critchlow was killed by Smoke Jensen, who is a visitor to our town. Critchlow had opened the contest by presenting a Dead or Alive wanted poster that had been issued by a marshal in Bury, Idaho. Before undertaking to print this story, this newspaper contacted, by wire, the current marshal of Bury, Idaho, and was told by the marshal that Kirby Jensen is not wanted in Idaho now, nor as far as that marshal is concerned, is he wanted anywhere else.

Witnesses to the gunfight have all stated that before the gunplay ensued, Mr. Jensen attempted to inform Critchlow that the reward poster was invalid, as he was not wanted. All the witnesses to the encounter are uniform in their declaration that Critchlow, unwilling to listen to Mr. Jensen's declaration, precipitated the gun battle that followed, and that Mr. Jensen was entirely justified in defending himself.

I hasten to put this story in the paper so that all might know the actual facts of the event. In this way it is to be hoped that the truth, published so that it is universally known, will prevent a repeat of the travesty of justice that condemned young Rusty Abernathy, and subsequently his mother, to death in a trial that defied all standards of legitimacy and fair dealing.

This editor has stated before, and by these published words I say again, that until our town has a new marshal and a new judge, independent of the improper influence of Silas Atwood, we will continue to be void of all semblance of justice.

Witherspoon had been absent from the marshal's office for the better part of the day, and Calhoun was alone when Elmer Welch, the undertaker, came into the marshal's office.

"Is the marshal here?" Welch asked.

"No," Calhoun answered. "But I reckon you have come here to see how much money the county is goin' to pay you to bury Critchlow."

"No. It isn't going to cost the county so much as one penny to bury him."

"Oh? Why not?"

"It turns out that Critchlow had enough money in his pocket to pay for his own burial," Welch said.

"He did, did he? Well, that was very nice of him to be so accommodating, don't you think?" Calhoun replied with a chuckle.

Welch smiled. "Yes, it was. And here's the thing, Deputy. Not only is Critchlow paying for his own burial, he's goin' to wind up makin' me a lot more money 'n just what I'd get for buryin' 'im."

"Oh? And just how, pray tell, is he going to do that?"

"Well, sir, it was Phil Dysart who come up with the idea," Welch said.

"Dysart? The photographer?"

"Yep. What he's plannin' to do is, he's goin' to charge people two dollars to get their picture taken while they're standing alongside Critchlow's body. And for an extra fifty cents, he'll give 'em a gun to hold, so that it'll look like they were the one that shot 'im."

"By now everyone in town knows that it was Smoke Jensen that shot 'im."

"It was, but forty or fifty years from now, who's goin' to remember that? And a feller could show his grandkids a picture of him standing next to Lucien Critchlow, holding a pistol, and they're goin' to think it was their grandpa who did it."

Calhoun laughed. "Yeah," he said. "Hey, I wonder if Dysart would take my picture like that? I've got my own pistol, though, I don't plan on givin' him a half dollar to hold his gun."

"Yeah, I'm sure he would."

"I can see how that'll make money for Dysart, but what are you gettin' out of it?"

"I get one dollar for every picture that is taken."

"You said there was some money in Critchlow's pocket?"

"Yes, after subtracting the cost of the burial expenses there was seventy-three dollars and fifty-seven cents left over and to tell the truth, I don't have any idea as to what to do with it. As far as I know, he doesn't have any kin anywhere close by."

"Leave it with the county and I'll write you a receipt for it. If there's no claim against it, we'll put it in a special fund to pay for any other indigent burials."

Welch grinned. "Yeah, I thought you might want to do something like that."

"Leavin' that money so other folks can get a decent burial is probably the only decent thing Critchlow ever did in his whole life," Calhoun said.

"I don't doubt that," Welch said. "Well, I'd better get back to the parlor. I expect business is going fairly well, right now."

* * *

"What's this money for?" Marshal Witherspoon asked when he stepped back into the office a little later and saw the bills lying on his desk.

"Welch brought it here," Calhoun replied. "He said that he found it in Critchlow's pocket, and he figured he ought to turn it back in to the county."

"Ha, imagine 'im doing that." Witherspoon gave Calhoun twenty dollars and stuck the rest into his pocket.

"What are you doin'?"

"What's it look like I'm doin'? I'm dividin' up this money between us."

"But don't you think that money should go to the county, to pay for buryin' someone that might need buryin'?"

"If that happens, the county will come up with the money. Of course, if you don't want that twenty dollars, I'll take it back."

"No, I didn't say I didn't want it. I was just wonderin' about it is all."

"Well, you can quit wondering."

"Marshal, do you think Critchlow just happened to find that poster somewhere, or do you think someone might of give it to him most especial so's that he would come after Jensen 'n try 'n kill 'im?"

Marshal Witherspoon stared at his deputy through eyes narrowed. "Now, why would you suggest something like that?"

"Never mind," Calhoun said with a dismissive wave of his hand. "There's more'n likely nothin' at all to it." He turned to leave.

"No, hold up a minute," Witherspoon called.

Calhoun stopped.

"You got somethin' stickin' in your craw, you might as well spit it out."

"Well, think about it, Marshal. Critchlow had all that money in his pocket, and for all that he was a famous gunman, me 'n you both know he was most like to be dead broke." Calhoun chuckled. "All right, so we finally catch him when he ain't broke, but he is dead."

"I think perhaps I should pay a visit to Mr. Atwood," Witherspoon said.

"So Critchlow got himself killed, did he?" Atwood asked, as he lit the ever-present cigar. "Well," he drew several puffs before he continued, "I can't say that the world has lost much."

"Did you pay Critchlow to kill Jensen?"

"What makes you think that?"

"He had a wanted poster in his pocket," Witherspoon said. "There was only one copy printed, and I gave it to you, so this had to be the same reward poster."

"All right, so what if I did pay him to kill Jensen? You haven't been able to do anything to get him out of the way, have you?"

"I haven't had any legal reason to go after him."

"There is that reward poster."

"Mr. Atwood, you and I both know that reward is bogus."

"We don't know that for sure," Atwood replied. "I mean, we didn't find anything that said it had been withdrawn, did we?"

"No. But if you ask me, Critchlow got hisself kilt for a reward that wasn't goin' to be paid."

Atwood smiled. "Well now, there's an idea. Maybe the wanted poster you've got on Jensen is no good, but it was Jensen who killed Critchlow. It seems to me like you could use that to arrest him for murder."

Witherspoon shook his head. "It wouldn't hold up. Ever'one in the saloon says that it was Critchlow who drew first."

"What difference does that make? They said the same thing about Rusty Abernathy, but we tried him for murder and got a conviction."

"It's not the same thing. There ain't nobody outside of Etholen that's ever even heard of Rusty Abernathy. Hell, people all over the country have heard of Jensen. Not even Judge Boykin could make it stick. Besides which, Jensen's got some kind of connection with Judge Turner, and Turner can overrule anything Boykin might say."

"We need to find some way to get Jensen out of the picture," Atwood said. "He has become quite a complication."

"Short of shooting the son of a bitch in the back, I don't know how we're goin' to do that," Witherspoon said. "I know I don't want to face him, not even if I had two or three more men with me."

"Then I'll just have to find someone who will be willing to face him," Atwood said.

"What makes you think you can find such a man?" Witherspoon asked. "Critchlow faced him, and you see what happened. I'll tell you the truth, Mr. Atwood, I'm not all that sure such a man even exists."

"I may have someone in mind."

"That's what you thought about Critchlow, isn't it?"

"Yes, but you know what they say. If at first you don't succeed, try, and try again."

Witherspoon chuckled. "Yeah, well, as long as it ain't me who's doin' all the tryin'."

After Witherspoon left, Atwood returned to the library to revisit an article he had read in the paper. It was a story that was reprinted from the *Morning Star*, a newspaper from the nearby town of Eagle Springs.

Gunfight in the Four Ten Saloon

Last Friday night, Milt Pounders, who has been making a name for himself through his prowess with a weapon, came to our fair city of Eagle Springs. His reason for coming soon became obvious, because he instigated a gunfight with Cain Conroy. Whatever their reason was, it was not well thought out because, while good, young Pounders was not good enough. All witnesses to the gunfight agreed that Pounders drew first, but even with that advantage, he could not prevail.

Cain Conroy drew his weapon with the speed of a flash of lightning, and as quick as one could think about it, Pounders was on his back on the saloon floor, his sightless eyes still expressing the shock of having been beaten. There are those who have made a study of such a thing, who insist that Conroy is the fastest, and most deadly, gunman ever to employ the pistol in its most baneful extreme.

Atwood smiled as he lay the paper aside. Critchlow had failed him, but he had an idea that Conroy wouldn't. He decided to send for him.

Eagle Springs, Texas

When Cain Conroy stepped into the Four Jacks Saloon, he moved quickly away from the door, then backed up against the wall, standing there for a long moment while he surveyed the room.

"Pedro," the bartender said to the old man who was sweeping the floor. "Mr. Conroy is here. Go into the back room and get his special bottle."

"*Sí*," Pedro said, and leaned the broom against the cold stove. He started toward the back at a shuffle.

"Hurry, man, hurry! Conroy don't like to be kept waitin'."

Pedro's shuffle increased imperceptibly.

Conroy walked over and sat at an empty table. He didn't have to say anything to anyone. He knew that his drink would be delivered, and he knew it would be what he wanted. A moment later the bartender approached with the drink in hand, and he poured a shot, then waited for Conroy's nod of approval.

There was someone standing at the bar who saw how everyone was treating the man who had just come in.

"Who is that feller?" he asked the bartender.

"You're new here, ain't you? Yeah, I know you are, 'cause ever'one in town knows that that is Cain Conroy."

"So that's Cain Conroy? Well, I ain't never met 'im, but I have heard of 'im."

"I should think you've heard of him. Why he's kilt hisself more'n forty men."

"Forty, huh?"

"At least that many. And truth to tell, they don't nobody really know just how many he has kilt. He might'a kilt a lot more'n that."

The questioner nodded. "Thanks," he said, turning away from the bar and taking a step toward the table where Conroy was sitting.

"Here, mister! Are you crazy? You don't want to go botherin' him now!"

The curious one didn't respond. Instead, he stepped boldly up to Conroy's table.

"Mr. Conroy?"

"Yeah, I'm Conroy."

"I've got a message for you."

"What kind of message?"

"I don't know, I didn't read it. I was just told to hand this envelope to you." He held the envelope out.

Conroy snatched the envelope from the man's hand, then opened it. A fifty-dollar bill fluttered out.

"What's this for?" he asked.

The man who had delivered the note, obviously a cowboy, shrugged. "I don't know. Like I said, all I was told to do was deliver this envelope to you, then wait 'n see what you said."

Conroy grunted, then read the note that accompanied the fifty-dollar bill.

> *Conroy, this fifty dollars is just to get your attention. I wish to make a proposal and if you accept it, there is much more money for you. If you are interested, Bo Willis, the man who delivered this to you, will lead you back to see me. If you are not interested, tell him so, and you may keep this money as compensation for the intrusion into your time.*

Conroy folded over the fifty dollars, then looked up at the cowboy. "Your name Bo Willis?"

"Yes."

"It says here that you're supposed to take me to see the man who wrote this note."

"Yeah, that would be Mr. Atwood," Willis said.

"Where is he?"

"He's got a ranch near Etholen."

Conroy tossed his drink down, then stood up. "Take me to him."

CHAPTER EIGHTEEN

"A thousand dollars?" Conroy said. "Am I hearing you right? You're offerin' to give me a thousand dollars to kill Smoke Jensen?"

"After you kill him," Atwood said. "There's also a ten-thousand-dollar reward for him. You can keep that money as well."

"No, there ain't," Conroy said. "There was paper on 'im oncet, but that was pulled a long time ago."

"How do you know?" Atwood asked, surprised that Conroy would know that.

"I know, 'cause I've done me some bounty huntin' from time to time, 'n I know there ain't nothin' out on him."

"Hmm, I heard that there was, but you may be right," Atwood said, making no mention of the bogus flyer he had printed. "But the thousand dollars is good, and it's coming from me."

"Fifteen hundred," Conroy said.

"Fifteen hundred? That's asking a lot, isn't it?"

"I know that Critchlow couldn't take him."

Atwood gasped in surprise. "You heard about that, did you?"

"Yeah. When you are in the business I am, you follow other folks who are in the same business. You hired Critchlow, did you?"

"Yes, but as you have pointed out, he was insufficient to the task."

"He was what?"

"He didn't get the job done."

"Yeah, well, the truth is, I figured the day would come when me 'n Critchlow would go up ag'in each other. Only Jensen beat me to it. I figure that ups the risk enough so that askin' for fifteen hunnert dollars ain't too much. Besides which, you must really want Jensen dead, or you wouldn'ta hired Critchlow in the first place. And if you want Jensen killed, it's going to cost you fifteen hunnert dollars, or you'll have to find someone else. Wait a minute, there ain't nobody else, is there?"

"All right, yes, I do want him killed," Atwood said. "And I'll meet your demand. But I would suggest that after you do the job, and I pay you, that you leave the area. With that much money you could go to some place like New Orleans, or Saint Louis, or even Chicago."

"Why would I want to do that? If I kill Smoke Jensen, I'll be about the most famous man in the whole West."

"Is that really what you want? You would be a marked man. Can you imagine how many people would want to kill the man who killed Smoke Jensen? You'll have them coming from everywhere, some who will want to avenge Jensen, and some who will just want the fame it will bring them."

"Yeah, well, I guess there is that to think about."

"I'm glad you understand. And of course, it will also be to my advantage for you to be gone, because that way, there will be less of a likelihood that I would be connected with it."

"When do I get the money?"

"I told you, you'll get it after you do the job. I didn't give Critchlow what I had agreed to pay him before the job, and it's a good thing I didn't. If I had, I would have been out the money. I didn't get where I am today by paying for failure."

"You just have the money ready when I come back," Conroy said.

"It'll be here for you."

"If it ain't, there'll be another killin' that I won't be paid for. But I'll be doin' that killin' for me . . . if you know what I mean."

"I fully understand what you mean, Mr. Conroy. You just do your job, and the money will be here for you."

Atwood walked out onto the front porch and watched Conroy until he rode away. Then Atwood sent for Al Booker, one of his men. But, like Willis, Booker couldn't exactly be called a cowboy. He was one of the nearly dozen or so men that Atwood referred to as his special cadre.

As soon as Booker arrived, Atwood gave him fifty dollars. "I want you to do a little job for me," he said.

Booker looked at the money. "It must be more than a little job if you're willing to pay fifty dollars for it."

"There's not that much to it. I want you to go into town and keep an eye on a man named Cain Conroy."

"Conroy?" Booker replied nervously. "That's the feller you sent Willis after, ain't it?"

"Yes, it is."

"Willis tells me that Conroy has kilt more'n fifty men."

"I really don't care how many he has killed," Atwood said. "I'm only interested in who he is going to kill."

"Yeah, well, what do you mean by 'keep an eye on 'im'? On account of I don't plan on me bein' the next man that he kills."

"Good, then that means you'll be very careful around him, doesn't it?"

"When you say around him, what exactly do you mean? I mean, how close do I have to get to him?"

"It would be better for you, and for me, if he doesn't even know you are around. If you can, keep an eye on him from some distance."

Booker smiled. "I don't mind keepin' my distance from him. But what is it, exactly, that you want me to do?"

"I've hired him to do a job for me, and I want you to tell me whether or not he does it."

"What is the job?"

"You don't need to know that."

"Mr. Atwood, I don't understand. If I don't know what his job is supposed to be, how will I know whether or not he has done it?"

"If he does his job, you'll know what it is. Everyone in town will know. And if nothing at all happens, oh, say within the next day or two, then you come back and tell me that nothing has happened. That's all you need to do."

"All right," Booker said. "That sounds like an easy enough job."

Etholen

Smoke, Pearlie, and Cal were in the Pretty Girl and Happy Cowboy Saloon when Sally and Kate returned from an impromptu shopping trip. Sally was carrying a package.

"Did you find something you liked?" Smoke asked.

"That isn't the question you ask," Kate said. "The question is, will *you* like it? Surely you know by now that women buy clothes, not to please themselves but to please the men in their lives. Is that not true, Sally?"

Sally laughed. "Now, Kate, don't you go giving away all our secrets."

"I know I will like it," Smoke said. "Anything Sally chooses, I will like."

"Ha, way to go, Smoke. That was exactly the correct answer," Pearlie said.

"Smoke, I didn't have lunch," Sally said. "Why don't you take me out?"

"We could get something here if you're hungry," Smoke said.

"I believe you said you were going to take me out."

"I did say that, didn't I?" Smoke replied.

"Katie and I ate at the Palace Café the other day, and it was a most pleasant experience."

"Oh, yeah," Pearlie said. "The food is real good there, I'll vouch for it."

Smoke laughed. "Your endorsement would carry some weight with me, Pearlie, if I didn't know that you had never found any place to eat that you didn't think was really good."

"Well, you tell 'em, Katie. I mean, you live here. I'm sure you know the place," Pearlie said.

"Yes, I've eaten there many times, and the food is quite good," Kate said, her words validating Pearlie's stamp of approval.

"All right, you've sold me on it. Let's go," Smoke said.

"Good, I'm starving," Cal said.

Until that moment there had been no mention that Cal was to be a part of the visit to the café, but after his comment, there was no way he would be excluded.

Pearlie cleared his throat. "Cal, if you're that hungry, we could just eat here," Pearlie suggested. The suggestion was pointed enough that Cal understood.

"Oh, uh, yeah, that's right. We could eat here, couldn't we?" Cal replied. "Maybe you two had better go on without me."

"The lack of your company leaves me bereft," Sally said.

"It leaves you what?"

Sally chuckled. "Never mind. Enjoy your lunch with Pearlie."

"Yes, ma'am, I expect I will."

"Smoke, can we stop by the hotel room so I can change clothes?" Sally asked as they left the saloon. "I'd like to wear my new dress."

"Sure," Smoke agreed.

* * *

Half an hour later, with Sally now wearing her new dress, she and Smoke approached the Palace Café, which was just down Waling Street a short distance from the saloon. They were assailed by delicious-smelling aromas as they approached.

"Well, if it tastes as good as it smells, I'd say the food is going to be very good," Smoke said.

There was a counter to the left as they entered, then eight smaller tables spread out through the dining room, and one long, banquet table at the back of the room.

The woman behind the counter was a very attractive redhead, who looked to be in her late thirties.

"Hello, Sue Ellen," Sally said.

"Hello, Sally," the woman replied. "It was so good to see you and Kate in here the other day. I'm glad she has been set free."

"I think everyone is."

"Well, almost everyone, if you know what I mean," Sue Ellen replied.

"Any table?" Smoke asked Sue Ellen.

"Yes, sir, you all just find an open table and seat yourselves," the woman said. "I'll be right with you. I hope you enjoy the food."

"Believe me, he will enjoy it, I guarantee," Sally said.

The Bull and Heifer Saloon was a block and a half away from the Pretty Girl and Happy Cowboy Saloon, on the corner of Cavender and Martin Streets. Bull

Blackwell, owner of the Bull and Heifer, wasn't exactly in direct competition with Kate Abernathy, because there was a vast difference in their establishments.

The Pretty Girl and Happy Cowboy Saloon featured blended whiskeys and fine wines, and was a genteel enough place that women could visit without danger to their reputation. The Bull and Heifer, on the other hand, used only the cheapest whiskey and beer . . . and no wines at all. The Bull and Heifer did serve a purpose though . . . it served a clientele who either couldn't afford the Pretty Girl and Happy Cowboy, or preferred a somewhat more coarse atmosphere when they were drinking.

The Bull and Heifer also offered something else that the Pretty Girl and Happy Cowboy Saloon did not. For a price, the girls at the Bull and Heifer would take a customer upstairs to their room, whereas the girls at the Pretty Girl and Happy Cowboy Saloon offered nothing but drinks and friendly smiles.

Cain Conroy, after arriving in Etholen this morning, had just taken advantage of the services offered by Lucy, one of the accommodating young women of the Bull and Heifer. At the moment, Lucy was sitting up in bed, covered to the waist only by the bed sheet. She was topless and smoking a cigarette she had just rolled for herself. Conroy was sitting on the edge of the bed, pulling on his boots.

"You know, honey, if you would like to spend the night with me, tonight, I'll give you a special deal since we've already had one visit today," Lucy said. "That is, if you can do it twice in one day," she added with a suggestive smile.

"I more'n likely won't be here tonight," Conroy

said. "I got me some business to take care of in this town, 'n once I do that, I'll be leavin'."

"Oh? What kind of business are you in, honey?"

Conroy chuckled. "You might say I'm in the arrangin' business, seein' as someone arranges for me to do somethin', 'n then I do it. This here job involves a fella by the name of Smoke Jensen. Do you know him?"

"Smoke Jensen? Yes, he's only just come to Etholen, but he's already made a name for himself. Why, he's killed two people, did you know that?"

"Two people? I heard that he kilt Lucien Critchlow. Who else has he kilt?"

"He killed Rufus Pardeen. Pardeen worked for Atwood."

"Do you know how I can find him?"

"He hangs out most of the time over at the Pretty Girl," Lucy said.

"Pretty girl?"

"It's the name of a saloon," Lucy said. "They call it the Pretty Girl and Happy Cowboy, but if you ask me, the girls that works there ain't no prettier than the ones that works here. And we're a lot more friendly, if you know what I mean," she added with a seductive smile.

Booker had seen Conroy go upstairs with Lucy, so he just stayed at the corner of the bar, nursing his beer and keeping his eyes on the stairs, waiting for the gunman to come back down. He wasn't up there for more than fifteen minutes, and Booker smiled. He knew Lucy, and he knew that she prided herself on how short she could make the visits with her clients. He watched as Conroy stepped up to the bar to order a drink.

"You got 'ny idea where I might find Smoke Jensen?" Booker heard Conroy say.

"I just seen him 'n his wife goin' into the Palace Café," one of the saloon patrons said.

"Where's that at?"

"It's just sort of catty-cornered across the street from the Model Barbershop."

"Can you see the Palace Café from the barbershop?"

"Well, yeah, I mean, it bein' just across the street 'n all."

"Thanks."

Conroy tossed the whiskey down, then left the saloon. He didn't notice Booker, who had been eyeing him from the other end of the bar. If he had noticed him, he wouldn't have paid any attention to him. He had never met Booker, and had no idea that Booker worked for the same man who had just hired him.

CHAPTER NINETEEN

"Haircut, sir?" the barber asked when Conroy stepped into his shop.

"Yeah. Which chair gives me the best view of the Palace Café?"

"You can see it well from here," the barber said, pointing to the chair. "Are you planning to eat there? It's a fine restaurant. But so is Dumplin's."

"Do you know Smoke Jensen?"

"Well, I can't say as I actually know him," the barber replied. "But I must say that since he has come to town, he has certainly made himself known." The sign behind the barber chair read EARL COOK, and after Conroy got into his chair, Cook put the cape around him.

"Would you know this Jensen feller if you seen 'im?" Conroy asked.

"Oh, yes."

"I'm told he's takin' his dinner in the Palace Café today."

"Indeed he is, sir. I saw him and his wife going into the place a few minutes ago. She's such a pretty thing.

It almost makes you wonder how somebody like Smoke Jensen could get himself such a pretty wife."

"What do you mean, somebody like Smoke Jensen?"

"Well, maybe you don't know that much about him. But since he came to town, he's already let people know he was here. First thing he did was he got Miss Kate out of jail."

Cook began cutting Conroy's hair.

"Who is Miss Kate?"

"Oh, she owns the Pretty Girl and Happy Cowboy Saloon. It's quite a fine establishment, I go in there myself, from time to time. Anyhow, there was some trouble there, her son killed one of Mr. Atwood's men, then he wound up being tried and sentenced to hang. But he escaped, and when he did, why Atwood got Miss Kate put in jail."

"Atwood did?"

"Yes, well, it was the judge who actually did it, but ever'body knows that Atwood controls the marshal and the judge in this town. Anyway, Smoke Jensen got Miss Kate out of jail, then he shot and killed Lucien Critchlow. I reckon you've heard of Critchlow, haven't you?"

"Yeah, I've heard of 'im."

"They say that Critchlow is the fastest gun in Texas; only, he wasn't fast enough. I can see now why they've written so many dime novels about Smoke Jensen. I bought one."

Cook put down the scissors and picked up a book. "I don't know how true this story is, but it's mighty exciting reading, I can tell you that, for sure," he said, showing the book to Conroy.

Smoke Jensen, King of the Western Range

"If you've never read anything about him, you should," Cook said.

"They ain't come back out yet, have they?"

"I don't think so. At least, I haven't seen them come back out. Anyway, I don't think they have been in there long enough to have actually eaten a meal."

"I've got some business with him, but I don't want to disturb him while he's eatin'."

"Yes, I think you are right to let the man eat in peace. You say you have business with him. Do you know Mr. Jensen?"

"No, I ain't never seen him before. If he comes out while I'm here in the chair, point him out to me, would you?"

"Why yes, I'd be glad to," Cook replied. Having put the book down, he was once more employing the scissors, and Conroy could hear them clicking beside his ear.

Conroy sat in the chair, then, under cover of the barber's cape, he pulled his pistol from his holster and held it in his lap.

"In the book I'm reading, it seems that Smoke Jensen is tracking down a young lady who was kidnapped by . . ."

"I don't like talkin' while I'm gettin' a haircut," Conroy said gruffly.

"Very good, sir. I shall be as silent as the sphinx."

Conroy had no idea what a sphinx was, or why it might be silent, but he was grateful that the barber had shut up.

"You sure he ain't come out yet?" Conroy asked after a few minutes.

"Oh, yes, sir, I'm quite sure."

* * *

Booker left the Bull and Heifer shortly after Conroy did, and now he was sitting on a bench in front of the Buckner-Ragsdale Emporium, keeping an eye on both the Model Barbershop and the Palace Café. While in the saloon, he had heard Conroy ask about Smoke Jensen, so he had a pretty good idea about what Conroy had in mind. If there was going to be a shoot-out between Conroy and Jensen, he would have a front-row seat.

Because Conroy had told the barber that he didn't want to talk, the only sound that could be heard in the barbershop at the moment was the click and snap of the scissors as Earl Cook worked. Then, Conroy broke the silence.

"You be sure and keep an eye open and let me know soon as you see Jensen."

"Yes, sir, I will," Cook said.

The sound of clicking scissors continued for another minute, then Cook stopped.

"Oh, there he is now, him and his wife," the barber said, interrupting Conroy's comment. "They're just now comin' out. She's such a pretty thing, don't you think?"

Even as the barber was talking, Conroy leaped up from the chair and rushed through the door.

"Sir, I'm not finished, you . . ." At that moment the barber saw Conroy raising his pistol to point at an unsuspecting Smoke who was looking toward Sally.

"Mr. Jensen! Look out!" the barber shouted at the top of his voice.

Smoke's reaction was instantaneous. With his left hand he pushed Sally down. He didn't have to push her all the way down; she was smart and reflexive, and she went all the way down and then rolled out of the way without any further effort.

Conroy fired, and Smoke felt the concussion of the bullet as it fried the air just past his ear and slammed into the door frame just behind him.

Conroy didn't even realize he had missed, because even as his bullet was burying itself in the door frame, Smoke had already drawn and fired, his bullet plunging into Conroy's heart. Conroy fell facedown in the middle of the street, the barber's cape spread out on the ground under him. His right arm was outstretched and his hand still wrapped around the gun.

The shooting, happening as it did right in the middle of town, began to draw a crowd as people came out of the Pretty Girl and Happy Cowboy Saloon, the Bull and Heifer Saloon, Palace Café, Dereck's Gun Shop, the Buckner-Ragsdale Emporium, as well as the feed and seed store.

Smoke leaned down to help Sally back to her feet.

"Are you all right?" he asked anxiously.

"Yes. I must say, though, that this was certainly not how I intended to break in the new dress I just bought."

"What happened here?" Marshal Witherspoon asked, hurrying up to Smoke.

"That fella over there took a shot at my wife," Smoke said.

"You say he shot at your wife?" Witherspoon asked.

"Well, it might have been at me, but Sally was standing right next to me, and I have to tell you that did get me some riled."

"What's that he's lying on?"

"It's a barber's cape, Marshal," Earl Cook said, arriving at that point. "He was getting a haircut, and he asked me to point Mr. Jensen out to him. Mr. Jensen, I'm so sorry. He said he had some business to do with you. I had no idea he intended to shoot you."

"No need for you to apologize," Smoke replied. "Your shout for sure saved one of our lives, either my wife or me."

"Jensen, this is the third man you have killed in my town in less than a week," Witherspoon said.

"This is the third man who has tried to kill me," Smoke replied.

"Do you know him?" Witherspoon asked.

"To be honest I didn't get that good of a look at him," Smoke said. "Let me see if I know him."

Smoke and the marshal walked across the thirty yards that separated them from the body, but, by now, they had to pick their way through the crowd that had gathered. Marshal Witherspoon turned him over so he could be seen.

"Do you know him?" the marshal asked.

Smoke shook his head. "I've never seen him before."

"His name is Cain Conroy," Booker said. By now

several of the citizens of the town had collected around the body, and Booker was one of them.

"You ever heard of 'im?" Witherspoon asked Smoke.

Smoke shook his head. "No, I'm afraid not. The name doesn't mean anything to me."

"Well, your name must've meant something to him," Witherspoon said. "That is, if you're tellin' the truth, 'n he shot at you first."

"Mr. Jensen is telling the truth," the barber said. He pointed to Conroy's body. "This gentleman was getting a haircut, and he asked me to point out Mr. Jensen when I saw him. When I saw Mr. and Mrs. Jensen come out of the café I mentioned it, and, without so much as a fare-thee-well, he leaped up from the chair with his gun in his hand. I had no idea that he had such a thing in mind."

"Booker, how come it is that you know him?" Marshal Witherspoon asked.

"I can't say as I actual know him," Booker replied. "It's more like I know of him. Anyhow, I seen 'im oncet when I was over in Eagle Springs, and then I seen 'im a while ago over in the Bull and Heifer."

"That's right," someone else said. "He was in the Bull and Heifer a few minutes ago, 'cause I seen 'im, too. 'Course, I didn't know who he was, then."

Atwood hadn't told Booker what he was supposed to be looking out for, but he did tell him that when it happened, he would know. Well, now he knew.

"So, Smoke Jensen shot Cain Conroy, did he?" Deputy Calhoun said with a little chuckle back at the marshal's office. "It looks to me like he's goin' to be a pretty hard man for Atwood to kill."

"What do you mean for Atwood to kill?" Witherspoon asked.

"Well come on, Marshal. Atwood is the one who wanted us to see if we could find a wanted poster on Jensen. We found one, I mean it was so old that I knowed soon as we found it that it warn't no good anymore. But we found it, 'n the next thing there was a new, fresh poster printed up, and since then there's been two gunmen who come after him, Critchlow and Conroy. You don't think they just took it on their own to try 'n kill Jensen, do you? Like I said before, Atwood had to be behind them. Leastwise, that's what I think."

"You know what I think?" Witherspoon replied.

"What?"

"I think there are some things you'd be better off just keeping your nose out of it."

"Well, yeah, I'll do that, Marshal. I was just talkin' is all."

"You talk too much. I've got something I have to check on. If Welch comes to ask you about Conroy's body, tell 'im he can have 'im, I don't need to do any investigatin'."

"All right," Calhoun said. "More'n likely there'll be money in Conroy's pockets, too, so I don't figure the county's goin' to have to pay for this one, neither."

Eagle Shire Ranch

"You came back pretty quickly," Atwood said when Booker returned to the Eagle Shire.

"Yes, sir, but there warn't no need to stay around no longer," Booker said.

"Good, good!" Atwood rubbed his hands together in satisfaction and smiled broadly. "That means Conroy did the job and will be back soon."

"No, sir, he won't be back soon. Fac' is, he won't be back at all," Booker said. "Conroy got hisself kilt."

"What?"

"Yes, sir. Turns out Conroy tried to kill Jensen; onliest thing is, Jensen wound up killin' Conroy."

"Damn!" Atwood said, striking his fist angrily into the palm of his hand. "Damn!"

"That was what you sent him to do, warn't it?" Booker asked. "You wanted him to kill Smoke Jensen?"

"Booker, do you like your job here?" Atwood asked in a sharp and challenging tone of voice.

"Well, yes, sir, I like my job here. I like it a lot."

"Then don't ask so damn many questions."

"No, sir, I won't ask no more," Booker replied.

While the two men were talking, Marshal Witherspoon rode up.

"Booker, find something to do," Atwood ordered. "The marshal and I need to talk."

"Yes, sir," Booker said.

Atwood waited until Witherspoon dismounted.

"Marshal," he said by way of greeting.

"I thought you might like to know that . . ."

"Jensen killed Conroy," Atwood said, interrupting him.

"Yeah."

"Maybe we're concentrating on the wrong person," Atwood suggested.

"What do you mean?"

"I've been doing some checking on my own," Atwood said. "It turns out there was also a reward offered for Kate's brother, Wes Fontaine. The reason he left Texas some time ago, it was because he had just killed a marshal. He's wanted for murder."

"It must have been a long time ago, 'cause I've been marshalin' for fifteen years, and I never even heard of him until he 'n the others come into town," Witherspoon said.

Atwood showed the wanted poster to Witherspoon and, like the original one for Smoke, this flyer was browned, with curling edges.

"That looks as old as the one for Jensen," Witherspoon said.

"It doesn't matter how long ago it was. It was for murder, and there's no statute of limitations to murder. Better yet, it's from Texas."

"That federal judge will just throw it out," Witherspoon said.

"No, he can't. Murder is a state crime, not a federal crime. He won't have any say-so on this one at all."

"He threw out the verdict on Kate and her boy, and those was both state crimes."

"That's because he found fault with the trial," Atwood said. "But we haven't had a trial for Wes Fontaine. In fact, there never has been a trial for him, because he disappeared and nobody knew what happened to him. We know where he is now. Get some new paper printed up for him, and I guarantee you that the federal judge will do nothing about it."

"Yeah, but if we try him, and . . ."

"Who said anything about bringing him to trial?" Atwood asked.

"All I asked you to do is get a wanted poster out on Fontaine. Only don't stop at just one this time. I want you to print up about a thousand copies and spread them around. Make certain they say dead or alive. That way anyone who wants to take on the job won't have to go up against him face to face. When it says dead or alive, you're just as dead if you're shot in the back as you are if you're shot in the front. And the reward is just as high."

"Who's goin' to pay the reward?"

"It's a Texas crime, so we'll get the state of Texas to pay it."

Witherspoon shook his head. "Mr. Atwood, look, I've gone along with you on just about ever'thing you've wanted."

"And you have been well compensated," Atwood replied.

"Yes, sir, I have, 'n I'm real grateful to you for that, too. But what you're sayin' now, put out a flyer that's near twenty years old, I don't know. What if that flyer was withdrawn, like the one on Smoke Jensen was? I mean for Jensen, that was a flyer up in Idaho, 'n it didn't much matter down here in Texas whether it was withdrawn or not. But this here was a Texas warrant, 'n if it's been withdrawn, the state ain't only not goin' to pay the reward, but they could maybe charge whoever kills Fontaine with murder."

"You aren't planning on trying to collect the reward on him, are you?" Atwood asked.

"Well, no sir, but I couldn't collect it anyway, bein' as I'm a marshal."

"Then what difference does it make to you whether whoever kills Fontaine is charged with murder or not? Now just get the new poster printed, and put it out like I told you to," Atwood ordered.

"All right," Witherspoon acquiesced. "If you say so."

"I do say so."

"But I can tell you right now, it ain't goin' to do you no good to print that thing. It ain't goin' to do you no good at all," Witherspoon said.

"Just do it, Witherspoon," Atwood said.

"Yes, sir, if you say so. Only, I don't think it's going to do no good."

After Witherspoon left, Atwood poured himself a drink and called for his butler.

"*Sí, señor?*"

"Sanchez, fetch Mr. Willis for me."

Sanchez nodded, then left on his task. A few minutes later Sanchez showed Willis into the parlor.

"You sent for me, Mr. Atwood?" Bo Willis asked.

"Yes, I've decided to make you the new marshal," Atwood said.

"You mean Witherspoon ain't plannin' on runnin' in the next election?" Willis replied.

"There ain't goin' to be another election. I'll have Judge Boykin appoint you."

"What about Witherspoon? You mean he's going to resign?"

"I'm afraid Marshal Witherspoon has become somewhat troublesome and argumentative," Atwood said. "Such a person can be deleterious to my long-range plans. His usefulness has expired and I need a new marshal, someone I can depend on. I can depend on you, can't I, *Marshal* Willis?"

A broad smile spread across Willis's face. "Yes, sir!" he said exuberantly. "You can depend on me, for sure."

CHAPTER TWENTY

"This ain't goin' to do no good," Calhoun said when Witherspoon ordered him to print up new posters for Pearlie. "This won't be no different from the posters that we printed for Smoke Jensen."

"It ain't the same thing," Witherspoon said. "Jensen wasn't wanted in Texas, Fontaine is."

"This was near twenty years ago," Calhoun said. "You know it ain't good now. Like as not, there don't nobody even remember it."

"It's murder," Witherspoon said. "It don't matter whether anyone remembers it or not. Now, get them posters printed up like I told you to."

"If you're goin' to arrest him, why do you need the posters printed?" Calhoun asked. "Why not just arrest him?"

"Who said anything about arresting him?" Witherspoon asked with an evil smile.

"This is Atwood's doin', ain't it? He don't want Pearlie arrested, he wants him kilt."

"What if it is?"

"It ain't right," the deputy replied.

"You want to turn your back on the money Atwood is givin' us 'n just live on the salary the city pays?"

"I'll get the posters printed," Calhoun said.

"Yeah, I thought you might see it my way."

It was dark by the time Calhoun returned to Etholen with the printed flyers. There was a huge difference between the daytime Etholen and the town at night. In the daytime the population was given to the normal pursuits of a small community, freight wagons rolling in out of town, the arrival and departure of trains on the Southern Pacific Railroad, and merchants and shoppers in the stores.

At night, though, the population of the town increased precipitously, and its character changed, tone and tint. The cowboys who came into town did so in quest of fun and relaxation from a long day of work on the ranch, and most found that fun in the town's two saloons. Liquor flowed, laughter, shrieks, loud voices, and occasionally gunshots sounded in the night. In some unfathomable way, the citizens of the town learned how to discern the difference between gunshots that were fired in celebration and those fired in anger.

Calhoun rode down the dark street, sometimes passing through the golden bubbles of light that came from the streetlamps or was projected into the street from lighted windows. He stopped in front of the marshal's office, then went inside.

"Here they are," he said, dropping the bundle onto Witherspoon's desk.

"I'll get 'em put out tomorrow," Witherspoon said.

"This ain't right. I mean especially if you ain't even plannin' on arrestin' him."

"Make your rounds and quit your bitchin'," Witherspoon said.

When Deputy Calhoun came into the Pretty Girl and Happy Cowboy Saloon a few minutes later, he was holding one of the reward flyers in his hand.

"Hello, Deputy," Peterson said. "Making your rounds?"

"Yeah," Calhoun said. "Listen, is Kate's brother in here?"

"You mean Pearlie? Yes, he and the others are all sitting around the table back by the piano. See them?"

"Yeah, thanks," Calhoun said as he started toward the table the bartender had pointed out.

"Hello, Deputy," Pearlie said when Calhoun approached. "Something we can do for you?"

"Mr. Fontaine, I've got something I think you should see."

"What is it?" Pearlie asked.

Without answering him directly, Calhoun handed Pearlie the paper he was holding.

WANTED
DEAD *or* ALIVE
For MURDERING *a* SHERIFF :

WES WESLEY FONTAINE
Alias: "PEARLIE"

$2,500 REWARD
Contact: MARSHAL WITHERSPOON, *Etholen, Texas*

"Damn," Pearlie said after he examined it.

"There's been about a thousand of these things printed up 'n Witherspoon plans to have 'em all posted tomorrow," Calhoun said. "I thought maybe you ought to know about 'em."

"Smoke, take a look at this. They've got paper on me, too. Where the hell did they come up with these things?"

"Where did they come up with it, Deputy?" Smoke asked after he looked at the document. "This one, like the wanted poster Critchlow had on me, has been freshly printed."

"Yeah, look, it even calls me Pearlie. I mean when this happened, nobody called me Pearlie."

"I got it printed over in Sierra Blanca," Calhoun replied. "Witherspoon sent me over there, 'cause he knew that Blanton wouldn't print it here."

"You got it printed?"

"Yeah, Witherspoon ordered me to do it. And Atwood ordered him," he added.

"You're not looking to arrest me, are you, Calhoun?"

"No!" Calhoun said quickly. "No, I'm not. Truth to tell, I don't think Atwood wants you arrested, either, which means the marshal doesn't want you arrested."

"Then I don't understand," Kate said. "If they don't want him arrested, why did they have these old posters reprinted?"

"They don't want him arrested, 'cause they want some bounty hunter to kill 'im," Cal said.

"Oh, Pearlie!" Kate said.

"Cal, must you be so blunt?" Sally scolded.

"Sorry, Miz Sally, but you know it's true," Cal replied.

"And he's right, ma'am. I'm pretty sure that's exactly why Atwood had them printed. I'm sorry to be the one to show you this," Calhoun said.

"No, you did right to show it to him," Smoke said. "Better to be approached with a reward poster than a bounty hunter's gun."

"Tell me, Calhoun, why did you show me this?" Pearlie asked. "Did Witherspoon ask you to?"

"Ha, Witherspoon would just as well want you to not know nothin' about it till some gunny took a shot at you," Calhoun said.

"Well, I appreciate the warning."

With a departing nod, Calhoun left the saloon.

"You shouldn't have come back to Texas. This is all my fault," Kate said.

"No, Mom, it's my fault," Rusty said. "I'm the one started all this when I shot Calley."

"Don't be ridiculous. If you hadn't shot him, he would have shot you."

"If it is anybody's fault, it is mine," Pearlie said. "I'm the one that killed Miller, and Marshal Gibson. And I'm the one that ran away after my name wound up on a wanted poster. I've put this off long enough. I think it's time I faced up to it."

"Maybe so, but not with Judge Boykin," Rusty said. "Boykin is an evil man who will do anything Atwood tells him to do."

"Rusty is right," Kate said. "You won't get a fair trial with Boykin."

"We could go see Judge Turner again," Sally suggested.

"That won't do any good, Miz Sally," Pearlie said with a shake of his head. "This happened in Texas, and unlike the dodger Critchlow had on Smoke, this one didn't cross state lines. Also I'm sure it has never been pulled back."

"Judge Turner can order a change of venue," Sally said.

"What's that?" Cal asked.

"It means he can order that the trial can be held somewhere other than in Judge Boykin's court."

"Well then," Rusty said with a wide smile. "That's something else. If you have a chance to have a fair trial, without Boykin having anything to do with it, then maybe everything will be all right."

Bo Willis, Al Booker, Emile Clark, and Johnny Sanders were in the Bull and Heifer Saloon when Willis saw Calhoun step in through the batwing doors.

"Well now," Willis said. "We ain't goin' to have to look for Calhoun, there he is."

"Hello, Deputy. How are you doin' tonight?" Bull Blackwell asked, greeting Calhoun when he stepped up to the bar.

"Hello, Bull."

"Good to see that you are visitin' my place tonight. I thought the Pretty Girl and Happy Cowboy was more your style."

"That ain't true. I come in here as much as I go in there."

"Hello, Calhoun," someone said, approaching the bar then.

Turning toward the voice, Calhoun saw one of Atwood's men. And "men" was the way he thought of it, because Willis wasn't one of Atwood's cowboys. He was one of the people Atwood called his special cadre, one of his gunhands.

"Hello, Willis."

"Why don't I buy you a drink, Deputy?" Willis asked.

"I don't know if I should. I'm on duty." Calhoun paused for a moment. "On second thought, maybe I'm not on duty."

"What do you mean?" Bull Blackwell asked.

Calhoun reached up to the star pinned to his shirt, took it off, then lay it on the bar. "I'm not on duty, 'cause I ain't the deputy anymore, seein' as I just quit. You know what I plan to do? I aim to get good 'n drunk, one last time. Then I'm goin' to quit drinkin' for real. I mean, if I ain't workin' for Wither-spoon no more, I don't see as I'll have any need to be gettin' drunk anymore."

Willis laughed. "There you go. Blackwell, give me 'n the deputy . . ."

"I told you, I ain't the deputy no more," Calhoun said.

"That is, give me 'n my friend a bottle. Come on, Calhoun, let's me 'n you get us a table 'n get drunk together."

Willis took Calhoun back to the table where, earlier,

he had been sitting with Booker, Clark, and Sanders. The table was empty now.

Booker left the saloon and went straight to the office of the city marshal. "Marshal?" Booker said.

Witherspoon was sitting at his desk in the marshal's office, playing a game of solitaire.

"Yeah? What's Atwood want now?" he asked without looking up.

"No, this ain't got nothin' to do with Atwood. Did you 'n Calhoun have a fallin' out over somethin'?"

"A fallin' out? No, what do you mean, a fallin' out? What are you talkin' about?"

"I don't know if he's mad at you over somethin', or if he's just suddenly got ambition. But he's over at the Bull and Heifer now, tellin' Willis that he's plannin' on killin' you the next time he sees you, then he's goin' to pin on your badge."

"The hell you say? Calhoun said somethin' like that? That don't sound like him. Unless he's drunk again."

"Well, he is drinkin', but he ain't drunk yet, so it ain't the whiskey that's talkin'. But as for what he's sayin', I'm tellin' you the straight of it, 'cause I was right there listenin' to 'im. He said next time he seen you, he wasn't goin' to give you no warnin' at all. What he was goin' to do was shoot you down like a dog. Them's his exact words. 'I'm goin' to shoot him down like a dog,' he says. Then, he says, he'll be the new marshal."

"We'll just see about that," Witherspoon said. "Where'd you say the son of a bitch was?"

"He's over at the Bull and Heifer. But I wouldn't go in there if I was you. I'm tellin' you, Marshal, he aims to shoot you on sight!"

"Hello, Clark," Willis said when Clark came over to the table. "Why don't you join me 'n my friend for a drink?"

"There ain't no time for that," Clark said. "I come here to tell Calhoun, he'd better get out of town."

"Get out of town? What for?" Calhoun replied.

"I don't know what it is that you done to get Witherspoon all mad at you 'n ever'thing, but he's tellin' ever'one that he's comin' over here to kill you."

"Now that don't make no sense at all. Why would he want to kill me?"

"I don't know, but if I was you, I'd get out now, before he comes over here."

"I'm not goin' anywhere. Besides which, I'm not the deputy anymore, so nothin' I do has anything to do with him."

Clark looked around to the others in the saloon. "Listen to me, all of you," he said. "I just told the deputy here that the marshal is gunnin' for him. I want it well known that I give him the warnin', and as to what he does about it, well, I reckon that's his business."

"And I want ever'one to know that I ain't the deputy no more, which means the marshal ain't got no truck with me no more," Calhoun said. He raised the glass of whiskey to his lips to show that he wasn't concerned. He had just begun to take a sip when

Witherspoon burst through the batwing doors, and burst through was the most accurate way of describing it.

"Where is that scum-sucking son of a bitchin' deputy of mine?" Witherspoon shouted. He already had his gun in his hand.

Calhoun put the glass down quickly. "Marshal, I . . ."

"Here I am, Calhoun! You want to shoot me?"

Even as Witherspoon shouted his challenge, he pulled the trigger. Immediately after, both Clark and Willis shot back at him. Within a matter of a moment, both the marshal and Calhoun lay unmoving on the floor of the Bull and Heifer Saloon.

"Son of a bitch! Did you all see that?" one of the saloon patrons asked.

"What was that all about?" another asked.

Clark and Willis still had the smoking guns in their hands. Willis put his gun away and checked Calhoun. "Calhoun's dead. What about the marshal?"

"He's deader 'n a doornail," Booker said, having come into the saloon immediately after the shooting.

"What was that all about?" Bull asked.

"I don't know," Willis replied. "You seen it same as we did. Witherspoon come in here just blazin' away. Hell, we didn't have no choice but to kill 'im. There was no tellin' how many people he would shoot afore he was all done."

CHAPTER TWENTY-ONE

The next morning, in a brief ceremony held in front of "Old Thunder," the cannon that the "officers and men" of Fort Quitman had donated to the town, Judge Boykin swore in Bo Willis as the new City Marshal of Etholen. Willis's first act was to appoint Clark as his deputy.

Almost immediately thereafter, Willis and Clark began strutting around town, showing their badges and exercising their new authority. Allen Blanton, editor of the *Etholen Standard*, called upon Mayor Cravens.

"That was sort of quick, wasn't it, Joe? I mean appointing a new marshal and deputy without even calling a meeting of the city council?" Blanton asked.

"We did have a city council meeting."

"And the city council wanted Willis and Clark? Hell, Joe, those two are Atwood's men, part of his special cadre. They don't even live in town."

"I know that, Allen, and believe me, if it had been up to me, they would not be wearing badges today. But there is nothing I can do about it. The city council appointed them, and you know as well as I do that all five of them are in Atwood's pocket. The vote on the council was five to zero."

"That's not right," Blanton said. "There's nothing right about that."

"Let's face it, Allen. Whether we like it or not, Atwood controls this town. And with the city council in his back pocket, I am as useless as tits on a boar hog."

"Maybe all it takes is a little reminder to the citizens of the town that, as Americans, we can control our own destiny," Blanton suggested.

"What do you have in mind?"

"You'll see."

Blanton didn't waste any time printing a scathing editorial in the *Etholen Standard*.

Marshal and Deputy Killed In Shoot-Out!

Yesterday in an act, the motive of which we shall probably never know, Marshal Seth Witherspoon stepped into the Bull and Heifer Saloon shouting vituperative challenges at Tim Calhoun. Even as he mouthed the scurrilous words, he was engaging his pistol with devastating effect. Deputy Calhoun dropped to the floor with a bullet in his heart.

Bo Willis and Emile Clark, both of whom were standing near the deputy, fired at the marshal, killing him instantly. Although there was no witness testimony, nor evidence to indicate that Witherspoon represented a threat, their claim of self-defense was immediately accepted by Judge Boykin, and no charge of homicide has been filed.

With the death of both Marshal Witherspoon and Deputy Calhoun, our fair community was left without the services of either, though a case could well be made that neither the marshal nor his deputy represented the people's interest in the first place. The absence of law enforcement did not last very long, however, for in a move that can only be described as bizarre, the city council, by unanimous vote, appointed Willis as our new marshal and Clark as our new deputy. The very men who had, by their action, rendered the vacancy available were selected to fill it. The city council wasted no time in making the appointments, no doubt directed to do so by Silas Atwood.

While this newspaper agrees that it is good to fill such a vacancy as quickly as possible, we do not agree that the wisest choice was made. Atwood's influence over Marshal Witherspoon had already been a point of concern by the good citizens of our town. Now that influence shall be even greater, for this paper believes that Willis and Clark have been appointed as the newest officers of the law in order to give Atwood even more control.

I would be remiss in my duty if I did not urge my fellow citizens to rise up against this usurpation and demand an immediate popular election to either

> sustain, or override, the action of the
> city council. We cannot allow Atwood to
> continue to exercise his tyrannical reign
> over our fair community.

"Just who the hell does Blanton think he is,
anyway?" Atwood shouted angrily, throwing the
newspaper down.

"I couldn't understand about half of them words,
but I was pretty sure they wasn't good ones. That's
why I brung the paper to you soon as it come out,"
Willis said.

"I think, perhaps, Mr. Blanton needs to be taught
a lesson," Atwood said.

"You want me 'n Clark to rough 'im up a bit?"

"No, I'll have Sanders and Booker pay his office a
visit. You're the marshal. It'll be your job to investigate, to find out who did it."

"Well hell, Boss, if Sanders and Booker does it,
there won't be no need to investigate. We'll know
who done it," Willis said.

"You won't know that they did it."

"Sure I will, you just told me you was goin' to have
them do it."

"Willis, I didn't make a mistake in making you the
marshal, did I? Please tell me you aren't that dumb."

"What do you mean? I mean, if Sanders and . . ."
Willis stopped in midsentence, and a smile spread
across his face. "Oh!" he said. "Oh! Yeah, I get it! I
ain't *supposed* to know who done it. That way I'll be
tryin' to figure it out."

"Aren't you the brilliant one, though," Atwood said.

"Yeah, I am pretty smart at that," Willis replied, not catching the sarcasm in Atwood's remark.

Allen Blanton was still at breakfast the next morning when there was a loud knock on the door. When he opened the door he saw Oscar Davis, his all-around handyman.

"Hello, OD. Lose your key?"

"No, sir," OD replied. "And truth is, even if I had, it wouldn't have mattered this morning. There was no key needed."

"Damn! Did I leave the door unlocked last night?"

"No, sir. That is, not that I know of," OD said. "Anyway you don't need a key to open the front door this morning because there is no front door. That's why I'm over here."

"What?"

"I think perhaps you should come take a look," OD suggested.

Five minutes later Blanton was standing in the front room of the *Etholen Standard*, looking at the disarray. In addition to the fact that the door was lying on the floor, all the glass of the front window had been broken, the composing tables turned over, the type trays emptied, and type scattered everywhere.

"Who would do something like this?" Blanton lamented.

"Do you really need to ask that question, Mr. Blanton? Don't you know who it was?" Smoke asked. Smoke was but one of several of the town's people who had gathered at the newspaper office, not only from curiosity, but, for many, a genuine desire to help put things back in order.

Blanton shook his head. "No, I don't know."

"Think about it, Mr. Blanton. Who has been the most frequent subject of your recent editorials?"

"Surely you don't think Atwood would do something like this, do you? I'll admit, he is a bit overly ambitious, but he is a wealthy and influential man. I just can't see someone of his social and economic status stooping to do something like this."

"I have been around a lot of wealthy men," Smoke said. "Believe me, a sizable bank account has very little bearing on their behavior."

"Yes," Blanton said with a troubled nod of his head. "You are right, of course."

"What happened here?" a loud voice called, and looking toward the front door, Smoke and Blanton saw the newly appointed Marshal Willis standing there.

"It's fairly obvious what happened here, isn't it?" Smoke replied. "Some of your friends took issue with Mr. Blanton's editorial."

"What do you mean, some of my friends? Are you telling me you think I know something about this? That's a damn lie, and you know it."

"You may well be right," Smoke replied. "Now that I think about it, it is foolish of me to believe that you actually have any friends."

Many of those who had been drawn to the scene laughed at Smoke's reply.

Blanton chuckled as well. "Thanks," he said. "I needed a laugh, especially now."

"What do you mean I ain't got no friends? I got

friends," Willis asked, not catching the sarcasm. "I got lots of friends."

"I'm sure you do," Smoke replied.

Blanton got down on all fours and began gathering the type that had been scattered all over the floor.

"We'll help you, Mr. Blanton," someone else said.

"Each of you just choose one letter to pick up at a time," Blanton suggested. "It will be easier to separate them that way."

"I've got the z's," someone said.

"Ha! Leave it to Doodle to do the least work," another said. "I'll do the x's."

"Wait a minute, wait a minute!" Willis called. "You folks ain't got no right to start pickin' up the type, or to do anythin' like that till I tell you."

"What do you mean till you tell us, Willis?" one of those in the crowd asked.

"This here is a crime scene, as I'm sure all of you know. 'N bein' as it is a crime scene, it needs to be left just the way we found it, till I'm through investigating."

"Willis, either help us get this place cleaned up, or get out of the way," Smoke said with an angry growl.

"Well, I was just . . . I mean . . ." Willis started to respond, but he realized that he wasn't going to be able to stop the cleanup of the newspaper office because by now at least ten of the citizens of the town were involved in putting it back together again.

Willis remained for no more than a moment longer, then he turned and left the office as even more townspeople joined the first group, picking up type and setting the press and furniture to rights. At least two people were reattaching the door, while a couple more were cleaning out the rest of the broken window so a new plate of glass could be put in place.

Smoke, Sally, and Pearlie had planned to go to El Paso to visit Judge Turner this morning, but they put the trip off, staying to help the rest of the town put the newspaper office together again.

"This is great," Blanton said as the newspaper office continued to be put back to normal. "I never would have expected anything like this."

"Mr. Blanton, you know what this tells me?" Kate, who had also joined the helpers, asked.

"What's that?"

"It tells me that you have a lot of friends, and that, despite everything, Etholen is a very nice town."

"Yes, it is, or at least it could be, if we could ever get out from under Atwood's thumb," Blanton replied.

"We will," Kate said. "I have no doubt about that."

It was late afternoon before the newspaper office was completely reassembled, with the type and composing tables back in place, along with a new door and new glass in the front window. Afterward, everyone who had showed up to help put the newspaper office together again gathered at the Palace Café for dinner. Sue Ellen Johnson, proprietor of the café, pushed several tables together so there was one long table to accommodate everyone.

"Who could have done such a thing as try and destroy the newspaper?" someone asked. "And what could possibly be their reason?"

"That shouldn't be all that hard to figure out," Cletus said. "I mean, all you have to do is read yesterday's issue, when he talked about Atwood. There's no doubt in my mind but that Atwood done it. Or leastwise he had some of his men do it."

"But Willis was one of Atwood's men before he become marshal, wasn't he? And now he's investigating it. If it was one of Atwood's men that did it, don't you think Willis would know that?" one of the men around the table asked.

The others looked at him.

"Oh," he said. "Yeah, he probably already knows, don't he?"

"If he didn't do it himself," another offered.

Blanton struck his fork against the glass and, getting everyone's attention, stood to speak.

"My friends," he said. "And you are, all of you, indeed my friends I will be honest with you. When Rusty Abernathy was convicted in the sham of a trial, and then Kate arrested and put in jail to take Rusty's place when he escaped, I had just about given up all hope for this town. Indeed, I had started looking into other towns where I could take my printing press and start my newspaper all over again.

"But now there are things that are giving me hope that our town will be able, not only to survive, but to escape from these oppressive shackles placed upon us by Silas Atwood and his gunhands. And the people we can most thank for that are here with us tonight. I'm talking about Smoke Jensen and his wife Sally, Pearlie Fontaine, and Cal Wood."

"Hear! Hear!" Joe Cravens said, lifting his glass

toward Smoke, Sally, Pearlie, and Cal, and the others joined the mayor in lifting their own glasses in salute.

Eagle Shire Ranch

"Are you telling me that the people of the town actually turned out to help Blanton get his newspaper office put back in shape?" Atwood asked, the tone of his voice showing his anger.

"Yes, sir, that's exactly what happened, all right," Willis said. "Why there musta been fifteen or twenty people there helpin', fixin' the door, puttin' in a new window, pickin' up all the type and such."

"I think the townspeople are feeling pretty emboldened right now, because Smoke Jensen and Kate's brother, what is it they're callin' 'im?"

"Pearlie," Willis said.

"Yes, Pearlie. Witherspoon didn't get any of the reward posters out for him, did he?" Atwood asked.

"No, sir, he never got the chance."

"As soon as we get them distributed, I have a feeling that Kate's brother will concern us no further."

Blanton had more to say in the next edition of the *Etholen Standard*.

ATTACK ON FREEDOM OF THE PRESS

As many of you know, the *Standard* offices were attacked last night. The vandals broke out the front window and knocked the front door off its hinges. Once they had gained access to the building, they scattered the type around and overturned the press. This scurrilous action was not only an attack on the newspaper, it was an assault on the free press, which means that every citizen of Etholen was as much a victim as was the *Standard*.

But this heinous attack aroused a wave of righteous discontent among the population. For, dear readers, dozens of right-minded citizens of our city came to my aid, and in so doing, expressed their belief in, and their willingness to defend, freedom of the press.

Now, and for some time, our fair city has been subjected to the heavy-handed activity of one Silas Atwood. Atwood, as our readers know, is a very rich man . . . one of the most affluent in West Texas, if, indeed, not in the entire state. This has given him a sense of entitlement, and no despotic ruler in the history of the European feudal system has ever been more tyrannical in the ruthless application of wealth and power than the owner of Eagle Shire Ranch, who used his position to force out all the other area ranchers, and now, through his control of our city council, judge, and city marshal's office, is, by fear and intimidation, doing all that he can to establish his own fiefdom in El Paso County.

We cannot let this happen, and it is my belief, as evidenced by the courageous reaction of our town when this newspaper was attacked, that the time will come when our citizens will arise and throw this despot out.

CHAPTER TWENTY-TWO

El Paso

On the very morning that Allen Blanton's defiant article appeared in the *Etholen Standard*, Smoke, Sally, and Pearlie went to the courthouse in El Paso to pay another visit to Judge Turner.

"Is the information on this poster true?" Judge Turner asked.

"If you are asking is it true that I killed Marshal Gibson, then the answer is yes, that is true," Pearlie said. "But it isn't true that I murdered him. I killed him in self-defense."

"Where, did this happen?" Judge Turner asked.

"Bexar County," Pearlie replied.

"Bexar, not El Paso?"

"No, sir. It was Bexar."

"But the information says contact Marshal Witherspoon in Etholen. By the way, I understand that he was recently killed."

"Yes, sir, he was."

"He was killed by the man who is now the marshal," Smoke added.

"When did this happen?" Judge Turner asked. He held up the poster. "It must be very recent, judging by this poster."

"It happened a long time ago, Your Honor," Pearlie replied. "When I was fifteen."

"But these reward posters are new."

"Yes sir, they are," Smoke said.

"Still, there is no statute of limitations on murder," Judge Turner said.

"It wasn't murder, Your Honor. It was self-defense," Pearlie insisted.

"That may be, but there is going to have to be a resolution to the charge."

"Yes, that's why we came to you," Smoke said.

"What, exactly, are you asking me to do?" Judge Turner asked.

"I want to go to trial, Your Honor, and get this behind me. But I don't want to be tried by Judge Boykin," Pearlie said.

"We're asking for a change of venue," Sally said. "We know that you can't arbitrarily dismiss all charges, but, as a federal judge, you can at least position us in such a way as to guarantee a fair trial."

"Yes, I can at least do that," Judge Turner replied. "Tell me the story of what happened. Don't leave anything out," the judge added.

As he had when he related the story back at Sugar-loaf, before they left to come to Texas, Pearlie laid out all the facts of that afternoon when he had gone into town with his friends with no more intention than to enjoy a cool lemonade.

When Pearlie was finished with his story, Judge Turner smiled, then held up his finger. "Come with me," he said mysteriously.

The four followed Judge Turner downstairs, then to an office in the back of the building. The sign on the door leading into that office read FIELDING POTASHNICK, JUDGE OF CIRCUIT COURT.

"Zeke," Judge Potashnick said when Turner took them into his office. "What can I do for you?"

"Fielding, I want you to conduct a trial for this young man," Judge Turner said.

"What kind of trial? And when?"

"A murder trial, and right now."

"Whoa, hold on there, Zeke. What do you mean, right now?"

"I am acting as his attorney," Judge Turner said. "And we waive trial by jury . . . we will accede to your finding."

"We'll need a prosecutor."

"Is David Crader in his office?"

"Yes," Potashnick said. "Wilma, step down to Mr. Crader's office, and tell him to meet us in the courtroom."

"Yes, sir," his clerk answered.

"I found an article about the incident in the newspaper morgue," Crader said two hours later, when he returned to the courtroom after learning what it was about. "I'm prepared to make my case."

Potashnick turned toward Judge Turner. "Your Honor, are you . . . ?"

"Your Honor . . . we can't be Your Honoring each

other all day," Turner replied. "As you are conducting this trial, I will refer to you as Your Honor. But as I will be acting as Mr. Fontaine's defense attorney, suppose you just refer to me as Counselor?"

Potashnick chuckled. "All right, Counselor it is. Counselor, are you ready to present your case?"

"I am."

"Mr. Prosecutor, you may begin."

"Your Honor, according to the information I have before me, Wes Fontaine, then a boy of fifteen, shot and killed two men within a period of one hour. And one of the men he shot was the marshal, who was attempting to arrest him for murdering the first gentleman."

"Have you any witnesses to call?" Judge Potashnick asked.

"No, Your Honor, I do not. As it happened nearly twenty years ago, and given the constraint of time since being assigned this case, I have been unable to find any witnesses, other than the printed witness of the newspaper article I have used as my source."

"Objection," Turner said. "A newspaper article is, by definition, hearsay evidence."

"But, Your Honor," Crader replied. "Hearsay or not, it is the only evidence Prosecution has. And, I hasten to point out that it is a contemporary account."

"Objection overruled. The newspaper account will be considered as evidence. Have you anything else?"

"No, Your Honor."

"Do you rest your case?"

"I do."

"Defense counsel?"

"Your Honor, Defense has a witness to the event, a

very good witness as he was also one of the principals to the case. I call the defendant, Mr. Wes Wesley Fontaine."

Pearlie was sworn, then he took his seat in the witness chair.

"You go by Pearlie, I believe? Do you mind if I address you as Pearlie?"

"No, sir, I don't mind at all."

"A moment ago, the prosecutor said that you killed the marshal when he tried to arrest you for murder. Is that true?"

"No, sir, that isn't true."

"What is untrue?"

"He wasn't trying to arrest me," Pearlie said. "Emmett Miller was the first man I killed. He drew on me, and everyone in the saloon saw it. When Marshal Gibson arrived very shortly thereafter, everyone in the saloon who had seen it told him that Miller drew first, and I had no choice but to defend myself."

"And did the marshal believe you?"

"Yes, sir, he did."

"But he attempted to arrest you, anyway?"

"No, sir, he did not."

"Then I don't understand. If he wasn't trying to arrest you, how is it that you wound up shooting him?"

Pearlie told how the marshal had ordered him out of the county, and when he said he didn't want to leave, that he had a good job and friends, the marshal said that he would either leave or get killed.

"When I said I wasn't going to go, he went for his gun."

"And you beat him?"

"Yes, sir."

"What happened then?"

"Everyone in the saloon told me that I'd better leave because I had shot a lawman, and it wouldn't matter if I was right or wrong. Shooting a lawman meant I would probably be hanged for it. So they all took up a collection for enough money for me to leave Texas. As I look back on it now, I think I should have stayed there and gone to trial. But I was a fifteen-year-old kid, I was scared, and I listened to everyone when they told me I should run."

Turner returned to the defense table and picked up a piece of paper. "Your Honor, I enter this as a defense exhibit. It is a wanted for murder poster issued on Wes, Pearlie, Fontaine, offering a reward of twenty-five hundred dollars, dead or alive."

"Let me get this straight, Counselor," Judge Potashnick said. "This is a wanted for murder poster, issued against your client, and you are putting this up as evidence for the defense?"

"I am, Your Honor. Its relevance shall come clear, shortly."

"Very well, let the clerk note that this is accepted as evidence for the defense."

"Is this an original poster, Mr. Fontaine?" Turner asked.

"No, sir. As you can see, it's clear that this poster isn't twenty years old."

"Yes, I can see that. I'm also interested in the way your name is listed here. Pearlie. When the incident in question happened, were you known as Pearlie?"

"No, sir," Pearlie replied.

"How did you come by the name Pearlie?"

"I figured I needed to change my name, in order to keep anyone from tracking me down."

"Where do you think this reward poster came from?"

"Objection, Your Honor, leading the witness," Crader said.

"Sustained."

"Let me restate the question. Do you know where this document came from?"

"I'm sure that Silas Atwood had it printed."

"Objection, Your Honor. That's not a definitive response."

"Objection sustained."

"I have no further questions, Your Honor," Turner said.

"Cross, Mr. Prosecutor?" Potashnick asked.

Crader started to approach the jury box, then, realizing that there was no jury, smiled sheepishly and came back to the witness stand.

"Mr. Fontaine, how old were you when this happened?"

"I was fifteen."

"You were fifteen, but you expect this court to believe that you, a fifteen-year-old boy, could draw faster and shoot straighter than an experienced marshal?"

"Yes, sir."

"Why is that? How were you able to draw faster and shoot straighter than an experienced law officer?"

"I had been practicing."

"So, you practiced drawing and shooting?"

"Yes, sir."

"Why?"

"I thought I might need the skill in order to defend myself."

"Isn't it also possible that you had this great skill, and you wished to show it off, and were willing to do so at the slightest provocation?"

"No, sir."

"But that is what happened, isn't it? In both cases, when you shot and killed Miller, and when you shot and killed the marshal, you could have avoided killing them?"

"Both Miller and Marshal Gibson drew first."

"After you provoked them into it."

"No, sir, I don't see it that way at all."

"You say your friends all took up a collection for you?"

"Yes, sir."

"And you left Texas?"

"Yes, sir."

Crader stroked his chin for a moment as he stared at Pearlie. "Mr. Fontaine, if what you are telling us is the truth, have you ever considered the irony of it?"

"The irony, sir?"

"Yes," Crader said. "According to you, the entire incident happened because you refused to leave Texas when the marshal ordered you to do so."

"Yes, sir, that's right."

"But you wound up leaving, anyway."

"Yes, sir."

"Wouldn't it have been better, under the circumstances, to have left when he told you to? As it turned out, you left anyway, and the marshal wound up getting killed."

"Yes, sir," Pearlie said contritely. "I've thought about that a thousand times over the last several years. And I wish to hell I had left when he first asked me."

"So you admit that you did provoke the marshal into shooting you."

"I . . ."

"No further questions, Your Honor."

"Redirect, Mr. Turner?" Judge Potashnick asked after Crader sat down.

Turner stood up but didn't leave the table.

"Mr. Fontaine, prior to the incident we are debating, how did you and Marshal Gibson get along?"

"We got along fine," Pearlie responded. "I guess," he added.

"You guess?"

"Yes, sir. Well, the truth is, I don't think the marshal even knew who I was. There was no need for him to. I mean, I had never done anything to cause him to know me. We never even spoke, at least, not before that night."

"Did you feel you had something to prove?"

"Something to prove?"

"Yes. When you went into town with your friends that night, did you have it in your mind that you were going to prove to the others that, even though you were only fifteen, you could take care of yourself?"

"No, sir. The only reason I went into town that night is because I wanted to have a lemonade, and I wanted to have it with my friends."

"No further questions."

"Closing statement?"

"None, Your Honor. Defense rests."

"Prosecutor?"

"Prosecution rests."

Potashnick looked out over the court and, for a long moment, drummed his fingers on the bench.

"Would the defendant please stand?"

Pearlie, and Judge Turner, acting as his defense counsel, stood.

"After careful consideration, I find the defendant not guilty, and hereby order the recall of any and all wanted posters that may be, or may come to be in existence, as it pertains to this particular incident.

"Court is adjourned."

With a big smile, Pearlie reached out to shake Judge Turner's hand. By the time he turned around, Sally had stepped up to the defense table, and she gave him a big hug.

"Oh, Miz Sally, do you know how long that's been hanging over me?" Pearlie asked. "I mean, I wasn't ever really worried about it, but still, it sometimes sort of nagged at me. And now, it's all over."

"It is indeed," Sally said.

CHAPTER TWENTY-THREE

Etholen

"I got a telegram for you," Dennis Hodge said, stepping into the marshal's office.

"You have a telegram for me?" Willis asked.

"You're the city marshal, aren't you?" the Western Union operator said.

"Oh, yeah, I guess I am."

"Well, then this is for you. It came for you about five minutes ago."

"Do I have to pay for it?"

"No, it's already been paid for. Are you going to take it or not? I have to get back over to the office."

"Yeah, sure, I'll take it," Willis said, reaching for the sheet of paper. He waited until Hodge left before he read it.

WES WESLEY PEARLIE FONTAINE FOUND
NOT GUILTY OF ALL CHARGES.
IMMEDIATE RECALL OF ALL REWARD
POSTERS ORDERED BY JUDGE F.
POTASHNICK.

"Damn," Willis said. "Atwood ain't goin' to like this."

"He ain't goin' to like what?" Clark asked.

"He ain't goin' to like it that we have to take up all them posters we put out on Fontaine."

"What do you mean?"

Willis showed Clark the telegram. "What the hell? Does this mean we have to go out 'n find all them posters we done put out?"

"That's what the telegram says."

"What if we can't find 'em all? What if some people have already took some of 'em, 'n is lookin' for Pearlie?"

Willis chuckled. "Well, now, it'd just be a real shame if someone was to kill 'im by mistake, wouldn't it?"

Booker laughed as well. "Yeah," he said. "A real shame."

"Look at this!" Cal said excitedly, holding out the telegram he had just received from Smoke. "Pearlie has been tried and found innocent already. Miz Kate, you don't have to worry about him ever again. Whatever happened all those years ago is behind him now."

"Oh!" Kate said. "Oh, I'm so happy!"

"I think the smartest thing I ever did was go to Colorado to find Uncle Wes," Rusty said.

"I agree," Kate said. "I just know, now, how foolish I was once I learned that my brother was still alive, and where he lived, that I didn't make any effort go see him long before now."

Reeves County, Texas

Dingus Lomax rode into Salcedo, stopped in front of the Longhorn Saloon, dismounted, and went inside. Stepping up to the bar, he slapped a silver coin down in front of him.

The sound of the coin made the saloonkeeper look around. The man waiting to be served looked like a piece of rawhide. He was smaller than average, with a craggy face and an oversized, hooked nose.

"What'll it be, Mr. Lomax?" the bartender asked, stepping up to him.

"Whiskey."

Lomax was a bounty hunter, who was well known for the dispassionate way he could kill. His very name instilled fear. He wasn't surprised that he was recognized by the bartender, but in his profession that was a mixed blessing. On the one hand, it often gave him an edge, by inducing fear in his quarry. On the other hand, it also forewarned them, so they could get away.

Lomax specialized in those fugitives who were wanted "dead or alive." So far he had hunted down and been paid reward money for seventeen such fugitives. Not one of the fugitives for whom the reward was paid had been brought in alive.

"Why should I bring 'em in alive?" Lomax replied when a marshal queried him about his method of operation. "They're easier to handle when they're dead, 'n besides which, I don't have to feed 'em."

When Lomax had ridden into the small town of Salcedo a few minutes earlier, news of his arrival spread quickly. Old men held up their grandsons to point him out as he rode by so that the young ones could remember this moment and, many years from now, tell their own grandchildren about it. Those grandchildren would ultimately tell their grandchildren that their grandfather had once seen Dingus Lomax, so that the legend of the man would span seven generations.

Lomax picked up his drink, then slowly surveyed the interior of the saloon. He was on the trail of Mort Bodine, and a chance remark he had overheard down in Wild Horse suggested that Bodine might have come to Salcedo.

The saloon was typical of the many he had seen over the past several years. Wide, rough-hewn boards formed the plank floor, and against the wall behind the long, brown-stained bar was a shelf of whiskey bottles, their number doubled by the mirror they stood against. Half a dozen tables, occupied by a dozen or so men, filled the room, and tobacco smoke hovered in a noxious cloud just under the ceiling.

At the opposite end of the bar stood a man wearing a slouch hat and a trail-worn shirt. Lomax thought this might be Bodine, and because the man looked away from him the few times Lomax glanced that way, he was sure this was the man he was looking for.

Hanging low in a well-oiled holster on Bodine's right side was a Colt .44 with a wooden grip. The man was slender, with dark hair and dark eyes, and there was a gracefulness and economy of motion about the way he walked and moved.

The longer Lomax studied him, the more he was convinced this was his man. Bodine, if that really was his name, had not turned around since Lomax arrived.

"Hey, you," Lomax called.

The man did not turn.

"I'm talkin' to you, Bodine. Your name is Bodine, isn't it? Mort Bodine? That who you are?"

Lomax studied him from the back and saw a visible tightening of the man's shoulders. Then, with a sigh, he turned around. "Yeah," he said. "I'm Bodine. You're Lomax, ain't you?"

"That's me," Lomax said with a smile. "There are wanted dodgers out on you," he added.

"Yeah, I know. I'm a little surprised to see you here, though. I thought you shot most of the men in the back."

Lomax's smile grew bigger. "Try me," he said.

"Draw!" Bodine shouted, going for his own gun even before he issued the challenge.

Bodine was quick, quicker than anyone else this town had ever seen. But midway through his draw, Bodine realized he wasn't quick enough. The arrogant confidence in his eyes was replaced by fear, then the acceptance of the fact that he was about to be killed.

The two pistols discharged almost simultaneously, but Lomax had been able to bring his gun to bear and his bullet plunged into Bodine's chest. The bullet from Bodine's gun smashed the glass that held Lomax's drink, sending up a shower of whiskey and tiny shards of glass.

Looking down at himself, Bodine put his hand over his wound, then pulled it away and examined the blood that had pooled in his palm. When he looked back at Lomax, there was an almost whimsical smile on his face.

He coughed, then fell back against the bar, making an attempt to grab on to the bar to keep himself erect. The attempt was unsuccessful, and Bodine fell on his back, his right arm stretched out beside him, his pistol still connected to him, only because his forefinger was hung up in the trigger guard. The old slouch hat had rolled across the floor and now rested in a half-filled spittoon.

Lomax turned back to the bar where pieces of broken glass and a small puddle of whiskey marked the spot of his drink.

"Looks like I'm going to need a refill," he said.

One hour later Dingus Lomax dismounted, then stepped over to the side of the road to take a leak. He was riding one horse and leading another. Mort Bodine was belly-down across the saddle of the led horse. It wasn't uncomfortable for Bodine, because he was dead. Bodine was wanted in Presidio County. The county seat was Marfa, but that was farther away than Lomax wanted to go, so he was headed for Wild Horse, which was the closest town.

As Lomax buttoned up his trousers, he saw a poster pinned to a nearby tree, and he walked over to examine it.

"Twenty-five hunnert dollars, huh? Seems to me like you coulda at least put a drawin' o' this feller, Fontaine, so that folks that might be after 'im would know what this here Wes Pearlie Fontaine looks like."

Lomax planned to turn the body over to the marshal, or the sheriff, whoever the local law was in Wild Horse, then he figured on going on to Etholen to find out whatever he needed to know about Fontaine.

"Pearlie," he said. "I reckon that's the name you go by. Is that the name you want on your tombstone?"

Lomax giggled at his question, then he swung into the saddle.

"Hey, Bodine," he called back to the body behind him. "You ever been to Wild Horse before? It'd be kind of funny, don't you think, if you ain't never been there before? Funny, I mean, 'cause you're likely goin' to wind up gettin' buried there instead of Marfa, 'n that's where you'll be for all eternity.

"'Course, when you stop to think about it, I reckon you wasn't all that different from me. I mean, I was born just outside Dayton, Ohio, but I ain't been back in Ohio for more'n twenty years now, 'n I don't reckon I'll ever go back. I don't know where I'll wind up planted, but more'n likely it'll be someplace just like you, someplace I ain't never been to before."

Wild Horse

"Which one of you's the marshal?" Lomax asked when he stepped into the marshal's office where two men were engaged in conversation.

"I'm Marshal Wallace," the larger of the two men said, looking toward Lomax. "What do you want?"

"Marshal, my name is Lomax."

"Lomax?" the marshal asked, the expression on

his face becoming more animated. "Would that be Dingus Lomax?"

"Yeah. Look, I got Mort Bodine outside, 'n ole' Mort has a fifteen-hunnert-dollar reward on 'im."

"And you're wantin' me to put him in my jail?"

Lomax laughed, a dry, high-pitched cackle. "You can put 'im in jail if you want to, onliest thing is, he's liable to start stinkin' in another day or two."

"What do you mean, he's liable to start stinkin'?"

"That's what happens to a dead body iffen you let it lie around long enough. When I told you I had Mort Bodine outside, I didn't tell you he was belly-down on his horse."

"I don't understand," the marshal said. "If he's already dead, what did you bring 'im to me for?"

"Damn, how long you been a marshal?" Lomax asked.

"What difference does it make how long I've been a marshal?" Wallace replied, clearly agitated by Lomax's question.

"The thing is, you can't have been one for too long, or you'd know what this is all about. You see, what you have to do is send a telegram back to the Pecos City marshal, 'n tell 'im that you are a lawman, and say that Bodine is dead, and I'm the one that kilt 'im."

"Lomax, I wouldn't know Mort Bodine from Mrs. Smith's housecat. How am I supposed to be able to say he's dead?"

"Maybe, for two hundred and fifty dollars, you might remember that you saw him somewhere before."

"But I ain't never . . ."

"Sure we did, Harold, me 'n you seen 'im back in Van Horn oncet, don't you remember?" his deputy asked.

"No, I don't recall that we . . ."

"You said to me, 'Carl, I do believe that feller over there is worth a hunnert 'n twenty-five dollars to each of us,'" Carl said very pointedly.

Wallace's frown deepened for just a moment, then he realized what his deputy was saying, and a broad smile spread across his face.

"Yes!" he said. "Yes, I do remember that now. Them was my exact words! Come on, Mr. Lomax, let's get a look at this dead prisoner of yours, so I can send word back to Pecos County that this Bodine feller has done been caught."

Lomax's smile was without mirth. "Well now," he said. "I'd say you two is pretty smart law officers. Yes, sir, real smart."

CHAPTER TWENTY-FOUR

Etholen

"I wonder if Katie's got any champagne in her place," Pearlie said as he, Smoke, and Sally rode back into town.

"Champagne?" Sally asked.

"Sure. Isn't that what you drink when you want to celebrate something? I'm that relieved that this has finally been cleared up after all these years that I plan to celebrate with champagne, and I want you all, and Cal, Katie, and Rusty to celebrate with me."

"That's a bit extravagant," Sally said. "But, under the circumstance, I think it may be appropriate."

They tied up in front of the Pretty Girl and Happy Cowboy Saloon, then, Pearlie let out a shout as soon as they stepped inside.

"Yahoo! Katie! Did you get my telegram?" Pearlie asked as he, Smoke, and Sally pushed through the batwing doors.

"Yes!" Katie said happily. "You're a free man!"

Kate, with her arms spread, and a wide smile on her face, hurried over to Pearlie to give him a hug.

"There's not one thing out of my past that's hanging over me now. Katie, I plan to buy a couple of bottles of champagne so we can celebrate."

"Mr. Peterson, how many bottles of champagne do we have?" Kate asked.

Peterson looked under the bar. "Six," he said.

"Open them up, Mr. Peterson. Open every bottle and serve it to anyone who wants it, until it's all gone."

"Champagne?" Cletus said. "Damn! I ain't never tasted any champagne in my whole life."

"Well, you're about to now," Rusty said with a happy laugh.

Over the next few minutes, corks popped loudly, glasses were filled with the bubbly beverage, and the patrons, Dolly, and the other Pretty Girls joined Pearlie in celebrating the outcome of Pearlie's trial.

"Oh! This tickles my nose!" Dolly said, giggling as she took the first drink.

"Sure, champagne always does that," Rusty said.

"Ha! You talk like you've drunk a lot of champagne," Cletus said.

"I've drunk it, before."

"Well, I've got two reasons to celebrate," Dolly said.

"What two reasons?" Rusty asked.

"One, because your uncle Pearlie got everything from his past taken care of, and one because it is my birthday."

"Today is your birthday?"

"Actually, tomorrow is my birthday," Dolly said.

"Well, happy birthday, tomorrow," Rusty said, lifting his glass. "How old will you be?"

"Rusty!" Sally scolded. "That's not something you ever ask a lady. Not even someone as young as Dolly."

Dolly laughed. "She's right, you know. But I'll tell you. I'll be nineteen tomorrow."

"Good, I'm a year older than you are," Rusty said.

"Why do you say good?"

"Because it's just good, that's all."

"Rusty?" Sally said. "I wonder if you would do me a huge favor and play Beethoven's Sonata Number Fourteen?"

"Oh, yes, please do!" Dolly said. "That's one of my favorites."

"Why, Dolly, I didn't know you liked classical music," Sally said.

"I didn't used to like it. Well, I can't say I didn't used to like it . . . it's just that I never actually heard any of it until I heard the kind of music Rusty plays. Now, I love classical music, and I could sit here and listen to it all day."

"Then, why don't you come over here and sit beside me?" Sally invited. "We can enjoy it together."

"Oh, yes," Dolly said. "That would be wonderful. Thank you!"

The celebration stilled, and the patrons of the saloon grew quiet, as Rusty approached the grand piano. Before he sat down, he addressed the saloon patrons.

"The piece I'm about to play, Beethoven's Sonata Number Fourteen, is sometimes known as Moonlight Sonata. Beethoven composed it and dedicated it to the Countess Giulietta Guicciardi, a pupil of Beethoven. He was in love with her, you see, and he proposed to her shortly after playing the piece in public for the first time. She loved him as well, but she was forbidden by her parents to marry him, so, sadly, the marriage never happened.

"Beethoven's Moonlight Sonata," Rusty concluded, then he held his hands over the keyboard for just a moment before he started to play.

The opening notes were haunting, the melody almost a whisper. The music filled the saloon and caressed the collective soul of the patrons. If there was anyone left in Etholen who was unaware of Rusty's talent, it took but a few bars of music to convince even the most skeptical that they weren't hearing a mere saloon piano player, they were listening to a concert pianist of great expertise. As Rusty's fingers caressed the piano keyboard, he created magic. It was as if, through his skill, he had actually been able to resurrect the great composer.

When Rusty finished, the applause was spontaneous, genuine, and sustained, from the Pretty Girls, who were also Dolly's friends, to the men who punched cows or drove freight wagons or worked for the railroad. Those who had never even heard of Beethoven were applauding as enthusiastically as Sally, Kate, and Dolly.

"Oh, Rusty, that was so pretty that it made me cry," Dolly said when Rusty came back over to her.

"Dolly is right," Sally said. "I've heard Ricardo Castro and J. E. Goodson in concert, and neither of them have anything on you."

Rusty beamed at the compliment. "I've heard both of them play as well," he said. "And while I can't agree that I play as well as they . . . I certainly do appreciate you saying so."

"Well, this has been a most enjoyable celebration," Sally said. "But, Smoke, if you don't mind, I'd like to clean up before dinner tonight, so I'm going back to the hotel."

"I've got a little trail dust I'd like to get off as well, so I'll join you," Smoke said.

When they returned to the hotel, they made arrangements to have a tub and hot water brought up to their room.

"You can go first," Smoke said, once the tub was filled with hot water.

"That's nice of you to let me have the clean water," Sally said.

Smoke chuckled. "Letting you have the clean water has nothing to do with it. I just want to see you naked."

"Smoke!" Sally said, dipping her hand down into the water and splashing some of it on him. "You're awful!" She laughed. "I have to admit, though, that I'm flattered you would still say something like that."

"Tell me, do you think Rusty has ever watched Dolly take a bath?" Smoke said.

"I don't know," Sally replied. She giggled. "But I'll bet he would like to."

"Ha! Now who is being awful?"

Blanton wasted no time declaring Pearlie's innocence in the *Etholen Standard*.

WESLEY FONTAINE FOUND INNOCENT

Why, readers may ask, does this paper print an article declaring the innocence of this man Wesley Fontaine? Recently questionable wanted posters have been freshly printed, and circulated, offering a reward of twenty-five hundred dollars, dead or alive, for Mr. Fontaine. I say questionable, because the event for which the reward was being offered happened many years ago in another county.

Upon learning of the existence of these posters, Mr. Fontaine presented himself before a valid court, requested, and was granted a trial. The result of that trial was absolution of any guilt implied by the reward circulars. As publisher of this newspaper, I feel it is my obligation to make certain that everyone knows the reward is no longer valid, and if you see one of these dodgers still posted, you should, as a matter of civic duty, destroy it, in order to prevent what could become a tragic mistake.

Mr. Fontaine, who is better known by the sobriquet "Pearlie" is the brother of Mrs. Kate Abernathy. Kate Abernathy is not only one of our town's most successful business leaders, she is also generous of spirit and resources. It was she, you might remember, who organized and was the major contributor to a special fund last year that made Christmas an enjoyable event for the less fortunate of our community.

Pearlie arrived in town along with Mr. and Mrs. Smoke Jensen in order to have overturned the unjust conviction of Rusty Abernathy and to free, from illegal incarceration, Pearlie's sister, the above mentioned Kate Abernathy.

Shortly after Smoke and Sally left, Willis came into the saloon, and he saw everyone laughing and toasting each other. Seeing the marshal, the mood changed quickly.

"Is there something we can help you with, Marshal?" Kate asked.

Willis pointed to the glasses several were holding. "What's that stuff you're all drinkin'?" he asked.

"It's champagne. We're celebrating my trial, Marshal," Pearlie said. "You may not have gotten the word yet, but I was tried and found innocent of all charges. So that reward poster that Witherspoon had put out is worthless."

"Yeah," Willis said. "I got a telegram tellin' me that." He looked over toward Kate.

"Have a glass with us, Marshal. Help us celebrate," Kate invited.

"A beer's fine," Willis replied with a growl.

As the others continued to celebrate, Willis stood alone at the bar, finished his beer, then left.

"You know what, Pearlie? I don't think the new marshal was all that interested in celebrating you being found innocent of all those old charges," Cal said.

"It didn't appear like he was, did it?" Pearlie replied with a chuckle.

"Hey, Cal," Rusty said a moment later when Dolly returned to work. "Dolly's birthday is tomorrow. Did you know that?"

"No, I didn't know."

"Yeah, she just told me. I'd like to buy her a birthday present. Would you come with me to help me pick something out for her?"

"Yeah, sure."

* * *

When Cal and Rusty left the saloon, they had to wait for a rider to pass before they could cross the street. The rider was Dingus Lomax who had just arrived in town twelve hundred and fifty dollars wealthier than he was when he woke up this morning. He hadn't actually been paid the reward yet, but he was told that the money would be waiting for him in the Bank of Wild Horse within three days. He decided that, while waiting on that money, he might as well investigate the twenty-five hundred dollars that was being offered for Fontaine, and for that, he had to come to Etholen.

If he could find Fontaine, that would make today the best payday he had ever had. And he decided that the best place to start would be with Marshal Witherspoon, since his name was on the dodger. Tying up in front of the city marshal's office, he stepped inside.

"You Marshal Witherspoon?" Lomax asked.

"Witherspoon is dead. I'm the marshal now," Willis said. "Who's askin'?"

"Lomax is the name." Lomax took the reward poster from his shirt pocket. "Tell me, Marshal, what do you know about this man, Fontaine? It says that Witherspoon is the one that's a' wantin' 'im. Bein' as you're the new marshal, are you a' wantin' 'im, too? Or has somebody done brung 'im in?"

"There ain't nobody brung 'im in yet, but . . ."

Willis was about to tell Lomax that the reward posters were being withdrawn, but he changed his mind. He knew that Atwood wanted Pearlie taken care of . . . so why not let Lomax do it?

Glancing down toward his desk, Willis saw the newspaper article proclaiming Pearlie's innocence, and he turned the paper over so that the story wasn't visible.

"But what?" Lomax asked.

"But there don't nobody need to bring 'im in 'cause he's here, in town, now," Willis said.

"He's here? You mean, you got 'im in jail?"

"No, he ain't in jail."

"Well, if he's in town, 'n he ain't in jail, how come it is that you ain't arrested him?"

"I was fixin' to go over 'n arrest 'im, but the onliest thing is, bein' as I'm the law, I can't collect on the reward. So I was thinkin' . . ."

"I know what you was thinkin'," Lomax said. "You was thinkin' that if you let me bring 'im in, that maybe I'd give you some of the reward money."

"Yeah, that's what I was thinkin' all right."

"Only thing is, if you know anything about me, you know I don't bring 'em in alive."

"Oh?"

"This here poster says dead or alive, don't it?"

"Yes."

"That means that when I bring 'em in, he'll be dead."

Willis nodded. "Yes, well, like you said, the reward is for dead or alive."

"Where is he?"

"If I tell you where to find 'im, I'll be expectin' some of the money."

"I'll give you two hunnert and fifty dollars."

"Uh-uh. Fontaine is worth twenty-five hunnert dollars. I want five hunnert."

Willis knew that there was no reward being offered, but he carried out the charade because he wanted Lomax to think that the poster was valid. That way Lomax would kill Fontaine. And because Atwood wanted Fontaine taken care of, Willis was reasonably sure that after he explained how it was all set up, the rancher would be generous to him, if not to Lomax.

"How 'bout if I give you three hunnert dollars?" Lomax asked. He smiled. "And all you have to do to earn that is sit here 'n wait for me to kill 'im for you."

"All right. He's in the Pretty Girl and Happy Cowboy Saloon," Willis said.

"What's he look like?"

"He's wearing a low-crown black hat with a silver band around it. 'N he's got on a yeller shirt."

CHAPTER TWENTY-FIVE

When he went into the Pretty Girl and Happy Cowboy Saloon a few minutes later, Lomax saw the man Willis had described. He was fairly tall, but then to Lomax, who was only five feet four inches, everyone was tall. The man Lomax saw was also wearing a yellow shirt, and though he wasn't the only one in the saloon with a yellow shirt, he was the only one with a yellow shirt and a black, low-crowned hat with a silver hatband.

"Yes, sir, what can I get for you?" the bartender asked, stepping down to greet Lomax as he stepped up to the bar.

"Whiskey," Lomax replied. He thought about asking the bartender if the man at the other end of the bar was Pearlie Fontaine, and he knew that someone with less experience would probably do just that. But he also knew if he did ask, it would draw attention to him, and, in his business, that wasn't something you wanted to do.

Because Lomax was nearly as good with a knife as he was with a pistol, that was sometimes his weapon of preference. It was more stealthy than a pistol, and as the reward poster specifically said, "dead or alive," there was no need to give his quarry any warning. Rewards were paid no matter how the subject was killed, and that same reward poster would insulate him against any murder charge, no matter how he killed him.

The knife was perfectly balanced for throwing, and, slowly and without being observed, Lomax pulled the blade from its sheath. He held the knife down by his side, waiting for the opportunity to present itself.

"You know what I think?" Pearlie was asking Peterson. "I think my nephew has his cap set for Dolly."

"You just now noticing that are you, Pearlie?" Cletus asked from the other end of the bar. "Why ole' Rusty's been sniffing around that little ole' girl ever since she come here. Ever'body knows that."

Pearlie turned toward Cletus, momentarily showing his back to Lomax.

"Well, you can't blame him, can you, Cletus? I mean she is a pretty little thing, and . . ." Pearlie raised his hand and when he did, he spilled some of his drink on his shirt. "Damn," he said about the spill. He took a step back from the bar to wipe it off, just as something flashed by in front of him. It was a knife! The blade buried itself about half an inch into the bar with a thocking sound, the handle vibrating back and forth. It missed him, only because of the fortuitous spill that had caused him to move.

Instantly, Pearlie drew his pistol and turned toward

the direction from which the knife had come. He saw a man with a gun in his hand standing at the other end of the bar. However, when the man saw how quickly Pearlie had drawn, he held his hands up, letting the pistol dangle from its trigger guard.

"No, no," he said. "Don't shoot, mister. Don't shoot!"

"Why the hell not?" Pearlie growled. "If you would've had your way, that knife would be sticking out of me instead of the bar."

"No, it wouldn't. If I'da been throwin' it at you, I woulda hit you. I was just wanting to get your attention is all," the man said.

That was a lie; Lomax had every expectation of seeing the knife plunge into Pearlie's back, and it would have had not Pearlie moved at that precise moment.

"Well, you got it," Pearlie said. "Now, what do you want?"

"Is your name Wesley Fontaine? You go by Pearlie?"

"Yep. Who are you?"

"The name is Lomax. Dingus Lomax. And I just wanted to make sure you was who I thought you was, is all. We need to talk."

"What do you want to talk about?" Pearlie asked.

"Oh, first one thing, then the other," Lomax replied.

"Mister, you aren't making a lick of sense," Pearlie said. "But if we're goin' to talk, I'd feel better if you hand that gun over to me."

"I can't do that, 'less I put my hands down."

"You can lower them."

Lomax lowered his hands, smiled, then slowly turned the pistol around so that the butt was pointing toward Pearlie. Pearlie had started across the floor for the gun, but before he went half a step, Lomax executed as neat a border roll as Pearlie had ever seen. Pearlie wasn't often caught by surprise, but this time he was . . . not only by the fact that Lomax would try such a thing, but by the skill with which Lomax was able to do it.

Pearlie had relaxed his own position to the point where he had actually let the hammer down on his pistol and even lowered the gun. Now he had to raise the gun back into line while, at the same time, cocking it. And he was slowed by the fact that he first had to react to Lomax's unexpected action.

The quiet room was suddenly shattered with the roar of two pistols snapping firing caps and exploding powder almost simultaneously. The bar patrons, also caught by surprise, yelled and dived, or scrambled for cover. White gunsmoke billowed out in a cloud that filled the center of the room, momentarily obscuring everything.

As the smoke began to clear, Lomax stared through the white cloud, smiling broadly at Pearlie.

"I'll be damn," he said. "I'm goin' to wind up in the boot hill of someplace I ain't never even heard of before today."

The smile left his face, his eyes glazed over, and he pitched forward, his gun clattering to the floor.

Pearlie stood ready to fire a second shot if needed, but a second shot wasn't necessary. He looked down at Lomax for a moment, then holstered his pistol.

"Pearlie! Are you all right?" Kate asked. She had

been back in her office when the shooting happened and, coming out quickly, was now standing next to her brother.

"You didn't know that fella, did you, Pearlie?" Peterson asked. The shooting had all happened so fast that neither Peterson nor anyone else in the saloon had had the opportunity to get out of the way.

"I never saw him before in my life," Pearlie said.

Cletus walked over to the body, squatted down beside it, then pulled a piece of paper from Lomax's pocket.

"Here's what this was all about, Pearlie," Cletus said. "Looks like this feller didn't get the word that you ain't wanted no more."

Pearlie looked at the reward dodger. "I can see right now that a court order calling them back isn't going to mean there's an end to it."

"You think she'll like this?" Rusty asked, holding up a cameo broach.

"Yes, I don't know why she wouldn't, it's really . . ." that was as far as Cal got in his response before they heard gunshots.

"That was from Mama's place!" Rusty said. He lay the broach back down and he and Cal ran across the street and into the Pretty Girl and Happy Cowboy Saloon.

As soon as they stepped inside they saw a body lying on the floor, with a few people staring down at it. Dolly and the other girls were standing down at the far end of the bar, looking on with horror-struck faces. Kate was next to Pearlie, with her hands on his arm, and the expression on both her face and Pearlie's left no doubt as to who did it.

"You did this, Pearlie?" Cal asked.

Pearlie sighed. "Bounty hunter," he said.

"Then you didn't have any choice. It's probably going to be a while, and I blame Atwood for putting out the posters in the first place."

"Atwood?" one of the bar patrons said. "The name on here is Witherspoon."

"Tell me, Doodle. Who controlled Witherspoon?" Cletus asked.

"Oh, yeah," Doodle said. "You're right."

When Willis stepped into the saloon a moment later, he fully expected to see Pearlie lying dead on the floor. Instead, the body he saw was the small, wiry man who had been in his office a few minutes earlier. He gasped in surprise and disappointment.

"What's goin' on in here?" Willis asked. "What's all the shootin' about?"

"This here feller just come after Pearlie," Cletus said, pointing to Lomax's body.

"You kilt 'im?" Willis asked.

"Yes," Pearlie replied without elaboration.

"You can't seem to stay out of trouble, can you, boy? I mean you just got yourself cleared of one killin', 'n here you've done kilt yourself another 'n."

"I didn't have any choice," Pearlie said.

"Seems to me like ever since you and Jensen, and," Willis paused, then glanced toward Cal, "this feller here, come into town, folks has been dyin' left 'n right all around you. And you always say you didn't have no choice."

"Willis, there were twelve people in here when this happened, and every one of us will swear that the man lying dead on the floor is the one who started this," Peterson said.

"You're askin' me to believe that Lomax come in here, 'n for no reason at all, just started shootin'?"

"How did you know his name?" Pearlie asked.

"What?"

"How did you know his name was Lomax?"

"Well, I, uh, just knew, that's all. He was a bounty hunter. Lot's of people know'd him."

"How did he know me?" Pearlie asked.

"What do you mean, how did he know you? Your name is on a thousand or so reward posters."

"Those posters have all been recalled."

"I just got the word to recall 'em today, there ain't no way in hell they could all be called in this quick." Willis smiled. "The thing is, boy, you're famous."

"My name, yes. But my picture isn't on any of the posters, so how did he recognize me? Mr. Peterson, did he ask you who I was?"

The bartender shook his head. "No, all he asked for was a whiskey."

"Willis told 'im who you was," one of the saloon patrons said. "Just afore I come in here, I seen that feller there," he pointed toward Lomax's body, "leavin' the marshal's office."

"Is that right?" Pearlie asked. "Did Lomax come to see you? Did you tell him what I looked like and where to find me?"

Willis's eyes darted nervously back and forth

between Pearlie and the man who had reported seeing Lomax leaving the marshal's office.

"No, I didn't tell him no such thing. I mean, yeah, he come over to see me 'n showed me that dodger 'n all, but I tole' 'im it warn't no good no more, that they'd all been called back." He smiled. "I even showed him the story that Blanton wrote 'n put in his newspaper today. I don't have no idee why he'd a' come over here after you, seein' as I told him you wasn't wanted no more."

"Get this body out of my saloon," Kate said.

"What do you mean, get this body out of your saloon?" Willis replied.

"You are the city law now," Kate said. "When something like this happens, it is your responsibility to take care of it."

"You two," Willis said, pointing to two of the patrons in the saloon. "Get his carcass down to the undertaker."

"Why should we do that?" one of the men asked.

Willis drew his gun. "Because if you don't, I'll have to find somebody to get three bodies moved."

With grumbling compliance, the two men picked up Lomax's body and Willis followed them out.

"Maybe I had better go tell Smoke what happened," Pearlie suggested a moment later.

"No need to. I'll go tell 'im," Cal promised.

"Cal, before you go," Rusty called to him. "That thing I showed you a while ago?"

"What thing?"

"You know. That thing," Rusty said, making a head motion toward the street.

Cal realized then that he was talking about the cameo broach.

"Oh, yeah, that thing," he said.

"You think she'll lik . . . uh . . . that is, do you think it'll be all right?"

"I think it'll be just fine," Cal replied with a smile.

"Then I'm goin' to go get it!" Rusty said with an even broader smile.

"Smoke? Smoke?" The call was accompanied by a relatively loud knock on the door.

"That's Cal," Sally said. Fresh from their baths, Smoke and Cal were dressed now and about to go out for dinner.

Smoke chuckled. "You can always count on him to show up in time to eat." Smoke opened the door, but his smile disappeared when he saw the expression on Cal's face.

"Cal, what is it?"

"Some bounty hunter just tried to bring Pearlie in," Cal said.

"Oh, Cal!" Sally responded in alarm. "Is he . . . ?"

"Pearlie's fine," Cal said. "But the man that threw down on him isn't so fine. Pearlie killed him."

CHAPTER TWENTY-SIX

In order to celebrate Pearlie's acquittal, Smoke invited Pearlie, Katie, Rusty, and Cal to have dinner that evening with Sally and him.

"Uh, Mr. Jensen, would you mind if Dolly came as well?" Rusty asked. "I'll pay for it. It's just that tomorrow is her birthday."

"Of course she can come as well," Smoke said. "And no, you will not pay for it."

They took their dinner at the Palace Café that evening, Sue Ellen Johnson putting them at a table that was long enough to accommodate all eleven of them, the extra numbers made up by the four other Pretty Girls from Kate's saloon.

The meal was enjoyable, and would have passed without incident, had it not been for three extraordinarily rude customers who were sitting at one of the other tables in the dining room.

"Hey, Clinton," one of the men said, speaking loudly enough to be heard at every table. "There ain't goin' to be no need for us to be a-goin' over to the Bull 'n Heifer tonight. Why put up with their whores, when all the whores from the Pretty Girl has come over here to us."

Clinton laughed. "Tell me, Reed, which one o' them whores do you like best?"

"I think I like that redheaded one down at the end of the table," Reed said. "What about you?"

"Me? I like that little black-eyed girl that's sittin' in front of the cake. Her name is Dolly, 'n I've had a few drinks with her, but she ain't never let nobody do nothin' but talk to her. What about you, Warren? Which one do you like?"

"Hell," Warren replied in a low, rumbling voice that rolled out across the entire dining room. "A whore is a whore, 'n I like 'em all."

"Who are those idiots, Katie?" Pearlie asked.

"I don't know their first names. The one with the beard is Clinton, the one with just the mustache is Reed, and the clean-shaven one is Warren. They work for Atwood."

"Yeah, they would," Pearlie said.

"Hey! If we buy you whores some coffee, will you come over here and drink with us?" Clinton called out.

Sally turned toward Clinton. "May I make an inquiry of you, sir?" she asked.

Clinton was surprised that the woman had spoken to him, even if he didn't know what she had asked.

"What?" he replied. "What is it you are wanting to do?"

"Please forgive me for not wording my question to your level of understanding. What I said was, may I ask you a question?"

"Oh. Yeah, sure, go ahead."

"I would be interested as to which characteristic Atwood most values in his employees. Would it be depravity or retardation?"

Clinton blinked his eyes several times. He had absolutely no idea what Sally had just asked him, but he did have an idea that she had just insulted him. When the others at the birthday table laughed, he knew he had been insulted and he stood up so quickly that the chair turned over and he started to reach for his gun. He stopped in mid-draw when he saw that Sally was pointing a pistol at him.

"You don't really want to carry this any further, do you, Mr. Clinton?" she asked.

Clinton stared at her for a moment longer, then reaching down he righted his chair and, once more, took his seat. Nothing else was heard from them until, about half an hour later, when the three men then left.

With the situation calm again, the celebration continued. That was when Rusty took the broach from his pocket and gave it to Dolly.

"Oh!" Dolly said. "Oh, this is the most beautiful thing I have ever seen. I'll be so proud to wear it!"

"Nobody will see it," Rusty said.

"What do you mean, nobody will see it? Why won't they see it?"

"Because, if you are wearing it, they'll have something even prettier to look at," Rusty said.

Dolly laughed self-consciously. "Rusty, you do say the sweetest things," she said.

* * *

When Willis rode out to Eagle Shire the next day to report what happened, Atwood invited him into the library.

"Who is the man you said Pearlie killed?"

"His name was Lomax," Willis said. "Dingus Lomax. He was a bounty hunter, and he come into town yesterday carryin' one o' them reward posters."

"So, you are tellin' me that all the reward posters on Pearlie haven't been pulled back, are you?"

"We've pulled back the ones that's still in town, but there is just too damn many of them still out that we ain't got back, 'n more'n likely a lot of 'em has done been took by bounty hunters like the one Lomax brung with him when he come into town."

"Did you happen to see Lomax before this happened?"

"Yes, sir, he come by the marshal's office to see what kind of information he could get from me about Pearlie."

"You mean to tell me, Marshal Willis, that a bounty hunter came to see you with one of those reward posters, and you didn't tell him that the posters had all been rescinded?"

"Uh . . . well . . . I thought . . ."

Suddenly, and unexpectedly, Atwood laughed out loud.

"You mean you ain't mad?"

"No, I'm not mad. You did just the right thing," he said. "Like you said, we can't call in all the posters, and if another bounty hunter wants to try Pearlie, or Smoke Jensen, well, who are we to stop him?"

"Yes, sir, that's just what I was thinkin'," Willis said with a relieved grin.

"I knew that Jensen was fast with a gun," Atwood said. "Now it would appear that Kate's brother, Pearlie, is also quite skilled with a pistol. So, even though there may be a lot of posters still out there, we can't depend upon them to get the job done, because if they attempt to face Pearlie or Jensen the result of such an encounter can be predicted."

"So, what do we do next?" Willis asked.

"Step out to the bunkhouse and have Clinton, Reed, and Warren come see me. I'll give them the task of taking care of Smoke Jensen."

"Why are you sending them, Mr. Atwood?" Willis asked, obviously disturbed that Atwood was giving the task to someone else. "What can they do that me 'n Clark can't do?"

"They can get killed," Atwood replied simply. "And right now it's to my advantage to keep you and Clark alive."

Willis frowned for a moment until he realized what Atwood was saying. Then he smiled broadly.

"Yeah," he said. "Yeah, I can see that. I'm all for stayin' alive."

"I thought you might understand," Atwood replied with a condescending smile.

"You wanted to see us, boss?" Warren asked.

"Yes. I understand you three men had an encounter with Smoke Jensen last night."

"Who told you that?" Clinton asked.

"I have ways of keeping track of things that I need to know."

"Yeah, we did. Well, it was more Jensen's wife than it was him."

"Yes, so I heard. She beat you to the draw."

Clinton held up his hand and shook his head. "Now she didn't do no such thing. She already had her gun drawed when she started mouthing off at me."

"Would you be interested in a little revenge?"

"Yeah," Clinton said. "Yeah we would. Or at least, I would."

"Warren? Reed?"

"She didn't pull 'er gun on me or Reed," Warren said.

"So, you have no interest in revenge?"

"Not particular," Reed replied.

"But, if it paid very well for you to help Clinton get his revenge, you might be more interested?"

Warren and Reed glanced toward each other, then smiled.

"Yeah," Warren said. "I think we might be."

"I told you men when I hired you that from time to time I would ask you to take care of a specific job for me. This is such a time. You would be killing two birds with one stone, so to speak. You would be taking care of a job for me, and you would be helping Clinton get his revenge."

"You said something about payin' really well?" Reed said.

"I did indeed, and I will make good on that promise as soon as you handle the job I'm going to give you."

"What do you have in mind?" Warren asked.

"I want you three men to kill Smoke Jensen."

"Smoke Jensen?" Reed asked, the tone of voice in his response showing his nervousness over the prospect.

"Yes, the way I have it planned, you will be killing Jensen and his wife. It should be an easy enough job for you."

"Mr. Atwood, I don't know what you know about this feller Jensen, but I've heard a lot about him," Warren said. "And believe me, from all that I've heard, he ain't all that easy to kill."

"His wife ain't goin' to be all that easy, neither," Reed added, "most especial when you think back on how fast she got that gun out."

Atwood smiled. "Yes, well, what if I told you that you wouldn't have to go up against either one of them? If you take this job, it will be as simple as shooting someone while they are lying in bed, in the middle of the night, sound asleep? Do you think you could handle the job then?"

"Asleep? Where are we going to find them asleep?"

"In their hotel room, tonight," Atwood said.

"How are we supposed to get to them if they're in a hotel room?" Warren asked.

"I will make all the arrangements you need. And I will pay each of you two hundred dollars apiece to do the job."

"Two hunnert dollars, 'n all we have to do is kill him while he's asleep?" Clinton asked.

"Not just him. You are going to have to kill both of them. Do you think you can handle that?"

"What about the law?" Reed asked.

"What law would that be?" Atwood replied. "I

control the city council, the marshal, and the judge. You don't have to worry about the law."

"Yeah, that's right, you do, don't you?" Reed said with a big smile.

"Mr. Atwood, I can tell you right now, you ain't goin' to have to worry none about Smoke Jensen no more after tonight," Warren said.

Atwood gave the men twenty dollars apiece. "Here's a little spending money for you while you're waiting."

CHAPTER TWENTY-SEVEN

"I think Dolly really appreciated her birthday gift from Rusty," Sally said.

"Yes, I think so, too," Smoke said. "I mean, the way she took on about it. Especially when I don't think it was really all that expensive."

"Expensive? What does that have to do with it?" Sally asked.

"Well, I was just talking about how much she seemed to appreciate it, way beyond what it was actually worth."

"Oh, Smoke, for heaven's sake, just how obtuse are you, anyway?" Sally asked.

"Obtuse? What are you talking about, obtuse?"

"It isn't how expensive it is . . . it's that Rusty gave it to her."

"Oh," Smoke replied, then it dawned on him what Sally was actually saying, and he smiled. "Oh," he repeated, mouthing the word this time in a way that showed he really did understand it.

"I'm glad I don't have to explain in minute detail. It renews my faith in you," Sally said.

"I like it that Pearlie has been able to reestablish a relationship with his sister," Smoke said.

"Not only his sister but finding a nephew that he never knew he had," Sally said.

The conversation was taking place in their hotel room. It was too early for bed, so Smoke and Sally were sitting in the two chairs furnished by the room, with a table lantern lighting the distance between them.

"Do Kate and Rusty remind you of Janey and Rebecca?" Sally asked.

Janey was Smoke's sister, and Rebecca was the niece he never knew he had until he discovered her one Christmas.*

"Well, Pearlie finding Rusty does remind me of my finding Rebecca, I suppose," Smoke said. "But if you remember, Janey and I had managed to make contact from time to time before she died, and the contacts weren't always that pleasant."

"I liked Janey," Sally said. "I think that if the situation had been different, the two of you would have gotten along well."†

"Maybe," Smoke admitted.

"Smoke, do you think Atwood is ever going to leave Kate alone?"

"If you mean do I think he will have a change of mind, no, he won't. But it isn't just Kate. He dominates the entire town."

"What do you think is going to happen?"

*A Lone Star Christmas.
†Sally met Janey in *Smoke Jensen, The Beginning*.

"I think Atwood is going to push this town too far," Smoke said. "And when he does, the town is going to fight back."

"Will the town win?"

"Yes," Smoke answered.

A soft breeze came up, lifting the muslin curtains away from the open window.

"Uhmm, the breeze feels good," Sally said.

"Yes, I'll sleep well tonight," Smoke said.

Sally chuckled. "What do you mean, you'll sleep well *tonight*? Smoke Jensen, you sleep well every night. Why, you can sleep outside in the rain. I know that, because I have seen you do it."

"Maybe, but some nights are better than others. Put out the lantern and let's go to bed."

Cal also had a room in the hotel, but Pearlie did not. Kate had an apartment at the back of the Pretty Girl and Happy Cowboy Saloon, and she invited Pearlie to stay in the spare bedroom. On the one hand, Pearlie felt, somewhat, as if he had abandoned Smoke, Sally, and Cal. But on the other hand, he felt good at being able to reestablish a connection with his long estranged sister.

Smoke and Sally might have turned in for the night, but Cal was still at the saloon visiting with Pearlie, Rusty, Dolly, Linda Sue, and Peggy Ann. Linda Sue and Peggy Ann, like Dolly, were part of the Pretty Girls that gave the saloon its name. At the moment, all six were sharing a single table.

"Seems like Smoke and Sally are turnin' in earlier 'n earlier now," Cal said. "They must be getting old."

"Ha!" Pearlie said. "I'd like to see you say that to Miz Sally's face."

"Well, I don't mean old, old," Cal said. "I just mean older than me."

"Honey, seems to me like almost ever'one is older than you," Peggy Ann said.

"Darlin', don't let these boyish good looks fool you," Cal said. "I've been rode hard and put away wet more than a few times."

Peggy Ann laughed. "I'm just foolin' you, honey. I'm sure you've had more than your share of experiences. But, you do have boyish good looks, and that I appreciate." Her words were teasing as she traced her fingers along his cheek.

"Well I'll be damn, Cal, who would have thought it? Peggy Ann just made you blush," Pearlie said with a little laugh.

"No, she didn't."

"Yeah, she did," Rusty said.

"Now quit it! I'm not blushing!" Cal insisted.

"Ya'll quit picking on him now," Peggy Ann said.

"Ahh, I'm not picking on him," Pearlie said. "Cal was just being modest when he said he had been ridden hard and put away wet. He could say more than that. Besides, he's my closest friend and he's saved my bacon more than once."

"I thought Mr. Jensen was your closest friend," Rusty said.

"I suppose that, by definition, you can have only one 'closest' friend," Pearlie said. "But in this case, the dictionary be damned, I have two closest friends."

"Me, too," Cal said.

"How long have you two been cowboyin' for Mr. Jensen?" Linda Sue asked.

"We don't cowboy for him," Pearlie said.

"What? But I thought you did."

"We are full-time riders for the brand," Pearlie explained.

"Isn't that the same thing as cowboying for him?"

Cal shook his head. "Most cowboys are temporary hands. Pearlie and I are not only full-time . . . you might say that we are partners with him."

"Partners? You mean, you and Pearlie own part of the ranch?"

Pearlie laughed. "No, we can't say that. But Cal and I have about a thousand head of livestock that we run on the ranch, along with Smoke's cattle. And he and I also have land claims that run adjacent to the Sugarloaf, and since they are without fences, you can't really tell where Smoke's property ends and ours begins."

The six visited for a while longer, then the three girls, declaring that they had to "earn their pay," excused themselves and began moving through the saloon, visiting, smiling, talking, and laughing with the other patrons.

"I know you two think it's prob'ly wrong for me to like a girl like Dolly," Rusty said. "But no matter what it looks like, she's not a whore. All she does is be nice to people."

"Rusty, there is no need for you to apologize for anything. I once had a, uh, friend like Dolly. Her real name was Julia McKnight, but her working name was Elegant Sue."

"Her working name? You mean she was like Dolly?"

"Yeah, only more so," Cal said.

"By more so you mean . . . ?"

"She really was a whore when I first met her."

"When you found that out, is that when you . . . what I mean, you said you once had a friend like Dolly. I take that to mean that you don't have her anymore."

"No, I don't."

"What happened?"

Cal was silent for a long moment before he answered. "She was killed," he said, the words barely audible.

"She was a sweet girl, Cal," Pearlie said, reaching over to put his hand on his friend's shoulder.

"Oh! Cal, I'm sorry! I didn't mean . . ."

"No apology needed," Cal replied. Then he let a smile replace the melancholy expression on his face. "Well, gents, I think I'll get on back to the hotel," he said. "I'll see you both tomorrow."

When Warren, Clinton, and Reed rode into Etholen that night, they stopped at the Bull and Heifer Saloon. They were met by one of the girls as soon as they stepped inside. The girl, who was known at Cactus Jenny, may have been attractive at one time, but the dissipation of her profession had hardened her features.

"Well, how are you boys tonight?" she said, flashing a smile. The smile disclosed a two-tooth gap, the result of a drunken cowboy. "Which one of you are going to buy me a drink?"

"Why do I have to buy you a drink?" Warren asked. "Seein' as how last time I was here you told me how much you love me."

"Honey, I love all the boys," Cactus Jenny said. "That is, I love 'em as long as they've got the money."

"Tonight, I got the money," Warren said.

Cactus Jenny smiled again.

"Don't smile so much," Warren said. "You can see where you ain't got teeth, 'n that ain't purty."

The smile left her face, replaced with a hurt look. "You say you've got money?"

"Yeah."

"Well then, let's just go upstairs." Cactus Jenny's invitation was even more business-like than usual.

Clinton and Reed watched Warren and the girl go up the stairs, then they turned toward the bartender and ordered a couple of beers.

"How long you reckon he'll be up there?" Clinton asked.

"About two or three minutes," Reed replied, and they both laughed.

"Atwood said he'd give us two hunnert dollars apiece," Clinton said. "You ever had two hunnert dollars before?"

"Not all at one time," Reed admitted.

"I ain't never had that much money, neither. What are you goin' to do with your money?"

"First we got to earn it."

"Hell, how hard can that be? I mean he'll be asleep, so it ain't like we're goin' to be a' callin' 'im out, or anything," Clinton said. "Besides which, if that bitch is lyin' there alongside 'im, I'm goin' to take particular pleasure in shootin' her."

"Shhh!" Reed said. "You want the whole world to know our business? Anyhow, from all I've heard about Smoke Jensen, this ain't the kind of job we want to mess up on. I know that I sure as hell don't want him comin' after me."

"How many men do you reckon Smoke Jensen has kilt?"

"I don't know. Twenty, thirty . . . maybe a lot more'n that," Reed replied.

"If he really has kilt that many, how come he ain't never been put in prison?"

"On account of folks say that ever'one he's kilt was tryin' to kill him."

"Like us, you mean?" Clinton asked.

"Yeah, like us. Well, no, not really like us. They say that he's some kind of a hero, on account of the way he is. They've actual writ books about him, did you know that?"

"No they ain't, you're just spoofin' me. They ain't writ no books about him."

"Yes, they have. I've seen them."

"Wow! You think we'll be famous after we kill 'im?"

"We plan on killin' the son of a bitch while he's a' sleepin', don't we? How's that goin' to make us famous? Besides which, when you kill someone like that, you don't particular want no one to know that you was the one to do it," Clinton said.

"Yeah, I reckon that's right. And I don't care how

good he is with a gun, there ain't nobody that can shoot in their sleep."

"Shh," Clinton said. "Bartender's comin' back this way again."

"You gents 'bout ready for a refill?" the bartender asked.

"We'll tell you when we're ready," Clinton said. "Don't be botherin' us none."

"I'm just trying to be helpful."

"Yeah, well, don't be."

Chagrined, the bartender walked away.

"How much longer you think Warren's goin' to be?" Reed asked.

"I don't know he . . . wait, here he comes now," Clinton answered.

Warren joined the other two at the bar.

"Damn, Muley, you smell like a whore," Reed said.

"Yeah, well I just been with a whore, so what the hell am I s'posed to smell like, roses? Anyhow, that's better 'n smellin' like horse shit, which is what you two smell like," Warren replied with a broad smile.

"How was she?" Clinton asked.

"How was she? Hell, why don't you find out for yourself? It don't cost but two dollars."

"No, thanks. I'll wait till we do this job 'n get the money Atwood's promised us, then I'm goin' to go down to the Pretty Girl 'n get me one of the women that works down there," Clinton said.

"Them women don't do nothin' but sit with you while you drink," Reed reminded them. "They ain't actual whores, 'n they won't none of 'em let you take 'em to bed. Don't you 'member, they was all in the Palace Café?"

"Yeah, I remember, and I also remember how snooty all of 'em was actin'. But I reckon if I offered one of 'em enough money, she'd go to bed with me, all right."

"Ha! As ugly as you are, it'll take a lot of money," Reed teased.

CHAPTER TWENTY-EIGHT

The three men moved from the bar to one of the tables where, for the next hour or so they "spent" the money they were going to get from Atwood.

"I'm goin' to New York," Reed said.

"What are you goin' there for?" Warren asked.

"You ever been around any of them Eastern dudes?" Reed replied. "Hell, you can push 'em around like babies. I figure if I go to New York 'n I've got a little money, it won't be no time a-tall till I got me a gang put together, 'n I can take anythin' I want."

"It'll take a lot more money than a couple hundred dollars if you're plannin' on goin' to New York."

"Well, who knows, I might just pick me up a little more money on the way," Reed said.

"I'm goin' to China," Clinton said. "I used to live in San Francisco, 'n near 'bout all them Chinese women is purty. Just think how many Chinese women there is in China."

"What time is it?" Warren asked.

Clinton pointed to the clock on the wall behind

the bar. "Accordin' to that, it's near onto midnight," he said.

"You think the son of a bitch is asleep yet?" Reed asked.

"I reckon he is," Warren replied. He loosed the pistol in his holster. "What do you say we go get this job done?"

Draining what remained of their beers, the three men left the saloon.

"First thing let's do, let's get our horses took care of," Warren said.

"Hell, can't we just tie 'em off in front of the hotel?" Reed asked. "That way they'll be there when we come out."

"I think we'd be better off leavin' 'em tied off over on Center Street. That'll keep 'em out of sight, 'n we can slip through between the buildings of the hardware store and the feed store. There ain't no light in between the stores, so we can get away real quick."

"What are we gettin' away from?" Reed wanted to know. "Jensen will be dead, 'n the law is on our side."

"I think it would just be better this way," Warren said.

"I agree with Muley," Clinton said.

For now, the three horses were tied in front of the Bull and Heifer Saloon. After they were mounted, Warren, Clinton, and Reed rode as if they were leaving, then once out of town, they doubled back on Center Street, which was one block over. They tied their horses off on a hitching rack that was in front of the apothecary, then came back to Waling Street by passing between the hardware and feed store. As Warren had said, it was very dark between the stores.

"Damn, I can't see nothin' in here," Reed said.

"That's good; it means nobody can't see us, neither," Warren replied.

When they reached the Milner Hotel, they stopped.

"See anyone watchin' us?" Warren asked.

"No, the onliest people that's still up is all in one of the saloons," Clinton said.

As if validating Clinton's comment, a woman's high-pitched squeal, followed by laughter, came from the Pretty Girl and Happy Cowboy.

"All right, let's go in," Warren said.

Low-burning lanterns sat on a table, illuminating the middle of the lobby but leaving the outer edges shrouded in shadow. The lobby was deserted, and the scattering of chairs and sofas that in the daytime were often occupied by guests were now empty.

Walking quietly across the carpet, the three men approached the front desk. The night clerk was sitting in a chair behind the desk. He had his chair tilted back on its rear two legs, leaning against the wall. His chest was rising and falling in rhythm with the snoring, which came in snorts, wheezes, and fluttering lips.

"What room are they in?" Reed asked in a low whisper.

"Atwood said they were in room two ten. That's up on the second floor, nearest the street," Warren replied. "Let's get on up the stairs, but be quiet about it." He pulled his pistol.

With guns drawn, the three men stepped softly back across the carpeted lobby and through the shadows until they reached the foot of the stairs. They were surprised when they reached the second floor, because in contrast to the lobby and stairwell, the hallway was incredibly bright. That was because there were four sconce-mounted kerosene lanterns on both walls, flanking the hallway.

"Let's get these damned lights out!" Warren ordered in a whisper, and Clinton went down one side of the hall and Reed the other side, snuffing out the lanterns one at a time. The hallway grew progressively dimmer as each of the kerosene lanterns was extinguished.

Sally had no idea what woke her up. One minute she was sleeping soundly, and the next minute she was wide awake, and alert. She had the strangest foreboding of danger, a sense that someone was close by, though there was nothing immediate to suggest that. Nevertheless, as she lay in bed she continued to experience a sense of unease. She looked toward the door, where she saw a narrow bar of light that slipped in under the crack. Had it actually dimmed slightly, or was this her imagination?

As she continued to stare at the light bar under the door, she realized that it wasn't merely an illusion, the light was progressively fading.

"Smoke!" she whispered. "Smoke, something is wrong!"

Smoke was awake instantly. "What is it?" he asked.

"I'm not sure."

Smoke needed no further explanation. Sally's intuition was enough.

"Out of bed!" he ordered quietly, and Sally reacted quickly. When Sally saw Smoke putting a pillow under the bed sheet, she did the same thing. She grabbed a housecoat, and when Smoke pulled his pistol from the holster that hung from the head of the bed, she drew her own gun.

Smoke moved quietly to the already open window, then raised it high enough so he and Sally could step through it. Their room opened onto the front of the hotel, and just below the window was the roof that covered the entry porch below.

"Out here," Smoke said, and after helping Sally through the window, he followed her out onto the roof.

"We should have slept out here," Sally said quietly and with an easy smile. "It's a lot cooler."

"Come on!" Warren said in a loud hiss. "That's his door down there!"

The three men moved silently through the now dark corridor toward the front end of the hallway.

"Are you sure his wife is goin' to be with 'im?" Clinton asked.

"Yeah, that's what Atwood said."

"Good. When the shootin' starts, she's mine. I'll show that bitch to pull a gun on me."

The conversation had been carried on in a very low voice as the three men made their way toward the room that had been identified as the room occupied by their targets. Now they were standing in front of a door to which had been attached, in white-painted tin numbers, 210.

"Shall we break it in?" Reed asked.

"No need for that," Warren said.

"How we goin' to get in?"

"Atwood not only give us the room number, he also give us the key," Warren said, holding it up for the others to see.

"How the hell did he get the key?" Reed asked.

"We're talking about Atwood, remember? He can get anything he wants."

Warren slipped the key into the keyhole, then turned it. It moved the tumblers, but as they were tripped they made a clicking sound that seemed considerably louder than any of them had expected. Startled, the three men stepped to either side of the door, staying there for a long moment to see if there was any reaction.

There was none.

"He must not have heard nothin'," Warren said, and reaching out to the cut-glass knob he turned it and, slowly, swung the door open. To his relief, it opened quietly.

"You two go in first," Warren ordered, making a motion with his hand. It didn't actually occur to the other two that by so doing, Warren was putting them in harm's way before he submitted himself to any possible reaction from someone who might be waiting just inside the room.

The room was slightly brighter than the hallway because of the pale moonlight that fell in through the open window. That allowed them to see the two mounds under the bedclothes, as well as a hat that was hanging from the brass bedpost.

"There's his hat," Warren whispered. "That means he's here."

"Of course he's here, I can see 'im in the bed," Clinton replied, pointing to the two covered mounds.

On a chair, near the bed, there was a dress.

"Look at that!" Reed said excitedly, pointing to the dress. "Damn, I'll bet she's nekkid!"

"Quiet, you fool! You want to wake them?" Warren said. He aimed at the bed.

"Now!" he shouted as he pulled the trigger. The other two began firing as well, and for a moment, all three guns were firing, lighting up the darkness with white flashes and filling the room with thunder.

In his room at the far end of the hall, Cal suddenly sat up in his bed. Those gunshots were coming from this very floor, and they were coming from the other end of the hall. Could they be coming from Smoke and Sally's room?

Cal reached for his pistol.

After firing three shots apiece, Warren called out to the other two men. "Stop your shootin'!" he shouted. "We've made enough noise to wake the dead, 'n the whole town is goin' to be comin' up here in a minute. We got to get out of here," he said. "Clinton, you check on 'em, 'n make sure that both of 'em is dead."

Clinton walked over to the bed and felt around, then gasped in surprise.

"Son of a bitch!" he shouted. "Muley, there ain't nobody here!"

"What? What do you mean there ain't nobody

there? If they ain't there in the bed, then where in the hell are they?"

"We thought we'd sleep out here tonight. I mean, it is a lot cooler," Smoke said. He was standing on the porch roof just outside his window, his large frame back-lit by the ambient light of the streetlamps.

"Son of a bitch! He ain't dead!" Reed shouted.

"Shoot 'im, shoot 'im!" Warren yelled.

With shouts of frustrated rage and fear, all three would-be assassins turned their guns toward the window and began firing. Bullets crashed through the window, sending large shards of glass out onto the porch roof. They found no target though, because Smoke had jumped to one side of the window as soon as he spoke, and by so doing was able to avoid the initial fusillade. The outside walls of the hotel building were of brick construction, so shooting into the wall beside the window would have been an exercise in futility.

After the first volley, Smoke leaned around and fired through the window. One of the would-be assassins went down as he stumbled backward into the hallway.

"Clinton! He shot Warren!" someone said.

"Come on, Reed! Let's get the hell out of here!" a second voice replied.

Cal had taken time to slip on his trousers before leaving his room and was moving up the hallway as quickly as he could. Although the hall lanterns had been extinguished, several of the doors had been opened, and the occupants were standing in the open door of their rooms. Some of them were holding lit lanterns, which cast enough light out into the hall for Cal to see his way.

"What is it?" one of the men asked.

"What's going on?" another questioned.

Cal saw two shadowy forms darting down the stairs, and he gave a passing thought to going after them, but frightened for Smoke and Sally, decided to check on their condition first.

When the remaining two men left the room, Smoke started to climb back through the window.

"Smoke, wait!" Sally called out to him. "You know they'll be coming out through the front door of the hotel."

"Yeah!" Smoke said with a chuckle. "Yeah, you're right."

"Smoke!" Cal shouted.

"We're out here, on the roof, Cal!" Smoke replied.

Cal hurried through the room to the window.

"Cal, watch your feet," Sally cautioned. "There's glass everywhere."

Carefully, because he was barefooted, Cal picked his way through the broken glass, then stepped out onto the edge of the porch. He no sooner got there, when two men ran out into the street.

"Hold it right there!" Smoke called down to them.

One of the men turned and fired, the bullet whizzing by Smoke's ear, much closer than he would have liked.

Smoke, Sally, and Cal returned fire, all three of

them shooting at the same time, and the shooter went down.

The remaining gunman darted across the street and disappeared into the darkness between two buildings on the other side.

Smoke stepped to the edge of the porch, preparatory to jumping down into the street.

"Smoke, wait! You're wearing your underwear!" Sally said.

"Yeah," Smoke replied with a chuckle. "I suppose I am at that."

By now others in the town had begun to react to the shooting. Several men came out of the two saloons, and a few even came out from the houses that fronted Waling Street.

In addition to the few hotel guests Cal had seen during his traverse of the hall, others had been awakened as well, and now several of them were gathered in the hallway, asking questions.

"What was all the shootin'?"

"What happened to the hallway lights?"

"Good Lord! There's a body lyin' right here on the floor!"

Smoke knew that someone from the law would be here shortly, so he pulled on his trousers and boots, then put on a shirt. Sally took the dress from the chair and slipped it on as well so that, dressed, Smoke and Sally joined as many as a dozen of the hotel patrons out in the hall, where the lanterns closest to Smoke's room had now been relit. Cal, who had been wearing only trousers, borrowed one of Smoke's shirts before he, also, stepped out into the hall.

"Well now," Cal said. "Look here. This is one of the men who was giving us trouble last night."

"Smoke, you don't think they came here because I . . ." she was about to say because she drew on them, but Smoke held up his hand to stop her.

"No," he said. "I don't think that had anything to do with it at all."

CHAPTER TWENTY-NINE

"What happened here?" the hotel clerk asked. "What was all the . . . oh, my goodness! Is that man dead?"

"Deader 'n a doornail he is, 'cause I just checked," one of the hotel guests replied to the question.

"Who is it? Does anyone know?"

"His name is Warren," Smoke replied.

"Make way! Make way! You folks get out of the way!" an authoritative voice was shouting as he came up the stairs. Deputy Clark pushed his way through the others until he reached the body.

"I'll be damn! This is Muley Warren," he said. "And the one lyin' dead down there in the street is Danny Reed."

"You know both of them, do you, Deputy?" the hotel clerk asked.

"Yes, I know 'em. They both ride for . . . that is, they rode for Mr. Atwood, out at the Eagle Shire Ranch. They don't ride none for 'em now, seein' as they're both dead."

"If they both rode for Atwood, what do you suppose they were doing here, in the hotel?" Smoke asked.

"I don't know what they was doin' here. Who kilt 'im, anyway?"

"I did."

"Damn, Jensen, that makes the fourth man you've kilt since you've been here. Pardeen, Critchlow, and Conroy. And one of them fellas that come with you, the one called Pearlie? Why, he kilt one, too."

"Actually, I've killed five," Smoke said dispassionately. "Don't forget the one that's lying out in the street. I killed Reed as well."

"Wait a minute, Smoke," Sally said. "If there are two bullets in him, one of them is mine."

"I was shooting, too, don't forget," Cal added.

Smoke chuckled. "I guess that's right."

"So you might say all three of us killed him," Sally said.

"What did you kill 'em for?" Clark asked.

"Come in here, and I'll show you," Smoke invited.

Clark followed Smoke, Sally, and Cal into the room, where Smoke showed the deputy the bullet holes in his bed.

"We killed them because they came into our room and tried to kill us," Smoke said. "We're sort of funny that way."

"Wait a minute, if they come in here 'n put these bullet holes in your bed, how come you two wasn't kilt?"

"Yes, that has to be disappointing to Atwood, doesn't it?" Smoke asked.

"What do you mean, disappointin' to Mr. Atwood?"

"You did say that these two men worked for Atwood, didn't you?"

"Yes, but . . ."

"I believe Atwood sent them here to kill me. And not just me, but my wife as well."

"Or maybe you was just finishin' the job you started last night," a new voice said. This was Marshal Willis, who had just arrived.

"What are you talking about?" Smoke asked.

"I was told you got into it with these three men last night."

"These *three* men?" Smoke asked.

"Yes. Wasn't all three of 'em at the Palace Café last night?" Willis pointed to Sally. "And didn't you pull a gun on 'em for no reason at all?"

"What three men would that be, Marshal?" Smoke asked. "There are only two men that I can see. Warren, here, and Reed, who is laying out in the street."

"Well, yes, but . . ." Willis stammered.

"You think there were three men who came to kill us?"

"Well maybe it was just these two," Willis said. "Thing is, they was three of 'em last night and I just sorta thought that . . . uh, maybe all three of 'em come in town together."

"To kill my wife and me," Smoke said.

"Uh, listen, you ain't goin' to leave town, are you?" Willis asked. "I'm goin' to need to investigate this."

"You don't have to worry about me leaving town, Marshal. I'm not going anywhere until this business with Atwood is settled."

"Settled? What do you mean, settled?"

"Settled," Smoke said, repeating the word without further amplification.

* * *

From the *Etholen Standard:*

ATTEMPTED MURDER THWARTED

Last night, as Mr. and Mrs. Smoke Jensen lay peacefully sleeping in their bed at the Milner Hotel, three brigands gained access to their room in the middle of the night. Once in the room the three men began shooting into the bed where they believed Mr. and Mrs. Jensen to be. Their nefarious scheme was foiled, however, because the Jensens, sensing not only their presence but their evil intent, managed to step out onto the porch roof, their room being at the front of the hotel, thus allowing their egress.

In the exchange of gunfire that transpired, two of the three attackers were killed, their names being Muley Warren and Danny Reed. The identity of the third man is unknown.

Reed and Warren were both in the employ of Silas Atwood, as was Jeb Calley, who readers will remember attempted to kill Rusty Abernathy. Marshal Bo Willis and Deputy Clark were also once employees of Silas Atwood, and one can't help but think that, though they are supposed to be servants of the public, they are still at the beck and call of their former employer. No villain in literature has visited as much evil upon others as Silas Atwood has upon our fair community.

"My name is in the newspaper this morning," Smoke said as he and Sally ate their breakfast. "I'm famous."

"Oh, for heaven's sake, Smoke, you have more than a dozen books written about you. You are already famous, so you don't need a story in a newspaper to make you famous."

"But you're famous, too, now," Smoke said. "Your name is in here as well."

"Let me see it," Sally said, reaching for the paper.

Smoke pulled the paper back from her. "Ha! Good to see that you have a little vanity."

"Give me the paper," Sally said again, grabbing it from him.

"'The two were having breakfast at the Palace Café. They had invited Cal, but he decided to have breakfast with Pearlie and Rusty.'

"Wow, he really is letting Atwood have it, isn't he?" Sally said when she finished the article.

"He hasn't printed anything about him that isn't true," Smoke replied. "This town is suffering under him."

"I just hope he doesn't wind up with his newspaper office damaged again. This time could be worse than the other time," Sally said.

"I've got a feeling that Mr. Blanton is not the kind of man who would let a little intimidation cause him to back away from printing the truth."

Of the three men who had gone into town to kill Smoke Jensen, only Tony Clinton returned to the Eagle Shire Ranch, and now, as Smoke and Sally were having their breakfast, Clinton was standing in the parlor of Atwood's house, nervously rolling his hat in his hands as he reported their failure to his boss.

"Let me understand this," Atwood said. "There were three of you. You attacked Smoke Jensen in the middle of the night, and you not only didn't kill him, but he, while asleep in his bed, managed to kill Warren and Reed?"

"That's just it, Mr. Atwood, he warn't in his bed. Him 'n his woman was outside, standin' on the roof of the porch, 'n when we went into his room, why they commenced a' shootin'."

"Still, there were three of you, which made the odds three to one."

"No, sir. They was three of 'em, too."

"Three?"

"Well, not at first. They was only Jensen 'n his wife at first, 'n both of them was shootin'. But by the time me 'n Reed got outside, they was three of 'em, 'cause another man had come out on the porch, 'n he was shootin', too. Me 'n Reed was outnumbered then, 'n when they kilt Reed, well, sir, I was bad outnumbered. Seemed to me like the best thing for me to do was get away, so's I could come back here 'n tell you what happened."

"If this happened last night, why are you just now telling me?"

Clinton didn't tell him when he first returned, because he was afraid to tell him.

"Well, I, uh, didn't want to wake you up, it bein' in the middle of the night 'n all."

"Well, I didn't need you to tell me what happened,

anyway," Atwood said. "Something like this, everybody in town will soon know, and it would get back to me."

"Does this mean I ain't goin' to get none of that money you was talkin' about?"

"Did you kill him, Clinton?" Atwood asked challengingly.

"Why no, sir, we didn't kill him. It's like I told you, he wound up killin' Warren and Reed instead."

"Then what makes you think I would give you anything? I've a good notion to take back the twenty dollars I did give you. The only way you can get the money I promised is by doing the job I asked. Would you like to go into town and try again?"

"No, sir, I wouldn't like that a-tall," Clinton said.

"I didn't think you would. But it makes me wonder, just what in the hell is it going to take to kill Smoke Jensen?" Atwood asked.

Slim wasn't proud to be riding for the Eagle Shire, and he knew that some of the other cowboys weren't, either. Most of them, that is, the real cowboys, had ridden for legitimate spreads before. It may have been that, from time to time they might have put a running brand on a few new calves that didn't exactly belong to the spread, or thrown an occasional long rope . . . but none of them had ever before worked for a man who was as ruthless as Silas Atwood. But they felt they had no choice. Atwood was so successful in his ruthlessness . . . that there was no place else for them to work, unless they left West Texas entirely.

Slim had seen Warren, Clinton, and Reed leave

last night, but this morning only Clinton seemed to be around. He wondered what happened to the other two men, but there was no way he was going to ask Clinton. Slim tended to avoid the men who lived in the special bunkhouse as much as he could. He wasn't sure what they did, and not long after he came to work at Eagle Shire, he asked some of the older hands about the mysterious group of men who occupied the other bunkhouse. It appeared to him that they did nothing for their pay, but he was told that it would be better if he didn't ask questions.

He was working on the windmill when he saw Bo Willis come riding up. Until very recently, Willis had been one of the men who lived in the special bunkhouse, but now he was the new marshal in town. Slim couldn't help but wonder how Willis had ever gotten the job. Slim's idea of a lawman was someone who looked out for the people, and from what he knew of Willis, the new man didn't give a damn about the people.

"Did Clinton come back here, or did he run off?" Willis asked.

"He came back," Atwood said.

"I wasn't sure he would, after what happened last night. I reckon he told you."

"Yes."

"Jensen kilt Warren and Reed."

Atwood had answered in the affirmative, but Willis didn't want to be denied the pleasure of telling him specifically.

"Yes, sir, he kilt Warren just outside his hotel room,

'n he shot Reed after Reed run out of the hotel 'n was already down on the street. Shot 'im from his hotel room, he did."

"Clinton said there were three of them shooting at him and Reed."

"Yeah, they was. Jensen, his wife, 'n one of them two fellers that come to town with 'em."

"His wife was one of the shooters?"

Willis nodded. "I expect she's right good with a gun. From what I heard, when Clinton 'n the others started raggin' on them whores from the Pretty Girl Saloon, why, Jensen's wife draw'd her gun quicker 'n Clinton did."

"So, what you are saying is it isn't just Jensen and Pearlie we have to worry about. It's four of 'em."

"Yeah. Well, I don't know how good the youngest one is, the one they call Cal. But turns out he was one of the ones shootin' last night."

"I expect he is about as good as the others."

"Yes, sir, I expect so, too."

"You know what I think?" Atwood asked. "I think you need some more deputies."

"What do you mean, I need more? Witherspoon never had but one deputy."

"Yes, but Witherspoon didn't have three, and maybe four gunmen to deal with. And Witherspoon wasn't collecting the special taxes."

"What special taxes?"

"The special taxes we'll need so I can pay you and your new deputies more money."

Willis smiled. "I like the idea of more money," he said. "But I don't understand what kind of special taxes you're talkin' about."

"We'll call it the Law Enforcement Capitalization tax. I'll have the city council put on the new tax for the protection of the citizens of Etholen. It will apply to all the citizens in the town in order to pay all the extra deputies you're going to put on," Atwood said. He smiled. "And you'll need the extra deputies to collect the taxes."

"Do you think the city council will go along with this new tax?"

"Of course they will, when they learn that the new taxes will allow the council members to be compensated for their service to the community."

Willis laughed. "Yeah," he said. "Yeah, I can see where they might go along with that."

"When you go back into town, I want you to take Booker, Sanders, Creech, and Walker with you. That will give you five full-time deputies, and if it actually comes to a showdown, I'll provide you with some additional support."

"I'm pretty sure the six us will be able to handle just about anything that pops up," Willis said confidently.

CHAPTER THIRTY

"All right, Willis, you called for a meeting of the city council," Mayor Joe Cravens said, when Willis, Mayor Cravens, and the five members of the city council were gathered in the city hall. "What do you want?"

"One of the first things I realized, after becoming marshal, was the need for deputies," Willis said.

"What do you mean, a need for deputies? You've got Clark," Mayor Cravens said.

Willis shook his head. "Just havin' Clark ain't enough. Maybe you ain't noticed it, but what with all the killin' that's been happenin' lately, why we practically got us a war goin' on here in town. It started with Rusty Abernathy killin' Jeb Calley. Then, his mama helped him escape. Then, the next thing you know Smoke Jensen come into town with Kate Abernathy's brother, 'n since they come to town, why they's been a lot more that was kilt, even Deputy Calhoun and Marshal Witherspoon."

"What the hell, Willis? You are the one who killed Witherspoon," Cravens said.

"Yes, 'n that's what I'm talkin' about. You might 'member that I kilt Witherspoon right after he kilt Calhoun, 'n with him still shootin' 'n all, why who knows who else he woulda kilt? 'N don't forget, Kate's brother was already wanted afore he even got here."

"It is my understanding that he was tried and found not guilty," Cravens said. "That means he is no longer wanted."

"Yeah, well, whether he's wanted or not, that didn't stop the killin', did it?" Willis said. "Two of 'em was kilt just last night. Smoke Jensen, his wife, and one o' them two fellers who come to town with 'im, shot 'n kilt Muley Warren 'n Danny Reed."

"After they broke into Mr. and Mrs. Jensen's room and tried to kill them," Cravens said.

"Could be. But even that proves my point," Willis said. "It's just that much more shootin'. Which is why we need to raise taxes so's I can put on more deputies."

"Raise taxes? Why, don't be silly, Willis. You know the town would never put up with having their taxes raised," Cravens said.

"It don't matter whether the town is willing to put up with it or not," Willis said. "The town don't have nothin' to say about it. All it needs is a vote by the city council to pass it."

Mayor Cravens sighed, then looked at Jay Kinder, who was Speaker of the City Council.

"I've got an idea that you are going to pass it," he said.

Kinder smiled. "And there's nothing you can do about it."

* * *

The first place to feel the manifestation of the new taxes was the railroad depot. Booker and Creech, two of the new deputies, set up a table in the waiting room of the depot, charged with the task of collecting a "visitor's tax" from all the arrivals.

"Visitor's tax? Why, I've never heard of such a thing," an arriving salesman said. "I travel to towns all over West Texas, and nobody has ever asked me to pay a visitor's tax before."

"Well, it's the law here in Etholen," Booker said. "And you'll either pay it or get on the train and go on to the next stop."

"How much is it?" the drummer asked.

"The town charges visitors a tax of a dollar a day as long as you are in town."

"All right," the salesman said. "I've got too many good customers in town not to call on them. I'll pay it. I don't like it, but I'll pay it."

"You!" Creech called to a passenger who walked on by the table without stopping. "Get over here! We haven't collected the visitor's tax from you yet."

"What do you mean, visitor's tax? My name is Ron Gelbman, and I live here. I own Gelbman's Department Store and I have lived here for as long as the town has been here. I'm just coming back home from a business trip."

"Then you're lucky," Creech said. "You only have to pay the tax for one day. Iffen you was just visitin', you'd have to pay a tax for ever'day you're in town."

"This is outrageous," Gelbman said as he paid the dollar fee.

Very quickly, the rest of the town learned that the taxes weren't limited to the visitors. The new taxes had an impact on everyone, sales taxes upon purchases, operating taxes on businesses, service taxes on people who provided services, from doctors to blacksmiths, and from lawyers to whores.

That same morning, one of the deputies came into the Pretty Girl and Happy Cowboy Saloon. Seeing Cal sitting at a table with Rusty, the deputy walked back to them.

"You ain't a resident of this town, are you?" the deputy asked.

"No, I'm not, but I'm sure you already know that," Cal replied.

"What are you doin' here, in Etholen?"

"I thought everybody knew by now, Mr. Booker. This is a friend of my uncle, and they are visiting my mother and me," Rusty said.

"That would be Deputy Booker. So, what you're sayin' is, he is a visitor."

"Yes, I just told you, he is visiting my mother and me. But why is this any concern of yours?" Rusty asked.

Booker pointed a finger at him. "Now, don't you go gettin' smart with me, boy. I'll throw you back in jail for mouthin' off at a deputy."

"Are you aware of the First Amendment, Deputy?" Cal asked.

"The first what?"

"The First Amendment to the Constitution. It guarantees all Americans the right of free speech.

That means that Rusty can say anything he wants to you, short of a physical threat, and you have no authority to put him in jail."

"Yeah, well, he ain't the one I'm concerned about anyhow. You're the one I'm concerned about. On account of because I don't believe you have paid your visitor's tax."

"My what?"

"Your visitor's tax," Booker repeated.

"What visitor's tax?" Rusty said. "I've never heard anything about a visitor's tax."

"That's 'cause it's a brand-new tax that the city council just put on today. We're collectin' from ever' man that visits the town. It's called the Law Enforcement Capitalization tax."

"How much is this visitor's tax?" Cal asked.

"It's a dollar a day, for ever'day you're here," Booker said. "Now, hand it over."

"You know what? I don't think there is any such thing as a visitor's tax."

Booker pulled his gun and, cocking it, pointed it at Cal. "You'll pay the dollar now, or I'll shoot you dead and take it from you."

"You'd shoot a man for a dollar?" Cal asked.

"It ain't just the dollar. It's the law," the deputy replied.

"Why do you suppose it is that I have the feeling you haven't always been such a stickler for the law?" Cal asked.

"It don't matter none whether I have or I haven't. Right now I'm a deputy city marshal, 'n I'm askin' you, polite like, to pay the taxes you owe."

"Polite like? Asking somebody at the point of a

gun doesn't seem all that polite to me," Cal said. "But here's my dollar."

Booker took the dollar.

"Do I get a receipt?"

"What do you need a receipt for?"

"Suppose one of the other deputies approaches me and asks for a dollar? If I just told them I had already paid it, they might not believe me. So, I'd like a receipt."

"Yeah, all right, I'll write you out a receipt."

"Where are them other two?" Booker asked as he handed the receipt to Cal.

"What other two?"

"You know what two. The ones that come with you, Jensen and Kate's brother."

"They aren't in town right now."

"Where did they go?"

"It's such a nice day, I think they just decided to take a ride through the country."

"When they come back, you tell 'em they owe me a dollar apiece."

"They owe you a dollar?" Cal asked. "And here I thought the tax was going to the town."

"You just tell 'em," Booker said gruffly as he left.

"Who are you?" the rancher asked suspiciously, as he stood on the front porch of his small house, holding a shotgun. Smoke could see the anxious face of a woman, and a child, through the front window.

"Mr. Barnes, my name is Smoke Jensen. This is Pearlie Fontaine. Joe Cravens suggested that we come talk to you."

"Talk to me about what?"

"So far you've managed to resist having your ranch taken over by Silas Atwood."

"If you're here to make me another one of those offers to buy my ranch, you can just forget about it," Barnes said resolutely. "It ain't for sale!"

"You don't understand, Mr. Barnes. We aren't here to take your ranch. We're here to help you keep it."

In the office of the *Standard*, Allen Blanton learned quickly that his business was no different from all the other businesses in town when he was assessed five dollars for every issue he published. Unlike the other businesses in town, though, Blanton published a newspaper, which gave him a voice, and he was using it.

After he finished setting the type, he leaned back to read it. Because he could read backward as easily as he could forward, he smiled as he read the opening paragraph of his editorial, to which he had added a title reminiscent of an earlier time in the nation's history.

TAXATION WITHOUT REPRESENTATION

Our forefathers fought a war of revolution against the British because they insisted upon taxing the colonies without giving the colonies any say in their own fate.

Unfortunately the people of Etholen are now facing the same thing because Atwood's bought and paid-for city council, in a closed hearing, which by its

> very nature prevented the attendance of our citizens, enacted a series of draconian taxes. That is, by any definition, taxation without representation.
>
> These taxes, once they are fully implemented, cannot help but have a most deleterious effect on the economy of our fair community.

Blanton stroked his chin. Was "draconian" the correct word? Yes, he was sure of it. But would all his readers understand it?

He reached for the word to remove it, then had second thoughts. He smiled. Let them learn a new word.

Suddenly there was the crashing sound of glass being broken in his front window, and looking around in fright, he saw a brick lying on the floor. There was a note tied to the brick, but before he picked it up, he stuck his head out the front door and looked around in an attempt to see who had done this.

He saw nobody.

Stepping back inside, he removed the note.

We are watching you.

"This is all it says?" Willis asked after reading the note that Blanton had brought to him. "Just, 'we are watching you'?"

"Yes."

"Nobody said anything to you?"

"No. I didn't even see anyone," Blanton said. "I

was about ready to start my print run when the brick crashed through the window."

"If you didn't speak to anyone, or even see anyone, how do you expect me to help you?"

"I don't know, but you're the marshal. Who should I ask to look into it for me? The doctor?"

Failing to catch the sarcasm, Willis handed the note back to the editor of the *Standard*.

"There's nothing I can do. I don't even know why you came to me."

"Neither do I," Blanton said, and again Willis missed the sarcasm.

CHAPTER THIRTY-ONE

It was just before noon, and business was slow in the Pretty Girl and Happy Cowboy Saloon, with only one man standing at the bar and nursing a beer. Peterson was behind the bar, polishing glasses, not because they needed it, but because he was wont to stand there and do nothing. None of the girls were working yet, and the only other people in the saloon at the moment were Cal, Rusty, and Kate, who were sharing a table.

"It was bad enough when Atwood had Witherspoon and Calhoun to run roughshod over us, but now he's got an entire army to do his bidding for him."

"Well, to be fair, Mom, Deputy Calhoun wasn't all that bad."

"I know but he had his hands tied so that, even when he wasn't drunk, which was most of the time, there wasn't much he could do for us."

"These taxes may turn out to be a good thing, though," Cal said.

"What?" Kate asked, surprised by the remark.

"What do you mean? How could anything good come from these taxes?"

"It might be just the thing needed for the town to fight back," Cal said.

Kate nodded. "Yes," she said. "You might be right."

"Say, Rusty, what do you say we go down to the Palace Café and have a good lunch?" Cal suggested. He glanced across the table at Kate. "Of course, that invitation includes you as well, Miz Kate."

Kate smiled. "No, I'd just be a fifth wheel, I'm afraid. You two go on, have a good meal, and enjoy yourselves. And tell Sue Ellen I send my regards, will you?"

"Yes, ma'am," Rusty said.

"There are four ranchers who haven't given in to Atwood," Rusty said. "Jim Barnes, Burt Rowe, Bill Lewis, and Tom Allen. I don't know how much longer they're going to be able to hold him off, though."

"Smoke and Pearlie are out talking to them now," Cal said. "I think once they know they have someone like Smoke on their side, that'll give them all the resolve they need."

"I've never met anyone like Mr. Jensen," Rusty said.

Cal smiled. "That's because there isn't anyone like Smoke Jensen."

The two were just finishing their lunch at the Palace Café when Sue Ellen came over to the table to visit with them.

"We made apple pie today, boys," Sue Ellen said. "Would you like a piece?"

"I'll say!" Cal replied. "With a piece of cheese on top, if you don't mind."

"Cheese, on apple pie?" Rusty said.

"You mean you've never tried it?"

"No."

"Miss Sue Ellen, put a slice of cheese on his pie as well," Cal said.

"What if I don't like it?" Rusty asked.

"Don't worry. If you don't like it, it won't go to waste. I'll just eat it for you," Cal offered.

Sue Ellen laughed. "Careful, Rusty, it may be that he's just setting you up so he can eat your pie, as well as his own."

"Ha! That won't happen," Rusty said.

A few minutes later the pie was delivered, and from the beginning, there was no question but that Rusty would eat it. He did so with relish, complimenting Cal on the suggestion and swearing that from now on, he would eat every piece of apple pie in just such a way.

They had just finished their pie when two of Willis's deputies came into the restaurant. Sue Ellen started toward them.

"Deputies Creech and Walker, can I help you gentlemen?"

"We've come to collect the tax," Creech said.

"Tax? What do you mean you are here to collect the tax? All my taxes are paid."

"We're talking about the new tax."

"A new tax? What is the tax for?"

"It's the Law Enforcement Capitalization tax," one of the deputies said. "You see, the town has added more lawmen for the protection of the citizens, 'n we're havin' to raise taxes to pay for it. Are you sayin' you ain't even heard of the new taxes?"

"Well, yes, I had heard that the taxes would be increased, but I assumed that would be from an addition to the sales and business taxes. I had no idea anyone would be coming around to ask for a direct payment. How much is this new tax?"

"It's ten dollars a week."

"Ten dollars a week?" Sue Ellen gasped in shock. "Why, that is insane! That would more than double the taxes I already pay. There is no way my restaurant can make enough to pay that kind of money!"

"Are you saying you aren't going to pay the taxes?" one of them asked gruffly.

"It's not so much that I won't pay them, as it is I can't pay them," Sue Ellen replied.

"You'll either pay the tax, or you're going to jail," the deputy said, reaching out to grab her.

"Let me go!"

"Let her go," Cal said.

"You stay out of this, cowboy. This woman is in debt, and what I do to her ain't none of your concern."

"You can't put someone in prison for debt."

"Who says I can't?"

"The Constitution says you can't. It's against the law."

"You know about the Constitution, do you?"

"I know enough to know that you can't put someone into prison for debt," Cal said. "Miz Sally taught me that."

"Yeah? Well, all I know is that Judge Boykin sent us

to collect the money, or put her in jail, one or the other, and that's what I intend to do."

"Which one are you? Creech, or Walker?"

"Creech, but that would be Deputy Creech to you, cowboy. Who are you?"

"The name is Wood. Cal Wood."

"You're one of them that come with Smoke Jensen, ain't you?"

"Yes, I work for Smoke Jensen, and I consider him a good friend."

"You folks have caused nothin' but trouble ever since you got here," Creech said.

"Deputy Creech, I believe you said that you have come for ten dollars?" Cal said. He took a ten-dollar bill from his wallet and held it up. "Well, here it is."

"It don't do no good for you to pay it. It's got to come from her," Creech said.

"It will be coming from her. Miss Sue Ellen, this is for the dinner my friend and I just had."

"Wait a minute, you're givin' her ten dollars? I know damn well there ain't no meal served in here that cost that much," Creech said.

"It was a very good meal, wasn't it, Rusty?" Cal asked.

"It was a very good meal. Especially the pie," Rusty answered. "Miss Sue Ellen, here's my ten dollars as well."

"I don't know what's goin' on here, but I don't like it," Creech said.

"It doesn't matter whether you like it or not," Cal replied. "You came here to collect a tax, didn't you? Well, here it is."

Sue Ellen came over to retrieve the money from

Cal and Rusty, forming a silent "thank you" with her lips.

"Now, give these men their ten dollars, Miss Sue Ellen, so they can be on their way."

Sue Ellen walked back to where the two deputies were standing, and she held out a ten-dollar bill toward Creech.

"Here is your blood money," she said.

Creech started to reach for the money with his right hand, but he lowered his right hand and held his left out toward Sue Ellen. It was that gesture, using his left hand, and lowering his right hand so that it hovered just over his pistol, that put Cal on the alert. Suddenly, Creech gave Sue Ellen a shove, as his right hand dipped down to his side to draw his pistol.

Creech had a broad smile on his face, thinking he had put one over on Cal, but that smile left when he saw that Cal had beaten him to the draw. Both pistols fired at the same time, but Cal's bullet found its mark. Creech's didn't.

Creech collapsed to the floor, took a couple of gasping breaths, then died. Cal swung his pistol toward Walker.

"Hold it! Hold it!" Walker shouted, stretching his empty hands out toward Cal. "I ain't goin' for my gun!"

The shooting had happened so fast that none of the diners had had time to react. There were nine others in the restaurant, and they had been watching all the talk about the taxes, but when the shooting started, all were still sitting at their tables, shocked at the sudden turn of events.

"You . . . you're goin' to go to jail! You shot a deputy!" Walker said, pointing at Cal.

"Creech drew first, Walker, and you know it," one of the diners said.

"We all know it," another added.

"You wait till Willis hears about this. You'll be goin' to jail, 'n that's for sure," Walker said.

"Go get 'im. I'll wait here," Cal said.

"We'll all wait here," a third diner said.

Walker left at a dead run.

"Oh!" Sue Ellen said, putting her hand to her mouth. "This is all my fault!"

"Nonsense," Cal said. "They came in here to demand a tax . . . a tax which you paid, regardless of whether it was fair or not. Anyway, I'm the one who killed him, so I'm the one at fault."

"You aren't at fault, young man," one of the other diners said. "Everyone in here saw what happened."

"Yeah," another said. "Creech drew on you and he didn't leave you any choice."

At that moment Walker returned with Marshal Willis.

"He's the one, Marshal," Walker said, pointing to Cal. "He shot Creech down while Creech warn't doin' nothin' no more'n collectin' the tax like we was told to do."

"You're under arrest for murder!" Willis said to Cal.

"It wasn't murder, it was self-defense. He drew on me," Cal replied.

"He's telling the truth, Marshal," Sue Ellen said. "I was in the process of paying the tax when Mr. Creech shoved me, rather violently I might add, to one side and drew his pistol. This gentleman," she pointed to Cal, "was forced to defend himself."

"That's right, Marshal," another said. "Everything this man and Miss Sue Ellen told you is the gospel truth."

"Yeah? We'll just see about that," Willis said. He moved his hand toward his pistol, but stopped when he saw how quickly Cal had drawn his own gun.

"You know what, Marshal? I would feel a lot more comfortable if you and your deputy would just use two fingers on the butt of your pistols, take them from the holsters, and lay them on the table there."

"Look here, you can't take our guns!" Willis said angrily.

"I don't intend to keep them," Cal replied. "Just leave them on the table there. In a few minutes, after we're gone, you can send one of your deputies in to pick them up."

"Yes, I got a visit as well," Kate said when Cal and Rusty returned to the Pretty Girl and Happy Cowboy to tell what happened. "Deputy Clark has just informed me that we are to add a fifty percent tax to every drink we sell, plus a twenty-dollar per week business tax."

"Twenty dollars a week? We can't afford that, can we, Mom?" Rusty asked.

"Not for very long," Kate said. "I paid him this time, but I won't be able to keep those payments up, especially as the fifty percent sales tax is going to wind up driving business away."

"What about the Bull and Heifer?" Rusty asked.

Kate nodded. "Yes, I spoke with Bull Blackwell, he has been hit with the same taxes. So have all the other businesses in town, from Buckner-Ragsdale Emporium to White's Apothecary."

"It's just another way of Atwood trying to take over our place, isn't it?" Rusty asked.

"Yes, but he won't get it. I'll burn the place to the ground before I let him have it."

"What do we do now, Marshal?" Clark asked after he retrieved the pistols Willis and Walker had been forced to leave at the Palace Café. "We can't just let that feller walk free, can we? He killed Creech."

"We goin' to tell Atwood 'bout this?" Walker asked.

"We're goin' to have to tell him," Willis replied. "There's no way we can avoid it."

"He ain't goin' to like it. He ain't goin' to like it none a-tall. Especially since we ain't made no arrest," Clark said.

"There wasn't no way I coulda arrested him. He got the drop on us when I wasn't expectin' it," Willis said.

"I think right now he's over at the Pretty Girl most by hisself," Clark said. "We could go get 'im, all of us. There ain't no way he could do anythin' against all of us, against just one of him."

"Yeah," Willis said. "Yeah, you're right. And this time, we'll make sure we have the law on our side. I'll get us a warrant from the judge."

CHAPTER THIRTY-TWO

"Didn't you just say that there were nine witnesses in the restaurant at the time of the shooting who would testify that Creech drew first?" Judge Boykin asked when Willis told him he wanted a warrant.

"Yeah, but what does that matter? You can just keep 'em from testifyin', like you did when Rusty was tried for killin' Jeb Calley."

"If we do that, Judge Turner will simply free him just as he did Rusty Abernathy. And I could wind up being removed from the bench. What good would I be, either to Atwood or you, if I'm no longer the judge?"

"What good are you now, if you say I can't arrest someone for shootin' one of my deputies?" Willis asked.

"Next time one of your deputies decides to try and kill someone, tell them to make certain they don't do it in front of a lot of witnesses."

"It just don't seem right," Willis said.

"If I were you, I would tell my deputies to continue

to collect taxes from the businessmen, and cause as little trouble as you can."

"Atwood ain't goin' to like it," Willis said.

Smoke, Sally, and Cal were having breakfast in the hotel dining room the next morning, discussing the run-in Cal and Rusty had had with the two deputies the day before.

"I hope it doesn't wind up causing even more trouble for Miz Kate," he said.

"How could it cause any more trouble than my killing Atwood's man Pardeen, or Critchlow, or Conroy?" Smoke replied.

"Or Warren or Reed, who also rode for Atwood," Sally added.

"Yes, Creech is just one more."

Sally chuckled. "It may be that Atwood will be defeated by attrition. He can't have that many more men who are willing to die for him, can he?"

"Well, he still has the marshal and all his deputies," Smoke said. "That is, the ones that are left," he added, smiling across the table toward Cal. "And Slim Pollard says he has at least ten more of what he calls his special cadre out at the ranch. And if that's so, that means that attrition has taken out less than half of them."

"Oh, there's Kate," Sally said with a broad smile.

"And Mayor Cravens," Cal added.

"May we join you?" Kate asked as they approached.

"Of course," Smoke replied as he stood. Cal stood as well.

"Smoke, Sally, I brought Mayor Cravens to talk to

you this morning, because he may need some help in the special election he is planning."

"You're planning to recall the city council?" Sally asked.

Mayor Cravens shook his head. "Unfortunately, we don't have the right of recall in Texas. But we *can* override the city council to repeal these new taxes they've put on the town. We can repeal them by veto referendum."

"By what?" Smoke asked.

"Veto referendum," Mayor Cravens repeated. "Our state constitution allows the citizens to call an election and vote on laws and ordinances passed by the state legislature, the county board of commissioners, or, and this is what pertains to us, city councils. The people can either vote to initiate a new law, or vote to repeal a law that's already on the books. In that case it would be called a veto referendum, and that's what we are going to do."

"Oh, that sounds wonderful!" Sally said.

"I just wished that women had the right to vote so I could vote for it," Kate said.

"Even if we can't vote for it, we can work for it," Sally said.

"Oh, I intend to do that," Kate said. "I plan to go around to see as many people as I can, to tell them of the election."

"Or you could have them come see you," Sally suggested with a smile.

"What do you mean?"

"You could have a meeting at the Pretty Girl."

"Yes, but I'm not sure we could get enough people to show up."

"Sure you can," Sally said. "If you had Rusty play the piano. And I don't mean just saloon tunes, I mean . . ."

"Yes! I know exactly what you mean!" Kate said enthusiastically. "Oh, yes, that's a wonderful idea. See, Mayor, I know they would be able to help."

By word of mouth, news was circulated that there was going to be an attempt to call a special election. At first, only those who could be fully trusted, and counted on to help with the process, were made aware of the plans. By midafternoon enough people had been notified that Mayor Cravens, who was behind the movement, suggested that the meeting be held.

At two o'clock that afternoon a sign was put up on the Pretty Girl and Happy Cowboy Saloon informing the public that it would be closed until four o'clock that evening. That didn't turn away too much business because it tended to be quiet in the afternoons anyway.

"Hey, Willis, somethin' is goin' on down at the Pretty Girl," Clark said.

"What do you mean?"

"I was goin' to go in 'n have me a beer, only they've got a sign up sayin' that it's closed."

"Closed? Ha! Maybe we've run her out of business. That should make Atwood happy."

"No, I don't think she's shuttin' down for good. Like I said, somethin' is goin' on down there."

"I'll check it out," Willis said, reaching for his hat.

As Willis approached the Pretty Girl and Happy

Cowboy Saloon he saw that Peterson, the bartender, was standing just in front of the locked door. A couple of men approached the saloon, spoke briefly with Peterson, then left. Then, a third man approached and after a brief conversation, Peterson unlocked the door to let him in. Clark was right . . . there was something going on.

Willis watched for a moment or two longer, and he saw Peterson allow two men and two women to go inside. His curiosity getting the best of him, he decided this called for a closer investigation.

"Hello, Marshal," Peterson said, greeting Willis with a friendly smile. "Here for the concert, are you?"

"The what?"

"The concert. You know, Rusty isn't just a piano player, he is a concert pianist, and this afternoon he's going to be playing classical music."

"Why is the door locked?"

"To keep people from just coming in, in the middle of the concert," Peterson said. He held up the key. "If you are in there, you wouldn't want your enjoyment of music to be interrupted like that, would you? Here, I'll open the door for you."

"No, no, never mind," Willis said, holding up his hand. "I heard him playing some of that highfalutin stuff before, and it makes drops of sweat break out on me as big as my thumbnail."

"Oh, that's too bad. Rusty is quite talented, you know. We are very lucky to have a musician of his caliber here, in Etholen."

"I can't understand how anyone could like that."

"You're sure you don't want to attend the concert," Peterson said. "Why don't you come on in, I know Miz Kate would be happy to have you. I'm sure she can get you a seat right down front."

"How long do you plan to keep the saloon closed?"

"Oh, the concert should last for about two hours, I suppose."

"Two hours? Two hours of that caterwauling noise?"

"We'll be open for business again by four o'clock," Peterson said.

At that moment Barney Easter, who was the manager of the stagecoach depot, arrived with his wife. Easter glanced toward Willis, his face showing his curiosity, and just a little concern as to why the marshal was here.

"Hello, Mr. Easter," Peterson said in welcome.

"Hello, Ray. We're here for the concert," Easter said. Those who had been specifically invited to the meeting had been told to use this as their password.

"I'm glad you brought the missus with you. I'm sure she is going to enjoy the music," Peterson said. He opened the door, then glanced toward Willis. "Marshal, you're sure you don't want to attend?"

Willis waved his hand dismissively. "I'll be back when it's all over," he said, and turning, he walked away.

Easter chuckled. "I was concerned for a moment, there. You handled that very well."

"There ain't nothin' goin' on down at the Pretty Girl except a concert," Willis said when he got back to the marshal's office. "Rusty Abernathy is goin' to be playin' some of that highfalutin music this afternoon."

"And you mean they's actually some people that will come to listen to that of a pure purpose?" Clark replied.

Willis laughed. "You'd have to tie me to a chair to keep me in there this afternoon."

Inside the saloon Mayor Cravens greeted those who had come, and explained how the meeting would be conducted.

"For reasons I'm sure I don't have to explain, we need to keep this meeting secret," Cravens said. "That's why we are using the concert as our cover, and we'll actually conduct our business between each song."

"They aren't 'songs.' 'My Wild Irish Rose' is a 'song.' I will be playing opuses, symphonies, and sonatas, all compositions of renowned composers," Rusty said with a chuckle.

Many of those present laughed.

"All right, then, between each, would it be correct to say musical offering?"

"Yes, that would be correct," Rusty said.

"Very well, between each musical offering, we will discuss our business," Cravens said. He looked toward Rusty. "If you would, maestro, play your first, uh, selection."

Rusty's first number was Prelude Number 15 Opus 28 by Chopin. The conclusion was met with a round of applause, then Cravens stepped up to conduct the first bit of business.

"I want to thank all of you for being here," he said. "What we do at this meeting may be the first step in getting our town back."

"Mayor, as I understand it, we are going to have some kind of an election," Fred Matthews said. Matthews was one of the partners of Foster and Matthews Freighting.

"That's right. We're going to have a special election."

"How are we going to get an election called without the city council approval?" Matthews asked. "I know every one of those men, and I know that none of them are going with this."

"We don't need the approval of the city council," Mayor Cravens replied. "All we need to call, and to establish, a special election is a petition signed by ten percent of those who voted in the last election. There are forty-nine people present in this room right now. Three hundred and ten voted in the last election, so that means we'll need at least thirty-one of you to sign the petition. And while you are thinking about that, Rusty will play something else for us. What are you going to play this time?"

"My next presentation will be Symphony Ninety-Four by Haydn," Rusty said.

Just as Rusty began to play, Willis walked by the front of the saloon and, hearing the music, shrugged, then walked away. If there were some people in town who actually wanted to spend time listening to such boring music, let them. He walked down to the Bull and Heifer Saloon, which seemed to be a little fuller than normal this afternoon.

"You're doin' a good business today," Willis said.

"Yeah, well, with the damn taxes you people have put on us, I need to," Blackwell said. "Don't know why I'm so busy though."

"It's 'cause they're havin' a concert down at the Pretty Girl," Willis said. "Rusty Abernathy is playin' some of that kind of music that just seems to go on forever. I reckon he's drivin' some of their customers away."

Blackwell laughed. "Well, I hope he plays all afternoon then."

Back at the Pretty Girl, the meeting continued.

"Tell me, Mayor, what do we do with this petition, once it's signed?" Barney Easter asked.

"We'll file it with Judge Boykin, and he will have no choice but to schedule the election," Cravens explained.

"Ha! A lot of good that will do. He's on Atwood's payroll, same as Willis."

"That doesn't matter," Cravens said. "We are going to make a certified copy of the petition and file that with Judge Turner, in the federal court. Since the right to vote is a federal law, he will be able to exercise authority over Boykin if Boykin denies the vote."

"How do we get a certified copy?" someone asked.

"It will be certified when Miss Delores Weathers signs it," Kate said.

"When who signs it? Who is Delores Weathers, and why would it be certified just because she signs it?"

"That would be me," Dolly said.

Everyone looked toward Dolly, who was sitting to one side with the other Pretty Girls that gave the saloon its name. And, as the other four Pretty Girls, Dolly was dressed in a way that emphasized her feminine attributes.

"You? How does your signing it have anything to do with it?"

"I'm a notary public. The petition will be certified as soon as I notarize it."

Mayor Cravens smiled and nodded. "That is true, ladies and gentlemen. Miss Weathers is, indeed, a notary public. If we are successful here, we can hold a vote next Tuesday that will repeal every tax applied to our citizenry since Willis became marshal. Rusty, you'd better start playing again, just in case Willis sends someone over here to check on us."

"All right," Rusty agreed.

Rusty's next selection was Symphony Number 6, Opus 68, by Beethoven.

The music not only provided cover for the meeting, it provided entertainment, and even those who were not used to listening to such classical selections found themselves enjoying the musical interludes between the business part of the meetings.

"Mayor, a moment ago you mentioned Willis. What about Willis and all his deputies?" Pete Malone asked.

Allen Blanton chuckled. "Tell me, Pete, do you really think those men have such a devotion to civic duty that they will continue to serve if they aren't getting paid?"

"They'll still be gettin' paid," Cletus Murphy said.

"They'll be gettin' paid same way they are now, by Silas Atwood."

"Yes, but it must be putting a drain on him, or they wouldn't have introduced this draconian tax schedule," Blanton said.

"What kind of tax schedule?" Cletus asked.

"Did you read my editorial?" Blanton asked.

"Yeah, and you used that word in there, too. What does it mean?"

"Burdensome," Blanton explained.

"Well, why didn't you say so?"

"So, what you're sayin' is, all we have to do is sign our names on a piece of paper, have that pretty little girl over there sign it, too, 'n we can call this election?" one of the men said.

"That's all we have to do," Cravens said. "And by my count, there are forty-nine of us here, so there shouldn't be any problem."

"Mayor, didn't you say you need ten percent of the people who voted in the last election?" Smoke asked.

"Yes."

"Well you can't count Pearlie, Cal, or me."

"Oh, that's right," Cravens said. "Nor can I count women who are here." Cravens made another quick count. "There are fifteen women, and you three, that means there are eighteen here who can't vote, and that leaves . . . oh, my, we are right up against it, folks. That means that every one of you who is eligible to vote is going to have to sign. We can't leave anyone out."

CHAPTER THIRTY-THREE

"Say, Joe, I hate to bring this up . . . but supposin' we sign this petition 'n get the election called, but it don't pass. That'll mean that Willis 'n his deputies is all still deputyin', 'n they're likely to come after those of us that sign, ain't they?" The questioner was Dave Vance, who worked at the R.D. Clayton stock barn.

"I won't lie to you, Dave," Cravens replied. "We may all be taking some risk in signing this."

"Some risk? Seems to me like we'll be takin' a lot of risk if we sign it."

"Dave, you've got to sign it," Cletus said. "You heard what the mayor said. We need thirty-one people to sign it, 'n thirty-one is all we got here."

"Just 'cause we all sign it, that don't mean it'll pass," Vance said. "If I was for sure it was goin' to pass oncet we hold the election, why I wouldn't think nothin' a-tall 'bout signin' it. But it seems to me like iffen it was goin' to pass, there ought to be more people here at the meetin'."

"Not necessarily," Blanton said. "This meeting was called on a spur of the moment, and we got nearly everyone we were able to contact. Besides which, the ballot will be secret, which means nobody will know how anyone voted, and can you think of anyone who might decide that they would want to vote *for* more taxes?"

"Yeah, well, that's all well 'n good 'bout it bein' a secret ballot 'n all. But oncet we put our names on this here petition the mayor is trying to get, why, that won't be no secret. Anybody who wants to know who signed it can just see our names there."

"They won't have to look up the petition to know who signed it," Blanton said. "I intend to publish every name in the paper."

"Why would you do a damn-fool thing like that?"

"Because I think it is a way of honoring those who are willing to do it."

"But puttin' our names on the thing means we are puttin' ourselves on the line, don't it?"

"Are you familiar with the Declaration of Independence?" Blanton asked.

"Well, yeah. Fourth of July and all that."

"The men who signed that document mutually pledged to each other their lives, their fortunes, and their sacred honor. Can we do any less?"

"No, by damn!" Cletus shouted.

"Dave, I know your history. I know that you put your life on the line at Antietam. You were there, weren't you?"

"Yes, but this ain't like that," Vance replied. "Then we had an army. We wasn't alone."

"You aren't alone here, Mr. Vance," Smoke said. "My friends and I have no intention of leaving here until Atwood and his men are no longer a threat to the town."

"There's your army, right there," Cletus said. "They've done took down seven of Atwood's men, all by themselves. Come on, I'll sign my name right next to yours, 'n I'll make my name bigger."

Vance paused for a moment, then he chuckled. "I didn't say I wasn't goin' to sign it. I was just commentin' on it is all."

"Rusty, perhaps you could honor us with another song . . . uh, I mean opus, while everyone is signing," Mayor Cravens suggested.

"Symphony Number Five, Opus Ninety-Five, by Antonín Dvořák," Rusty said.

As the music filled the saloon, Mayor Cravens sat behind a table and invited all the men to come up and sign the petition. Vance was the last one to sign, and several stared at him accusingly until he signed, making the total of signatories thirty-one, the minimum amount needed to bring about the desired result.

Mayor Cravens had them sign three copies: one to file with Judge Boykin, one to file with the state, and one to keep back, "just in case Boykin or Willis decided to destroy the petition."

Once Rusty's final presentation was completed, a smiling Mayor Craven held up the piece of paper.

"Gentlemen, enough signatures have been collected for the election to be held on Tuesday next," Mayor Cravens said when all had signed. "And this is the amendment for which you will be voting."

Clearing his throat, the mayor began to read:

"The ordinances and laws establishing the taxes created by

the Law Enforcement Capitalization Act are hereby repealed. Only such taxes as the sales and property taxes that were enacted on August 1, 1877, concurrent with the establishment of the community of Etholen, will stay in force.

"*This repeal will take effect immediately following the ballot count upon the day of the election.*"

"Yes!" someone shouted, and again there was loud and enthusiastic applause.

"Now, gentlemen, your task will be to contact as many men as you possibly can, tell them of the election coming up next Tuesday, and make certain that they vote for it."

"Why do you address only the gentlemen present? And why do you limit the contact to the men only?" Kate asked.

"Mrs. Abernathy, I don't mean to be exclusive," Mayor Cravens replied. "But, in the interest of expediency, we must concentrate only on those who can vote."

"Joe Cravens, do you really think that the women of this community have no influence over the men who do vote?" Kate asked.

Cravens laughed, then raised his finger. "You have made an excellent point, Kate," he said. He looked back out over those gathered. "*Ladies,*" he said, coming down hard on the word 'ladies' "and gentlemen, contact everyone in town, men and women alike, tell them of the election, and suggest, strongly, that they vote for this amendment."

"Mayor Cravens," Blanton called out to get attention. "I will write an article about the meeting for the *Standard,* but in order to be assured of maximum publicity, I think I should also print off circulars advertising the election and post them around town."

"I think that would be a great idea, Allen. Tell me how much that would cost and I'll have the city . . . no, wait, there is no way we'll be able to get the city council to approve it. I'll pay for it out of my own pocket."

"We can take up a collection here to pay for it," Dave Vance said. "I'll put in my part."

Blanton shook his head and held out his hands. "Gentlemen, it isn't going to cost you anything. The cost of the paper and ink is negligible. All I need from this august body of community-oriented souls is your permission."

"I think, without fear of objection, that you have the universal approval of all of us," Cravens said. "As well as our appreciation."

"Hear! Hear!" several of the others called out.

As soon at the meeting and concert was over, Allen Blanton hurried back to the newspaper. The first thing he did, was print the circular he had spoken of at the meeting.

IMPORTANT NOTICE
to the CITIZENS OF ETHOLEN:

A SPECIAL ELECTION
TO REPEAL TAXES !
will be held on
TUESDAY, JUNE 8.

VOTE <u>YES</u> TO APPROVE THE MOTION.

With the circular printed, Blanton turned his attention to the story he intended to run in his newspaper. The next issue was due on the following day, and it had already been put to bed, but this story was important enough that he pulled the Associate Press article about the fire that burned the Whitney Opera House in Syracuse, New York.

Blanton didn't even attempt to write the story first before setting it. Instead he wrote the story and set the type at the same time. Then, the story having been set, he read over it to satisfy himself that he had caught the mood of the concert and the meeting.

OF GREAT CIVIC INTEREST TO OUR COMMUNITY

Several concerned citizens of Etholen gathered at the Pretty Girl and Happy Cowboy Saloon today to hear a concert of classical music brilliantly performed by Rusty Abernathy. Mr. Abernathy, who is a concert pianist of exceptional talent, was in perfect form as he played selections by Beethoven.

But as it turned out, as great an event as the concert was, there was even more afoot. During the concert, a proposal was made that there be an effort to call a special election. The proposal was met with enthusiasm and support, and enough signatures were gathered on a petition to authorize . . . no to demand . . . that an election be held on Tuesday June 8. The election will be on a proposed amendment, which will have the immediate effect of rescinding the Law

Enforcement Capitalization Act, thus relieving the citizens of Etholen from the crippling burden of taxes, which have been levied upon us by the city council.

In affixing their names to the petition, these brave men have assured a spot for themselves in the history of our city . . . and no doubt schoolchildren far into the twentieth century will be able to recite the names, which I now list:

Roy Beck, Lonnie Bivins, Allen Blanton, Rusty Abernathy, Arnold Carter, Mayor Joe Cravens, Andrew Dawson, Lou Dobbins, Dan Dunnigan, Barney Easter, Benjamin Evans, Ken Freeman, McKinley Garrison, Ron Gelbman, Bert Graham, Cole Gunter, Ed Haycox, Doodle Higgins, Michael Holloway, Roy Houston, Ed James, Robert Jamison, Gerald Kelly, Ray Kincaid, Luke Knowles, David Lewis, Pete Malone, Jim Martin, Ray Peterson, Cletus Murphy, and David Vance.

These thirty-one names are enough to guarantee the election will be held. They have done their part to free Etholen from the yoke of oppressive taxes. Now, this newspaper urges every citizen to do his civic duty and vote "yes" on the amendment.

"What?" Judge Boykin said when Mayor Cravens put the petition before him. "What is this?"

"It is a *mandamus* that an election be held on Tuesday week, to vote on this act," Cravens said.

"What do you mean it is a *mandamus*? A *mandamus* can only come from a superior court!"

"In this case . . . Your Honor"—Cravens set "Your Honor" aside so that the words dripped with sarcasm—"it is a *mandamus* from the people, and, as I'm sure you know, in our form of government the people are our superior. This is a petition with the required number of names, calling for a special election. You have no choice . . . the election must be held."

Boykin looked over toward Smoke, who had come to the office with Cravens to deliver the petition.

"Is your name on here? This is your doing, isn't it?"

"Why, Judge Boykin, you know I'm not a resident of this town. I can't vote, so if my signature was on there, it would be invalid," Smoke replied.

Judge Boykin smiled smugly.

"I could just tear this up, you know. Then where would you be?"

"We would be just fine," Smoke said. "We have sent a copy to the state, and we have an extra copy. On the other hand, if you would do something so foolish as to tear up this petition of the people, you will be dead."

"What do you mean I would be dead?"

"Let me explain it to you. If you tear up that petition, I will kill you where you stand," Smoke said calmly.

"What? You would say something like that to me? I am a sitting judge, sir! A sitting judge! You wouldn't dare threaten me, sir! You wouldn't dare!"

Smoke chuckled dryly. "I didn't threaten you," he said.

"What do you call that, if not a threat?"

"I would call it a promise."

"Cravens, you heard him! You are my witness! I intend to serve him with a warrant for threatening to kill me. That is a ten-year sentence!"

"What are you talking about?" Mayor Cravens asked. "I didn't hear any such threat."

"That you, an elected mayor, would countenance such a thing as a threat against a sitting judge is unconscionable."

"Where are you going?" Smoke asked.

"I'm going to get someone to come in here as a material witness."

"No, you aren't," Smoke said. "You are going to sit back down and listen to what Mayor Cravens has to say."

"Well I . . . I never . . ." Judge Boykin sputtered.

"Sit down," Smoke repeated, but he didn't raise his voice. It wasn't necessary for him to do so.

"Go ahead, Mr. Mayor," Smoke said to Cravens.

"Judge Boykin, I am also serving you with a court order, setting aside the Law Enforcement Capitalization Act until its status can be determined by the election next Tuesday," Mayor Cravens said.

"Court order? What court order? I've issued no such order."

"Oh, I'm sorry, I should have been more specific. This order comes from Judge Turner of the West Texas Federal Court. And that means you will do it, sir," Cravens said.

"See here, you have no right to do this!"

"How is it that you are a sitting judge, and yet you know so little about the law?" Smoke asked.

"Don't you presume to lecture me about the law, sir," Judge Boykin said.

"I am a member of the bar, as you know, but don't worry, I won't. I could no more get you to see your duty than I could teach a pig to sing."

"I . . . I . . ." Boykin sputtered.

"We'll be going now, Judge," Mayor Cravens said. "We have a campaign to run." Cravens smiled. "Come to think of it, I suppose you have the same campaign to run. I expect we had all better get busy and let our republic form of government work its course."

Atwood held up the newspaper. "Are you telling me that the nonsense Blanton has printed in his newspaper is true? Is there actually going to be a vote against the taxes?"

Atwood was sitting in the parlor of his house, along with Willis, Clark, Judge Boykin, and Jay Kinder, Speaker of the City Council.

"I'm afraid so," Judge Boykin said.

"Can't you stop it?"

"How?"

"I don't know. Issue an order or something."

"If I did, Turner would just issue an order that would override it."

"Maybe if we conduct a rigorous enough campaign, we can convince the people that we need this tax base to keep them safe," Kinder said.

Atwood glared at him. "Are you serious? We are going to be able to convince people to pay more taxes? Why the hell did I select you as the speaker of the city council? My God, you are dumber than a day-old mule."

"Mr. Atwood, you have no right to talk to me like that," Kinder said, obviously stung by the harsh comment.

"I put you and the entire city council in office, Kinder. You belong to me. And that means I can talk to you any way I want."

"Well, what are we going to do?" Judge Boykin asked. "You're right, we aren't going to be able to convince them to vote against their own best interests."

"It depends on what you mean when you say convince them," Kinder said.

Boykin glanced over toward him. "What do you mean?"

"If they are frightened enough, perhaps they'll vote the way we want them to vote."

"We aren't going to be able to frighten them," Judge Boykin said. "Not as long as Smoke Jensen is here."

Atwood smiled. "My point, exactly."

CHAPTER THIRTY-FOUR

In all the time he had been in the newspaper business, Allen Blanton had only put out two "Extra" editions; one when Custer and his men were killed, and one when President Garfield was shot. Now he was about to put out his third.

EXTRA ! EXTRA ! EXTRA !

By court order the taxes demanded by the Law Enforcement Capitalization Act have been set aside. That means that, already, businesses that have been crippled by the taxes can reopen, and the additional tax burden upon the citizen has been lifted.

It is important to understand, though, that this relief is temporary, pending the outcome of the election on Tuesday. Therefore it is incumbent upon each of us to use the power of the ballot to make this relief permanent.

When the deputies learned that they would no longer be able to collect taxes, they saw it as an end to their gravy train, and they returned to the marshal's office to complain to Willis.

"I'll tell you right now, Willis," Booker said. "If the money is shut off, I don't intend to be a deputy anymore."

"Who said the money is goin' to be shut off?" Willis asked.

"Well, if we can't collect the taxes no more, just where do you expect the money to come from?"

"Mr. Atwood said not to worry, that he has come up with an idea. So let's wait and see what his idea is."

"You mean like his idea of havin' someone kill Jensen?" Clark asked. "Because that idea sure hasn't worked out, has it?"

"Just wait a while, and see what he has in mind."

Everyone responded to the upcoming election, as well as the court order setting aside taxes, by posting signs outside their places of business.

OPEN *for* BUSINESS *as before*
NO TAXES

The result was a flurry of business activity all over town, but no business bounced back as far as the Palace Café. It was so crowded that there was a waiting line to get a table. It wasn't just the businesspeople who celebrated the suspension of taxes, the mood of the town had greatly changed, and men and women strolled up and down the boardwalks, recognizing each other with smiles and friendly greetings.

Pearlie and Cal were nailing up election circulars all over town:

VOTE: **YES** !
to repeal taxes!

TUESDAY, JUNE 16

"How many more of these things do we have to put up?" Cal asked.

"I've only got about four or five more," Pearlie replied. "Why so you ask? Do you want to go get a beer?"

"Yeah," Cal said. "Let's go over to your sister's place."

Pearlie chuckled. "You're not fooling me, Cal. It's not a beer you're after. You just want to talk to some of the Pretty Girls."

"Well, that's why your sister named her place the way she did, isn't it?"

The two laughed as, with all the election circulars now put up, they started back to the saloon.

When they stepped inside, they saw Rusty and Dolly sitting together.

"Well now, Rusty, just how is this young lady supposed to earn her keep if she spends all her time with you instead of visiting with the cowboys?" Pearlie asked.

"She doesn't spend all her time with me," Rusty replied.

"Well, you can't prove that by me. Seems like every time I look up, I see the two of you together."

"Oh, she visits with the cowboys. But she spends

her quality time with me," Rusty said with a broad smile.

"Would you like Linda Sue and Peggy Ann to join us?" Dolly asked, flashing a smile at Pearlie and Cal.

"Yeah, that would be nice. We'd like some quality time, too," Cal replied with a laugh.

Smoke and Sally were also in the Pretty Girl, sharing a table with Kate and Mayor Cravens. A burst of laughter came from the table where Pearlie and Cal were holding court.

"It's good to see people laughing again. I've not seen a mood this ebullient since Atwood started taking over everything," Cravens said.

"It's because of Smoke," Kate said. "He, my brother, and Cal came riding in on white horses, dressed in shining armor, and nothing has been the same since."

"And don't forget Mrs. Jensen," Mayor Cravens said. "She is the one who has taken our fight to the courts."

"There's no way I'm going to leave Sally out of this," Kate said. "If Smoke, Pearlie, and Cal are knights in shining armor, Sally is the crown princess they serve."

"Let's not celebrate too early," Smoke said. "We've had a few victories against Atwood, but I don't think he's ready to give up just yet."

"Oh, believe me, I know you are right," Mayor Cravens said. "But we have had so few victories against this . . . tyrant, is the only way I can think of him, that it is good to celebrate the ones that we do have."

* * *

Unlike Kate Abernathy, Silas Atwood didn't see Smoke Jensen as a knight in shining armor. But like the owner of the Pretty Girl and Happy Cowboy Saloon, he did see Jensen as the architect of the resistance that he was now facing. The court-ordered revocation of the Law Enforcement Capitalization Act, and the upcoming election, which would surely overturn it, was the latest setback.

From shortly after Jensen arrived, Atwood had correctly assessed him as a problem and had tried to eliminate the problem by eliminating Jensen. And the only way to eliminate Jensen was to kill him. So far every effort had failed, and Atwood was beginning to believe all he had heard about Smoke Jensen. Jensen wasn't a man who could be bested in a gunfight. If he was going to be killed, Atwood was going to have to come up with another way, but just what way would that be?

José Bustamante was a killer, but he was not a gunman in the classic sense. He was an assassin, pure and simple. When Bustamante learned there was a wealthy Texan who was willing to pay well to have someone killed, he started to contact him but decided instead to just go see him. Thus it was that, when he arrived at Atwood's house, he was unexpected. Dismounting in front of Atwood's house, one that Bustamante would call *casa grande,* he didn't bother to knock on the door. Instead, he sat on the porch swing and remained there for well over half an hour before Atwood, who had no idea that Bustamante was there, came outside.

"Who are you?" Atwood gasped when he saw a Mexican sitting cross-legged on his swing, a *sombrero* resting on his knee.

"I am Bustamante."

"How dare you sit on my front porch without permission. What are you doing here?"

"You sent for me, señor."

"What are you talking about? I didn't send for you."

Bustamante took a piece of paper from his pocket and showed it to Atwood. It was a letter Atwood had written to an acquaintance, an acquaintance he could trust.

> *From time to time in my business, I may have occasion to use a person who is possessed of a particular talent, as well as the predilection to use it without question or compunction. If you know such a person I would be most anxious to hire him.*

Atwood had sent the letter, but he had sent it six months earlier, long before Smoke Jensen had arrived on the scene. As it turned out, this was exactly one of those "times" he had mentioned in the letter. If this Mexican really was such a man, it was an unexpected and fortuitous piece of good luck that he should arrive here, now, when Atwood's need was even greater than it had ever been.

"Where did you get this letter?" Atwood asked.

"A man I did a job for gave me the letter," Bustamante said.

"Are you good with a gun?"

"I do not have a gun."

"You don't have a gun?"

"No, señor."

"Then there has been some misunderstanding here. Apparently you don't know what I am looking for."

"Do you want someone keeled, señor?"

"That's a hell of a question to ask."

"Do you want someone keeled?" Bustamante asked again.

"What if I do? How are you going to do that without a gun?"

"I do not need to be good with a gun, because I do not use a gun. For me, señor, killing is not a sport, it is a *profesión*," Bustamante said.

Atwood stroked his chin as he stared into the dark, obsidian eyes of the Mexican who had not yet risen from the swing.

"There have been others who have tried to kill Smoke Jensen. But they have all failed."

"I am not like the others."

"Yeah, maybe you'll do after all. All right, put your tack in the bunkhouse. Use that one," he said, pointing to the smaller of the two buildings. "The other one is for the cowboys. This one is for men who do . . . special jobs for me."

Bustamante nodded but said nothing. He led his horse into the barn, removed the saddle, found an empty stall, then he took the blanket in which he kept his tack with him to the bunkhouse Atwood had pointed out to him.

Clinton and two other men were in the bunkhouse.

Bustamante saw a bunk on which the mattress was in an "S" roll, and he dropped his blanket there.

"Hey you, Mex!" Clinton called. "What are you doing in here?"

Bustamante didn't answer.

"I'm talkin' to you, Mex. You're in the wrong building. If you've just signed on, you need to be in the other bunkhouse."

"I seen 'im talkin' to Mr. Atwood a couple of minutes ago, Clinton," one of the other men said. "If he come in here, I reckon it's 'cause Atwood told 'im to."

"Is that right, Mex? Did Atwood tell you to come in here?"

Again, Bustamante didn't answer.

"What's the matter with you? Don't you speak English? *No habla Inglés?*"

Bustamante stared at him but said nothing.

"You know what I think? I think maybe he's deaf," one of the other two men said, and the others laughed.

Clinton pulled his pistol and pointed it at Bustamante. "Let's find out. Mex, here's what I'm going to do. I'm going to count to three, 'n if you don't say somethin' to me before I get to three, I'm goin' to shoot you dead. You *comprender*, Mex?"

"I am Bustamante."

A wide grin spread across Clinton's face, and he put the gun back in his holster. "Well now, Loomis, Hicks, what do you think of that? Our little brown friend can talk after all. Bustamante, is it?"

"Si."

"I don't know what Mr. Atwood was thinkin' when

he hired a Mex, but let me tell you how it's goin' to be. As long as you are in this bunkhouse, with us, you stay the hell out of my way. I don't like Mexicans. *Comprender* that, Bustamante?"

"*Sí.*"

It may have been close to midnight, Bustamante had no way of knowing, though he knew it was quite late. And, because of the chorus of snoring coming from the others, he knew that everyone was asleep. Getting up from bed, Bustamante removed his knife from its scabbard, then lit a candle. By the wavering light of the candle, he walked quietly across the wide, unfinished plank floor until he reached Clinton's bunk. Clinton was lying on his back, his mouth open, and snoring loudly.

Holding the candle in his left hand, and the knife in his right, Bustamante made a quick slice, with the blade cutting halfway through Clinton's neck. Clinton's eye popped open, and he remained conscious just long enough to be aware of what happened to him. He opened his mouth wider, as if to cry out, but because the larynx had been destroyed, he could make no sound. Blood gushed from the wound and began to pool on both sides as Clinton's eyes glazed over.

Bustamante went back to his own bed.

CHAPTER THIRTY-FIVE

"What the hell!" Loomis shouted the next morning. "Hicks! Boyle! Jones! Come here! Look at this!"

Loomis was standing over Clinton's bunk, looking down at his cut throat, his open, but unseeing eyes, and his blood-soaked pillow and blanket.

"Son of a bitch! Who did this?" Boyle asked.

"I don't know. Someone must've come in here last night," Jones said.

"I think it was the Mex," Loomis said.

"The Mex?" Boyle asked. "Who are you talkin' about?"

"That's right, you 'n Jones wasn't here when he come in yesterday. He says his name is Bustamante."

"It couldn'ta been him," Hicks said. "Hell, look down there! He's still here, lyin' in his bunk. He wouldn' still be here iffen he had done this."

"Then who did do it?"

"Did you hear about Clinton?" Slim Pollard asked Hog Jaw Lambert. Like Slim, Hog Jaw was one of the working cowboys on Eagle Shire. The two of them were riding fence line.

"Clinton? Ain't he one o' them gunmen that Atwood's brought onto the place? What about 'im?"

"He was found dead in his bunk this morning."

"Damn! You mean he died in his sleep?"

Slim chuckled, a macabre laugh. "Yeah, if you call gettin' your throat cut dying in your sleep."

"Someone cut his throat?"

"He didn't cut it himself."

"Who did it?"

"Nobody knows."

"That's a hell of a way to die," Hog Jaw said.

"Yeah, I suppose it is. But I'll be honest with you, Hog Jaw. I don't feel one bit sorry for the son of a bitch."

Hog Jaw looked around quickly to make sure that there was no one close enough to overhear them.

"No," he agreed. "I don't feel sorry for 'im, either. I wonder if it has somethin' to do with what's goin' on between Atwood and town right now?"

"It could be. You know he, Reed, Clinton, and Warren went to town together the other night. Clinton was the only one who come back."

"Yeah," Hog Jaw said. "They say that fella Smoke Jensen kilt 'em. I wonder if he come out here in the middle of the night 'n kilt Clinton?"

"I doubt it," Slim said. "So far ever'body Jensen has kilt has been face to face. It ain't like him to sneak up in the middle of the night 'n kill someone."

* * *

Atwood was certain that Bustamante was the one who killed Clinton, but he didn't ask him about it. And, if he was being honest with himself, he didn't really care. He had sent Clinton into town with two other men for what should have been an easy job . . . to kill Jensen in the middle of the night. Clinton and the other two had failed. If Bustamante could kill Clinton, in a bunkhouse that was filled with Clinton's friends, and neither be caught nor discovered, then this might just be the man he needed.

"You're right," Atwood said to Bustamante after sending for him. "I do want someone killed. His name is Smoke Jensen, and you will find him in town."

Smoke was in the Bull and Heifer Saloon, campaigning for the election.

"Hell, yeah, I'll vote against the taxes," someone said. "I don't like payin' extra for my drinks."

"And for ever'thing else you have to buy, too," another added.

"Mr. Jensen, have a beer on the house," Bull Blackwell said. "I think the best thing that's happened to this town is you comin' here."

"Hell, I think he ain't done nothin' but bring trouble to the town," someone said.

"You would say that, Hicks, you're ridin' for Atwood."

"Yeah? So, what if I do?"

"He ain't really ridin' for 'im. He ain't a cowboy," Slim Pollard said.

"If you mean I don't walk around with cow dung on my boots the way you 'n the others do, then yeah,

I ain't a cowboy," Hicks replied. "But there's other jobs Mr. Atwood needs done besides cowboyin', and he hires special people for that."

"I think I've run across some of these special people you're talking about," Smoke said. "As a matter of fact three of them came into my hotel room the other night intent upon killing my wife and me."

"Yeah, well, I wouldn't know nothin' about that," Hicks said.

"No, I'm sure that you don't. Mr. Blackwell, thank you for the beer," Smoke said, lifting the empty glass toward the bartender.

It was very dark outside with only the moon and dim squares of light around the few lampposts keeping it from being as black as the inside of a pit.

From the other end of the street Smoke could hear Rusty playing the piano, and he recognized the song "Lorena."

From the shadows of the Mexican quarters on the south side of the tracks, Smoke could hear a guitar and trumpet. They were playing different songs, yet, somehow it all seemed to blend into a melody that was distinctly here and now.

A dog barked.

Somewhere a baby cried.

Smoke could see the lights of the Milner Hotel and started toward them. Sally was already there, probably reading, and he was anxious to get back to her. He knew that most wives, being displaced from home for as long as Sally had been, would probably start showing their displeasure. But Sally was supportive in every way, and he was glad she had made such good friends with Pearlie's sister. It was almost as if Kate, like Pearlie, had been invited into the family.

He felt the assassin coming for him before he heard him, and he heard him before he saw him. A man, obviously a Mexican, suddenly materialized from the dark shadows between the buildings and sprang toward him, making a wide slash with his knife. Only that innate sense that allowed him to perceive danger when there was no other sign had saved his life, for he was moving out of the way at the exact moment the man started his attack. Otherwise the attacker's knife, swinging in a low, vicious arc, would have disemboweled him.

Despite the quickness of his reaction, however, the attacker did manage to cut him, and as Smoke went down into the dirt, rolling to get away, the flashing blade opened up a long wound in his side. The knife was so sharp and wielded so adroitly that Smoke barely felt it. He knew, however, that the knife had drawn blood.

The Mexican moved in quickly, thinking to finish Smoke off before he could recover, but Smoke twisted around on the ground, then thrust his feet out, catching the assailant in the chest with a powerful kick and driving him back several feet. But the Mexican was good, skilled and agile, and he recovered quickly, so that by the time Smoke was back on his feet, he was once again facing the knife wielder.

Smoke reached for his pistol, then realized with a shock that his holster was empty! The gun had fallen out while he was on the ground! He was unarmed and having to face someone who obviously knew how to use a knife.

The attacker, realizing that Smoke was defenseless, flashed a self-satisfied smile and made another swipe with his knife. Smoke managed to avoid the knife and thrusting out with the heel of his hand, he hit the man in the forehead, driving him back a few feet.

Smoke looked around on the ground to try to find his pistol as his attacker charged him again. Then Smoke heard a gunshot, and he saw a black hole appear in the forehead of his assailant. The Mexican went down, and Smoke turned to see Sally standing behind him, holding a smoking gun.

"I was getting tired of waiting," Sally said. "So I decided to come see what was keeping you."

"You mean you were actually going to go into the Bull and Heifer?"

"If necessary," Sally said, putting her gun back in the holster. "It looks like I made a good move."

"What? You mean this little fracas? Ahh, I was handling it all right."

"Yeah, I could tell," Sally replied with a chuckle. "You're bleeding like a stuck pig. We'd better get that taken care of."

"Nothing to it, I just need . . ."

"Smoke? Smoke? Smoke? Are you all right?"

When Smoke opened his eyes he saw Sally, Pearlie, and Cal looking down at him.

"Why are you asking me if I'm all right?"

Sally's smile was one of relief. "Because you are lying on your back in the middle of the street."

Pearlie, Cal, Kate, Rusty, Dolly, and Mayor Cravens were at Dr. Pinkstaff's office as he treated the wound in Smoke's side.

"How is he, Doc?" Pearlie asked.

"Well, he lost a lot of blood; that's why he fainted," Dr. Pinkstaff replied.

"I didn't faint," Smoke replied. "That's what women do when they see a mouse, or something."

"Well, if you didn't faint, what were you doing lying in the middle of the street?" Sally asked.

"I just . . . I just went to sleep rapidly," Smoke said.

Dr. Pinkstaff laughed. "If he's still got a sense of humor, he'll be just fine. I'm giving him a saline transfusion and he's going to need some rest until his blood builds back up. And you'll need to keep the wound clean."

"What do you mean by rest?" Smoke asked.

"By rest, I mean rest. I don't want you on your feet just yet. I'm going to keep you here for a while."

"How long is a while? I plan to be up and about by Tuesday."

"If you do what I tell you, I think I can promise you that you'll be back on your feet by then. I'm going to give you a solution of chloral hydrate to help you sleep tonight."

"Wait a minute," Smoke said. "That stuff will knock me out, won't it?"

"Yes, but I think it is necessary. At least for tonight."

"I'm not going to take it."

"Yes, you are," Sally insisted.

"Bustamante is dead?" Atwood said.

"Yeah," Hicks said. "Welch has him down at the undertakin' place now, and he wants to know if you are goin' to pay for his buryin'."

"No, why should I pay for it?"

"I guess he thinks you should pay for it 'cause he worked for you."

"I paid for Pardeen, Creech, Warren, Reed, and Clinton because they were good men who had worked for me for a long time. Bustamante was only here for a few days, and he did nothing while he was here except possibly kill Clinton. I see no reason to pay for his burying."

Hicks laughed. "Yeah, that's what I told Welch."

"How is Jensen?"

"From what I hear he was cut up pretty bad," Hicks said. "He's most likely goin' to spend the night in the doctor's office."

Hick's words caused a broad smile to spread across Atwood's face, and he struck his open hand with his fist.

"We've got 'im!" he said. "If he is in the doctor's office tonight, he is helpless!"

"Want me to take care of 'im?" Hicks asked.

"Yes, and if you are successful, I guarantee you, you will be amply rewarded."

* * *

It was two o'clock when Cal came to relieve Pearlie at the doctor's office. Sally had stood watch until midnight, and Pearlie from midnight until two.

"How's he doing?" Cal asked.

"He's in there sleeping like a baby," Pearlie said.

"It's probably the first good night's sleep he's had since we left home," Cal said.

"There's coffee on the stove," Pearlie said as he left.

Cal looked in on Smoke, then took a seat. After several minutes he started getting very sleepy, and remembering Pearlie's reminder of the coffee, he went into the other room to pour himself a cup. He took a sip, then walked back to his guard position and saw someone standing over Smoke's bed.

"Pearlie, what are you . . . ?" It wasn't Pearlie!

The intruder turned and fired at Cal, who had leaped to one side as soon as he realized it wasn't Pearlie. Cal fired back, and the intruder went down. Hurrying to him, Cal looked down, then kicked the weapon away.

That action wasn't necessary. The man Cal shot was dead.

CHAPTER THIRTY-SIX

Smoke was fully recovered by election day, and he, Pearlie, and Cal were watching the polling place to make certain that there was no intimidation of the voters. Sally, Kate, Sue Ellen, Dolly, and the Pretty Girls had set up a table near the polling booth, and they were serving lemonade and cookies. Cletus and Doodle, having just voted, were availing themselves of the refreshments offered.

"These cookies is so good, I think I'll vote two or three times," Cletus said.

"Don't even joke about that, Cletus," Mayor Cravens said. "We're going to win this election, hands down, and I don't want even a whisper that could give them a challenge."

"No, sir, I won't say nothin' like that no more," Cletus said. "Long as I can have me some more of these cookies."

"Of course you can, Cletus," Kate said. "But leave enough for the others to be able to enjoy as well."

"What about them fellas?" Doodle asked, pointing

to a group of men. "You aren't going to give them any cookies and lemonade, are you?"

Doodle was pointing toward Marshal Willis and his deputies.

"Of course we will," Sally said with a broad smile. "These refreshments are for everyone who votes. Would you like a cookie, Marshal?"

"Yeah," Clark said, starting toward the table.

"Clark!" Willis said sharply, shaking his head.

"No," Clark said. "We don't want none of your damn cookies."

"That would be 'we don't want any of your damn cookies,' to be correct about it," Pearlie said.

"Why, yes, Pearlie, that's very good," Sally said with an approving smile.

Willis, Clark, Booker, and Walker voted, then walked back down to the marshal's office. A few minutes later, the four men were seen riding out of town.

"Ha!" Rusty said. "Looks to me like Willis and his deputies have given up. They're leaving town!"

"They're goin' to win that election, Mr. Atwood," Willis was saying half an hour later. "There ain't no way they ain't goin' to win."

"What time will the voting poll close?" Atwood asked.

"They said they're goin' to keep it open till five o'clock."

"Then we haven't lost the election."

"Yeah, we have, you don't have no idea how many has already voted. And you know damn well they're votin' to get rid of the taxes."

"The votes have to be counted to make the election official, don't they?"

"Well yeah, but . . ."

"All we have to do is see to it that they aren't counted."

"How are we goin' to do that?"

"You let me worry about that."

When Slim Pollard dismounted, he walked over to the refreshment table where Smoke stood talking with some of the townspeople.

"You can't vote, Slim," Cletus said, "on account of you don't live in town. I wish you could, though, I've got a feelin' you'd do the right thing."

"Yeah, well, I hope I'm doin' the right thing now," Slim said. "I'm leavin'; I can't ride for the Eagle Shire no more. Atwood just ain't a man I can work for."

Doodle laughed. "Hell, Slim, you just now learnin' that?"

"Well, I don't know, maybe I have know'd about it for a while, 'n always before I kinda turned my head away from it. But I can't look away from what he's got planned now."

"What he has planned now? And just what would that be?" Smoke asked.

"He plans to come into town to stop the election."

"Stop it? How does he expect to do that?" Smoke asked. "The election is half over already."

"He plans to kill as many townspeople as he can, then he's goin' to steal the ballot box before the votes can be counted."

"Why, he's insane if he thinks he can razz an entire town," Peterson said.

"That's not as far-fetched as you might think," Smoke said. "Remember what Quantrill did with Lawrence."

"Yeah, that's right," Mayor Cravens said. "Mr. Pollard, how many men will Atwood have with him?"

"He'll have Willis an' his deputies, that's four, plus at least ten others from the ranch, and maybe a few more."

"I know he has a bunch of gun hands," Cletus said. "I didn't know he had that many."

"Some of the cowboys may ride with him," Slim said. "Not many, but a few."

"Why would they do that?" Mayor Cravens asked.

"Some will because cowboys just naturally have a loyalty to the brand they ride for, and some will because if you want to be a cowboy in this part of the county, now, Eagle Shire is the only job there is."

"What will we do, Mayor?" Doodle asked.

"I don't know," the mayor replied. "If there are that many of them coming into town, I don't see how we can possibly stand up to them. When it comes down to it, they will just about have us outnumbered . . . at least as far as young, fighting age men are concerned. And most of them know how to use guns. I'd be willing to say that there aren't more than nine or ten in all of Etholen who have ever used a gun before, let alone in battle."

"Smoke, we aren't just going to give in to them, are we?" Kate asked.

"Not by a long shot are we going to give in to them," Smoke replied. "Actually, it's good that this is all going to come to a head now. I said I wasn't going to leave until this business with Atwood was settled, and I meant it. I figure that, before nightfall, it will be settled."

"Do you really think we can hold him off?" Doodle asked.

"I'm not interested in just holding them off. We need to finish this business with Atwood, once and for all."

"But how are we going to do this? He's probably got us outnumbered, and all of his men are experienced fighting men."

Smoke glanced toward the courthouse and smiled.

"That may be. But we've got something he doesn't have."

Cletus Murphy, Roy Beck, Lonnie Bivins, Allen Blanton, Rusty Abernathy, Arnold Carter, Andrew Dawson, Barney Easter, Ken Freeman, Ron Gelbman, Bert Graham, Cole Gunter, Doodle Higgins, Michael Holloway, Ed James, Robert Jamison, and Gerald Kelly dug the trench and rampart, and felled a couple of trees to add a revetment. The result was a defense position that was in place between the town and Eagle Shire.

"What do you think, Smoke?" Allen Blanton asked. "Looks to me like you could hold off an army." Blanton had been in charge of digging the fortification.

"I think you and the others did a great job," Smoke said.

"As long as they don't decide to circle around town and come in from the other side," Blanton suggested.

"Damn! If he does that we are in a peck of trouble," Cal said.

Blanton chuckled. "Don't worry about it, I know Atwood. He's not really all that smart, certainly not smart enough to think about going around the town."

"I hope you're right," Smoke said. "Cletus, Doodle, you two stay here with Pearlie, Cal, and me. The rest of you men can go on back into town now. I thank you very much for all the work you did in building this fort so quickly. You did a great job."

"I am the mayor of this town," Joe Cravens said. "I intend to stay as well. It wouldn't be right for me to desert my post now."

"All right, you can stay."

"And me," Rusty said.

"Rusty, if something happened to you, I'd never be able to face my sister again," Pearlie said.

"How is that any different from the last twenty years, Uncle Pearlie?" Rusty challenged.

Pearlie stared at Rusty for a long moment, then nodded. "You're right," he said. "You can stay."

"I don't have a gun," Rusty said.

Smoke pointed to the three cloth bags that Sally and Kate had sewn for them. "Yeah, you do," he said with a smile.

Fourteen men left Eagle Shire with Atwood. Calling upon his experience when he was a lieutenant in the Windsor Regiment during the war, Atwood rode at their head and had his men follow him, in a column of twos. When he was no more than a mile from town, he halted his men.

"Willis. Ride ahead and take a look around."

"You mean go by myself?"

"Of course go by yourself. You're the marshal of the town, you aren't going to attract any attention, especially if you are by yourself."

"All right," Willis agreed, though somewhat hesitantly.

Disengaging from the others, Willis rode ahead at a trot. He had just come around the last curve in the road, when he stopped. Ahead of him, and just to the side of the road, there appeared to be a couple of tree trunks, and he could see the head and shoulders of three men sticking up just above the improvised fortifications.

"Ha!" Willis said, a wide smile spreading across his face. Turning his horse around, he urged it into a rapid, ground-eating trot, until he got back to Atwood and the others.

"There's only three of 'em!" Willis said when he returned.

"Ha! Yes, that would be Jensen, Kate's brother, and the other man who came with them. I thought that might be the case," Atwood said, slapping his closed fist into his hand. "They've been so successful in dealing with my men before that they've grown arrogant and overconfident. Well, we are about to teach them a lesson. Unfortunately the lesson won't do them any good because they're going to die learning it."

"Smoke!" Cal called down from the tree he had climbed. He was holding a tin can in his hand, and a long string stretched from it to Smoke's position in the entrenchment. Smoke put the can to his ear.

"They are about a half mile away," Cal's tinny, but easily understood voice said.

Smoke put the can to his mouth. "Start giving me a countdown, by yards, when they are about fifty yards from the marked tree."

Smoke looked over toward Rusty. The first of the three cloth bags of powder had been pushed down into the breach of the gun, and a hollow cannon ball that had been filled with powder had been loaded. The cannon ball fuse protruded through the touch-hole, and Rusty was holding a burning wick. The cannon was laid in on three selected targets, the marked tree being the first one.

"One hundred yards," Cal said, and he began counting down in ten-yard increments. When he got to twenty yards, Smoke called out to Rusty.

"Ready!"

Rusty moved the wick closer.

"Ten yards," Cal said.

"Fire!"

The cannon roared and belched fire. Quickly the barrel was sponged out, and a new sack of powder and a new cannon ball put in place.

"What the?" Atwood shouted when he heard the sound of the cannon being fired. He had heard such sounds before, but it had been more than twenty years in his past.

The preliminary explosion was followed by another

explosion, this one loud and ear-splitting, coming from the road behind him.

"Arghhhh!"

Men screamed in fear and pain.

"Forward at a gallop!" Atwood shouted, remembering enough of his battle experience to know that the best defense was to gallop out of the kill zone.

"Fifty yards from the double rock!" Cal said into the tin can, marking the second firing point.

"Fire!" Smoke shouted when Cal indicated that they were ten yards from the double rock.

This time the cannon ball exploded in the road far enough behind Atwood and the men who were advancing with him that no one was wounded.

"Yes! Faster, we can outrun them!" Atwood shouted.

Back at the entrenchment, Smoke had the gun moved up onto the rampart and the barrel depressed. This time, instead of being loaded with an explosive cannon ball, the barrel was filled with cut pieces of horseshoes that had been prepared by the blacksmith. Cal had come down from his position in the tree and he, Pearlie, Smoke, Cletus, and Doodle were in the trench, with rifles at the ready.

"Hold your fire until after the cannon has fired," Smoke told the others.

They could hear the sound of thundering hooves, then the riders came around the last bend in the road. Here, they spread out in a long front. Smoke had no idea how many they had started with, but he counted twelve. The twelve attackers started shooting, and Smoke and the others could hear the bullets whistling over their heads.

"Fire the cannon, Rusty!" Smoke shouted, and again, the cannon roared.

Smoke could see the bits of iron, hurtling toward Atwood and his men in a cloud of death. Four men went down under the fusillade.

"Now!" Smoke shouted, and he and the other four men began firing as rapidly as they could jack new rounds into the chambers. Within seconds, there wasn't one man left in the saddle.

EPILOGUE

Etholen, the following June

Smoke, Sally, Pearlie, and Cal were met at the depot by Allen Blanton, the newspaper publisher.

"I hope you don't mind being met by me instead of your sister or your nephew," Blanton said. "But, as I'm sure you can imagine, they're quite busy right now."

"Yes, I imagine they would be," Sally said.

"I know they're thrilled that you folks could come," Blanton said. "Actually, the entire town is. You folks are heroes around here, you know."

Smoke shook his head. "No more so than anyone else who took part that day . . . and that goes for the people who voted, and for people like you, Cletus, Doodle, and others who helped to turn out the vote."

"I've got something I want you to see before you go to the hotel," Blanton said.

A short while later, with their luggage loaded onto a small wagon that was being pulled behind a phaeton carriage, Blanton drove them to the Milner

Hotel. But, before reaching the hotel, they stopped at the flagpole in front of the courthouse. The cannon was still there, but the sign beside it was much larger, and the name of the cannon had been changed.

THE CANNON
"SMOKE"

MANNED IN BATTLE
by Joe Cravens *and* Rusty Abernathy
under the COMMAND *of*
SMOKE JENSEN
and with the HEROIC SERVICE *of*
Wes "Pearlie" Fontaine, Cal Wood,
Cletus Murphy, *and* Doodle Higgins

**Brought FREEDOM *and* INDEPENDENCE
to Etholen, Texas**

"Well, I'm very honored, Mr. Blanton. And I know that Pearlie and Cal are as well."

"Yes, sir, we sure are," Pearlie said.

"So, Cletus is the new city marshal now?"

"Cletus is the new marshal, Doodle is his deputy, Mr. Peterson is our new mayor, Joe Cravens the judge, and Rusty, Bull Blackwell, Fred Matthews, Dave Vance, and I make up the new city council."

"My," Sally said. "It looks like the town has been reborn."

"Yes, ma'am, but not just the town," Blanton said. "The whole county. Atwood's ranch has been broken up. Some of it has been given back to the people he stole it from, and some of it was sold at auction. Slim

Pollard and Miner Cobb bought some of it, with a bank loan, and they're doing just fine."

"Well, here we are," Blanton said a few minutes later when they stopped in front of the hotel. "I'll see you at the wedding tonight. I don't know who is the most excited, Miss Kate or Miss Dolly."

The wedding was held at the Pretty Girl and Happy Cowboy Saloon, which was well decorated for the event. All the tables had been taken out, and the chairs arranged so that there was an aisle down the center.

The priest, Mr. Peterson, the groomsman, and Joe Cravens, the groom, were standing at the front, where an altar had been constructed. Rusty was sitting at the piano.

After the bride's maids processed up the aisle and took their position, Rusty began playing Mendelssohn's Bridal March.

Smoke, Sally, and Cal turned to watch the bride, Kate, being escorted up the aisle by her brother, Pearlie. When they reached the altar, Kate moved over to stand next to Cravens, while Pearlie hurried back down the aisle where he met Dolly and escorted her up the aisle as well, all the while Rusty continued to play the Bridal March.

Then, when Dolly reached the altar, Rusty got up from the piano and hurried over to join her.

"Dearly Beloved, we are gathered here in the sight of God and these witnesses to join this man Joseph Cravens to this woman, Katherine Abernathy, and this man Rusty Abernathy, with this woman Delores Weathers in holy matrimony."

The next day

Smoke, Sally, Pearlie, and Cal were sitting at a table in the dining car on the train, on the way back to Colorado. They had ordered their food, but it hadn't yet been delivered.

"I thought the wedding was just beautiful," Sally said. "And, Pearlie, you looked so cute, escorting your sister and Dolly down the aisle."

Cal laughed. "Yeah, you were cute," he teased.

"And I'm so glad you have a family now," she added.

Pearlie reached across the table to take Sally's hand, then he took Cal's hand. At a nod from Pearlie, Cal reached across the table to take Smoke's hand, and he took Sally's other hand in his.

"Heck, Miz Sally," Pearlie said. "I've had a family all along."

"Yes, you have," Sally said, raising Pearlie's hand to kiss it.

"Lord, Smoke, you're not goin' to kiss my hand now, are you?" Cal asked.

Their laughter drowned out the train's whistle.

Keep reading for a special excerpt . . .

The First Mountain Man
PREACHER'S HELLSTORM

For the sake of the son he never knew,
Preacher goes on the warpath.

Long ago, the legendary trapper known as
Preacher took shelter with the Absaroka and
fell in love with a girl called Bird in the Tree.
Twenty years later, he rescues a woman and
her son from an ambush by the hated Blackfoot.
The woman is Birdie, and the valiant young warrior
is Hawk That Soars—Preacher's son. Now the
greatest fighter on the frontier is about to go to war
to protect a family he never knew he had.

Led by the vicious war chief Tall Bull,
the Blackfoot are trying to wipe out the Absaroka.
Hopelessly outnumbered by vicious warriors,
Preacher and his son launch a war that will stain
the Rocky Mountain snow with Blackfoot blood.

Coming soon from Pinnacle Books!

CHAPTER ONE

Moving slowly and carefully, Preacher reached out and closed his hand around the butt of a flintlock pistol.

The night was black as pitch around him, but Preacher didn't need to be able to see to know where the gun was. He had committed all his surroundings to memory before he rolled in his blankets and dozed off.

Another pistol lay next to the one Preacher grasped, and a flintlock rifle and a tomahawk were there as well. The pistols were both double-shotted and heavily charged with powder.

Let the attackers come. Preacher was ready to cry havoc and let slip the dogs of war, as his friend Audie might say. The little fella had been a professor once and was fond of quoting old Bill Shakespeare.

On Preacher's other side, the big wolf-like cur he called Dog growled softly. Preacher sat up and put his other hand out, resting it on the back of Dog's neck where the fur stood up slightly.

Dog knew enemies were out there in the night. He

was eager to tear into them, but he wouldn't attack unless Preacher gave him the go-ahead.

Preacher waited and listened.

He didn't know what had roused him and Dog from slumber, but the rangy gray stallion known as Horse stood not far away, head up, ears pricked forward, so he'd sensed whatever it was, too.

Preacher's almost supernaturally keen eyes had adjusted to the darkness well enough for him to see the stallion and also the pack mule he had brought from St. Louis. The mule's head was down as it dozed.

A breeze drifted through the trees and carried voices to Preacher's ears. He couldn't make out the words, but the tone was familiar.

The voices were Indian, but they weren't on the warpath. If they had been stalking an enemy, they would have done so in grim silence. In this case, they sounded amused.

Preacher was on the edge of Blackfoot country, which meant he didn't see anything funny about the situation. For more than twenty years, he had been coming to the Rocky Mountains every year to harvest pelts from beaver and other fur-bearing animals, and nearly every one of those years, he'd had trouble with various Blackfoot bands.

In fact, it was the Blackfeet who were responsible for the name he carried to this day.

Early on in his frontier sojourn, he had been captured by the Blackfeet and tied to a stake. Come morning, he would be tortured and eventually burned to death.

However, something had possessed him to start talking, much like a street preacher he had seen back in St. Louis, and when the sun rose he was still going at it, spewing out words in a seemingly never-ending torrent.

Crazy people both intrigued and frightened the Indians, and they figured anybody who started talking like that and wouldn't stop had to be loco. Killing somebody who wasn't right in the head was a sure way of bringing down bad medicine on the tribe, so they had scrapped their plans to roast the young man known at that point as Art. They let him go, instead.

Eventually, word of the incident got around—the vast wilderness could be a surprisingly small place in some ways—and the other mountain men started calling him Preacher. The name stuck. He didn't mind. By now he never thought of himself any other way.

His war with the Blackfeet had continued over the years. He had killed countless numbers of warriors, some in open battle, some by creeping into their camps at night and slitting their throats with such stealth that no one knew he had been there until morning.

They called him the White Wolf, they called him the Ghost Killer, they probably had other names for him as well.

And the Blackfoot warrior who finally killed Preacher would be the most honored of his people.

Preacher figured to keep on frustrating that ambition, just as he had for a long time now.

So as he sat there where he had gone to ground to sleep for the night, more than a mile away from where he had built a small fire to cook his supper, he knew he didn't have any friends in these parts. Those warriors who were barely within earshot would love to kill him if they got the chance.

For a moment he considered stalking them, becoming the hunter, but when he thought about it he realized they weren't hunting him. He hadn't seen a soul in more than a week. They weren't looking for him.

They were on their way somewhere else, bound on some errand of their own, and already their voices had faded until he could barely hear them.

"Wouldn't make sense to borrow trouble," he whispered to Dog. "Sooner or later it always finds us on its own."

Dog's fur lay down. Horse went back to cropping at some grass. The crisis had passed.

Preacher rolled up in his blankets and went back to sleep, confident that his instincts and his trail companions would awaken him if danger approached again.

The rest of the night passed without incident. Preacher slept the deep, dreamless sleep of an honest man and got up in the morning ready to press on.

He was headed toward an area where he hadn't been in quite a while, hoping to have good luck in his trapping.

For more than thirty years, since a party of men under the command of a man named Manuel Lisa had started up the Missouri River in 1807, men had been coming to these mountains in search of pelts.

After all that time, beaver and other fur-bearing varmints were becoming less numerous, and it took more work to find enough of them to make a trip to the Rockies profitable.

That was why Preacher was expanding the territory where he trapped. He didn't really care that much about the money. His needs were simple and few. He loved it here. The mountains were his home and had been ever since he first laid eyes on them. He would be here even if he never made a penny from his efforts.

If a fella was going to work at something, though, he might as well do the best job of it he could. That was Preacher's philosophy, although he would have scoffed at calling it that.

After a quick breakfast, he saddled Horse and set out, leading the pack mule. Dog bounded ahead of them, full of energy.

Snow-capped peaks rose to Preacher's right and left as he headed up a broad, tree-covered valley broken up occasionally by meadows thick with wildflowers. A fast-flowing creek fed here and there by smaller streams ran through the center of the valley. That creek and its tributaries would be teeming with beaver, Preacher hoped.

At the far end of the valley about forty miles away rose a huge, saw-toothed mountain. Something about it stirred a memory in Preacher.

Whatever the recollection might be, it proved elusive. After a moment, Preacher gave a little shake of his head and stopped trying to recall the memory.

It would come back to him or it wouldn't, and either way it wasn't likely to change his plans.

He intended to make his base of operations at the upper end of the valley, near that saw-toothed peak.

He would work the tributaries one at a time, down one side of the valley and then back up the other.

That would take him most of the summer, and then in the fall he would pack up the pelts he had taken and head back to St. Louis, unless he decided to pay a visit to one of the far-flung trading posts established out here by the American Fur Company and sell his furs there.

If he did that, he could spend the winter out here, as he had done many times in the past, finding some friendly band of Indians who wouldn't object to having him around—

He straightened abruptly in the saddle, peered toward the saw-toothed mountain in the distance, and said, "Well, son of a . . . No wonder it seemed familiar to me." He grinned and shook his head. "Wonder if any of 'em are still around."

Maybe he would find out.

Preacher didn't get in any hurry traveling up the long valley. By the middle of the next day he was about halfway to the point where he intended to set up his main camp. He still hadn't seen another human being, although he had come across plenty of deer, a herd of moose, and a couple of bears. He left them alone and they left him alone. From time to time eagles and hawks soared overhead, riding the wind currents between the mountains.

When the sun was almost directly overhead, he stopped to let Horse and the pack mule drink from the creek. Hunkering beside the stream, Preacher set his rifle down within easy reach, then stretched out his left hand and dipped it in the water, which was icy from snow melt. He scooped some up and drank, thinking nothing had ever tasted better.

The current made his reflection in the water ripple and blur, but he could make out the rugged features, the thick, gray-shot mustache, the thatch of dark hair under the broad-brimmed felt hat he had pushed to the back of his head.

A few feet away, Dog lifted his dripping muzzle from the creek and stiffened. Horse stopped drinking as well.

Preacher acted like nothing had happened, but in reality, his senses had snapped to high alert. He listened intently, sniffed the air, searched the trees on the far side of the creek for any sign of movement.

There! Some branches on a bush had moved more than they would have if it was just some small animal rooting around over there.

Preacher still didn't rise to his feet or give any other sign he had noticed anything. All he did was carefully and unobtrusively move his hand toward the long-barreled rifle lying on the ground beside him.

Two figures dressed in buckskin suddenly burst out of the brush and trees on the other side of the creek and raced across open ground toward him. Preacher snatched up the rifle and came upright with the swift smoothness of an uncoiling snake.

He brought the flintlock to his shoulder and slid his right thumb around the hammer, ready to cock and fire.

He held off as he realized the two Indians weren't attacking him. One was a woman, brown knees flashing under the buckskin dress, visible above the high moccasins she wore.

The other was a young man who carried a bow and had a quiver of arrows on his back but wasn't painted for war. He probably could have outrun the woman, but he held back, staying behind her as if to protect her.

A second later, Preacher saw why. At least half a dozen more buckskin-clad figures raced out of the woods in pursuit and let out blood-curdling war cries as they spotted not only their quarry but also the white man on the other side of the creek.

CHAPTER TWO

Instantly, Preacher shifted his aim. He cocked the hammer and pressed the trigger.

The hammer snapped down, the powder in the pan ignited, and the rifle boomed and bucked against his shoulder. The mountain man's aim was true. The heavy lead ball smashed into the chest of the man in the forefront of the attackers and drove him backward off his feet.

Preacher dropped the rifle butt-first on the creek bank so dirt wouldn't foul the barrel. His hands swept toward the pistols tucked behind the broad leather belt around his waist as he shouted, "Get down!"

The young Indian man tackled the woman from behind and bore her to the ground. Preacher's pistols came up and roared. Smoke and flame spurted from the muzzles as they sent their double-shotted loads over the heads of the fleeing pair.

That volley cut down three more of the attackers, although one of them appeared to be only wounded as a ball ripped through his thigh. Preacher dropped the empty pistols next to the rifle. He had two more pistols in his saddlebags, loaded and primed, but it would take too long to reach them.

Instead he jerked his tomahawk from behind his belt and charged across the creek, water splashing around his feet and legs as he charged. Dog was right beside him, growling and snarling.

Like a streak of gray fur and flashing teeth, the big cur leaped on one of the attackers and brought him down. The man began to scream as Dog ripped at his throat, but the sound was quickly cut short.

At the same time, the young man rolled up onto one knee, put a hand on the woman's shoulder for a second in a signal for her to stay down, and then plucked an arrow from the quiver on his back and fitted it to his bowstring. A loud twang sounded as he let fly.

Then, following Preacher's example, he dropped his bow and grabbed his tomahawk as he bounded to his feet.

Four of the attackers were still on their feet, but one of them staggered as he clutched the shaft of the arrow embedded in his chest. With five men down, that meant the original party had numbered nine.

Preacher, Dog, and the young man had cut the odds more than in half, but they were still outnumbered.

In Preacher's case, that wasn't hardly fair.

He moved like a whirlwind, lashing out right and left with the tomahawk. The stone head crashed against the head of an attacker, splintering bone under the impact. The warrior dropped, dead before he hit the ground.

Preacher pivoted and launched a blow toward a second warrior, who managed to block the mountain man's stroke with his own tomahawk. As the weapons clashed, the man launched a kick at Preacher's groin. Preacher twisted and took the man's heel on his thigh instead.

A few yards away, the young man went after the uninjured warrior, but the man with the wounded thigh lurched into his path instead. The young man's tomahawk came down and split the man's skull, cleaving into his brain.

The dying man fell forward, tangled with the young man, and brought them both to the ground.

Preacher whirled to the side as his opponent tried desperately to brain him. The mountain man's tomahawk swept around and slashed across the attacker's throat.

Flesh was no match for sharpened flint. Blood spouted from the wound as the man choked and gurgled. He dropped his tomahawk and put both hands to his ruined throat, but he couldn't stop the crimson flood.

His knees buckled and he pitched forward.

Preacher turned in time to see the youngster struggling to get a buckskin-clad carcass off of him. The last member of the war party bent over both of them, tomahawk raised as he looked for an opening to strike.

Preacher threw his 'hawk. It revolved through the air, turning over the perfect number of times for the head to smash into the Indian's left shoulder and lodge there.

The man staggered back a step and dropped his

own tomahawk. He turned and ran toward the trees, obviously realizing he was the one who was outnumbered now, and wounded, to boot.

The young man finally succeeded in shoving the dead warrior off of him. He sprang to his feet, grabbed the tomahawk the fleeing man had dropped, and flung it after him.

The throw missed narrowly as the 'hawk whipped past the man's head. A heartbeat later he disappeared into the trees.

Preacher started after the man, not wanting him to get away, but to do that he had to pass the woman, who reached up, grabbed his hand, and said, "Preacher!"

That stopped him in his tracks. He looked down at her, wondering how she knew him.

Of course, he was known to many of the tribes, up and down the Rocky Mountains from Canada to the Rio Grande. He was an enemy to some but a friend to many.

This woman looked up at him with a clear, steady gaze. Since she was holding his hand already, Preacher tightened his grip and easily lifted her to her feet.

The young man who had come out of the trees with her picked up his bow and turned toward them. A frown creased his forehead.

Preacher didn't pay much attention to the youngster. His attention was on the woman as something stirred inside him.

She was a handsome woman, close to his own age. He could tell that by the faint lines on her face and the silver threads among her otherwise raven-black hair, which was cut short around her head. The years had thickened her waist slightly, but her body was still strong and well-curved under the buckskin dress.

By the woman's short hair and the beading and other decorations on her dress, Preacher could tell she was Absaroka, a tribe with which he had always been friendly. The young man's clothes and the long hair that hung far down his back marked him as a member of the same tribe, and when Preacher looked back and forth between them he noted an even stronger similarity.

Unless he missed his guess, this woman was the boy's mama. He could see the resemblance in their eyes, and in the cut of their jaws.

Something else about the youngster struck him as familiar, too, but damned if he could say what it was. He had never laid eyes on the young man before today, he was pretty sure of that.

He couldn't say the same for the woman. He looked at her and wanted to call her name, but he couldn't quite do it. The words wouldn't come to his tongue.

She spoke instead, saying in the language of the Absarokas, "Preacher. It really is you."

"Reckon it is," he replied, equally fluent in her tongue even though he hadn't been born to it.

"I prayed to Gitche Manitou, the Great Spirit, that we would find you. When we fled from our home, it was to look for you. But I did not dare to dream fate would bring us together again."

"I know you," Preacher said as he looked down into her dark eyes. "But I can't quite remember . . ."

He saw what looked like a flicker of pain in those

eyes and wished he hadn't said it. Clearly, whatever had happened between them had meant more to her than it did to him.

It had been a long time ago, though. He knew he hadn't seen her in recent years. The memory was too dim and faded for that.

But it had stayed alive and clear in her mind. A faintly sad smile touched her lips as she said, "My name is Bird in a Tree."

Preacher drew in a deep, sharp breath as the memories flooded back. He said, "I knew a girl named Bird in a Tree, but it was many, many years ago. I called her Birdie . . ."

"I am she."

He put his hands on her shoulders, looked at her, and remembered everything.

He wasn't much more than a boy, but already he had battled river pirates on the Mississippi and fought the bloody British at the town of New Orleans with Andy Jackson. He had traveled to the mountains, made friends with the trappers, and become one of them himself.

He had befriended some of the Indians as well, and now as winter settled down a band of Absaroka had invited him to stay with them. Preacher had come west to experience everything life had to offer, and this would be new to him.

He had hunted with some of the Absaroka braves and brought in fresh meat for the village. They gave him his own lodge, small but comfortable enough with a good fire pit and a couple of bearskin robes.

He was sitting next to the fire on his first night in the village when someone pushed back the deerskin flap over the lodge's entrance.

A young woman stepped into the lodge and let the flap fall closed behind her. She stood there without saying anything until Preacher asked her, "What do you want, girl?"

"I am Bird in a Tree," she said. "I have been sent to cook for you, care for you, and warm your robes."

Preacher's heart began to slug harder in his chest. He'd had a little experience with women—well, one woman, anyway, the girl called Jennie—and he knew what Bird in a Tree was talking about.

She was beautiful, too, with slightly rounded features, smooth, reddish-tinted skin, and hair black as midnight cut short in two wings that framed her face. Not many men would be able to look at her without wanting her, and Preacher was no exception.

He found himself struggling to find words to say, though, and she must have taken his hesitation for indecision or even disapproval. She bent, grasped the bottom of her buckskin dress, and pulled it up and over her head.

She wasn't wearing anything under the dress except fringed moccasins that came almost to her knees. Her skin looked even smoother everywhere else than it was on her face. Preacher wanted to touch it and find out. The curves of her body were enticing in the firelight. The dark brown nipples that crowned her small but firm breasts were hard and insistent.

Preacher's blood began to hammer even harder in his veins.

Bird in a Tree dropped the dress she held and moved a step closer to Preacher.

"Do you not find me to your liking?" she asked.

He had to swallow and lick suddenly dry lips before he was able to say, "Birdie, I find you very much to my liking."

Her solemn expression disappeared as she smiled.

"Birdie," she repeated. "Will you call me this name when we are together?"

"If that's what you want."

"It is what I want," she said as she came toward him and he stood up to meet her. Her voice dropped to a whisper as she added, "And I want to warm your robes many times."

"I reckon that's mighty fine with me," Preacher said. His arms went around her and drew her to him.

Before the night was over, he found himself wishing the winter would never end.

But of course the winter had ended. All things did, after all. And the next winter, after another trapping season, Preacher had gone back to St. Louis instead of staying in the mountains.

Since then, he had been to many other places, but never back to the valley where that particular band of Absaroka lived. For several years, he had thought of Birdie from time to time, but gradually she had slipped from his memory.

It was hard to keep track of everything when a man lived such a long, full, adventurous life.

Now as he stood there looking at her, the time they had shared came back to him, and he smiled warmly as he said, "Birdie, it's mighty good to see you again. I'm glad the Great Spirit has brought us together after all these years."

"I thought you would return . . ."

"Life took me other places," he said, knowing that sounded a mite weak, but it was the only answer he had. The only honest one, anyway.

"The memory of what we shared never faded."

"I remember it well," he told her. That was true. He remembered it now, whether he had earlier or not.

The young man stepped toward them, drawing Preacher's attention again. The youngster was downright glaring at him now, for some reason.

Birdie laughed. "It is like one peers into still water, and the other gazes back."

Preacher's head jerked back toward her as he said, "What—"

"Preacher, this is our son, Hawk That Soars."

Connect with

Visit us online at
KensingtonBooks.com
to read more from your favorite authors, see books
by series, view reading group guides, and more.

for sneak peeks, chances to win books and prize packs,
and to share your thoughts with other readers.

facebook.com/kensingtonpublishing
twitter.com/kensingtonbooks

Tell us what you think!

To share your thoughts, submit a review,
or sign up for our eNewsletters, please visit:
KensingtonBooks.com/TellUs.